E. C. de Calabrella

Evenings at Haddon Hall

A Series of Romantic Tales of the Olden Time

E. C. de Calabrella

Evenings at Haddon Hall
A Series of Romantic Tales of the Olden Time

ISBN/EAN: 9783744676915

Printed in Europe, USA, Canada, Australia, Japan

Cover: Foto ©Andreas Hilbeck / pixelio.de

More available books at **www.hansebooks.com**

EVENINGS

AT

HADDON HALL,

A Series of Romantic Tales of the Olden Time.

WITH ILLUSTRATIONS BY

G. E CATTERMOLE.

LONDON:
GEORGE BELL & SONS, YORK ST., COVENT GARDEN,
AND NEW YORK.
1893.

CONTENTS.

EVENINGS AT HADDON HALL

IN the most singular and romantic, and withal the most beautiful, of the divisions of our all-beautiful England—the district of the Peak—is situated one of the noblest of those architectural relics of the times of Chivalry and Romance, which any country, even England itself, can boast—a relic that is preserved by its owners with as pious care, and made the object of as many pilgrimages of admiring interest, as the shrines of saints are wont to be, in countries where saints were needed to supply the place of those social virtues of which the "merry England" of the olden time was the chosen home. At the period when Haddon Hall was the proud seat of the Vernons, the old English hospitality of our barons and feudal chiefs rendered superfluous that less gracious and grateful dispensation which had previously borne the name of *Charity* — a name that the wiser benevolence of the times we speak of had, in England at least, banished from the vocabulary used to interpret between man and man. At this period, the princely hospitality of the Lords of Haddon Hall, demanded for its due dispensation the constant services of a retinue of seven score of domestics, and an annual outlay that would have ex-

B

hausted the treasury of many of the reigning sovereigns
of less favoured countries.

It is within the precincts of this princely abode of the
Vernons and the Mannerses that those simple revels are to
take place in which we would fain interest the imagina-
tions of our readers, with a view to their due appreciation
of those exquisite specimens of high art which it is our
pleasant office to be the medium of introducing to the
world, and which owe their inspiration to the stately times
to which those stately relics belong — times when, depre-
cate them as we may, by our meaningless epithets of
" rude," " barbarous," " uncivilized," and the like, gave
rise to nobler achievements of human intellect, brighter
phases of human character, more beautiful examples of
human virtue, and more signal evidences of the heights to
which our common nature is capable of attaining, than are
even " dreamt of in the philosophy," much less realised in
the practice, of our own ultra-civilized day — times, too, to
which the highest art and the purest literature of our own
day are frequently compelled to resort, in search of those
types of excellence, those traits of heroism, and those
symbols of intellectual and moral beauty, for which the
enamoured seekers look in vain in that more " cultivated"
era to which they appeal.

But let us not, in our desire to be just to the illustrious Dead, do an unjust thing to the illustrious Living—
least of all let us do this on the threshold of that spot
which, it may be, is destined to be hallowed by the revival
of those very institutions to which the " good old times "
owed all their goodness, and " merry England" all her
extinct merriment. If the social life of England is destined
to see the present "winter of her discontent" melt into the
genial spring-time of hopeful promise, and happy perform-

ance, by a recurrence to those antique usages, the birth of which was coeval with the antique halls to which we are conducting our readers, it will be (under Heaven) through the instrumentality of what the wise world is at present pleased to consider as the "dreams" of a scion of that noble house to which those halls belong. If we err not greatly, the name of MANNERS will, at no distant period, be associated with that noblest and happiest of all revolutions, a recurrence to those wise simplicities of social life which mark the youth of all nations, and which too seldom survive it.

It is, then, to Haddon Hall, with its noble recollections, its happy associations, and the still happier promises and prophecies of what may belong to its future destiny,— that we desire the reader to accompany us in imagination, while we endeavour to place before him, in a light worthy their unequalled beauty, results of the pictorial art which nothing but scenes and social institutions like those of Haddon in the olden time could have inspired, and which, in the presence of more modern localities and associations, would lose half their interest, and all that dignified propriety and appropriateness which are the crowning graces of high art.

Haddon Hall was built before the Conquest; and the extensive and elaborate alterations, and vast additions, made to it at so many different periods, afford a signal proof of the estimation in which this noble baronial mansion was held, both for its internal magnificence, and the beauty of the surrounding scene. To have demolished any portion of this dignified and time-honoured structure, would have been held sacrilege by the whole neighbourhood; indeed, there were so many legends and superstitious connected with the various parts of it, that it has always been an object of veneration, and sometimes of terror, in the country around. Even to some of its massive trees there were tales attached, which were handed traditionally from generation to generation, but never whispered beyond the precincts of the domain. Some of these are now about to be disclosed for the amusement of our readers. In the meantime, we must be allowed to complete our descriptive sketch of the spot at that particular period of its existence (we will not specify precisely how many or how few years ago) at which we have chosen to make it the scene of our revels.

The mansion was approached by a massive portal between two towers, near the angle of the lower ward; at the upper side of which, was the principal entrance to the body of the mansion, many of the earliest features of which have been studiously preserved. The great banqueting-hall in particular remained nearly in its primeval state, and contained many antlers, casques, and bucklers of various ages, from its foundation. This hall opened, at the lower extremity, immediately into the kitchen, from one part, and from another into the buttery, whence the substantial viands were formerly served. Near the door of the latter, there still remained (and remains) a curious instrument attached to its post, resembling a handcuff, — in which, it is supposed, the wrist of any recreant who refused to quaff the generous goblet presented to him, was confined in a position raised above his head, so that the contents of the goblet which he had rejected might be poured down his sleeve; for, in those simple times, it was deemed as much a duty to do honour to hospitality as it was to dispense it: you might stay away from the generous revels; but if you chose to be present at them, you were expected to yield to those influences which, for the time, made all equal. In this hall, in former ages, the lord of the soil sat at the high table, surrounded by his family; while his vassals and retainers occupied two long tables flanking the walls.

On the occasion we are about to signalise,—which was in celebration of the birthday of his only child, a beautiful girl of fifteen years of age,—the then lord of this princely domain occupied the same seat, and the customs and ceremonies of the antique time were preserved, as far as they could be rendered consistent with modern luxuries and refinements; as, for instance, the rushes, which had formerly strewed the floor, were now replaced by magnificent carpets from the Turkish looms; the bare oaken forms by cushioned, high-backed, and richly-carved chairs; the pewter or wooden trenchers, by massive services of plate. Many ancient goblets had been preserved, and were held in far greater veneration than any of the splendid additions of gold and silver plate which adorned the gorgeous sideboards. The ancient arras had been kept through each generation with great care, and still decorated the walls.

The upper end of this hall communicated with the guard-room, leading to a spacious staircase of old black oak, in the walls of which were many niches containing suits of armour and military trophies. The ceiling was of massive oak, panelled, and decorated with gold and brilliant colours, and emblazoned with the numerous armorial bearings of the noble ancestors of the family. The large bay window, by which the staircase was lighted, projected from the centre of the broad landing, and contained rare specimens of ancient painted glass. At each end of this landing were doors, communicating, the one on the right to the state apartments, and the other, on the left, to the private apartments. These continued in opposite directions round the great quadrangle, meeting on the opposite side in the chapel.

The first apartment on the right was an ante-chamber; the second, a spacious and lofty room, or audience-chamber, opening directly into the great gallery, — the proportions of which might, at first sight, appear somewhat too narrow, but this apparent defect was amply compensated for by three deep and spacious recesses, the farther end of which was composed of alternate casements and mullions of stone. The upper compartments of these casements were nearly filled with the finest old stained glass, while the lower portions were left clear, with the evident object of gaining an uninterrupted view into the tilt-yard; in the wide arena of which many a tournament had been held, in those days when every word and action of a true and loyal knight had some reference to their lady-love; when they styled themselves servants, or slaves of love — "*serviteurs, ou servants d'amour;*" — and in this adopted character of slaves, they often suffered themselves to be led to the place of combat by their fair mistresses, by small chains, or rich ribbons, fastened to the head-pieces of their horses. In the same quality, the knights wore the colour and livery of their ladies, and certain devices, which were only understood by each other; and these "*devices d'amour*" are the principal origin (according to Saint Palaye) of the unintelligible words to be found in the arms of many noble houses.

The gallery, of which we have spoken, had been the favourite resort of the family of each possessor; and whether occupied by a large or small party, had always a cheerful and commodious aspect. Many a game of blind-man's buff had been played at one end of it, by the young aud buoyant of spirit, without disturbing the gravity of some political discussion that was being carried on by the diplomatists of the day in one of the recesses, or deranging the whist party of some dowager intent on the odd trick.

From time to time, Haddon Hall had been honoured by many royal visits; and the descriptions preserved in the record-tower, of these entertainments, prove that they must have been of the most sumptuous character.

In latter years, the banqueting-hall had been used only upon great occasions; and the party lately assembled to celebrate the birthday of the young heiress, having been reduced to a comparatively small circle of relations and intimates, the grand apartments were abandoned, and the well-stored library became the resort of the remaining guests, among whom might be found that happy mixture of society nowhere to be met with in such perfection as in an English country-house. There were persons of various nations, holding eminent positions — ministers and diplomatists,—distinguished members of the church, the bar, and the senate,—learned orators and statesmen,—men of nigh literary and scientific accomplishments,—members of the army and navy,—some students from the universities; and, as might be expected, in company with such an assemblage of high-bred gentlemen, a goodly knot of fair, accomplished, and amiable women were also present.

The season had advanced to the middle of March. The weather was unusually severe; snow was lying deep on the ground, forbidding egress from the mansion. This circumstance, which at first threatened to throw a gloom on the party, became unexpectedly the source of much interest and amusement. Ennui had begun to make itself felt, and the question of—What *shall* we do to pass the time? had been whispered confidentially from one to an-

other, till everybody seemed to have learned it by heart ;
when, at last, the lovely daughter of the house, the Lady
Eva, who was turning over a portfolio of " rich and rare "
gems of art by George Cattermole, suddenly exclaimed—

" Will some one come and explain what these beautiful
pictures mean ?"

The question, simple as it might seem, involved a point
of critical difficulty, *felt* by most of those to whom the
inquiry was addressed, but not readily to be solved by any
one of them, without more thought than they seemed
disposed to give to the subject. All present, not excepting
the Lady Eva herself, appreciated the extraordinary beauty
of the designs which lay before them ; but all, and she in
particular, were evidently perplexed, and some were even
annoyed by the vague and unsatisfactory feeling which
always attends the inspection of a design, of the precise
subject of which we are ignorant. All felt that the
designs, which were by this time eagerly spread out upon
the library table by the Lady Eva, were exquisite works
of art ; and all, like her, the more they examined them,
became the more anxious to learn the particular subject of
which each picture was an illustration.

The artist himself not being present to reply to the
repeated (mental) cry, on all hands, of " Explain! Explain !"
the case seemed a hopeless one, when a lady—(there is
nothing like female wit for solving a knotty point, for if no
other course is left, she will *cut* the knot, and solve it that
way)—a lady exclaimed—" It would be easier, I suspect,
to *invent* an illustration of each of these beautiful designs,
than obtain, even from the artist himself, an intelligible
account of the incidents of which *they* are illustrations."

The vivacious fancy of the lovely Lady Eva seized the
idea almost before it was fairly expressed, and she eagerly

exclaimed,—"Oh, do invent some stories ! How delightful it will be ! Who will begin ?"

At first, the eagerness of the fair girl did but rouse the attention of all present to the object of her anxious interest. But to look upon works of art like those in question, and not to feel the interest and curiosity they excite "grow by what 'tis fed on," is impossible. Every one was presently absorbed in the careful examination of the several designs, with a sort of half unconscious desire to arrange his or her thoughts or feelings respecting each of them, into some tangible and intelligible narrative form ; and before the Lady Eva, in her anxious culling of the designs, with a view to the commencement of the pleasant project, had found time to repeat her question, of " Who will invent some stories ?" several of the members of that accomplished company had made up their minds that the project should not fail for want of *their* assistance.

Just at this point, the first dinner-bell rung, to the no slight chagrin of the eager and excitable Eva ;

> " And when a *dinner*'s in the case,
> All other things, you know, give place."

At least, it is so in that true home and temple of Hospitality, an English country-house. But they often give place, only to be entertained with double zest for the delay. At all events, in the case we are treating of, the apparent interruption to the project did but forward, rather than retard it, and even before the lady guests had quitted the board, it had been fully determined, on all hands, by a sort of tacit compact, felt rather than expressed, that the Birthday Revels of the lovely daughter of their host should be signalized by something more likely to be remembered pleasantly and profitably in her after years, than the inanities of a quadrille, the twirlings of a waltz, the tramplings of a polka, or the small-talk proper to the intervals occurring between such frivolities.

Accordingly, by the time our party had re-assembled in the library that same evening, a desultory conversation between the most gifted members of it, especially those among them who had some practical knowledge of the use of the pen, had arranged the general features of the simple plan on which to carry out the fortuitous suggestion of the young Queen of the Revels of Haddon Hall; leaving the minor details of the plan to the momentary suggestions of its originator, and thus affording her the double delight of feeling that she was in some sort the architect of that monument which was destined, in after years, to mark her happy advent to that loveliest of all the phases of female life, the debateable point which intervenes between the fresh dawn of roseate girlhood, and the bright sunrise of incipient womanhood.

It only remains for the recorder of these " Evenings at Haddon Hall" to relate, in the fewest possible words, the simple steps by which the Lady Eva was led, almost unconsciously on her own part, to work out the inartificial plan which her eager and excited imagination had originated. And first, of the first Evening.

EVENING THE FIRST.

IT must be noted that the Lady Eva, who was, perhaps, even better acquainted with the history of her father's noble place than any one else present, had, while waiting somewhat impatiently in the library for the advent of the last lagging guests from the dinner-table, in her nervous restlessness, several times passed to the moon-lit windows of the fine old room, and looked forth vaguely on the great court below, tracing the massive shadow of one of the old towers, as it lay in heavy blackness on the otherwise bright space. But on the last occasion of her looking forth, a thought seemed to flash like a sudden light upon her eager fancy—she started from the window— clapped her fair hands, as if in an ecstasy of mingled pleasure and excitement, and exclaimed aloud,—

"A Tournament! The very thing! How delightful! *That* shall be the subject of our first story."

While speaking, she betook herself to the table where the beautiful drawings, on which her mind was so intent, were spread in bright confusion, and selected from among them five, which evidently owed their origin to the times when noble feats of arms held the place of those ignoble sports—(our male readers will forgive us the phrase, bearing in mind the sex, and, it may be, pitying the simple tastes of the recorder of these simple Revels)—which have mainly helped to banish chivalry from the land.

"There !" continued the lovely child, worthy herself to stand for an effigy of one of those "ladyes-fayre" who figured in the times which now filled her eager thoughts ; "There ! somebody shall make a story about those five beautiful designs, and call it ' The Tournament.' "

"Mark you her absolute *shall ?*"   It was final, on the present occasion, as the "shall" of beauty is, and (sometimes) ought to be.   Turning with the quick tact of youth to the individual of all that company best fitted, by his studies and tastes, to carry her happy thought into effect, the Lady Eva went up to him, and, holding out the designs, exclaimed — raising her beseeching eyes to his face with one of those radiant smiles which are so resistless in the early bloom of girlish beauty, —

"There ! you shall be my knight-errant of the evening, and lead the Revels.   You know what a number of pretty things you have told me of the brave knights and beautiful ladies who used—I don't know how many hundred years ago—to grace our old court-yard below, and turn its present dreary and dreamy silence into a scene of noisy revelry.   Nay, it was only yesterday you were telling me anecdotes of some of the wearers of those very helmets, and the wielders of those very swords and lances, that hang uselessly on the walls of our old banqueting-hall. If you could make, or remember, all those delightful little stories and anecdotes from merely looking on a few battered casques and rusty weapons, surely these beautiful drawings must inspire you with whole volumes.   Come— take them !   Look at them for five minutes, and then *improvisez* me a Tale of Chivalry that shall make them all as intelligible as if *they* were executed for *it*, not it for them.'

The appeal was not to be resisted—at all events, not by the young and enthusiastic student and admirer of that age and its attributes to which the appeal applied. He took the drawings that the Lady Eva held out to him; examined them one by one, carefully and intently, for a few minutes, and then, the company having hushed itself to silence for the expected result, he proceed to relate

THE TOURNAMENT.

The ravages of war seldom leave enduring traces on the earth. Often a field of battle, with all its agonies and terrors, is known only by the richer harvest that waves on its breast. Nature, which banishes so soon from a nation's mind and heart the memory of great calamities, is careful, at the same time, to efface all material vestiges of them. Even walls, that have been carried by storm and blackened by fire, soon cease to exhibit distinct signs of strife. Luxuriant vegetation covers the stains of blood and smoke; creeping plants and shrubs insinuate their roots in crevices made by the shock of artillery, and gracefully crown the battlements and towers that have been partially overthrown by the repeated assaults of an armed host. When this transformation is complete, hardly, to an un- practised eye, can the slow and peaceful ravages of time be distinguished from the work of destruction accom- plished by man. A generation does not elapse before the castle that has been overthrown by an enemy, and that presented at first frightful images of war, shows the same aspect as one that has been suffered to go to decay from the protection of its walls being no longer needed, and that stands, even in ruin, a monument of peace.

Many dismantled castles of the character thus indi-

cated were to be seen in England in the reign of the fourth
Edward, after the long and disastrous civil wars.   In the
county of Derby there was one calculated to strike the
eye, from its magnitude and the peculiarity of its site.   It
was built on a natural elevation, which, from having been
gradual, had by art been rendered rugged and abrupt,—
the steep pathway, by which access alone could be gained,
having been jealously guarded from the possibility of successful attack ; but overthrown defences alone now marked
the care that had been taken to render the fortress
impregnable.

From the height there was a noble view, over woodland, meadow, and river, till the prospect was bounded by
a chain of irregular hills, which, in all aspects of light and
shade, mingled so naturally with the hue of heaven, that
it was difficult to tell where earth ended and sky began.
To the east these hills were softened down into a series
of gentle undulations ; and here, at the extreme range of
vision, rose the walls and turrets of a castle, belonging to
the house of Lenorde.   Between this powerful family and
that of the Fauconvilles there had long been bitter and
deadly enmity.   The clear stream that separated the two
domains, and served as their frontier, suggesting, with its
pellucid waters and richly fringed banks, only images of
peace, had often ran red with the blood of the retainers
of the two great rivals.   There was perpetual and, as it
seemed, inextinguishable strife between them, and each
lord could refer to a long list of injuries, treasured up
with as much care as the noble deeds of his ancestors, to
justify the continuance of the feud, and the call for reta-
liation.   It was remarked that, in all disputes of the
state, these houses invariably took opposite sides.   Tradition traced their hatred (so long will hatred survive its

first occasion) to a quarrel that had taken place on a point
of precedent when the Conqueror was preparing in Nor-
mandy his invasion of the English shores. From this
insignificant source had descended the broad tide of
quarrel that had caused so many calamities, and that
seemed widening and augmenting as it pursued its course
unchanged through all the mutations of time. At no
period within memory had the two families been at peace.
As the fortunes of one sank, those of the other commonly
rose; but never had either possessed sufficient power to
wholly crush his opponent. An ancient prophecy, suggested, doubtless, to some bard by the hope of gaining
his lord's favour, or of pleasing the popular prejudices of
those with whom he lived, ran that friendship between the
two houses should be fatal to both. The superstition was
cherished on each side, and guarded in remembrance with
as much care as an article of faith: it well answered
its end, and caused the prospect of even a temporary
arrangement, or the slightest approach to conciliation, to
be regarded with horror, as an omen of evil.

In the long wars of the Roses, the two chiefs then at
the head of their respective houses, found ample opportunities of gratifying their animosity. Deadly injuries
were mutually given and received. In the conflict, both
champions were weakened, and shared in the fluctuations
of the sides they embraced, but years elapsed before one
could boast of a superiority over the other. When, at
last, fortune determined the victory, she did so decisively.

Sir Richard de Lenorde and the Baron of Fauconville
were in the prime of life when the war first broke out.
Sir Richard, more renowned for policy than deeds in arms,
espoused the cause of York, destined in the end to be
victorious. His rival, of more chivalrous character, and

one of the best knights of his age, remained steady in his allegiance to Henry the Sixth. When, at length, the White Rose was in the ascendant, Sir Richard, whose influence was strong with his great leader, the Duke of York, persuaded him to bend for a time all his strength to the subjugation of one of his bravest and most dangerous opponents. An army, rapidly collected, advanced, without notice of its approach, and surrounded Lord Fauconville's castle. The brave chief, without hope of relief, saw himself doomed to inevitable ruin. Throughout the land there ran a rumour that a terrible example would be made of the powerful and malignant Lancastrian. His defence was worthy of his fame. Disdaining a submission, which he knew would be fruitless, he boldly defied his enemies, and knowing who had brought this overwhelming force against him, sent a formal challenge to his foe, Sir Richard de Lenorde, demanding that the fate of the siege should be decided by a mortal combat between them, in view of the besieging army and the defenders of the castle. The days were past when such a chivalrous defiance would be accepted, and the answer returned was stern and contemptuous :—" We have met as equals, often enough," it said ; " when we face each other next, it shall be for the moment that elapses before the headsman strikes his blow. It is not for a rebel to prescribe terms to his conquerors."

Braver knight never mounted steed or guarded fortress than the good Baron of Fauconville. But unavailing are the efforts of the highest will against the might that overmasters it. In vain does the captive, with stout heart and strong hand, strive to rend the massive walls that enclose him ; in vain does the pilot oppose skill and resolve to the strength of wind and wave. The lord of the beleaguered castle disputed every inch of ground with his foes, but they were numerous, active, and determined. Slowly they gained the outward defences, and advanced to the very walls: force did much; famine more. The whole garrison became exhausted or disabled, and on the morning when the grand assault was made, not a hundred men were on the walls to meet it. There was a bloody and desperate struggle, hand to hand, upon the ramparts. Fighting to the last, though wounded and faint, the Baron was surrounded by a host of foemen, and struck to the ground. Then all was lost, and the castle given to rapine. Utterly helpless, but with a spirit still unconquered, the Lord of Fauconville was led into the presence of his hereditary foe. An order for his execution had been obtained from York, who was enraged by the length of the siege, and the loss of his troops. In the sight of weeping captives and the triumphant host stood the fatal block, with the executioner wielding his keen axe beside it. Disdaining to ask for mercy, the brave lord advanced with firm and steady pace to his death, haughtily returning the exulting glances of his pitiless foe. Once only his frame shook with a strong convulsion, and his features lost their composure. It was when Sir Richard de Lenorde rudely seized from a matron's arms the infant son of Fauconville, the sole hope of his house, and triumphantly held him in view of his captive father. For an instant, the chief hesitated; nature was strong within his breast; and he almost decided to dash through his guards, snatch his son from the polluting grasp that held him, and die with him in his arms; but his pride forbade him to give this last triumph to his enemy. With a strong effort, he mastered his emotion, and commended his child to God. As he reached the elevation where the apparatus of death was displayed, he gazed round on the lovely view, every object of which

c

was endeared to him by some early recollection. Then, raising his noble form to its full dignity, and casting back the masses of hair from his pale but high and haughty features, he exclaimed, in tones that were heard widely round, and fell distinctly on the listening ear of his inveterate rival—" Sir Richard de Lenorde, had I fallen by thy hand in the fair and open combat of man to man, I would have forgiven thee with my dying breath, and have prayed that the quarrel between our houses might cease. Thou hast taken a mean advantage of me; this is butchery, not conquest ; my blood be on the head of thee and of thy children."

The whole assembly, awe-struck, heard the curse, which, spoken by dying lips, seemed to breathe the spirit of prophecy. Then, calmly placing his head on the block, the baron held his hand aloft, a sign for the headsman to strike. As the axe flashed in the air, and descended, a scream of grief and agony burst forth from a thousand faithful hearts. It was the death-wail of the greatest and bravest warrior of an illustrious line.

Motives of policy, mingled, perhaps, with some touch of pity for the orphan's helplessness, prompted Sir Richard to spare the child. Were he removed, the house of Fauconville would not long remain without an enterprising leader, who might renew the strife. From this danger the knight felt secure, so long as he kept the true heir in his custody. The result showed his prudence. In his hands, the young lord became a hostage of peace, and the wide domain, that had so long been the heritage of the Fauconvilles, was quietly submitted to Sir Richard's authority.

Years went by, and the curse of the dying lord bore no fruit. In the increasing prosperity of the house of De

Lerorde, it faded away from the memory of all but a few of the most devoted adherents of the murdered baron. Sir Richard helped to place the crown on Edward's brows, and to give the last fatal blow to the Lancastrian cause at Barnet. His son, a noble youth, was one of the favoured attendants of Edward's court, and the old knight lived full of years and honour. As the defeated party gathered round the new monarchy, they began to acquire influence, and the connexions of the Fauconville house threatened to call De Lenorde to account. But he had anticipated their clamours. A grant from the crown — how procured little mattered — gave him title to the Fauconville lands, with the exception of some few acres reserved round the castle; and another royal order constituted him the guardian of the young lord. To all appearance, he performed his part fairly; the castle was partially restored, though its defences were carefully left unrepaired, and the remaining portion of the child's inheritance was ostentatiously placed under careful stewardship. The policy of Sir Richard was to give no pretence for clamour, and he succeeded.

Had the character of the young lord been other than it was, the old knight might have played a bolder and more daring game. But as the youth advanced to manhood, there seemed nothing to fear from him. Gentle, almost timid in disposition, he took little delight in warlike exercises, preferring more peaceful pastimes, with hawk and hound.

Educated in a religious house, he had caught something of the monkish taste for learning, which his politic guardian took care to encourage. He gave the boy's dreamy tastes free indulgence, and let him wander as he willed amid rural solitudes. With a pleased eye, he saw that one of his girls was the chosen companion of the youth's excursions. To the knight's thought, there was nothing unnatural in an union between the two houses. Such alliances were of common occurrence, since the wars had finally ceased; and were Edmund Fauconville wedded to the Lady Alice de Lenorde, the last fear would be removed from his mind of being called to account for the blood he had shed, and the lands he had usurped. He watched over their growing passion, laughing, as he fancied that the youth was more girlish in his heart than his companion. Fate denied him the full accomplishment of his wishes. He sickened; and, warned that his end approached, summoned his family around him. He placed first the hand of the timid Edmund in that of his own bold, spirited son, Sir Raoul, though both youths shrank from the contact, and then motioned the young lord to embrace the sorrowing Alice, who knelt by the bed-side. The youth complied; but it seemed when he again rose, and shook back his dark waving hair from his thoughtful features, that the dying knight's spirit was mightily disturbed, as his eye caught the earnest and fixed regard of the youthful baron. He gave a deep groan, as if his soul was troubled by some grievous remembrance. The priest, who hung above him to catch his last accents, heard him murmur—"How few years have made us even! May the curse lie with me in my grave!" With these words he sank back and expired.

IT is beautiful to see young and loving hearts happy in the present, and confident in the future, dreaming neither of gloom nor cloud, having no foreshadowing of coming ill, fancying that the clear blue sky of a summer's night, with its myriad stars, is an image of life and its pleasures.

Then only does hope exist without fear, and indulge its happy illusions without dread of their fading.

Two beings in the very brightness and dawn of youthful maturity wandered together through the sweet scenes of nature that surrounded their castle homes. The chequered shade of forest trees shielded them from the ardent sun, and a stream, now deep and silent, which they compared to their love—now shallow and babbling, which they likened to joys less pure than theirs, filled the air with a delicious murmuring, and gave the promise, if not the reality, of refreshing coolness. The youth and maiden spoke of their prospects and plans without reserve. After their marriage, they would reside together in the abode of his fathers. It was less splendid, less luxurious, than the dwelling she had been accustomed to, but it had the remains of former grandeur, and they could make of it what they pleased. As the day declined, he led her willing steps up a steep pathway, conducting to the height, where the castle walls, though the battlements were overthrown, and the defences gone, threw bold masses of shadow down the eastern slopes. The girl marked the ruins with a smile.

" Ah, how beautiful," she said, " are these large masses of stone, covered with fresh moss, and blooming with wild thyme and oxslip !"

The youth's cheek was flushed, but he did not answer, and the girl went on—

" We have lost nothing by nature's gain. These walls, they tell me, did but provoke war, without contributing to the happiness of those who dwelt within them. Look, here is the *home* entire."

It was so ; whatever damage had been done by rude assault to the domestic apartments of the castle, had been

repaired.   Little was wanting to the noble mansion, save
in the interior the restoration of the rich furniture and
decorations which had once adorned it.

He guided her through the large and lofty halls, magnificent even in their desolation, and led to rooms which
had been partially refitted, enjoying her exclamations of
surprise that so much had been done since her last visit ;
and thence to the chapel, where, in fair order, were ranged
the tombs of his ancestors.   Not one was wanting.   The
young lord knelt for a moment before the sculptured effigy
and graven words which told of the valiant deeds and
virtues of his sire.   He died, said the tablet, in defending
his castle from an assault led on by the great Duke, father
of King Edward.

"A noble death, Alice!   He was a knight of high renown, and won his spurs in France, fighting by the side
of the renowned King Henry.   But, come ; I have yet a
greater surprise for you!"

They traversed a long and wide gallery, at the end of
which a massive door admitted them into a noble hall
The effect was singular.   Through a richly-stained western
window, the setting sun cast a flood of brilliancy upon the
floor, reflecting the arms of the Fauconvilles, and the pictured representation of their most famous deeds.   Around
the walls were many suits of polished armour, looking—so
cunningly were the plates of mail arranged—like stalwart
knights, ready to grasp the spears which stood beside
them.   In the centre, an aged man, with white hair, yet
with grim and stern aspect, sat before what seemed a huge
oaken frame-work, which served him as a board on which to
pursue his labour.   Arms of all kinds, in good order and
well polished, were disposed in fantastical devices on the
panels of the hall.   A portrait, representing a head full of

dignity and command, rested against a carved cabinet. The likeness to the youth, who gazed on it with melancholy aspect, was striking. Beside it was a shield, with the stain and dent of many a combat marked upon its disc.

The girl rallied her lover on his warlike tastes. She expected to have seen a library, rather than so fine a collection of arms. Was he thinking of arming his vassals, and going to the approaching tournament? There was something in the tone of raillery in which she spoke that displeased the old man.

" And why," he said, " should the Lord of Fauconville not be at the tournament as well as Sir Raoul de Lenorde? When were his fathers found at home, when honour was to be gained abroad? But I forget," he added, with a grim smile; " these tournaments are mere holiday shows now, where men tilt with headless spears, and lay on blows with blunted swords. Had knights done so in my young days, 'twould have been long before we won Agincourt !"

" This old man, Alice," said the young lord, bending over the chair in which she sat, " was my father's most trusted follower. All that you see here is his work, not mine. Here he exercises me in arms, and cases me in a coat of mail; then from this window looks into the court-yard below, to see how lightly, with my suit of steel, I can leap upon a steed or bear a lance. We must not thwart him, though sometimes he extends too widely the privilege of age."

The old armourer's ears caught the last words; they heightened the displeasure which clouded his face, from the instant he saw who accompanied his lord.

" The privilege of age !" he said, with something of sarcasm. " Ay, there is reason to complain of it, when we see nothing of the privilege of youth. In my days of

manhood, those who bore noble names thought it a pri
vilege to do feats of arms, to avenge the wrongs of their
house—to mount the war-steed when a challenge was sent
abroad—to wear coats of mail like those, not silken garments—to ride with their followers at their back, not stroll
for ever through chambers that idleness keeps empty of
trophies."

The youth's brow had darkened, though he retained
his temper.

" He rails at me often thus, Alice, though scarcely so
sharply; yet he knows that I can wield both spear and
brand. How now, Stephen!" he exclaimed, in a louder
voice, "is this fitting speech for thy lord's son ?"

There was deeper sarcasm in the old man's tones than
he had yet ventured on, as he answered the question with
another—" For my lord's *son ?* "

" Ay, for your lord's son ; I understand your meaning,
old man. Would you have me prove my title to my name
by always railing and quarrelling ? Is it not enough that
I am prepared to defend my right, if need be ? You have
ceased this reproach since last my rapier struck yours from
your hand."

" Ah !" said the armourer, " it is a pity you can be
brave to no one but your father's old servants."

This was too much even for Lord Edmund's gentle
temper, and he was about to make an angry reply, when
the Lady Alice interposed. She spoke gently and sooth-
ingly to the old man.

" You have seen much of brave service, good Stephen,
and have been witness to many noble deeds—can you recall
the memory of none of them now ?—or do you think us
unworthy to hear them ? Tell us of a tournament in your
time, as you think ours so foolish."

The armourer seemed little appeased by the lovely girl's gentleness. He neither looked at nor spoke to her, but turning to the young baron, who had then taken a blade from his bourd. said—

"One noble tilting I have in memory, if my lord would desire to hear it, though it may be thought a reproach to these prudent times. Ah, St. George! men thought little of broken bones in those days. Those who were present at that field will not soon forget it."

"Well, let us hear your story. Alice, there is an hour of sunshine yet; the evening will be sweet and cool; some May yet lingers on the bushes; the mavis and the nightingale will give you their song as we return. I have a palfrey for you here. Do you mind, dear love, a half-hour's ride after sunset?"

A blush and a sweet smile were the answer.

The old man commenced his tale.

"It was after the return of our brave King Harry from France—oh! that the son of so great a king should have been such a weakling! I mind the time well; for throughout the land there was nothing but joyance and idleness, I say, it was when brave King Harry—whom the saints keep!—was newly returned from France, that the court, from very wantonness, began to quarrel. Some knights there were, proud of their looks and glittering dresses, and their fame, who would, if they could, have behaved over pertly to the ladies of Queen Katherine's state. They were checked soon enough. I warrant they repented quickly of their forwardness, when they saw how it was resented. The rumour ran that one young malapert had his ears boxed by a noble lady, to whom he was too free of speech.

" These young coxcombs were mightily incensed when they saw the laugh turned against them. In revenge, they spread abroad rumours unfavourable to the reputation of the court ladies—ay, and in gross terms too—declaring that the maids of honour were not worthy of their titles, and that the dames who surrounded the throne were neither so fair nor so virtuous as they might be. You may be sure these springalds were soon called to account. But, to do them justice, there was no lack of spirit among them; and, banded together, eight-and-forty knights, of good repute in arms, who had won honour in France, and seen the princes and chivalry of that land fly before them, declared they would maintain their avouch with lance and sword, on foot or on horseback, in silken doublet or coat of mail, against the like number of gentlemen of birth, who would come against them. Ha! ha! they might want prudence, they might be too quick in quarrel, but braver men never bore shield. Their blades were ever ready to their hands, and their seat in their saddle as firm as the roots of an oak in the ground. And that was known all over merry England; so that their hardihood was applauded, and none cared to take up the glove they had thrown down.

" When the ladies saw that knights were wanting to champion their cause,—for the graver sort would have nothing to do with this mad-cap quarrel—they wept for very shame and vexation, and vowed, that if the defiance were not met, they could show their faces round the throne no more. Some gallant youths declared they would do battle for the ladies' fair fame against all comers; but the challengers stuck to their terms, and said, an equal number must meet them in the field—eight-and-forty against eight-and-forty; and that until their number was completed, they held their challenge unaccepted, and the ladies disgraced.

"Oh! honour and virtue were dearly prized in those days! No son forgot his father's fame—no daughter, her mother's purity. These ladies then put on weeds, declaring their fair repute was dead, and that they would weep for it, as loving wives weep for a well-loved spouse. The joy of the court was gone; no more silken bravery—no more laughing looks—no more merry, quick-glancing eyes—no more mirth and pageantry. Those who came to Westminster then thought the nation was in mourning. There were old men living who said, nothing so sorrowful had been seen since the great plague of 1349. Wherever these noble and beauteous ladies went, there were the sounds and sights of woe; and, to make the matter worse for them, the king swore by St. Denis he would not interfere, but leave the gallants of his realm to fight out the quarrel as they pleased.

"There was one young lord who took up the ladies' cause in a manner that won for him the good-will of all the women in the land. He dared the leader of the challengers to combat with what weapons, and in what guise he pleased; and when he was refused, swore by the Holy Virgin—and the brave youth kept his oath—that he would never quit his coat of mail till he had formed a band to meet the boasters, and had fairly broken a lance with their leader. Beauty and glory were his cry. Ah! that was a time when such a cry would be carried over the world.

"It is likely you may not recollect that the Princess Philippa, daughter of great John of Gaunt, was wedded to the brave and good king of Portugal, Don John, as they called him. I saw her, when a boy, as she went in a stately litter to Dover. We gave her a true English cheer; she waved her delicate hand to thank us, and then drew aside the silken curtains of her carriage—I mind them

well, worked with cloth of gold—and let us catch the last
sight of her lovely face.   Her hair, the colour of the silk
the worm weaves, hung in glossy ringlets about her face
and fair shoulders, and her eyes were as blue as the skies
above, or as mariners who have ventured far to sea say the
ocean is beyond sight of land.   This princess thanked us
with gentle courtesy.   Oh, the noblest in the land could
then sometimes spare a smile for the lowest!

"A noble queen did this gentle princess make; and
the youth of her adopted land loved her as though she had
been born of their own soil.   When she heard what was
passing in England, she sorrowed too—for she never forgot
dear England, that had such pride in her; and then she
dressed herself in weeds, and said she must needs mourn
for the disgrace that had fallen on the daughters of her
own native country.

"When the queen's grief was told, all the hot blood of
that southern land was on fire.   More knights crowded to
court than when an expedition was threatened against the
Moors.   They swore, by all the saints of their land, that
they would die or change the mourning garments of their
queen into the gayest colours that the loom could fashion.
The king would let no more than forty knights depart,
and those were chosen by lot from the very chivalry of the
land.

"Eight English knights, on the ladies' part, went to
meet them, and at their head the brave young lord, who,
over his polished mail with its gold studs, wore a scarf of
crape, to signify that he mourned, too, till the fair fame
of the court dames was established.   As the goodly procession moved to London, there poured forth, from town
and hamlet, thousands to welcome it.   The knights passed
beneath arches of welcome, and not a lady in all the land

was there who thought herself too noble or tender to walk
before them, and cast flowers for their horses' hoofs to
trample. I warrant, in those times, no brave man ever
wanted encouragement from ladies' eyes.

" The king himself received them at Westminster, and
lodged them in his palace. Who will forget that he slept
himself in a tent, and waited on these knights as though
he were a humble squire? Night and day, the ladies
worked for them banners, favours, and scarfs. I saw myself, Sir John Maxwell, Lord Mayor of London, ride in his
scarlet cloak, with all his officers and aldermen about him,
the golden mace, and the weighty sword of the city, such
as a stalwart man could scarcely wield,—I saw them all
go to Westminster, to pray the king that the tournament
might take place within the city walls. The king was
proud it should be so, and the lord mayor charged himself
with the whole expense of fitting up Smithfield, where so
many knightly games had been played in times past.

" Where would you find such a goodly company now
as assembled then? That was before Englishmen had
taken to cut each other's throats. The flower of all the
kingdom assembled that day, for it was bruited far and
wide that such a tournament had never been seen in England before. The people lined the road-side by thousands,
the hedge-rows were trampled down, and every tree
swarmed with life. As you came to houses, you saw
balconies decorated with cloth of gold and gems, and ladies
ready to shower the most precious things they had in the
warriors' path. No one knew how rich was London till
that day. You could not see the colour of the houses for
the tapestry that hung adown them.

" Had you seen the procession, you would have
thought our brave king was just going to take possession

of the France he had won. There were archers and men-at-arms to clear the way; but as they went by, the city youth broke into the road again, that they might mingle in the procession, and swear, in after-times, they had taken part in it. Then, there were trumpeters and heralds stiff with their gold embroidery, and the king-at-arms, looking more magnificent than any monarch ever seen — a body of knights in glittering steel came next, and after them the judges of the field — more archers to clear the way for the challengers — eight-and-forty of the bravest knights in the land, armed cap-à-pié, with their steeds dancing for delight as the trumpets sounded and the shouts of the people shook the air. The ladies in the balconies and windows cast down their eyes; but many an admiring glance did those knights gain that day, I'll engage; for where could there be collected a band of fairer and braver youths?

" ' Room, there — room !' Ah, then came the glory of the pageant. The king himself — the darling of the land — shame to it that it forsook his son ! — the king came, in the midst of his brilliant court, armed in mail from head to foot — I lie, his noble head was bare; a page bore his plumed helmet before him, and bent beneath its weight. Not a man who looked on the king that day but would have died for him, so loyal in those good days were the people. Those who shouted before, now wept; those who danced, knelt down ; those who tossed their caps into the air, now raised their hands to heaven, to implore God's blessing on his royal majesty.

" The Knights of Portugal rode next the king. Well do I mind their order — five a-breast, each with an English leader, and the gallant young lord, who had worn mail night and day for three months past, at the head of all

As they came on, the ladies all welcomed them as their champions; benisons were showered on their heads by gentle lips, and look where they would, they saw only loving glances and sweet smiles. Flowers and favours were rained thick upon them; hands were clapped, and scarfs waved in ecstasy. Every one said those knights must triumph.

"Then, last, in their mourning weeds, came Queen Katherine, and her maids and matrons, looking more lovely for their show of grief, more fair for their sombre garments.

"The day would close before I could tell you all the gallant actions of the field. The challengers well maintained their fame, yet still they were always worsted. The combat of the two leaders was most expected, for their fathers were rivals before them. When they met, at last, and rode proudly round the lists, the very sound of applause was hushed in anxiety, and spectators hardly dared to draw their breath. The young lord who championed the ladies' cause was such a stripling as thou art now; thy years were his; yet he had then won honour which, had he died that hour, would have rendered his name famous for ever. As he looked round, before closing his vizor, there was many a lady there who vowed she would mourn for that handsome youth till her death, should he perish in the combat; and the Virgin had endless gifts promised her shrine to bear him harmless.

"The chargers they rode seemed to know the sound of the trumpet, and to be eager for the strife as their lords. They met in the middle of the field, with a shock that wellnigh appalled the stoutest heart there. Not for an instant was the conflict doubtful. The challenger, man and horse, rolled over and over on the plain; but the ladies' champion remained erect in his seat, his feet in the stirrups, his crest untouched, and the point of his opponent's lance borne harmlessly in his shield. He rode round the ring as gaily as before the encounter. For one instant surprise kept the spectators mute ; no one had ever seen a victory more complete. Then rose a shout, which was heard that noon at Westminster. The queen crowned her champion, and the king threw round his neck a chain of gold and gems.

" Fifty years are passed since then, but I can live on the memory of that hour. I shared in the triumph of my lord — my hands removed that armour from his honoured frame, never to be stained in conflict more — my —— "

" Thy lord! — thy hands !" impatiently exclaimed the youth, interrupting the armourer ; " what is this ? — what mean the tears that are flowing down thy cheeks ? Old man, you torture me. Speak, — this instant — speak, I command you !"

" I have said it," said the armourer, solemnly ; " the victor was thy father."

" And the vanquished knight ?" breathlessly asked Alice.

" Lady, he was Sir Richard de Lenorde. Hear me yet. Now or never must I speak — now that a great truth, too long concealed, is struggling for utterance within me. Young lord, let go that hand. Her sire never forgave thine the issue of that day. He shunned him in open conflict, but he plotted his destruction. My lord died not with his sword in his hand, but with his head on the block. Sir Richard de Lenorde gave the order for his execution, and stood by to see him die. The curse thy noble father left upon the head of him and his — the curse that still rings in my ears — has yet to be fulfilled."

With these words, the old man rose, and abruptly left the hall.

The Lady Alice, almost fainting, laid her hand upon the young lord's shoulder for support. He clasped her to his breast—all the tumult of his feelings giving way to love and pity. In the gloom of night that had gathered round them, he vowed again that no power should part them, and that he would be true to her even in death. He knew not yet the power of the malignant star that ruled his destiny.

No change could be noted in the grim features of the old man, when in the fresh air of morning he resumed his well-loved toil. He polished, filed, and riveted as before, and seemed to have no other thought than for the careful execution of his labours.

A light but firm hand laid on his shoulder caused him to start. He looked up, and saw fixed on him the pale and eager gaze of his young lord.

" Stephen, your tale was harshly told. It should have been given to my ear alone. But you are faithful. Is there yet more to be disclosed ?"

" What more do you think I have to tell ?"

" Nay, I know not. Old man, you have maddened me, and I will be content with no half confidence. Let me know all your thought."

The rigid features of the armourer relaxed, and he changed at once from the stern monitor of vengeance, to the old and devoted adherent.

" Dear lord, the living likeness of him I loved more than words can tell, I see in thee the only prop of this great house. Why should you stay here, when fame and renown are to be won abroad ? Why be an outcast from the court,

D

where friends are gathering to serve you? Why not appear before Edward's throne — men name him generous — re-assert your rights, and rescue from disgrace and obscurity an honoured name?"

A single night had aroused in the youth's breast all the warlike ardour of his race. He mused for an instant, and then said —

" Well, Stephen, say on."

"The rumour runs that the king is quick to be caught by address in warlike exercises. Who can have better claim to excel in them than you? If this hand, that taught you, be weak, it has the skill and cunning of sixty years' practice."

" You would have me, Stephen, take part in this tournament — this gaudy reflexion of the past. Well, what more ?"

" My honoured master, have I not proved to you my devotion and love? Let me implore you, as you regard the memory of your dead father, as you prize your own safety — no, no, I know you regard not that — as you would preserve the noble name that has descended to you, separate yourself from the enemies of your house, bid them defiance — a marriage with the De Lenorde ——"

" Peace, old man ! that matter is beyond you. I will go and demand justice from King Edward on his throne — demand the lands of which our house has been despoiled. Answer me not. See what arms you have ready for my use."

The armourer, with trembling hand, swept from the oaken board on which he worked the implements of his trade. Touching a hinge in front, a piece of planking was removed, and a lock exposed to view. Taking from his dress a large and curious key, he presented it, kneeling, to his lord.

The young baron seized and applied it to the lock; it turned, but the huge chest refused to open and disclose its secret. The old man took a ponderous hammer, and pointed to the head of a spring in the lid, which seemed merely one of the studs intended to give solidity to the structure. Lord Edmund grasped the hammer, swung it above his head, and let it fall with a tremendous stroke on the bolt-head. Loud was the clang; and as it died away, almost with the sound of a solemn and deep-toned note of music, the lid rose, and discovered the contents of the chest to the gaze of the startled lord.

Within, extended at full length, was a suit of gorgeous armour, disposed in the attitude of the sculptured effigy on the tomb of the last Baron of Fauconville. The gauntleted hands were raised as in prayer, and the vizor was down. The casque was surmounted by a noble plume; the cross-handled sword lay by the figure's side, and a shield hung at its feet.

The armourer was the first to break the silence.

"Such a figure, Lord Edmund, was thy father on that day when he overthrew Sir Richard de Lenorde. That armour was treasured for the heir of his house. See, I have kept it faithfully; there is on it no spot. In the sack and ruin of the castle, I saved this from the spoiler's hands."

As if under the influence of a magic spell, or as if he expected to view his father's form beneath the mail, the young lord, with a tender but eager hand, raised the polished breast-plate. A scroll of silver only lay in the hollow. It bore this inscription —

'𝕿is 𝖙𝖍𝖊 𝖑𝖞𝖓𝖎𝖓𝖌𝖊 of 𝖙𝖍𝖎𝖘 𝖒𝖆𝖎𝖑𝖊
𝕿𝖍𝖆𝖙 𝖒𝖚𝖘𝖙 𝖒𝖆𝖐𝖊 𝖎𝖙𝖘 𝖒𝖎𝖌𝖍𝖙𝖊 𝖆𝖇𝖆𝖎𝖑𝖊.

"The lining!" cried the youth, as the meaning of the
couplet flashed on his mind; "yes, the heart it covers,
not the steel itself,—the hand that grasps this sword, not
the inanimate blade, must win the victory. I am ready to
fulfil my part. Stephen, do thine. Come, encase my body
in this mail."

"Nay, my good lord, there is time yet. These games
are some days distant."

"As did my noble father, so will I. By the cross, I
swear, this armour shall not leave my limbs till it is taken
from my corse, or I have restored the fortunes of my
house!"

As the young lord spoke, his resolve inspired his features, lent fire to his eye, and, thrilling in his breast, expanded his whole frame with energy. The armourer saw
that was no time for remonstrance or advice. Piece by
piece, he encased his young lord's graceful and noble figure
in the brilliant steel, light, yet brought to the finest temper,
and polished as the purest mirror. Hammer and pincers
closed the rivets fast. The transformation seemed hardly
less wonderful than those recorded in the fables of old;
the peaceful dress gave place to the guise of full-armed
war. Completely locked up in the suit of steel, Lord
Edmund moved with dignity and ease, and raised the
cross-handled sword to his lips to seal his oath. The
kneeling armourer would have placed the gold spurs of
his father to the youth's heels—

"Not yet—not yet, good Stephen, I have to win them
first. By the grace of God and the Virgin, they shall not
long be wanting. Prepare for my journey. See that I

g> with the state befitting the Baron of Fauconville. Let these old walls see me ride forth in pride, as did my ancestors. If my train be scanty, there is more need for me to enlarge it. Let those beware who would stand between me and my birthright. On the second morning from this day, Stephen, I depart."

Again it was evening when the lovers met. But the sun shone no longer for them as formerly. Shades of fear and mistrust had gathered around their future. Lord Edmund was cased in steel, and felt not the gentle pressure of the hand of his betrothed. He answered her earnest entreaties —

"Dearly as I love you, Alice, all your persuasions are in vain. I have had visions of this hour before, but they were visions only of brightness. I dreamt of glory to be won without pain. Now I feel that the path I have to tread is a harsh one, but I will not shrink from it; the honour of my name must be vindicated; it is better I should die, than that its lustre should be tarnished."

"Why should you expose yourself to needless peril by going to the court, where the enemies of your house are so powerful? Remain here till the king requires your service in a foreign land; the delay cannot subject you to reproach."

"You are mistaken, Alice; there is not a vassal of my father's house, whose silence does not cast bitter scorn on my inaction. I understand their moody manner now. Why was there no friend to inform me earlier of this cruel truth?"

"For what good end could you have known it, Edmund? Other families have suffered as greatly, — ay, much more than thine. Your face is darkened; yet recol-

lect, in those pitiless wars how readily men devoted each
other to death—how little of mercy was shown on either
side."

"Peace, Alice, peace, for mercy's sake ; your accents,
sweet and gentle as they are, put me to torture. I know
what you would say. Your father sheltered my childhood. Well, but he repaid himself by my inheritance.
He protected my youth. True, but he believed he had
nothing to fear from me. He let us love, Alice, caring
nothing for the bitterness of this hour."

"You repent your love. You would have me absolve
you from your vow. So be it ! I have strength as well
as you, Edmund."

"No, Alice, no, as Heaven is my judge ! I love you
dearer, purer, truer than ever. But a blighted name you
shall never share. There are friends of my house around
Edward's throne. They believe me a fool or a coward ; for
rumour has been busy in throwing shame upon me. When
I appear in arms, that shame shall be dispelled ; my sword
shall hurl the slander down the throats of those who dare
to breathe it."

"Most of all, do I fear a quarrel between you and my
brother. He is hot in temper, and stands high in Edward's favour."

"That is well. He will assist me, then, to recover my
heritage."

"Let the king decide that. But, Edmund, you will
shun Raoul ? Promise me only that, and I will see you
depart with less pain."

On the part of the young lord there was a momentary
hesitation, and it was easy to see, from the heightened
colour of his brow, that strong passions were working
within his breast. At last he answered,—

"I will neither shun nor seek him, Alice. For your dear sake, I will give him no occasion of quarrel. And should we meet in the lists, what then? You hear how old Stephen despises the bloodless contests of these days. Calm your fears, love. Dark and terrible is the cloud that has come upon us; but who knows how soon it may break, and reveal again the pure sky? I hold you to your promise. To-morrow you will see me depart."

With that they separated.

Forth went the rumour round the country that on the Baptist's morning the Baron of Fauconville would ride from his castle in state to King Edward's tournament. Various were the emotions this intelligence excited. The adherents of the house of De Lenorde heard it with incredulity and ridicule, not unmingled with a feeling of fear. The old vassals of Fauconville were clamorous in their expressions of joy and triumph, and scrupled not to avow their belief that the time was come for the restitution of their house to its ancient splendour. Anxiety and expectation brought to the castle-yard a large assembly, who beheld with some surprise an image of the former fame and power of the barony in the preparations made. Some dozen of well-appointed men-at-arms stood ranged around the ground, ready to mount horse at their lord's command. A herald, with the arms of the Fauconvilles richly blazoned on his coat, and mounted on a gay steed, was giving orders for the departure, and a crowd of old retainers were preparing to welcome with applause the approach of their lord. If there was nothing grand in these arrangements, they were yet more imposing than had been looked for. Whatever was done, was in excellent order, and no more had been attempted than could be properly effected.

From the domestic apartments of the castle a door led to a balcony, which had formerly been distinguished for its rich gothic tracery: much of its ornament still remained, and it had been newly fitted with crimson cloth. Those most experienced in the past history of the house pointed out this balcony to their younger auditors, and told how in old times the lady of the castle had there stood to take leave of her lord, and to watch his departure through the castle postern, till he was lost to view in the woodland of the plains.

The faithful Stephen, with joints too stiff for active motion, remained beside this balcony, watching with keen eye that nothing was wanting in this hour, which he knew would be so eventful in the life of his lord. His grandson, a fair boy, partly supported the aged man, whose pride helped to keep him erect and stern. His two sons were in the young baron's train.

The hour of departure had arrived, and the herald sounded a cheerful blast on his trumpet, which, waking echoes so long undisturbed in the neighbourhood of those walls, filled the heart of every Fauconville with triumphant expectation. At the instant, Lord Edmund, mounted on a noble and completely appointed war-horse, rode into the yard. Two pages were at his side, one with a goblet of gold, the other bearing a light steel cap, rapier, and gloves for use in his journey. To the affright of some, and the amazement of all, the Lady Alice entered the balcony, to bid her knight "God speed." With graceful courtesy the young warrior urged his steed to the place where she stood. There was a momentary parting, and some words said of sweet delight, which brought the red blood brightly to the lady's face. In her aspect, hope seemed to have part, though her eyes were downcast and her hands

clasped. The page presented his lord with the cap, gauntlets, and rapier he bore. The young baron cast them to the ground. "Thus," he said, "will I travel,— in this guise will I remain till my fame as a knight will allow me to lay aside my father's helm and sword." He stooped to raise the goblet presented him on a salver, touched it with his lips, then waving for the last time his hand to his betrothed, he set forth with high and gallant bearing on his dangerous mission

Never had the English court been more gay than in the period immediately preceding King Edward's pro-jected invasion of France. The horrors of civil strife were over, and the whole kingdom rejoiced in its return to peace and security. The beauty of ladies, the valour and grace of knights, again became the theme of troubadours. Banquets and revels succeeded to strife and intrigue. The halls of royalty, brilliantly illuminated, echoed to the ring of joyous laughs, the tread of light feet, the strains of sweet music, the whispers of devoted love. Again quaint masques and gorgeous pageants enlivened the night, and tourneys, jousts, and other martial exercises, gave entertainment to the day. All appearance of mourn-ing was banished: the dresses found most favour that were most rich and fantastical. In hall and bower there fluttered the rarest materials, the gayest colours. Men said that the age of gold had at once succeeded to the age of iron, so gay, splendid, and luxurious, was the monarch's reign. Whoever was distinguished for courtly accom-plishments and grace of person found ready favour in the king's eyes. Full of his projected invasion of France, he sought to collect round him the most ardent and bravest spirits of the realm. The adherents of Lancaster ceased

to be objects of suspicion; their cause was utterly lost;
its princes cut off, its chiefs slain, its hopes and resources
alike gone. The victorious Edward reigned without fear,
and was inclined to show himself the king of the nation
rather than of a party.

Accomplished in all knightly exercises, beautiful in
person, gay, young, and graceful, the monarch delighted
in all the pomp and pageantry of the tournament. He
had ordered one to take place with unusual magnificence
at Westminster, and had invited all persons of gentle
blood to take part in it without distinction. Regulations
were issued to protect the combatants from unnecessary
danger, as the king wished the pageant to be distinguished
by superior address and agility, rather than by the number
of combatants slain and maimed. The gallant youth of
the kingdom looked forward to the martial show without
the slightest apprehension for the result, and fair ladies
anticipated the display of their lovers' heroism and splendour, without dread that they would be thrown lifeless to
the plain before their eyes.

The pageant was graced by the presence of King
Edward himself, who, with his beautiful queen, Elizabeth,
sat prepared to award favour to the successful knights.
The spacious amphitheatre of seats which had been prepared was crowded with fair and noble spectators, who
manifested their interest in the exercises by the bursts of
applause with which they rewarded unusual dexterity.
The better to prevent accidents, barriers were placed in
the arena, on each side of which the combatants were to
run, that they might avoid those fierce shocks of horse to
horse and man to man, which, in former times, had so
often been attended with fatal consequences.

The tournament was to last three days. To accommodate the crowd who desired to take part in it, the king ordered that no knight should combat on more than one day, and that each day should have its victor. The three conquerors were allowed to demand boons of the king, such as a great monarch might grant; and as it was known that on such occasions Edward was profuse in his liberality, the fortunate knights might well hope to gain the highest prizes in the gift of the crown to bestow.

Near the person of the king there sat one lady, whose bold and brilliant beauty attracted universal homage. Her countenance bore the aspect of that high command acquired by distinguished birth and early indulgence. Her eyes were dark, lustrous, quick, glancing, and full of passionate fire. Her voluptuous mouth and ripe lips, and her cheeks suffused with lively colour, gave to the haughty fair one an appearance of almost masculine beauty, but that her bust was so full and swelling, and that her raven hair fell in the richest profusion of waves about her neck. One seat lower, at her feet, was a gentleman in the prime of manhood, dressed in the richest style of that extravagant period, but whose natural nobility of look and goodly form carried off the bravery that might have made another appear ostentatious. He was in conversation with the proud lady, his face turned admiringly to hers.

" Do you tilt to-day, Sir Raoul ?" she asked.

" Good troth, I know not whether any knight will appear worthy my lance."

" What ! do you esteem your skill so highly ?"

" Nay, I rate not myself. Do you name one who has gained an advantage over me, and I will abandon to him the right of basking in your smiles."

" Well, Sir Raoul, I shall remember your words ; and

when I see a champion worthy your might, then will I
summon you to horse."

"And then will I prove myself worthy your favour."

"You will obey my command, to tilt or to refrain ?"

"Most faithfully : the Lady Elgarva shall be mistress
of my actions, as she is of my heart."

The haughty beauty exercised her privilege capriciously.
Many spears were fairly shivered that day, many an adventurous youth was hurled from his saddle into the dust
of the arena ; yet, though continually fresh knights
crowded forward, she kept Sir Raoul at her feet till a stout
knight, Lord William Audley, was proclaimed the victor.

Those who chose to conceal their titles were at liberty
to do so ; yet, though the practice was generally adopted
of choosing some motto or characteristic denomination,
the combatants seldom failed to be recognised by their
arms or manner ; for those who were accustomed to such
exhibitions could as readily detect a knight by his horse-
manship or bearing, as in these days an author is recognised by his style, or an actor by his voice, whatever
masquerade he may assume. But on the second day, a
young warrior appeared in the lists, with a plain shield,
terming himself " L'Inconnu," who baffled the speculations of those who boasted a knowledge of every good
lance in the kingdom. This young unknown, slight in
figure, but of most graceful bearing, and gorgeously
armed, obtained a decisive advantage over the knight who,
up to the period of his arrival, had maintained his good
fortune against all comers. There were some stout and
practised warriors who generously declined to combat
with so youthful a champion ; yet he shewed that their
forbearance was little needed. In three several encounters

with soldiers of high repute, he worsted them all, hurling the last, Sir Thomas Aspinall, who boasted much of his might, with force to the ground. The king loudly applauded the feat, and smiled upon the young victor as he rode round the barriers.

What prompted the graceful unknown, after each success, to single out the Lady Elgarva for his homage? Was it her brilliant beauty, or was it that Sir Raoul de Lenorde was at her feet? Had he forgotten so soon his vows to the lady of his love, the promise he had given her, the scroll that indicated it was the heart and cause of the warrior that won his triumph more than lance or shield? It was even so. In his hour of pride and victory, he saw only the enemy of his line; revenge dictated his homage to the haughty beauty; every tribute of admiration he offered her was a challenge to the knight who looked admiringly into her eyes. Still the Lady Elgarva kept Sir Raoul inactive, though he fumed to contend with the audacious champion. The young victor bowed with grave dignity to the acclamations of the crowd, after his last and most signal triumph, and bent low as the crest of his steed to the king's mark of admiration; then he looked up to the gallery where the Lady Elgarva was seated, and respectfully lowered to her the point of his lance. The proud beauty's cheek was flushed, as the eyes of the whole assembly were bent towards her; but her love of distinction was not yet satisfied. She spoke hastily to her lover, at her feet,—

" Now, quick, arm! Meet this champion. He will try thy prowess!"

Sir Raoul sprang to his feet; his arms and charger were at hand; but before he was prepared, the king, wishing to spare L'Inconnu too severe a trial of his force, gave the signal for the day's proceedings to end. Sir Raoul arrived only in time to see the successful unknown again lower his lance to the Lady Elgarva, while he was proclaimed by the heralds the victor of the day.

The contests of the third and last day were more numerous than on either of the preceding ones. Sir Raoul, fired by his disappointment, and the consciousness that Lady Elgarva's eyes were on him, early gained a superiority, and maintained it until the close of the contest. Those most experienced in martial exercises, and among them Edward himself, declared him to be one of the most accomplished soldiers in the realm.

A magnificent banquet was prepared for the evening; but in the meantime the king prepared to redeem his promise. The three victors were summoned before his throne, that the whole assembly might be witness with what readiness the king would grant whatever was demanded of him.

" What boon hast thou, Sir Raoul de Lenorde, faithful son of a faithful father, to ask of thy king, he will not freely grant ? Speak thou, and speak all freely."

" My liege, I beg of your grace's favour the hand of the Lady Elgarva Montacute."

" Ah ! St. George ! thou hast spoken well. The richest heiress in our gift; whose lands, too, lie not far from thine own, and a queen for beauty. Richer gift never sovereign accorded to a subject. De Lenorde, she is thine ! Now, Lord William Audley, speak thou. I need not tell thee to ask fearlessly. Thy modesty, man, I know will not be a barrier to thy preferment."

" Faith, your majesty, I have so great a love for your royal person, that I would fain be with you always. And as your grace's master of the horse——"

" Ho, enough. I would I had entered the lists myself,

rather than allowed thee to remain conqueror. Sir Edward Ashley, here. Make out the patent; Lord William Audley, my new master of the horse. This good soldier's bluntness has saved me a world of trouble in choosing from a crowd of applicants."

" Indeed, your grace," answered the staid minister of the king, " I think there be never a place vacant but there are a hundred seeking to fill it."

" And now, Sir L'Inconnu, since that is thy title, raise thy vizor; show thy face to thy king, and ask, if it be thy will, a richer boon yet. What, so young and fair ! By the rood, if thou followest me to France, and wield thy lance there so well, thou shalt have a duchy of our new kingdom. Thy eye is as keen as a hawk's, and thy hand as true to thy aim as his stoop on the quarry. What, noble boy—for noble I'll swear thou art—is thy petition ?"

" First, the honour of knighthood from your majesty's hand."

Lord Edmund could hardly have presented a request which the king would have received with more pleasure. The monarch expressed surprise that he had not already received the accolade from a more renowned sword than his. Then as the youth knelt, the king questioned him of his name, heard it rather with satisfaction than displeasure, and bade him rise, Sir Edmund, Baron of Fauconville.

" Now, ask again. I owe thy house no ill-will. Thy father died cruelly enough, as I have heard, before I drew sword. Thou art welcome to our presence. Say, what seal shall I put to thy allegiance ? What hast thou to ask from thy king ?"

The youth again fell on his knee.

" Justice, my gracious liege !"

" Ah—how ? Your words are wide."

"The restoration of my house's lands."

The king bit his lip angrily. These demands, which were becoming more frequent, perplexed him extremely, and for an instant he hesitated to reply. His petitioner eagerly watched the changes of the king's face, and seeing him still pause, poured forth a passionate appeal in behalf of his suit.

"Good, my liege, pardon my too great boldness! Hear me for an instant. My father fought for the king he served, as I would combat for your majesty's right this hour. He met his foes fairly in the field; he gave quarter where it was asked; he slew no prisoners; he struck no defenceless man; when the battle was over, he gave his hand to his foe; he fought with the chivalry your highness loves. The ancient foe of his house came against him treacherously and basely. To avenge a private quarrel, to wipe away a disgraceful defeat, he engaged your royal father's arms against my sire. What wonder that he fell! He was murdered in cold blood; his lands were usurped by his enemy. Pretending to be my guardian, he stripped me of my heritage, and left me only a ruined castle, and as many roods of land as might support a yeoman. Your highness knows what part the house of Fauconville has played in this kingdom's history. The name must perish without your gracious aid; I will not transmit it impoverished and disgraced. My dread lord, I am careless of myself; I desire only my house's honour. Grant me this boon. Make men respect your justice as they fear your might, and declare that the reign of vengeance is at an end."

The king was moved by the earnest words of his petitioner.

"Sir Raoul de Lenorde," he said, "I have heard of

this before. Restore to this young lord his lands, and I pawn thee a king's word, thou shalt lose nothing by thy act."

"My liege," answered Sir Raoul, boldly, "his father dared to brand thy father as a traitor, and justly died. He should be thankful for the clemency that has spared him."

The young lord's eye flashed with indignant fire, as he said —

"Dost thou, the son of the spoiler, justify the robbery? Shame on thy false heart ! Was it for this I took thy hand ?"

"Had I not, boy," contemptuously replied Sir Raoul, "been some moments too late for the combat yesterday, I would have quelled thy braggart spirit, and sent thee to beg cure of a leech, instead of lost lands from his highness."

"Be silent, on your lives, I charge ye," commanded the king, as he rose. "Sir Raoul de Lenorde, see thou that our bidding is fulfilled."

As the king turned to depart, Sir Raoul said, scornfully and aloud —

"A beggar is a traitor's fit descendant !"

"And this," exclaimed the young lord, quickly drawing his mailed gauntlet from his hand, "the fit answer to such a taunt."

He struck his rival with his steel glove as he spoke, fiercely across the mouth ; a stream of blood followed the blow. Swords were drawn ; but, at the king's command, his guards promptly interfered, and the fiery youths were removed in custody to await the king's pleasure.

Edward retired, enraged at the insult offered to his presence. For a short space he remained alone in moody displeasure ; then he summoned to him some of his chief

E

nobles, and announced his decision. As the rivals desired nothing so much as a personal encounter, he commanded that, on the morrow, they should engage in mortal combat, in the arena that had witnessed their triumph and their quarrel. If the vanquished escaped with life, the king's decree was, that he should die by the hands of the executioner. His estate was to be forfeited to the crown, and his title declared to be extinct. The friends of the two disputants heard this decision with awe; yet as it appeared just to both, and moreover would gratify the monarch's love of show, no one dared dispute it.

Heralds published abroad the king's pleasure, and announced the approaching combat. Then was it seen how slight was the interest felt in a mere pageant compared with that entertained for the game in which life was to the victor, and death to the vanquished. The old taste of London for bloody encounters seemed at once to revive, as the news ran through the city that a mortal duel would be fairly fought before the king. The merits of the combatants were keenly discussed, and places eagerly demanded. The hearts of court ladies beat with anxious thrill for the event of the morrow; each had her favourite, and such wagers as ladies lay were freely sported on the result. The barriers were to be dispensed with, the weapons were to be keen and sharp. All knew that one of the combatants must die.

Never had lists been graced with a goodlier show of spectators. There was something superior even to novelty in the excitement of this combat. As nobles sat together in the balconies, as groups crowded in the space below, they ceased not averring to each other that one of the combatants must die.

As it was told how gallantly they handled their weapons

--how nobly they rode — how fairly they had overthrown all opponents—how equally they were matched in skill and dexterity, it was still repeated that—one must die.

When the enmity of their line was spoken of, and the calamities that flowed from it were numbered,—when it was related that these knights were the last of their race, —it was answered, the feud must now cease for ever, for that—one must die.

The monks who attended to shrive the warriors and prepare them for the combat, exhorted them to leave no sin upon their souls, as on that morning — one must die.

King Edward himself, as he sat in his chair of state that day, knew that the affront to his presence would be dearly expiated, for that of the offenders — one must die.

The Lady Elgarva sat by the queen's side, her white bosom heaving. with strange excitement, and her eyes darting keener lustre, as she whispered in the ear of her royal lady, that—one must die.

Now, indeed, was the strife of four hundred years to terminate. Now, for the first time, the two sole representatives of their houses were to meet face to face, with the knowledge that the feud must end that day, and that of them — one must die.

In the spacious galleries not one place was vacant, when the monarch and his train appeared. The arena was cleared, and all was announced to be in readiness. The king raised his hand, the marshal of the lists shook aloft his truncheon, the heralds sounded a charge, and amid the silence of death, the champions appeared from opposite sides of the barriers.

The titles of the knights were read, and answered to with firm and steady voice. Each had his vizor up, and

gazed steadily upon his opponent.   They crossed from side
to side, passing each other in the centre of the ring.   Then
it was seen how much more powerful in frame was De
Lenorde, and how faint was the chance that his youthful
antagonist could successfully meet his assault.   As they
almost touched, they gave one to the other a grave and
courteous salute, while their noble chargers, as if this
were a day of festive pride, shook the ground with their
hoofs as they pawed it, and champed the bit and tossed
the head till the white foam flew over their steel frontlets.

The marshal, with his assistants, placed the knights in
line directly face to face, and the steeds, when their positions were assigned, seemed changed to marble, so still
and motionless did they stand.   Their riders took their
spears from the hands of their squires.   Lightly poised in
their hand for a moment, and held aloof, they were then
fixed in rest; the vizors were drawn down; the moment
of conflict approached.

The spectators drew their breath thickly ; some maidens
turned pale, sickened, and slowly fell from their seats.
There were none to heed or help them.   Every eye was
fixed on the arena, and on those motionless figures of man
and horse.

The marshal caught the king's eye ; it signified impatience.   The truncheon was raised : the heralds sounded,
once, twice—still there was no motion,—thrice—and as
if lightning had descended from heaven, and animated
those erect and splendid forms, they sprang at once into
vigorous and rejoicing life ; the chargers bounded impe-
tuously forward ; the earth trembled with the shock : they
met in mid-way.

There are sights of an instant—of a point of time too

minute to have a name—that are impressed for ever on the brain. Such a sight was the meeting of those noble youths.

Each aimed at the crest of his adversary, and each aim was true. Frightful was that crash of bounding life. The stout spears were shivered, but not before they had done their office. The helmets of the champions rolled far away, as the gallant steeds were thrown back on their haunches by the shock. Through the head and brain of the Knight of Lenorde went the well-directed spear-head, and borne back, he fell from his steed heavily, with his face to the dust. Firm in his saddle remained Lord Edmund, though not unscathed. The lance of his opponent, in carrying away his casque, had deeply gashed his throat, and his charger, freed from all control, carried him wildly round the barriers.

They raised the dying man, and took the fainting victor from his saddle. Then there was a buzz and movement, and the king rose, disturbed by a tumult at his back. Frantic with haste and eagerness, the Lady Alice De Lenorde fell at his feet. She had come too late. The Lady Elgarva caught up her magnificent train, and proudly swept past the hapless girl, as she fell senseless to the ground.

They bore the wounded lord to his paternal home, for there he was resolved to die. They laid him in that hall where he had first listened to the armourer's tale, when his heart was full of love and hope. He chose that chest for his bier, and his casque for his pillow. When told his wound was mortal, he refused to part with his coat of mail: in his harness would he die. He commanded that thus he might be laid beside his father.

Priests brought him the sacramental cup and the sign of redemption, and monks sang chants for his departing soul. The few faithful servants of his house were there, clamorous in grief, and some who claimed a dearer interest in him by birth, stood around him, and wept for the loss of so brave and true a knight. But the dying lord had voice and eye for one alone,—for that fair girl, the playmate of his childhood, the love of his youth, who hung entranced above him, answering only with the sobs of a bursting heart his prayer for her forgiveness. One last, last kiss was their parting pledge of love, ere the priest bade the knight fix his failing sight on the emblem of salvation. He turned his head; but when he no longer saw his beloved, darkness settled round him, and the monk who held the ready cup, raised his eyes, and said— " Peace be to his soul—he is dead."

With a broken spirit, the Lady Alice retired to a convent. She lived only long enough to see the heritage of her father and her lover shared by strangers; but the Lady Elgarva flourished for years in splendour and pride, the ornament of the court, and told, in after times, what noble rivals had contended for the light of her smile.

" Well !" exclaimed the Lady Eva, looking round, exultingly, at the conclusion of the foregoing story—" well, was I not right ? Are not those beautiful pictures tenfold more beautiful, now that we know what they mean ? For we do know what they mean, through that story, better than all the explanations in the world could have taught us.

" Come !" exclaimed she, after a pause, seeing that nobody volunteered to proceed with her project—" come ! *you* shall be the next on my list of story-tellers,"—turning, as she spoke, to the lady of a distinguished diplomatist,

who sat near her. "We know that *you* can make pleasant
stories, even out of painful subjects. Look at this poor
prisoner; he reminds me of *your* prisoner in *Maurice of
Saxony*. Do tell us a pitiful story about him!" And her
soft eyes seemed to be suffused with tears as she looked at
the picture.

· "But why, my pretty Eva," replied the lady so addressed, "why desire to hear more on a theme, the mere
mention of which has cast a melancholy hue on your late
happy face? Let us pass by the prisoner, and go to some
more pleasant subject."

"Oh, no! no!" cried the enthusiastic girl; "I like
to be unhappy sometimes—I mean, in stories and books;
it makes me so much happier afterwards. You *must* tell
us a story of this poor captive."

There was no reply to this earnest appeal from the
lovely Mistress of the Revels; and the lady to whom it
was addressed, proceeded, after a brief but thoughtful
pause, to relate the story of

ANDRIANI.

THE numerous islands which lie scattered on the bosom
of the beautiful Lago di Garda, were reposing under the
cool shadows of a gloomy evening early in the September
of 1259, while a soft breeze drifted at intervals dark and
vapoury clouds athwart the moon, confounding in occasional and partial obscurity the cottages and buildings
which were dotted along the shore, with the fruitful
orange, olive, and the luxuriant vine, whose tender stems.
bending under the burthen of their rich clusters, twined
and interlaced themselves in graceful garlands and festoons

from branch to branch of the mulberry groves, which were
grouped around these lovely retreats.   A small and lowly
islet, situated apart from its more congregated neighbours,
presented no other habitation — and, indeed, its circum-
scribed limits admitted none of greater pretension — than
a rude shed, canopied by a clump of pines, from the rough
hewn logs of whose paternal arms it had been fashioned,
apparently without the aid of any other implement than
the woodman's axe.   This cabin not unfrequently afforded
temporary shelter to the fisherman, while perseveringly
watching his carefully-laid nets and baited lines, till the
dawn should decide his success, and probable gain for the
coming day, by the fortunate capture of the delicious
carpione.   The south wind moaned capriciously and by
soft gusts, like the sobbing of wayward infancy, among the
tall flags and rushes which girded this islet, bending their
pliant spear-like forms till their taper tips, in their rustling
obedience to the breeze, kissed and rippled their dark and
watery bed, scaring from sedgy nooks and mossy banks
the wild water-fowl, which, startled as the waving reeds
grated above them or swept their drowsy pinions, dived
and darted from their osiery lairs in search of a haven
more secure from the molesting sounds which invaded
them.   Moving lights from the villas were dancing, like
wandering meteors, upon the ruffled waters, when a man
issued from the hut, and with crossed arms planted himself against the trunk of an ilex, which the lightning
of the summer's storm had not spared, and patiently
mused, till one glimmering beacon from the mainland
alone outlived its fitful companions.   Disburthening himself from his cloak, he cast it over his arm, and descending
the grassy slope to the narrow landing-place, threw it into
a small skiff which lay moored to the bank ; casting a rapid

glance over the wide waters, he lightly bounded into the
bark, and pushing it from the shore, rowed swiftly in the
direction of the signal, for the appearance of which he had
been so anxiously watching. Before he had passed more
than two-thirds across the lake, the beacon-light wavered,
and was scarcely perceptible. Resting upon his oars, he
surveyed the distance he had yet to make, then untied a
handkerchief from his neck, which he tore in half, and
muffling the filling of his sculls, pursued his course. The
cottage which it was his object to attain lay about two
hundred yards from the margin of the lake, and some three
or four miles above the castle of Il Garda. Humble as it
was, and poor as its appearance bespoke its inmates, con-
cealment seemed to be their main care, for, with the aid
of evergreen shrubs and climbing plants, it was nearly
hidden from observation. To judge by the countenances
and movements of those inhabiting this isolated dwelling,
poverty was around them, but peace of mind did not
lighten the evil; for penury, apparently, was the least of
their anxieties for the future. A hale, though elderly man,
whose garb denoted him to be a fisherman, was measuring
a small chamber with impatient strides; the net which
he had commenced repairing was thrown aside, for his
uneasy thoughts evidently did not admit of any continuous
occupation. Every now and then, he stopped short, and
placing his hands at each side of his face to shade his eyes
from the bright-burning lamp within, looked forth from
the casement, which commanded a view of the waters. A
maiden was seated somewhat apart from him; her face was
buried in her outspread hands; their whiteness, with the
delicacy of her form, proclaimed her peasant's dress to be
rather a disguise than the accompaniment of her station.
Although her face was concealed, and for many minutes she

did not vary her posture, her ready ear was evidently
watchful of, and took in every sound. When her companion closed the casement with an exclamation of impatience, a heavy sigh told of intense disappointment; that
sigh was responded to by a female, who arose from her
spinning-wheel, and laying aside her distaff, approached
her husband; for such he was. Gently touching his arm
she whispered, "You are a poor comforter, my Giovanni;
doubtless, he waits and watches until others are at rest."
Then, herself advancing to the window, she again drew
him towards it, and pointed to a dark object which was
gliding close in shore. Answering to her quiet intimation,
he replied, "It is not he;" then hurriedly lifting his cap
from the table, and removing the light further from the
window, unbarred the door.

"Oh, do not leave us, good Giovanni!" cried the
maiden, starting to her feet, while her dark eyes were
earnest with fear and entreaty. "If the doom with which
I am menaced were death only, I would say, Fly, and
leave me to my fate; but you well know it will be worse
—oh, ten thousand times worse than death, Giovanni!"

Here terror usurped her power of further speech, and
contracted her brow with agony. She clung wildly to
him. Respectfully he raised the distracted suppliant from
his shoulder, and, in a tone of mingled tenderness and
reproach, said, "Leave you, signora!—have I deserved
such a suspicion?"

"Oh, I mean not thus," she replied, energetically and
hurriedly; "for well I know that to succour me you are
ever heedless of your own safety: already, to protect me,
you have left all, and by your unshaken fidelity to the survivors of our crushed house, you have lost all. Reproach!
Oh! no, no!"

"Speak not thus, signora! I have done my duty; I have fulfilled my promise. But no more of this, dear lady; suffer me to quit you for a few moments only. Our beacon-light may have induced the brave Andriani to believe that he could join us with safety, and I much doubt if there are not watchers at this moment to intercept him."

An impatient tap at the window further alarmed the group, and the trembling girl was almost sinking to the floor with affright. Giovanni paused, and bent forward in a listening attitude. "Open for Andriani!" were the welcome sounds which reached his ear. He lost no time in admitting the visitor; but a stranger presented himself, and dread again pervaded the party, who feared to question the intruder. The open and anxious expression, however, of his fine features assured Giovanni, that, unaccountable as his appearance among them at such a moment might be, he did not come unwarranted, or with any hostile purpose.

Albina, who was still clinging to Giovanni's arm, raised her eyes to him, and demanded, in tremulous accents, "Are you come to aid?"

"I am indeed, fair lady; but there is little time for explanation. By Andriani's desire I have closely watched, in Verona, the movements of him who there holds sway. His secret purposes are well known to me. Thus, being apprised of your peril, I prevailed with the boatman to allow me to steer the bark which now lies moored to the willow by the shore, and which is destined, when Eccelino and his followers have secured you, to carry you down the lake. He has chosen this method for your transportation in order to screen from his wife and from the public eye an act of lawless violence, which might lead to further conspiracies against his power and life."

Giovanni struck his forehead, and looked upon **Albina**
in despair, at a loss how to evade the immediate danger
which seemed to menace them.

"Thus," answered the young stranger, responding to
his thoughts; "we must secure the boatman, and make
good speed up the lake. At the foot of the mountains we
shall find the assistance which Andriani, whom I have for-
warned, has doubtless provided for this emergency."

"Ready!" replied Giovanni, with energy, at the same
time thrusting a stiletto into his belt, and taking down a
broad-sword, which hung from the wall, concealed behind
his cloak.

"Oh, take me with you!" cried Albina, again appealing to her protector, and looking imploringly in his face.

"Are you prepared," he asked, "to witness strife, perhaps bloodshed, signora?—But hark!" A hasty step,
and the watchword, "Andriani," scarcely preceded the
entrance of our islet boatman.

"Thanks—thanks!" he said, pressing the stranger's
hand. "Albina, we must fly!" The appeal was answered by her throwing herself into his arms. The previous intention of the party was briefly explained to him.

"Hold!" he exclaimed, as they were leaving the cottage; "we need not this delay. Your weary and slumbering companion, my friend, is bound hand and foot in his
bark, and both are by this time far adrift upon the lake,
his sculls broken, and scattered on the waters. Farewell,
Giovanni; we must trust to your adroitness to delay and
mislead the tyrant."

While he said this, Giovanni took up the cloak which
he had thrown aside, and with the aid of his wife carefully folded it round their charge, who was quickly embarked, and the boat vigorously and rapidly plied up the

lake. They had scarcely departed, when the tramp of horses drew forth an exclamation from Giovanni; "The Virgin be praised—they will miss their aim!"

He had time only hastily to resume his net, and Benita her distaff, when Eccelino and his followers burst into the cottage, filled the small apartment, and Eccelino, advanc ing, cried, "Arise, old man!"

Giovanni did as he was bid, at the same time feign · ing surprise at the unwelcome intrusion. He carefully gathered up his net, and hung it over the wooden bench on which Benita was sitting, then coolly eyeing his unbidden visitors, bowed to their leader.

"What is the signor's pleasure?" he demanded. "If he comes in quest of fish from our lake, I am sorry to say that I can neither supply a carpione for his supper, nor earn my own breakfast for the morrow," pointing to the rent net.

"You know better, fellow; men come not armed to barter for fish. Where is the maiden who abides here — the famed bandit's sister? It is her we seek."

"No maiden harbours here," he replied, with a look of astonishment; "the signor is mistaken."

"It is false, knave! You shall pay for this." And seizing Giovanni by the collar, he shook him rudely, and bade him precede him in his search through the premises, while he sent two of his men to the shore.

"You see, signor, I spoke truly; the maiden whom you seek is not under this roof."

"Then thou knowest, knave, of her hiding or escape; either, doubtless, of thy contriving."

"You wrong me, signor," he answered, respectfully. "My faithful Benita and my net are all I possess."

"He speaks falsely!" cried one of the tyrant's myrmidons. "The boat sent under Matteo's care rides over the waters at the will of the waves."

"Old man, you shall speedily answer for this falsehood! Bind him, fellows!" cried Eccelino; "let him be food for the fishes."

"As I hope for the Holy Virgin's protection," cried the now terrified Giovanni, "I have not left my cottage since noon to-day; busy in repairing the fractures of my net—the only means of my subsistence,—I have neither found leisure to launch a boat nor handle an oar. Spare me, I beseech you!"

Giovanni did not expect the mercy which he craved from a man who notoriously never showed any. He cast a significant glance from the net to his wife, who, alert to his purpose, lifted it from the bench and placed it over his arm. A whispered communication, as she did this, passed between them, and she fled from the cottage. The old man now stood more resolute and erect, while a smile, almost amounting to defiance, curled his lip.

"As I left the shore," chimed in again the former speaker, "two men were manfully rowing a skiff up the lake, but were then scarcely a mile from the land."

"Doubtless," observed Giovanni, calmly, "they were fishermen, anxious to cast their net before the troubled waters shall render their labour useless. We poor fishermen," he added, "are obliged early and late to pursue our calling; for ours is a precarious subsistence, hanging upon the chances of wind and weather."

"Ha! ha! you are plausible, old man; but it will not avail you. Speak out, 'tis the only hope I give you for your life."

"Signor," he replied, "I trust not so, for how could I foretel your purpose or your coming? Bear me blameless, I beseech you, and seek her, for whom you inquire, elsewhere."

Eccelino, whose dark features were working with wrath, deigned no reply to this appeal; but, turning to his men, who were grouped around him, pointed to Giovanni and repeated his command.

" As he will not speak, do my bidding, fellows; and then to horse." While he was uttering this sentence, Giovanni had been imperceptibly gathering his net in his right hand, his eye continuing steadily fixed upon the speaker, from the hard lines of whose countenance, which grew sterner and sterner, he saw that further parley or remonstrance would be instant death. As the men advanced to obey and seize him, he sprang suddenly upon the table, and casting the net dexterously over the bystanders, at the same time kicked the lamp to the other side of the room, and without a pause, darted through the casement.

The rowers exerted their utmost efforts; the wind was rising each moment, the waters became more and more disturbed, and threatened to swamp their light bark. Few words were spoken. Albina, reclining at the bottom of the boat, and, drenched with the spray which continually broke over them, endeavoured, with straining eyes, to penetrate the gloom which was increasing on all sides, and assure herself that they were not pursued. At lengthened intervals the pale-faced moon, for a few brief moments, shone forth, as if, by her transitory light, she would display to them the rising surges around them, and their consequent danger; then merging herself again behind piled mountains of dense and purple clouds, left them to combat with their peril, without a beam by which to steer their course.

The dreary prospect thus momentarily presented to

their view, served the more to stimulate the energies of the unflinching boatmen to continued and increased exertion. They well knew that as yet the troubled waters were only lashing themselves into the utmost terror of their fury, and that when the acme of their foaming rage should overtake their light bark, which for some time they had with difficulty steered across the agitated waves, it must fill and sink in the storm.

On the morrow, perhaps, the blue waters would array themselves in sunny smiles, and calmly ripple over the victims of their wanton anger, as if in mockery of human weakness when contrasted with their now overwhelming power; then, in playful gambols, cast their lifeless prey from their cold embrace, and convince the ruthless tyrant, who would capture to destroy, that his passions were baulked, and his cruelty forestalled.

Rapidly-following flashes of lightning were succeeded by, and left them in, total darkness; the distant thunder rolled and echoed among the rocky mountains; the boatmen, in tenderness to their helpless charge, were silent, nor did Albina impede their strenuous exertions by expressed terror or useless complaints. One involuntary exclamation alone escaped her, as a flash of forked lightning, which swept along the whole range of the horizon, and rendered every object for a moment perfectly visible, blinded her.

"Thank Heaven!" exclaimed Andriani, as the transient illumination left them, " we are under the lee of the mountains." They had, indeed, nearly gained the head of the lake, and were entering into smoother water. By the repeated and vivid flashes which danced and played on every object around, they descried figures moving on the shore. To this point they steered.

"Hold! they see us," cried Leonisio, laying his hand on the arm of Andriani, who was preparing to give the signal of their approach. While they were yet some yards distant from the intended spot of their disembarcation, two troopers, with led horess, dashed into the water, breasted its violence, and gained the boat.

"Either this is a frantic freak, Antonio," said Andriani to the foremost man, " or immediate danger has prompted it."

"The latter," quickly replied Antonio. "Mount, and haste away. Our scout reports that they will soon be upon us. I have posted our party in advance, to parry their first attack ; they greatly outnumber us already, and doubtless their leader is not far behind."

Andriani made no reply; but, as Leonisio steadied the boat, lifted Albina on one of the led horses. "Now you, Count, to the saddle, and follow ; to your protection I trust Albina ; I will keep the jackals at bay, and head my faithful followers, who are prodigal of life and limb in my service."

Leonisio hesitated. "My friend, it must be so," added Andriani; "here you can do me little service ; in accompanying and guarding her, much. Antonio will be your guide."

Leonisio paused no longer, but springing on the animal held for him, gained the landing-place with his precious charge. A few strokes brought Andriani's bark to the shore, and as few moments saw him armed, mounted, and in full career to join his band, repel the attack of his enemy, and cover the retreat of the fugitives.

With desperate haste they urged on their flight; heavy sighs were the only responses Albina was able to give in reply to Leonisio's encouraging words. What torture of

F

heart did the reflection bring, that the brave Andriani was
left to stem the fury of that powerful and unrelenting foe,
the scourging-rod destined for a time to lash Brescia,
Padua, and Verona, and track his way with cruelty and
bloodshed.   Her companion answered to her tears and
sighs, (for hers was the mute eloquence of grief,) by
assuring her that Eccelino could not yet have joined the
party he had sent forward early in the day, possibly to
watch Andriani's movements, even if he intended to do so,
which he doubted.   His speech and tone were gentle and
persuasive ; he warmed into enthusiasm when he spoke of
Andriani's courage, forethought, and intelligence ; he further urged his presence of mind and aptitude at stratagem,
qualities which had served him in many hair-breadth
escapes and encounters, and would, he trusted, avail him
now as they had done.   Such arguments were judiciously
brought forward by snatches only, when he found that
Albina's grief and terror were enfeebling her frame.

Day dawned as they reached the intricacies of the
mountains, and they were obliged to slacken their pace ;
for here a torrent, hissing, roaring, and tumbling through
a deep ravine, was to be forded, there a perilous cleft, between two perpendicular rocks, to be crossed.   The intimate knowledge which their guide possessed of such passes
alone ensured their safety : one false turn would have precipitated them headlong to destruction.   The storm during
their progress had passed away, and the moon once more
rode unclouded in the heavens.   A stony steep at last
brought them to the face of an overhanging rock, which
rose like a wall before them ; a sharp turn inwards round
its angle, led them to a passage which did not admit two
a-breast.   At its termination, there was just sufficient
room to turn their horses, and to pursue a still longer and

narrower path which fronted them, and which after ascending and descending, introduced them, when the watchword
had been given, into a wide and open space, resembling a
rude but roofless cavern ; for slanting rocks were still piled
toppling a hundred feet above them. A mountain spring
came leaping down the craggy heights; then overflowing a
? atural basin, crept away among the numerous fissures, to
fill some cavern pool, or feed a never-failing stream. The
day was breaking, as Albina was lifted exhausted from her
horse, and consigned to the care of two females, who, like
others, had fled with their husbands from Eccelino's barbarity, to join Andriani's band in the mountains. One of
the troopers had been sent back, when the fugitives had
gained the narrower defiles, to seek his leader, and carry a
report of their progress; but when he reached the scene of
the night skirmish, neither friend nor foe in life was there.
Filippo found two of his comrades in the sleep of death ;
one had expired clutching the throat of an enemy, with
whom apparently he had been in contention when he received his own death-wound. He turned and wept, for it
was his brother. A wretched peasant, who had come to
glean a harvest from the dead, assisted him to bear the
corpse to the bark which Andriani had left upon the shore;
they sank the body in the deep water, cased in its heavy
accoutrements, without a funeral rite, and then accorded to
its gory companion and foe the same watery grave. The
peasant could tell him nothing, for he had issued from his
hiding-place after the fight was done. These melancholy
obsequies performed, Filippo retraced his steps; as he
gained the mountains, his companions gradually joined
him; where was their leader? Their downcast looks
answered, " a prisoner."

When Leonisio had arisen, he satisfied himself that

another outlet from their fastness existed, but too dangerous
to be attempted, save in a case of utmost need. Seeing
the band enter one by one, he anxiously waited to greet
his friend; but the despairing looks he encountered were
heralds to the sad news they brought. Could they tell
aught of him? Only this, that, too eager to lead on his
men, he had rushed a-head of them, was surrounded, and
made prisoner. In this strait, he called to them to save
themselves, and report to Leonisio his condition. Had
Eccelino come up with them? No; but it was their belief
that Il Garda would be Andriani's prison. Leonisio turned
mournfully away, and placing his foot on a projecting stone,
for a few moments gave himself up to thought. His reflections were soon matured; he changed his position, and
gazed upwards at the sun, which was shining brightly
upon their retreat, then called the men around him.

"A good omen," he said, cheerfully, pointing to the
heavens; "refresh yourselves, my men; at nightfall, disperse near the passes, and wait until a signal shall call
you together; I must enlist two of you to accompany me;
Antonio, you must remain with six others to guard our
charge."

All who were not disabled volunteered their services,
but lots were drawn. While Leonisio hastily broke his
fast, a fresh horse was brought from one of the caves
which opened upon this arena ; and with a heavy heart he
again descended the mountain.

Exhausted by fatigue, wounded and shackled, the unhappy Andriani lay stretched on his stone pallet, in a
dungeon of the castle of Il Garda. The fates had torn out
the bright page of hope from the tablets of his future
fortune, and the prospect of a scaffold was before him. The

licentious tyrant—he who in the plenitude of his abused
power had ordered the execution of Count Bonifazio di
Panego, his brave father,—the execrable Eccelino, the
spoiler of his house and lands, would perpetrate the last
act of the tragedy, and in his person extirpate his house
and name. How impotent was he now to redress these
wrongs! how subdued, how crushed and sunk were those
high aspirations which had goaded and sustained him
to seek for restitution, retribution, or revenge! The cold
dew gathered on his brow like the unwholesome damps
which exuded and were dripping from his prison walls.
He clenched his hands in agony across his forehead, as he
recalled the scenes of misery and bloodshed his young and
innocent years had witnessed, and the narrow escape of his
loved Albina from dishonour; but he had saved her, nor
did he doubt the devotion and fidelity of his followers, the
friendship of Leonisio, or their united valour and endeavours
to secure her preservation in those secret haunts and fast-
nesses which had so long sheltered him; then other thoughts
as tender, but more selfish, stole over his weary senses : the
vision of his Fiorenza rose in her beauty before him ; her
beaming eyes seemed to gaze in sorrow upon him, her
parted lips to pour forth words of constancy and consolation
to him. In airy dreams again he trod with her the tranquil groves which had often witnessed their youthful sports;
again he wearied his young voice in rivalry of song with
hers; then hanging their lute upon a branch of the sober
cypress, which, clothed with dark, impervious foliage,
spread widely its evergreen arms of fan-like form, whiled
away the hours of noontide heat in listless indolence under
its friendly shelter; or, wandering among the brakes and
dells, sportively caught in their tiny palms the liquid gems
which parted from the cascade above, broke upon the lower

rocks, and dashed far and wide among the lichens, ferns,
and creeping plants which trailed or waved their bright
green leaves in contrast to their gray and stony cradles.
Then sterner visions invaded these peaceful fancies of
childhood's happy and thoughtless spring-time days; blood
and deadly strife were mixed with fantastic scenes of splendour; while gnawing reptiles fixed upon his heart, grotesque and horrid masks chased him round lordly courts
and halls, through devious paths and mountain steeps to
the brink of a precipice; he groaned and awoke. A muffled figure with folded arms was standing beside his pallet,
and watching his countenance as each unreal and wayward
fancy passed over it. His name pronounced aroused him;
he raised himself upon his elbow, and endeavoured to
recognise the person before him, for surely it was a voice
which had once been familiar to his ear — a voice whose
friendly tones had relaxed into discord since the harmony
of his own fortunes had been broken.

"Andriani," repeated his visitor, "chance brought me
to Il Garda, as you were led a captive through its gates;
I have come to save you, if you will."

" If you have the power to release me from the tyrant's
clutches, Count Bonifazio, it must be done at your will, not
mine ;" and he fixed his bright, keen eye upon him.

" I will it, Andriani, if, without delay, you accede to
my conditions; Eccelino knows not yet of your capture."

" Name them, Count," he replied; " I am not indifferent to life, and will purchase it on honourable terms."

" Renounce, then, your contract with Fiorenza," said
the Count, sternly. "Count Bonifazio's daughter shall
never be the bride of an outlaw."

" Does Fiorenza demand this of me ? Does she, too,
abandon the oppressed and deserted Andriani?"

"She does, Andriani, for your life's sake—to spare the Count Panego's son from an ignominious death."

Andriani rose, his eyes flashed with the fiery resentment of his heart. "Did Panego's son, Count Bonifazio," he demanded, energetically, "deserve an ignominious death, when, foremost among your followers, he fought by your side,—when, with your son, the brave Leonisio, more than once he defended your castle walls? Did he deserve an ignominious death, when he cleft in twain the soldier whose sword was at your breast, and when anew you swore to keep inviolate his contract with Fiorenza? Was he an outlaw until you made peace with that tyrant, who, amidst the tears and lamentations of all Padua, sent the noble Panego to the scaffold? who drove the persecuted and forsaken Andriani to the mountains, to seek a precarious subsistence for himself and those true, though humble few who still faithfully adhered to him? Has Andriani's arm slain the impotent and helpless? Has Andriani's tongue given forth the barbarous fiats of torture, mutilation, and, after, death to the weak and defenceless? Hath he constructed in his mountain holds horrible prisons and infernal machines for human suffering, and torn the lacerated and quivering limbs from his innocent victims? Hath he saturated each impress of his foot with blood, and made his name an accursed watchword for barbarity? It is not the outlaw, Count, whose alliance you now scorn, but the beggar! A beggar, beggared by that scourge and monster of mankind, your kinsman, Eccelino!" He paused, then in a hoarse tone added, "If Fiorenza renounces me for such heinous crimes, let her declare to Andriani that Andriani is unworthy of her pure love— let her denounce the proclaimed outlaw, and forswear her

often-plighted faith; if she refuse this, there is truly but
but one remedy."

"Name it," cried Bonifazio, with eagerness.

Andriani approached him, and bending forward, whispered, "Send the son of your bosom friend to the ignominious death with which you threatened him; his
constancy and hers will well deserve such a punishment."

The Count was staggered, and could find no reply. He
knew that he had a noble heart and a lion spirit to deal
with; he could find no ready arguments to contravert the
painful and upbraiding truths which had been spoken; he
turned away, and motioned as if to depart. Andriani
watched his receding figure. "Hold, Count, yet one
word; you shall now hear *my* conditions."

The Count Ricciardo returned. "The love of life,"
he thought, "will yet subdue Andriani's haughty mind."

They gazed for a few moments in silence at each other;
the trace of passion and the flush of anger had passed from
the prisoner's countenance; he stood pale, but proud and
erect, before the Count, who waited with impatience for
his proposition. "Speak quickly, young man, for time
wears; by special favour from the governor, I have obtained access to you; I may not tarry."

"Release me, Count," said Andriani, calmly. "Leonisio, mark me, has sworn to revenge my death; release
me, Count, for that time may come, when Andriani's arm,
and Andriani's mountain horde, may serve you and his
country well. I will not abandon my contract with Fiorenza,
nor Fiorenza's love; neither, till better fortune — if I
live — shall again invest me with Panego's honours, and
Panego's lands, will I claim Fiorenza for my bride. I
would live, but live with honour; I fear not death."

"You trifle," returned Count Bonifazio. "You forget," he added, with emphasis, "that death dissolves all
contracts."

"So it would appear, noble sir, for even your sworn
friendship and brotherhood were buried in Count Panego's
grave."

The Count winced; the reproach stung him, and came
home to his heart; nor could he stifle the full remembrance
of the oaths by which he had bound himself to protect the
unfortunate prisoner before him, the son of his murdered
friend. He would fain save him, but upon his own terms.

"You are mad!" he at last exclaimed. "When, like
a wild bird, you chose the mountains for your haunts, why
did you daringly quit their heights to invade our peaceful
valleys in search of prey?"

"Ha! ha! peaceful valleys, say you, Count?—peaceful valleys? Know ye that the putrid atmosphere from
your blood-stained lowlands, rises like a noxious vapour to
taint and infect the pure ether of our cloudless skies?
You ask why did I leave my mountain-heights for your
pestiferous valleys? I will tell you, Count Ricciardo di
Bonifazo," and he powerfully grasped the Count's arm.
"I left them to save Count Panego's daughter from the
wanton pursuit of Verona's ruler; to save her, that tongue
should not report—that eye should not see—Albina di
Panego the leman of her father's murderer. Yes, the
eagle left his eyrie to snatch the innocent lamb from the
vulture." As the last sentence left his lips, his nervous
grasp on the Count's arm relaxed, his countenance assumed
the hue of death, and he sank back on his pallet senseless.

When Andriani awoke from his stupor, and feebly
raised his head, the lamp was newly trimmed, food was
placed by his pallet, and his manacles removed.

Before Bonifazio had entered his dungeon, the pangs
of hunger for some hours had gnawed him, and further
spent by emotion, even his hardy frame could endure no
more, but sank, completely subdued.   He stretched his
hand to the pitcher of water, slaked his burning thirst, and
eagerly devoured the provision at his side.   The day was
waning into night, but he had no guide to passing hours.
He had slumbered, and ere the Count's departure, had
been deprived of sense, but how long he had thus remained
he knew not; possibly, some kindly feeling had prompted
Ricciardo to wait till he showed symptoms of recovery from
his deadly swoon ; perhaps he tarried with the hope that
he might never wake again; for unless he would consent
to abandon what was dearer to him than life, Fiorenza's
love, the Count's interest did not tally with his preservation, and then he thought how scenes of strife change men's
minds—ambition unrestrained, their kindlier natures—
how does it warp their first and better purposes !

He rose, and ascended the steps which led to the
strongly-secured door, but no human effort could move it.
He sat himself down upon the upper stair, his head bowed
upon his bosom.   The Count, doubtless, had left him to
his fate, but would not Leonisio, when his men brought in
news of his capture, seek him ?   Perhaps the knowledge
of his captivity would only reach him when too late.   But
how useless were these reflections of mingled doubt, hope,
and despair, to amend his condition !

With a heavy sigh he once more returned to his
wretched pallet, and, taking up his lamp, determined to
examine the extent of his prison.   As he did so, its light
gleamed on the polished blade of a dagger, which pro-
truded from his resting-place of stone and straw.   A ray
of hope again crossed his mind ; he tried its edge ; and

minutely inspected it. The word "Hope" was barely discernible upon its bright surface. He placed it in his bosom, and a thousand wild conjectures rapidly succeeded each other in his thoughts. Was this weapon conveyed to him to provoke his despair to suicide, or as a protection against secret assassination? He would not believe that the Count, however anxious he might be to rid himself of his claims upon him, or however unwilling that the affianced husband of his daughter should be led to public execution, would instigate the one, or sanction the other atrocious measure. He was bade to hope. In what anticipation could he indulge, if the news of his capture should reach Eccelino? for how would that tyrant exult if he could satisfy and satiate his own hatred and revenge upon the plea and show of justice! In those deep vaults no sound could reach him; there all was solitude and silence, nor did his lamp illuminate one third of his unexplored and spacious, but dreary prison. It was possible there might be some other available outlet, and he now proceeded to put into execution his intention, and ascertain its limits. He passed through numerous intersected arches, springing from short and heavy columns, doubtless, in part, supporting the castle towers above, until he arrived at the massy wall which enclosed him. With patient scrutiny, he held his lamp in every direction; his foot stumbled, the ground was no longer level; it was a newly-made grave that had endangered his falling, and the consequent extinction of his lamp. He shuddered, and imagined himself a partner in the same lone prisoner's grave, or one beside it. It had been made and closed, apparently in haste, for a pick-axe was lying close by, as if hurriedly cast aside. A small iron grating, immediately but high above this dungeon sepulchre, imparted new hope to our

prisoner. With the implement so happily offered to his
hand he contrived to excavate a footing, and assiduously
bent all his force to remove the bars from their sockets.
The work was nearly completed, one bar only remaining
before a free passage would crown his efforts, when advancing footsteps told him how useless his labour had
been. There was no time to quit his position, for two
persons stood directly beneath him. The ponderous instrument was in his hand; should he hurl it at them? The
aim was sure, and one thus disposed of, the other would
soon succumb to his strength and prowess. He raised his
arm, but before the fatal stroke was given, the lamp, which
his supposed assailants had lifted from the grave, shone
upon the upturned features of Leonisio! With one bound
Andriani was at the side of his friend—one sentence alone
was exchanged—Albina was safe. Leonisio's companion,
meanwhile, was examining the work which the prisoner
had commenced. "Since the signor," he observed, "has
opened this barrier, it may be a better and a safer way for
us, and may hereafter save my neck, if I should fall into
the governor's hands, by drawing suspicion from me as
having aided in his escape."

They lent their united efforts, the remaining bar was
soon removed, and the party found themselves in a vault
nearly resembling the one they had quitted.

"Have you the key?" demanded Leonisio, as he
advanced to the door. His attendant looked blank.

"And if I had," he answered, "there are strong bolts
on the other side."

"Then we must hew a passage through the walls,
cried Andriani; and with both hands he raised the pick-
axe, which he still retained, above his head.

The other arrested his arm. "Hist, Signor! this

prison has not of late been used, I bethink me the door
may not be closed;" at the same time he advanced before
Andriani, and pulled at a strong iron ring, which was in-
serted near the lock. The door yielded, and they entered
a passage hewn in the solid rock. Singly and in silence
they pursued its tortuous windings, which were at last ter-
minated by a grated portal. Here a justly-fitted key, produced by their conductor, gave them exit upon a narrow
and low platform, where a sentinel was making his solitary
turns. Before the soldier had time to give the alarm,
Andriani rushed upon him; assisted by his companions,
he disarmed, and thrust him within the passage, then
closed and locked the grated door upon him. It was still
dark when they descended the slimy steps which led to
the water. Leonisio struck his sword sharply against the
wall; upon the repetition of the stroke, two boatmen
appeared from behind the lee of a buttress, and quickly
steered their bark alongside the rocky stairs. As the released Andriani turned his eyes to look back upon the frown-
ing aspect of the stronghold from which he had escaped,
he breathed more freely: they gained the shore as the
dawn began to break, and ere the sun had shed his full
influence on the tops of the mountains, Albina was in
Andriani's arms.

Their escape had been too rapid to allow of observation, question, or rejoinder. As they passed onwards,
according to the preconcerted signal decided upon by Leonisio, the band by degrees left their hidden lairs, and congregated round their leader. Albina looked inquiringly
in her brother's face; his exhausted condition and disordered appearance told plainly of some bygone fearful
struggle, and her speaking eyes demanded an explanation
which she dared not trust her voice to ask.

"He has saved me, Albina," pointing to Leonisio;
" how, you must demand of him, my sister."

" I would ask him," she replied, " I would thank him,
but my gratitude overmasters my power to do so." Her
thick voice and falling tears confirmed the simple assertion.
Leonisio looked upon her; he now saw her in all the
freshness of her beauty, heightened by feeling and tenderness, drawn from the pure sources of affection, sisterly
love and gratitude, and he rejoiced as he contemplated
this lovely work of nature, that the service which in
friendship he had rendered, might allow him some claim
for a return of that love which was springing in his bosom.

It was now Albina's turn to assist in administering to
their wants, for, in truth, the whole party needed refreshment and rest.   While they partook of the former,
Andriani related his capture and escape, but in considera-
tion of Leonisio's feelings, touched lightly upon his interview with the Count in his prison. " And now, my friend,"
he said, as he concluded, "you must take up the tale, for
by what means or agency you effected my deliverance, I
have yet to learn."

" Willingly," replied Leonisio. " When I quitted this
airy castle of yours, I had hardly shaped my plans, save
that on your rescue I was determined ; I hoped, as in fact I
did, to meet my father at Il Garda, on his way to Verona.
I desired to be immediately conducted to his presence, but
I did not find him in the quarter assigned to him. While
searching for him I encountered Niccolo, who is my foster-
brother, and bound to me by the strongest ties. From
him I learned that for some months he had been entrusted
with the charge of the state prisoners; that Eccelino had
arrived at the fortress during the night, sought some hasty
refreshment, and then returned immediately to Verona ;

that you had been brought in soon after dawn, a captive, and just at the moment of my father's arrival; and that he, Niccolo, was then waiting his return from your prison, whither he had conducted him, to carry your supply of food. I knew Niccolo could not and would not refuse me any service I might demand from him; hastily, I scratched the word 'Hope' upon my dagger, and enjoined him to place it where you would find it, and then appointed him, these duties performed, to meet me at midnight at the same spot. I again went to seek my father; when he entered his apartment, where I had been waiting for some time with restless impatience, I strongly urged your claims upon us, and from him heard the full detail of your stormy interview. I found that he was ill at ease with himself: pride had veiled his better feelings, but had not smothered them. Your reproaches, while they angered, had also shamed and grieved him; and Eccelino's infamous attempt to carry off your sister had disgusted him, while it justified your descent from the mountains, and your encounter with his troops in her defence. He confessed that the shade of your murdered father seemed to hover between yourself and him in your lonely dungeon, and that on leaving you in that exhausted state, he had commanded Niccolo to remove your chains, and supply you with sufficient and proper food. Fiorenza's positive refusal to break her plighted faith with you, unless at your demand, as the last sacrifice which she could make to save your life, had maddened him. He left her at San Bonifazio, with the determination to seek and force you into compliance, if possible. When thus fortune assisted his measures, and placed you in his power, he procured permission to visit you. Fortunately, the soldiers who brought you to Il Garda had not yet departed from that fortress.

From this conversation I gathered, that although he wou.d bend you to his purpose, he was loath to denounce you to his kinsman, with whom, as you know, he is frequently at warfare. I left him, with the assurance on my part, that I would keep inviolate my faith, and hold sacred my bond of friendship with you in flood and field. I ordered the two men who accompanied me, members of your own band, to station their boat at any point which Niccolo should indicate. He agreed to accompany me to your dungeon; the rest you have already told."

While Leonisio thus simply and briefly narrated the means he had taken for Andriani's escape, Albina's eyes were bent upon his glowing countenance; to the gratitude which was thrilling in her bosom, she dared not give expression, lest other feelings, more tender, should form themselves into words, and give too strong an essence to her speech. She was hardly conscious herself, of the struggle which was passing within, but Nature loves not control; the blushing cheek was the tell-tale of the guileless heart. On his return, Andriani had ordered a dozen men, under the command of Antonio, to keep watch in the mountain passes, to act as scouts, and to collect forage. The peasantry were willing enough to supply those who protected, but did not molest them.

The gray of evening was now throwing its shadows on every recess and cavern opening, while the projecting rocks caught the golden tints which departing day had yet to give, when our trio were once more assembled in their roofless hall. The laugh and jest, with recollections of early days, for a time kept them in conversation; but, by degrees, their spirits and thoughts partook of the fading tints around them. Andriani's were far away, with his peerless Fiorenza; Leonisio dwelt with concern upon his separation from Albina on the morrow; and Albina was occupied with similar regrets, and mingled fears for the fate of the faithful Giovanni and Benita : thus, by degrees, they sank into silence. A sudden movement among the men at the entrance of the passage, where they were on guard, and where others were also grouped, roused Andriani from his reclining position. Antonio entering, followed by four of his companions, and leading three persons captive, sent the angry blood into Andriani's cheek.

"Leonisio," he cried, turning to his friend, who had also quitted his seat by Albina, "this is not our usual mode of warfare ! What means this, Antonio; and by whose authority do you make war on women?"

"Abate your displeasure, I pray, Count," replied Antonio respectfully, at the same time advancing, somewhat alarmed at the wrath which was quivering on his commander's lips and darting from his eye. "We found these persons wandering among the mountains : they stated that their feeble escort had been dispersed, and their baggage plundered, by some loose and disorderly stragglers from Eccelino's troops. While these marauders were intent upon rifling the booty, with the assistance of the brave old man who was part of their convoy, they fled, and reached the shelter of the mountains. He gave me reason to believe, by the extravagant marks of joy which he exhibited, when, in answer to his questions, he found you were rescued, and by his acquaintance with our password, that he was one whom you would gladly see; his only desire, he said, was to join you ; he implored me also to protect those with him. I consented so to do, if they would not hesitate at the perils of our way, and permit themselves to be blindfolded. Thus, carefully guiding them, I have brought them hither."

G

While he was yet speaking, Andriani motioned for his unexpected visitors to be brought forward.

"You have done wisely, Antonio, although not exactly the booty I expected you to bring."

"Not less welcome, I will vouch," cried Giovanni, stepping forward.

"Far, ah, far more welcome, my faithful friend!" cried Andriani, greeting him most cordially, "for in truth, Albina and myself have had many misgivings on your account."

"Indeed, indeed, we have, my good Giovanni!" cried Albina, while the warm and grateful tear dropped upon the old man's hand, which she fervently pressed. Giovanni's features lighted up with a beam of satisfaction, and an arch smile played round the corners of his mouth, as he turned his head over his shoulder; but a painful throb sent the colour from Albina's cheek, as she saw one of Antonio's female captives locked in Leonisio's arms, and leaning on his shoulder. He was tenderly bearing his burthen towards them, but she had not the power to quit the spot, and give the fugitives the greeting their situation demanded. Andriani caught but one glimpse of that fair form, when, with a bound, he was at her feet, "Fiorenza! my beloved Fiorenza!"

The rocks around echoed the passionate exclamation, "Beloved Fiorenza!" The icy chain, which, for a few moments, had rivetted Albina, was broken, and, with unfeigned joy, she pressed Fiorenza to her bosom. Leonisio resigned her to Albina's care, and took Giovanni aside, for an explanation of this unexpected meeting. Andriani cared only that she was there, and all he loved around him.

At this blissful moment, years of adverse fortune, sorrow, strife, and struggle, seemed to be repaid, and blotted from his memory. Giovanni related his escape from Eccelino : he had concealed himself till the tramp of horses assured him that the tyrant had taken the road back to Verona ; he then returned to his cottage, provided himself with some necessaries and provision, and having sought Benita at the house where she had taken refuge, obtained a horse, and went in quest of Andriani. On his way, he heard of his disaster ; then changing his course, he did not pause until he reached San Bonifazio, hoping that the Count would exert himself to save the son of his lost friend, but he was gone ; he then entreated to be admitted to the presence of the Lady Fiorenza, who was nearly distracted by the intelligence which he brought of Andriani's danger. She knew that it was her father's intention to visit Il Garda ; she insisted, therefore, upon setting off immediately to seek him ; and to urge her entreaties in favour of the prisoner, reckless of the danger, inconvenience, or even the displeasure of her father, which so prompt and bold a measure might bring upon her : indeed, there was no time to dwell upon evil consequences, as little for preparation ; she dared not weaken the force left to guard the castle. Attended, therefore, by one female, by Giovanni and three varlets, with two horses for baggage, she commenced her journey.

They had halted to take some refreshment, and were again pursuing their route, with unabated haste and diligence, when Giovanni slackened rein, and in alarm pointed out the advance of a party coming upon them, and which, he well knew, would treat friend or foe alike. He counselled Fiorenza to fly, before the distance between them should be lessened, and abandon their light baggage to the plunderers. To this, without hesitation, she consented. The attendants were to remain till the marauders gained sight of the booty, and then disperse themselves. They hoped the bait thus placed in their view would, for a few minutes at least, arrest their greedy attention. Meanwhile, they sought the mountains, where they wandered until they fell in with Antonio. Scouts were still out, and others were immediately dispatched, some in disguise; such were to make their way, if possible, to Brescia. During their absence, means and measures were considered for the safe convoy of Fiorenza back to the castle of San Bonifazio, whither it was decided Albina should accompany her. The morning would bring in those now out upon service, and Andriani considered his force sufficient to guarantee their safety against any of Eccelino's straggling parties whom they might encounter. Precious to the lovers were the few hours thus accorded to them; each flying moment rivetted more firmly the links which bound them in strong affection to each other. Andriani, to the last moment of the evening, lingered by Fiorenza's side; and when fatigue constrained Albina and herself to seek rest in the rude lodging which a cavern could afford them, he set about his arrangements for the following day; then snatched a short repose, far too anxious for the safety of those who under his guidance were to be lodged in security, to lose in indulgence the early hours, which would give him an opportunity of reviewing his preparations. Leonisio and himself were still in discourse, and debating every means which prudence could suggest against accident, when they were joined by those in whom all their thoughts centred. The joy of the preceding day was sobered down almost to melancholy, for a brief space only intervened ere they must part, and all beyond was uncertainty. The necessity for their separation was not cheered by any brighter prospect to relieve the present and positive evil of its dull truth. Andriani's activity, however, had left him leisure to enjoy the good that yet remained, in the society of Fiorenza. All, finally, was ready, and they only awaited the return of the scouts sent out on the previous evening.

As the sun began to glance his rays across one side of their craggy abode, Andriani and his friend experienced some uneasiness. None of the men had returned, and until some information was obtained, they could not venture to descend the mountain. Meanwhile, time was wearing apace, and Andriani felt that his asylum was ill suited to the propriety and habits of those who, in peril, had sought it as a refuge. Fiorenza dreaded her father's anger, if he should return and learn from others the imprudent journey she had undertaken; but if she could reach San Bonifazio before him, Leonisio would seek him, and mollify his displeasure. Leonisio and Albina, whose love, although ardent, was still young and unforbidden, were rather anxious for others than themselves.

" The signal at last !" cried Andriani.

The heavy stone which closed the passage was rolled back, and two of the scouts brought in their report, that the mountain passes were clear; nought but fishermen's barks were moving upon the lake, nor was there any evidence of impediment to cause them further delay. This intelligence was confirmed by those who had been sent in other directions, and arrived soon after the first comers.

" I would fain see them all in before we depart," observed Andriani, appealing to Leonisio, "and learn the news from Brescia and Verona."

He was not kept long in suspense, and the short delay gave further proof of his prudent judgment. The last scout reported that Eccelino had been wounded in the foot at Cassano, and had been carried to Vimercato; Azzo d'Este, with the Ferrarese and Mantuans, also the Marchese Oberto Pelavicino and Buoso da Duora, with the Cremonese, were leagued in arms against him, while himself was expected, when his wound was cured, to advance with the Brescians and meet this formidable coalition. It was believed the Count San Bonifazio was with the Marchese Azzo d'Este; but to this fact no one could speak positively.

While the men gave these details, a crimson hue flushed Andriani's care-worn features; he turned his eyes, which were full of hope, brightness, and intelligence, towards Fiorenza, at the same time exclaiming, " Heaven be praised! Andriani's arm shall not be wanting in the fight."

No obstacle appeared now to offer itself to immediate departure, but as the aspect of affairs was changed, it was necessary to make some alteration in the disposition of his force, and give some fresh directions to those who were to be left in guard over his secret stronghold. Giovanni would not consent to remain behind; he had shared, as a faithful retainer of their house, their fortunes, and would do so still. As they approached the drawbridge of San Bonifazio, Fiorenza turned to Andriani; the tear stood quivering in her eye; she pointed to the barrier but a few paces before them. Her voice trembled as she said, " Andriani, here we must part; you go to quell a tyrant revenge the death of a father, release your fellow men from horrible oppression, and, reinstated in your honours and your rights, claim the guerdon of my hand; it must be, nor can I say a word to stay your purpose, which patriotism, duty, and plighted love enjoin. Heaven be with you! Till your return, my prayers shall unceasingly be offered in your behalf: if," and the words almost choked her —

"if you fail, and fall, Andriani, you will leave to the church the legacy of my plighted vows to you, and a willing bride."

One interchanged long look of love, one pressure of united hands, and Fiorenza, giving a slight jerk to the rein of her horse, with Leonisio passed the bridge. A sobbing adieu from Albina, and Andriani was left alone to watch their receding figures as the portcullis was lowered, and the closing gates shut them from his view. He was still lost in mournful meditation, when the tramp of Leonisio's horse, in recrossing the bridge, aroused him. With a heavy sigh, in silence he wheeled round, and the friends proceeded at a brisk pace towards the theatre of war. As they came within sight of the Adda, they found that the hostile parties had already commenced their fierce contest. They rushed forward at the head of their small band to that part of the field where their presence was most needed, and the fight was hottest. Eccelino had already passed the ford; raging with fury, he was clearing the way before him till his further progress was almost impeded by the dying and the dead which he had heaped around him. Andriani marked him well; fighting his onward course through a medley of friends and foes, panting and bleeding, he at last attained and faced his deadly enemy. Raising himself in his stirrups, and throwing up his visor, he cried, in a voice which rang with an echo amid the clash and din of arms, " For Andriani the Avenger !" Then spurring on his charger, he whirled his sword three times in circles above his head without the intermission of a second, and ere the tyrant could raise an arm to parry the deadly assault, the crashing strokes descended in rapid succession upon his helmet. The Brescians, before wavering, now gave way and fled, and Eccelino

remained in the hands of his opponents. Shouts and exe-
crations hailed the capture of the wounded monster; crowds
flocked in to view him, pursuing him with revilings as he was
carried forward to Soncino. It was with difficulty that the
enraged populace were kept back ; they clamoured that he
should be delivered to their vengeance. They would willingly have anticipated the moment which should rid them
of a tyrant, who by his cruelties had goaded them to madness. This act of retribution his captors forbade. The
wounds given by Andriani's arm, although mortal, left
him a few days' respite for repentance, a brief mercy which
he despised. Without one solitary prayer or requiem, he
was deposited under the portico of the Palace of Soncino,
while all Lombardy feasted and sent up their voices in
rejoicing and thanksgiving that he was taken from the
world, and that a country which he had deluged with crime
and blood was freed from his oppression.

Andriani had fulfilled his compact ; with his sword he
had severed the yoke of tyranny. No more a wanderer or
an outlaw, but noble among the noblest, wealthy among
the wealthiest, and brave beyond the bravest, in all the
freshness of his glory, he sought her whose constancy and
truth had shone like a hallowed light to cheer the midnight
of his adverse fortunes. He claimed the plighted hand of
his Fiorenza, which was no longer withheld from him ;
neither did Count Ricciardo di Bonifazio frown upon the
union of his cherished Leonisio with the richly-dowered
sister of Andriani Conte di Panego, the gentle and lovely
Albina.

Giovanni and Benita stood foremost at the sacred altar,
round which were grouped those faithful followers who had
not deserted the persecuted children of the murdered Conte
di Panego.

EVENING THE SECOND.

No sooner had the party assembled in the library, on the second evening, than the Lady Eva occupied herself in searching anxiously among the designs that lay before her; presently she fixed upon two as dissimilar from each other in the associations they were calculated to call up in the mind of the spectator, as terror is from gentleness, or grief from joy: the one representing, with marvellous truth of effect, the burning of a vessel at sea; the other, the return of a minstrel to his home.

" There !" exclaimed she, "who will be able to tell *one* story about *two* such pictures as those ? One of them almost making you weep with pain and terror,—the other with pleasant thoughts !"

Holding out the two designs, she looked around, and her glance rested on a lady who had written on various subjects. " Ah !" she exclaimed, as she placed the two designs in the hands of that lady, " you, whose imagination is a perfect *prism*, you can find no difficulty in portraying in their true colours even two objects as dissimilar as light from darkness."

It seemed to have already grown into a tacit understanding that the Lady Eva was to have her way implicitly during the six evenings allotted to the .engthened celebration of her birthday; and the lady to whom she had thus addressed herself, though evidently reluctant to be called so early into the field of emulation with so many accomplished persons as she saw around her, seemed still more reluctant to disappoint the excited expectations of the eager child whose beseeching glance was fixed upon her. She paused for a brief space; examined the pictures with an attentive care; and then proceeded to relate

THE FORTUNES OF THE GLENGARY.

In one of the remotest parts of the northern division of Scotland stood the ancient castle of Glengary. To the eyes of a Lowlander, its situation might appear too insular, too lonely, for the cheering intercourse of society; but the lairds of Glengary had been used to behold in the girdle of heath-clad mountains and the fall of rushing waters which skirted their domain, features of grandeur and attraction undreamt of by any but their own clan. The hills were to them emblems of the strength and durability of their race. The lofty pine and the dark brown heather were to their eyes more picturesque than the richly wooded vales of England's garden scenery.

The character of the kilted clan of Glengary seemed to partake of this wilder scenery, and their nerves and sinews to be braced to the hardier exercises and amusements of the clime. The noble chieftain, Sir Norman Ramsay, had from boyhood lived on the estate, and had from infancy been beloved by all the vassal train. He had married young. For many years but one child, a son, had been born to him, and this son was preparing to enter

the army, when the birth of his sister brought desolation
on the poor father's heart, by taking from him the cherished
wife of his affection.

Not only was the husband's cup of sorrow full, and his
tenderest feelings rent asunder, but the son's support and
protection against his own turbulent nature were buried
in his mother's grave. From that hour his fierce passions
seemed beyond control. Her influence over him had been
great; it was the influence of a calm and gentle mind,
leading a proud and wilful spirit by the flowery chain of a
tender mother's love; effecting by a tearful caress what
the father's firm reason and unbending principle often
failed to accomplish.

For a few weeks after their mutual bereavement, a
gentler intercourse seemed established between parent and
child. But at length Allan received orders to join his
regiment; and for years they did not again meet. Indeed,
till Marian was entering her fourteenth year, her brother
was a stranger to her. Her tender age, her girlish beauty,
made a favourable impression on him. She listened with
delighted wonder to his description of those warlike scenes
in which he had borne a part, and his vanity was flattered
by the deference with which she treated him. The dis-
parity in their age prevented his naturally jealous and
envious temper from taking umbrage, when Marian was
folded to their father's heart, and caressed as his best loved
one; or, if a pang was felt, it was subdued by finding
Marian's arms round his own neck, and her young and
glowing cheek pillowed on his shoulder, as soon as released
from her father's embrace.

In their rambles over their native hills, Marian would
beseech Allan to talk to her of their mother—the mother
she, alas! had never known; and on these occasions,

Allan's stern mind would melt to childlike softness while speaking of her virtues, and remembering her endearments.

Ere his leave of absence had expired, Allan had gained strong hold on Marian's heart, and many an hour did she weep bitterly after his departure, while she thought of how long they might remain separate. She wondered that her father did not seem to share in these regrets; for she dreamed not that, while kind and gentle to her, Allan's conduct had been selfish and overbearing to their parent.

Nor was Sir Norman the only one on whom her brother's bursts of ill-controlled temper broke forth. Marian had often witnessed that to the poor old and now infirm steward, who had been the firm and attached servant, the faithful and zealous friend, of his father and grandfather, his manner was ungrateful, and oftentimes insolent. To the minstrel, whose service dated from before Allan's birth, and whose loudest strain was poured forth to proclaim it through hill and dale, making the very cairns resound with that event, he was bitter and impertinent; and to Marian, who loved these faithful followers with a love second only to that she felt for her father, this conduct was painful to behold. It had been one of her privileges to support the steward as he strolled through the house, imagining he was still directing its concerns, though, in reality, he was oftentimes too feeble to direct his own tottering steps. On such occasions, the young girl would spring to his assistance, and, leaning on her arm, he would linger in the different apartments, whiling away the time with old traditions of her ancestors, whose portraits were dispersed about the house. Age seemed to have made itself manifest in the mortal frame of Angus; while his mind remained unimpaired, his memory had perhaps lost something of its freshness; it no longer retained passing events with accuracy; but those long gone by were firmly and faithfully imprinted on it.

Fergus the minstrel had been brought up and had been taught by Angus to string into poetry the wondrous deeds of the Glengarys, and then wander forth to sing them. Between each ramble he was wont to pass his days with Angus, occasionally tuning his lay in the presence of Sir Norman and the gentle Marian, who would listen to his warlike strain, till the deeds of her ancestors would tinge her cheek with pride, or her eyes would fill with tears at the relation of some pathetic scene in which they had been engaged.

For neither of these attached followers did Allan feel kindness or sympathy, and in a second hurried visit which he paid them quite unexpectedly, he avowed to Marian his dislike to the steward. " How can my father tolerate that old drone's impertinence !" he exclaimed. " It is to be hoped, ere I come into possession, he will be laid in yonder kirk-yard, or he will have to provide himself with other lodgings, I can tell him."

Soon after his son's first visit, Sir Norman received some startling news respecting a law-suit instituted by a perfect stranger, a man wholly unconnected with his family, claiming a right to, and seeking to dispossess him of, his personal estate, of which estate he had taken possession at his father's death, not only as next of kin, but under a will found among his father's papers—a document which was regarded merely as a proof of the extreme care which characterized all the late Sir Archibald's proceedings. It is true that, soon after Allan's birth, he had received some anonymous communications, recommending him to be frugal, and to put aside something for a future

day, as the property he considered his own, and his right
of succession to it, might be contested, on the arrival of
certain parties from abroad. No credit, however, and but
little thought, had been given by Sir Norman to these
communications at the time they were made; but now that
a suit was actually commenced, they naturally recurred to
his mind. Still, as his agents had written him word that
this action seemed an act of insanity, and that he could
not possibly be harmed by its prosecution, as not a shadow
of a case could be made out, he did not, knowing the overbearing and imperious temper of his son, even mention the
matter to him on his second visit. For some months
nothing more was heard of it, and Sir Norman supposed
the parties must have been imposed upon, and had since
discovered the truth; but suddenly it appeared that some
new and conclusive evidence had started up, and that it
would be prudent to take such precautionary measures as
had till then been deemed needless. Among other demands, his agents begged to inspect the title-deeds by
which he held his estate.

Sir Norman Ramsay was a man of great precision and
exactness in all his arrangements. Everything around
him breathed order and regularity, and though ill disposed, on the receipt of his solicitor's letter, to trust the
deeds demanded into any custody but his own, he determined to inspect them himself, and proceeded to remove
them from the strong chest in which he had placed them
many years before,—when, to his utter dismay, he could
not find a single document but some of comparatively re-
cent date, while those he sought were coeval with the
mountains which girded his estate.

"Who can have done this act?" he mentally exclaimed,
"and for what purpose? To whom but to me and mine,

can these deeds be of any value ?" These were his first questions; but in another moment, the conviction of the important use that might be made by his opponent of his not being able to produce them, threw a different light on the loss, and as he sank heavily into a chair, he said aloud — " I am a ruined man !"

At this moment, Marian, who had been seeking him, appeared at the door. Calling her to him, he folded her to his heart with even more than his usual fondness; and when he released her, two large drops glistening on her shoulder evidenced a father's grief at the thought of his child's future poverty :—for Sir Norman was so unnerved by the discovery of this act of treachery, that he looked at once to the worst, and already saw his estate wrested from him, and his children reduced to the mere pittance which his late wife's fortune would ensure them. His gentle daughter had been his first thought ; she was too young, too artless, to understand the loss of fortune, but he could not look on her, all lovely as she was, without a shudder at the change which seemed lowering on her youth. Then he thought of his son, whose haughty bearing, whose un-controlled mind, whose hitherto thoughtless expenditure, rendered him little fit to struggle against so great a reverse. Last of all came the thought of his poor wife, his children's mother; and for the first time did he seriously thank that Almighty power which had seen fit to call home her gentle spirit ere such a blow fell on the objects of her tenderest love.

After the first amazement had in some degree subsided, Sir Norman carefully examined the iron chest in which these deeds had been deposited. Twenty-five years had intervened since he had referred to them ; but on several different occasions, when he had placed new documents in

the chest, he felt positive of having always seen them lying
at the bottom of it. The closest examination could discover no sign of force having been used to gain possession
of them; the iron clasps were as firmly attached as ever,
the lock was uninjured, and from the peculiar construction
of its wards, it could not have been forced without some
marks of violence; and the key had always been deposited
in the bureau from whence Sir Norman had that morning
taken it.

The more he reflected on the circumstance, the more
mysterious it became. For some days he was silent to
every one on the subject, but on receiving a second and
more pressing request from his agents, he determined
on revealing his loss to old Angus, ere he proceeded to
Edinburgh, to make it known to his men of business. Accordingly, the evening before he was to commence his
journey, he summoned Angus to his study, and began
relating his fearful discovery, and the use which might
be made of the extraordinary abstraction of these deeds.
"You must tax your memory, my old friend," said Sir
Norman; "you must try and remember every event which
can throw light on this malicious prosecution."

The old man's face was bent down as he approached
his ear, to prevent whatever his master might have to confide to him from being heard by others, and therefore Sir
Norman could not observe the impression caused by his
relation of these facts; but as he ceased speaking, he
heard a sort of gurgling in the throat, and saw Angus fall
forward from his chair, his hands clasped, his eyes rigid
as in death. There was a struggle for utterance, but
speech was denied; and ere Sir Norman could summon
assistance, he became aware that his poor old servant
was dying.

The steward was conveyed to his bed, and every means used to restore him, but for many hours he remained senseless. Sir Norman watched by him, but hearing that Marian appeared inconsolable, he went to appease her grief, and remained absent some hours. For a short time the dying man seemed to revive; he made signs to be raised, but fell back. The minstrel, who had been kneeling by his bed, approached his ear, and Angus articulated with difficulty some words, to which the other listened in silence. What these words might be, none but themselves could know, for they were uttered low and indistinctly, and in a foreign tongue. That they were of fearful import, the convulsed features of the dying man, the pale and terrified looks of the minstrel, afforded evident proof.

The dawn had broken; the glorious luminary poured one bright ray through the oriel window: it fell on the pale and distorted features of Angus, and revealed to the Glengary, who just then opened the door of the apartment, that the spirit of his old servant was no longer of this earth. A few wild notes which broke from the harp of the minstrel sounded his requiem.

Sir Norman delayed his journey to the metropolis while his daughter's preparations were made for accompanying him; for he could not think of leaving her unprotected by his presence. Angus, old and infirm as he had become, would, from his faithful attachment, and his mental vigour, which was always devoted to the good of the family he served, have been considered sufficient safeguard during his absence. Hitherto Sir Norman had not supposed that he had an enemy on earth; but now it was too apparent that some one or other stood in that relation towards him. It was impossible for Sir Norman not to connect the awful

H

visitation which had befallen Angus with the topic on which
he was speaking at the instant it occurred, and for a moment, perhaps, a feeling almost amounting to suspicion
arose, as he thought of the sudden seizure, and remembered that till he mentioned the discovery he had made,
old Angus appeared in his usual health. But Sir Norman
was too just and too honourably-minded to harbour mistrust
of one whose long service and tried honesty for three gene-
rations had secured him the respect of laird and peasant,
and whose impartial fulfilment of the duties of his situation
had earned for him the attachment of every one for miles
round the estate; and, with a feeling of self-reproach for
having even glanced in thought at such a possibility, the
chieftain banished all mistrust, and attended in person the
old man's funeral.

Sir Norman and his daughter had scarcely arrived in
the capital, when, spite of every effort which had been
made for the recovery of the lost deeds, the day of trial
was fixed without any clue to them having been gained.
True, Allan had written to his father and to their man of
business, declaring his positive belief that old Angus had
been bribed to sell them to the enemy; and, in the same
letter, he had not scrupled to denounce the minstrel as his
accomplice, and to urge that he should be forthwith seized
and examined. Sir Norman was indignant at his son's
petulant interference, and resented his defamation of the
old steward's character. Marian was thunderstruck when
she heard the charge. "Impossible!" she exclaimed.
"Suspect Angus of a fraud upon my father! As well
might Allan or myself be accused of it." And no argument that could be adduced, nothing that could be advanced, shook her faith in the integrity of the old man.

Meanwhile, the men of business looked at the probabilities of the case; and as they could find nothing more likely, would have given credit to the accusation against Angus, had it not been that, through some underlings connected with their own and the adversary's office, they had obtained information which gave them reason to suspect that the missing deeds were not in the possession of Mr. Muir; and that a deed of sale of the reversion of the estate after his death, executed in proper form by Sir Archibald Ramsay, was all their case rested on. They, however, considered it their duty to secure the minstrel's person, and for that purpose sent to Glengary; but he was nowhere to be found; and this circumstance rather gave colour in their minds to the accusation.

The suit was now pressed on by the wealthy stranger as rapidly as the forms of law would admit; and at length the day of trial arrived. In the opening of the case, the late Sir Archibald's will was described as a nefarious act. No longer did Sir Norman, who was in court, regard the decision of this suit merely as the question on which his inheritance rested. All thoughts of poverty or wealth, of lands and vassals, were absorbed in an overwhelming desire to clear his father's memory from the stigma cast on it. Home, fortune, position, influence, all became nothing but as they might tend to that one end. Sir Norman resolved that no tongue but his own should defend his father's honour; and though unfavourable impressions had spread themselves over the minds of their firmest supporters, on his admitting the impossibility in which he found himself to produce the title-deeds of his estate, and a smile of incredulity had been visible on the countenances of some while he related the manner in which he had discovered their loss, still, as he proceeded, his calm and lofty tone, his simple but forcible language, his expressions of outraged honour, so feeling and so emphatic, were carrying conviction to the hearts of his hearers;—when suddenly a stir was heard—a buzz, a press, a general commotion, was perceived—and then a man rushed breathless into court, and presented some documents to the prosecutor's counsel, who appeared completely taken by surprise, but in an instant recovered himself sufficiently to declare that, in his hand, he held the title-deeds, so plausibly declared by Sir Norman to have been, till lately, in his iron chest.

The suit was at an end. There could be no pretence for withholding the verdict from the prosecutor. The deed of sale might have been a forgery, but the possession of the title-deeds of the estate spoke for themselves, and Sir Norman left the court, not only a ruined, but a broken-hearted man. In vain did his daughter speak in those soothing tones from which he had never before turned away. Her own senses were so bewildered by what had occurred, that she hardly knew what to urge in mitigation of her father's anguish; but when she prophesied that the villany practised against them must, sooner or later, be brought to light, he would catch her to his heart, and pray God that she might live to see her grandfather's name avenged.

As soon as they could remove from the capital, the unhappy father and daughter retired to a small cottage, situated in a glen near to their ancient home. A very small income—being a life-interest in his late wife's fortune—was all Sir Norman could now call his own.

Mr. Muir, perhaps, felt how little his presence would be tolerated at Glengary; for there appeared no sign of his coming to take possession. The house remained closed, the park neglected, and silence reigned where many a scene of festive mirth was remembered, and many a banquet had been spread for all who came as guests, and whence, within the memory of living man, never had the poor or wayfaring been turned away without relief or hospitality.

At first, each week passed in their cottage seemed an age, both to Sir Norman and his daughter; but week succeeded week, months had nearly swollen into a year, and no change seemed likely to occur. Sir Norman evidently pined, and his state of health gave great alarm to his daughter. A change of scene, a warmer climate, was advised, and Marian proposed to her parent to remove from their humble home.

Then came the galling pinch of poverty. True, they had no debts to cripple or retard their movements. Their flight might be taken without fear of any opposing creditor; but the means for a long journey were wanting. Marian's heart beat quick, and her eye flashed with something like indignation, as she asked herself—"Shall my father's health, perhaps his life, be sacrificed for want of a small portion of that wealth his hand has so often bestowed on others?" She knew that the means would be found, were the want made known. Not one of his clan but would have given their last shilling to prove the love they felt for their chieftain. But Marian could not become a supplicant, even for her father, while any other means remained untried.

While in the capital, Sir Norman had given her the jewel-case of her late mother, and told her to wear any of the more simple ornaments it contained. She had removed from it a locket containing her father and mother's hair, with the date of their marriage engraved on it, which she had since constantly worn, but had never since opened the case. Now she flew to it, and while taking from it each separate ornament, many of them costly ones, she

fancied her mother's sweet and gentle spirit was hovering
round her. "I must not tell my father," thought she,
"that I am about to sell his gift, for he might not permit
it; but, once converted into money, he will not refuse
his child the happiness of seeing him restored to health
by the exchange."

Marian had no friend to whom she could confide her
plans, and alone she could not hope to execute them; so
the trinkets remained for the moment unsold. But as Sir
Norman became more feeble, and the second summer was
rapidly passing away, Marian grew wretched under the
sad prospect of her father's being exposed to the rigour of
another winter in that northern climate. "Could I but
persuade him to go to London," said she, "there I might
find a purchaser for these diamonds, which, by their dazzling lustre, seem to reproach me for letting my father
fade."

Marian's pleadings were in vain, so long as she entreated her father to seek further medical advice for himself; but when the restless anxiety she felt began to act
on her own health—when her cheek became pale, her
tone languid, and her step lost its buoyancy—the fond
father saw sufficient cause for a visit to London, and their
journey was instantly arranged.

Ere Marian could leave the neighbourhood, she felt
an irresistible desire once more to behold the home of her
infancy. She knew that strange stories were afloat—that
the old house was said to be haunted—that unearthly
sounds were declared to have been heard by those who
had ventured within its walls. But Marian, strong in innocence, and firm of purpose, feared no evil results from
her intended pilgrimage, save that she might be refused
admittance.

The owner of the neighbouring manse, to whom she confided her wish, agreed to conduct her to the village, and aid her in this act of harmless deceit, for she cared not to disturb her father's mind by mentioning it.

Early one fine autumnal morning they departed for the village, when, leaving her companion to see that his horse was taken care of while he went to visit some sick person, Marian proceeded on foot to the entrance-gate. It was open; she passed quickly into the neglected park, and by a short cut made her way, with some difficulty, towards the house. Its windows were closed, and an air of desolation reigned around. She rang the bell. Its sound seemed to terrify her. How often had she listened to that deep-toned bell, when expecting her father or Allan to return from some field sports! Then its peal seemed joyous; now it sounded like a mournful knell, and as it reverberated through the empty halls, each echo proclaimed aloud their fallen fortunes.

She remained some time within the porch, but no one responded to her call, and with a shudder she turned from the door which was wont to be thrown open to welcome her entrance. Buried in thought, she proceeded at random till she found herself at an angle of the building, near which she remembered there was a small door, that had been used by the old steward, when he wandered from his own apartment into the park, without coming through the house. On approaching, she found it a-jar, and, well versed in all the windings which to another would have been intricate, she made her way to that part of the dwelling which the family had occupied.

Arrived in her father's room, Marian paused. How many thoughts and reflections rushed on her mind! Her heart beat—her head grew giddy. Something like fear

took possession of her mind, but she tried to shake it off.
True, she was alone; but who had so great a right as herself to be there—there, in the home of her childhood —
there, in the halls of her ancestors—there, where the blood
of her forefathers had been shed, to maintain their right of
possession against the Lowlander and the Saxon? What,
then, had *she* to fear within those walls? Their desolate
appearance—their untenanted state—did it not prove that
no stranger could find in them a home? Her father had,
by treachery, been driven from his habitation: but no
other had found in it a shelter.

More tender thoughts quickly succeeded this burst of
pride. In one room, some kind word of her father's was
remembered; in another, some stirring tale of former
years, in which her ancestors had taken part, had been
related by the poor old steward. She was now in the
banqueting-hall, and casting her eyes around, she beheld
the small gallery in which the minstrel had been wont to
sing the deeds of other days. That gallery now vacant—
her father an exile from his home—her brother far away
—the old steward's memory attainted by foul suspicion—
the minstrel supposed to have fled from justice,—her
heart sank—her head drooped—the maiden's proud feelings were quenched, as, friendless and forlorn, she stood
leaning for support against the large buttress of the projecting chimney.

The wind was high, and rushed mournfully through
the dreary pile; but at intervals it seemed to bring a
sound of music on its wing. Marian listened breathlessly
—it came nearer—she threw back her long and silky
ringlets to hear more distinctly. Could it be? she asked
herself. Did she dream, or had the recollections of former
days bewildered her senses? The music became clearer,

and Marian no longer doubted but that it was the minstrel's harp, the minstrel's voice. When it ceased, Marian sprung forward, crying, " Fergus, Fergus, it is I !—it is your chieftain's daughter who speaks ! " But no answer was given. She ran wildly to the spot whence the sounds had appeared to come, and then to the part of the building formerly inhabited by the minstrel, but neither sign nor sound of human existence could she discover.

The morning was far advanced, and fearing to alarm her father by her long absence, she forced herself to quit the house by the same door she had entered, and crossing the park, regained the village, where the curate awaited her. Marian's heart was too full for speech, and silently they returned to the cottage.

The following day Sir Norman and his daughter commenced their journey. They remained in London some weeks, during which time they received several visits from Allan, who came there, he said, to meet them. But he was no longer the same Allan, Marian's childish heart had enshrined as the bright reality of her glowing imagination. He was changed in appearance, changed in manner, changed in temper, and the hours he spent with them, instead of giving his sister pleasure, were rather anticipated with dread, and remembered with pain. Once, when he had seemed less reserved, she ventured to tell him of her visit to the castle, but had not proceeded far when his vehemence frightened and arrested her relation. She felt, if the mere mention of her visit had such an effect on him, how little he would enter into her feelings—how little would he comprehend the sounds she had heard.

Marian had often wished to speak of the minstrel's strain ; but her father's weakened nerves, his shattered

health, rendered her fearful of mentioning it to him. She
had looked forward to Allan's being with them as the moment when she might relieve her own bewildered mind, by
giving him her confidence, and seeking, through the aid
of his stronger reason. a solution of those thoughts which
seemed too weighty for her own. But this hope was soon
dissipated : Allan sedulously avoided all reference to former years, and on more than one occasion gave Marian to
understand that any allusion to the two " old rascals," as
he called them, who had compassed their ruin, would
banish him from her sight.

Silenced rather than satisfied, Marian came to the painful conviction that her weight of responsibility would
neither be lightened nor shared by her selfish brother.
There were moments when he would look at her, as she
pursued her quiet domestic occupations, with a fixed stare
almost like insanity, place his hands before his face, and
rush from the house like a maniac. But his whole conduct was so strange and inexplicable, that, in her despair
of unravelling it, Marian thought but of concealing its
existence from her father. Alone she was left to devise for
that father's comforts ; she felt that on earth there was no
helping hand, no friendly counsel, to sustain her; and,
firm in the pursuit of her one paramount duty to her
invalid parent, she sought, with trust and perfect faith,
that support from above which is promised to the lone
and the helpless.

Had Allan performed the fraternal part Marian had so
joyfully anticipated, she might not have relaxed in her
own personal exertions; but, assuredly, she would never
have acquired that energy of character which marked her
after-life. Trusting to human aid, she would have faltered
and trembled under every fresh evil; but now her mind

had sought a higher trust; she was calm and resigned, leaving the event of all in the hands of her heavenly Father, while she fulfilled, with strict and scrupulous devotion, her care and duty to her earthly one.

Marian requested the physician who attended Sir Norman to recommend her to a jeweller of established repute, and Dr. R——, surmising that it was rather an errand of sale than a desire to purchase, made it a point of conscience to speak of one whose just and liberal dealings were known to him.   Early one morning, she set out to find her way into the city, where the address given her pointed out the residence of this merchant.

It was a dark and gloomy morning; the atmosphere was dense and yellow with a November fog; the multitudes she met, the many who hurried by her, all wore the appearance of urgent business; but there was an air of animation and bustle which made Marian contrast her sad and secret errand with what appeared their cheerful pursuit.

Many hours of the previous night she had sat contemplating the riches she was about to part with.   To her the objects she looked upon were full of sweet and happy recollections ; to their next possessors they would have no value beyond their intrinsic worth.

As she approached the spot which she had set out to seek, she involuntarily found herself slackening her pace, and as she pressed the case, concealed by the ample folds of her cloak, closer to her form, a doubt of her ability to go through her task arose ; but in the next instant she remembered her father's harassing cough, and proceeded at her utmost speed, till she beheld the name she had been directed by the physician to ask for, in large letters over a low, heavy-looking house.   Some articles of massive silver in either window convinced her that she had found the residence she sought.

On entering the shop, no one approached to speak to her—indeed, she had proceeded to the entrance of an inner room ere even her appearance seemed to be remarked. Stooping down, she inquired of a man who was employed in piling silver dishes one on the other, if Mr. Needham was at home. The man looked at her for an instant, and then, without quitting his occupation, said, "You had better go forward and inquire."

Mechanically she repeated the question to the next person she saw, who answered it by inquiring if she was known to Mr. Needham.

"No," she replied; "but I have a note for him from the gentleman who recommended me to come here."

"Will you let me see the note?" said the man; "perhaps I can attend to your business, without disturbing Mr. Needham, who is particularly engaged."

Marian paused: the physician had told her to deliver the note herself to Mr. Needham, but it appeared he was engaged. As she was hesitating, the door of an adjoining apartment to that in which she stood was opened by a venerable-looking man, who came forth, accompanied by a younger one; on perceiving a stranger, they both paused, and the elder one inquired if she had been attended to. There was something so kind and respectful in the accent of the speaker, that Marian at once regained her self possession, as she replied—

"I have a note from Dr. R——, which will explain my business; but I hear Mr. Needham is engaged."

"I am Mr. Needham," said her companion, "and will attend to you in five minutes. Do me the favour to be seated."

Marian presented the note, and as Mr. Needham perused it, she perceived a look of commiseration steal over his countenance. When he closed it, he looked kindly at her, and said—

"Pray walk into this room, where there is a fire; I will not keep you waiting."

"In less than five minutes, Mr. Needham joined her, and, drawing a chair to the table, inquired how he could serve her, adding that Dr. R——'s note led him to conclude that she might wish to change or dispose of some ornament. What a relief to Marian, to have the want, so painful to proclaim, thus considerately anticipated! She unlocked the box, which she had placed on the table, and replied—

"These were my poor mother's jewels; they were given me by my father, in happier days. Since then, our circumstances have become changed, and I wish to sell them."

A pause of some moments ensued. Mr. Needham's eyes remained fixed on the case, when Marian timidly added—

"Will you become their purchaser?"

"My dear young lady," replied Mr. Needham, as with almost paternal affection he looked at her, "have you well weighed the sacrifice you are making—are you aware of the value of these jewels?"

"Oh, yes," said Marian, as she burst into tears, "they were my mother's!"

Inexpressibly touched by her reply, he continued, "Surely a portion of these would be sufficient for any momentary difficulties?"

"Alas!" interrupted Marian, "ours are no momentary difficulties. My father's health has been for many

months si..king under accumulated and unmerited losses ;
an expensive journey, a residence in a warmer climate, are
necessary for the preservation of his life, and this case
contains the only means by which it can be accomplished
without injury to others, which my father will never listen
to."

Mr. Needham looked kindly and encouragingly, as he
said, " May I wait on you to-morrow, or would you prefer
returning here ?   It is a business I should like to reflect
on."

" I will come here," replied Marian ; " for my father
must not know of my intention; at least, not till it is
beyond recall."

" Be it so, then," returned her auditor.   " I must,
however, beg you to reflect well on the act you contemplate, and I will consider if, and how far, I can assist
your views.   Meanwhile, will you trust me with this case,
that I may examine its contents ?"

" Assuredly," replied Marian ; and she arose to depart
and hurry home, her heart full of thankfulness for the
hope held out of her project being crowned with success,
and of gratitude to the kind physician who had recommended her so feelingly to the jeweller's notice ; for she
felt convinced it was to his note she stood indebted for
the amenity shown her by Mr. Needham.

In part, her conjecture was right.   Dr. R——'s note
had interested Mr. Needham in her favour ; but it was her
own modest demeanour, her own unassuming but exemplary sacrifice, which rivetted the merchant's good opinion,
and disposed him to serve her to an extent and in a
manner she little expected.

On reaching home, Marian found that her father had
risen late, and been so engaged with her brother, that he

had not asked for her. When she entered the sitting-room, she found Allan about to leave it. The livid pale-ness of his countenance terrified her. As she watched him descend the staircase, he seemed hardly able to support himself. She called to him to stop, but her voice fell un-heeded, as he rushed from the house. In her father's manner, no agitation was apparent; and, fearful of alarm-ing him, she refrained from speaking of Allan's haggard look.

The next morning, when she repeated her visit to the city, she found Mr. Needham evidently watching her arrival. He conducted her into the room she had before occupied. The jewel-case was on the table. Mr. Need-ham drew two chairs to the fire; and when seated, he observed, after a moment's hesitation,—

"I am about to speak candidly to you, lady, though I hope, not so abruptly as to distress or offend you. An ornament in that case has revealed to me your name and family; and the few facts you yesterday related leave me in no doubt as to your father having been once known to me."

"You know my father, sir?" interrupted Marian. "Oh, then, I am indeed fortunate in my application; for you must be satisfied that I am only doing my duty in parting with these memorials of former years."

"Your conduct is noble," said Mr. Needham; "and I reverence the motive, though I cannot permit the act it would impel."

Marian started, and became pale as death. Her hopes, which had been raised almost to certainty, seemed at once dispelled. Mr. Needham watched the effect of his words, and continued —

"No, my dear young lady, I cannot, indeed, allow such

a sacrifice, the extent of which you do not know : but though I cannot become a party to your wishes, I must endeavour to prevail on you to adopt the plan which suggests itself to me. We will place your seal on this case of jewels, which must remain in my custody. I will advance the sum of 500*l.* for your journey and first year's expenses, and will bind myself for three succeeding years to place 300*l.* more in the hands of any banker where you may be residing, or as you may by letter direct. If, at the expiration of four years from this time, you cannot repay me the sums advanced, these jewels will become my property."

"But I have no prospect," exclaimed Marian. "There is no possibility of my ever repaying the money. Indeed, sir, I cannot accept your generous offer. You might become a considerable loser, for the jewels may not be worth so much money."

"Well, well, that is my concern."

"But all this is so unexpected, so extraordinary," again interposed Marian, "that I dare not concur in it unknown to my father."

"And yet," replied Mr. Needham, "you would have sold, irrevocably sold, without his knowledge, the very objects I propose to you to leave in my hands as a guarantee? Ah, young lady, like many others you have been deceiving yourself, and have fostered a plan of your own suggestion, till you have ceased to perceive the real act of irretrievable disobedience it necessitated ; though you start from one far less complete, and with a chance of becoming less fatal, when proposed by another. Surely, the mere possibility of being able, at some future day, to regain these jewels, ought to be acceptable, considering them as a sacred treasure to a daughter's heart."

Marian now burst into tears. Could Mr. Needham, could any one, suppose that she did not feel the sacrifice to be one, only to be thought of as the means to enable her to fulfil a yet more sacred duty?

The worthy merchant allowed her to weep unrestrainedly for some time, and then taking her hand, he said, " Forgive me for having distressed you. I did it for your good. I see so much to praise and admire, that I felt it a duty to point out an equivocation which seemed unworthy of you. Do not let us lose time. I have prepared a receipt, which also contains my written promise not to open or deliver this case to any one within four years, without your order. You must, in exchange, give me your acknowledgment for 500*l.* as the first instalment of a bond which I have ordered my solicitor to prepare, and which I shall also get signed by my son, the young man whom you, perhaps, remarked with me when I so accidentally found you waiting here yesterday ; for as this transaction must be one of a private nature, without any reference to the firm of which I am a member, I wish my son to become aware of its existence, in order that no difficulty or misunderstanding may arise in case of my death within the four years."

Marian signed the papers Mr. Needham placed before her. She was so deeply penetrated by his conduct, as to be unable to express her thanks. To a less practised observer, or to a mind less prone to indulgence, she might have appeared ungrateful ; but Mr. Needham had, in his lifetime, conferred too many benefits not to be an experienced judge of the impressions they produced, and Marian's tearful eyes and trembling frame were surer proofs to him of her gratitude than the most elaborate thanks, or the most eloquent language, she could have

J

uttered. When all was concluded, he draw her arm within
his, and said he would have the pleasure of conducting
her home, as his carriage was at the door.   During their
drive, he entreated her to lose no time in disclosing to her
father the transaction she had completed.   " It will be
freed," he observed, "from every unpleasant feeling to
both of us as soon as he is our confidant."

"Oh! Mr. Needham," cried Marian, " how can I ever
thank you, much less repay you, for such magnanimity?"

" By giving me your solemn promise that you will not
undertake any other affair of moment without consulting
me upon it."

" I promise solemnly and faithfully," said Marian. She
looked up as she said this, as if to ratify her vow in
heaven — when, standing close to the door of her home,
at which they were just arrived, she beheld, to her extreme astonishment, Fergus the minstrel!   The carriage
stopped.   As Marian descended, she cast a hurried glance
around, but the minstrel had vanished.

The news of old Angus's sudden death had reached
Allan (or, as he was more usually called, Master) of Glengary, while sitting in his room with a man who had for
some months been his shadow.   Wherever he went, Major
Jarvis was sure to follow him.   He had become his friend,
his adviser, almost, it might be said, his master :— it was
the knowledge of Allan's haughty spirit which alone
prevented his appearing to be so ; for he feared to rouse a
feeling which might snap the link between them before he
had drawn it round his victim too tightly for escape.   But
the assumption of power was all that was wanting — the
reality of it was absolute.

" Good God !" exclaimed Allan, on opening his father's

letter - - "what a frightful catastrophe! and may 1 not
have been accessory to it? Oh, how much better would
it have been to have lost all hope of retrieving my difficulties, than that the life of a fellow-creature should have
been sacrificed!"

"You talk in enigmas, Allan," said Jarvis; "what
has happened, and what are you reproaching yourself
with?"

But Allan was in no mood to answer; for a few
moments the better part of his nature was in the ascendant, and his heart really sympathized in his father's distress at his poor old servant's loss; but, unhappily, too
much guilt had already tainted his mind; he had become
too much the slave of evil passion not to turn from this
goodly thought. With Allan, virtue was a solitary star,
shining but for an instant, making the surrounding darkness visible. Jarvis, who had remained contemplating
him in silence, now put his hand on his shoulder, saying—

"Come, cheer up, Allan; whatever has befallen you,
I, for one, will stand by you to the last — ay, even through
shame and disgrace!"

He had touched the right chord. Allan started up.
"Disgrace!—shame and disgrace! no, no; no chance of
that now; the only tongue that could have dared to accuse
me is hushed in death. Jarvis, old Angus is dead!"

"And you tell it me in that rueful tone?" exclaimed
the other. "Why, Master of Glengary, are you a man,
and rejoice not at your escape? While that old driveller
lived, there was no certainty of your not being suspected;
now, you are indeed free from detection. Shew me the
herald of this good news." And without waiting for permission, he took up Sir Norman's letter, and read it
through.

"Dreadful! is it not?" said Allan.

"The man who could have any feeling but joy in its perusal could be no friend of yours, Allan. But you do not seem prepared to take advantage of this, as you assuredly must do."

"How is that?" said Allan, who had relapsed into deep thought.

"Why, you must boldly accuse him of having sold the missing deeds to your father's enemy, and make his death appear a sudden revulsion of his conscience."

"But did you finish my father's letter? did you see that the minstrel may now know whatever Angus suspected?" asked Allan.

"True," said Jarvis; "but he must be accused as his accomplice; his absence at such a time would almost fix the charge on him. Shall I spirit him away?"

"You are ever ready, Jarvis, and I have had too many proofs of your talents, not to trust implicitly to you to advise me for the best; but for some time past a thought has tormented me—and yet——"

"Out with it, man," cried Jarvis, "unkennel this thought; let us look at it, and see if it cannot be made a scourge for others instead of ourselves."

"I will tell it you," replied Allan; "there is a reluctance and a shuffling in the manner of old Isaacs, whenever I refer to those deeds, which alarms me. 'They are voluminous,' he says, 'and extracts from them must necessarily be long—or this being the vacation time, he has few clerks at home,' or some such excuse, instead of fixing a time for their return."

"Well, and what is the hurry for their return, except that you are kept out of your money? But I can help you on a little longer."

"Isaacs does not want to keep the money back; he has even given me a part," interrupted Allan.

Jarvis remained silent, while reflecting on what his friend had said, and endeavouring to find a cause for the Jew's parting with the money before he was obliged to do so. "Why," thought he, "should he care to retain possession of the deeds?" but as he could imagine no cause, he resolved to go and see the Jew next morning, for the purpose of interrogating him; and turning to Allan, he carelessly inquired if he would accompany him to a party to which they had both been invited; but Allan declined, preferring, for once, to pass the evening alone, to joining the heartless set in whose society he had lost, not only his money, but that feeling of honour and integrity which can alone command the respect of others, or ensure our own.

Allan sat musing over a dying fire, the expiring embers of which gave out fitful and uncertain light. A shade was over the only candle which had been placed by his orders in a distant part of the room, and there was just sufficient light to distinguish the surrounding objects, to which habit had familiarized the sight, but barely enough to recognise any new ones. Many preceding events of his life became present to his imagination. The look of pity and mistrust with which old Angus had appeared to watch his every word the last day he was with his family seemed before him. Some sound made him start; footsteps seemed to approach, he fancied that the door was opened softly. An indistinct dread of harm seized on Allan, and rooted him to his seat. He felt that some one was near him — so near, that their very breathing had become audible; but still he sat spellbound, till, from the receding step, and the door being again closed, he imagined himself once more alone.

On looking round, no form was visible; but on the table a letter had been placed. Approaching the candle, Allan tore the letter open and read—

" When the missing is restored, then only shall Allan of Glengary know peace !"

Who could have written those words ? His secret must be known to some one, whom he did not even suspect. And at this thought, his stern, unbending mind, became harrowed by fear. Again he sat down and tried to reflect calmly; but it could not be—and the night was spent in feverish and restless musings.

The day broke, and he thought of retiring to bed, but soon after fell asleep in his chair. His servant, surprised at not hearing him, went to his room, and not finding him in his bed, entered the sitting-room. A noise purposely made, roused the sleeper, who exclaimed— " Go instantly, William, and tell Major Jarvis that I wish to see him ! — Fool, fool that I was," added he, as his servant left the room, " to fall asleep, when these hours of delay may prove fatal !"

As he paced the room with impatient step, his eye caught sight of himself in the glass. Turning hastily, he stood for some moments contemplating the haggard features it reflected, and then with a shudder sat down, and burying his face in his hands, remained immovable till William's return. " Major Jarvis's compliments, and he will be here in half an hour," was the message he received; to which he merely replied, without altering his position, " Leave me till he comes."

Somewhat more than an hour intervened, and then Major Jarvis's voice, humming a popular air, was heard. It grated on Allan's ears, and seemed to rouse him to anger, for it was in a harsh and almost rude tone that he exclaimed—" Jarvis, my patience is almost worn out, waiting for you!"

Jarvis's quick eye perceived that something more than usual disturbed his host, and changing his gay and cheerful tone to one of interest, he replied—

"I should have been more expeditious, had you sent word that you were impatient for me.   But what has happened, my dear fellow? you look as if you had been up all night."

"And so I have," said Allan; "nor did I fall asleep in my chair till after daylight.   And yet, during the night, some one entered here—some one stole on my privacy; and I—fool, dotard that I am—let them escape to accuse and ruin me!"

"Why, you are still dreaming, Allan! Some one entered here—some one came to do you mischief—and you let them go without interruption? Why, this is the coinage of an overwrought brain."

"And this letter," cried Allan, as he held it to his friend—"is this, too, madness?"

Upon reading the few words it contained, Jarvis said—

"Allan, there is something in all this I do not understand.   Do be calm, and tell me, if you can, if any one entered your apartment, or how this letter was conveyed to you?"

Allan then related the sensation he had experienced, his conviction that some one was near him, and the inability he felt to move or speak, and that on rousing himself he had perceived the letter lying on the table.

"Know you the writing?" asked Jarvis.

Allan shook his head.

"Then all rests on conjecture," observed Jarvis; "and the only way to come at the truth will be to consider, first, who can be acquainted with the circumstance that letter alludes to; and, secondly, for what purpose you are informed of their knowledge. The latter will be more puzzling than the former to decide on, for I entertain no doubt that the minstrel must be the person. But what his design may be is not so clear."

"As I thought," exclaimed Allan; "all is lost!"

"And I see everything gained," replied Jarvis.

"The minstrel is aware of what Angus suspected. But dead men's suspicions furnish no proofs. He must be accused as Angus's accomplice, which will appear probable to those who were present at their last interview. But though accused, he must never be brought to justice. Some way must be found to dispose of him; but the first step is the accusation. Write boldly to your father."

"My father will never believe harm of either of his servants."

"He must be made to believe it, or at least to act as if he did. Give him no choice; but write yourself to the man he has employed to defend the suit, stating your belief that Angus was the thief, and desire them to secure the minstrel as his accomplice."

Allan mechanically wrote as Jarvis dictated, but once or twice urged the latter to go to Isaacs, and induce him to give certain documents into his possession.

"We will go together," replied Jarvis, "when your letters are finished." Not that he expected any argument would induce the Jew to grant such a request; but he wished to form his own conclusions as to whether he had any hidden motive for detaining them, beyond the common trick of swelling his bill by making delays in the business.

On arriving at his house, they were told that he was particularly engaged, and could not be spoken with. The same occurred on the next and many following days; but when, at the end of a month, Allan did get admittance, he found old Isaacs' manner, which had before been cringing to sycophancy, abrupt and insolent. He gave Allan no time to make his request, but poured forth a stream of abuse, calling him a swindler, who had taken advantage of his unsuspecting nature, to rob him of his money under false pretences, which had well-nigh involved him in a suit with an honest and injured man.

Allan remained for some time silent with astonishment, but at last said, haughtily—

"You are under some misapprehension, Mr. Isaacs. I have borrowed money from you, but on your own terms, be it remembered; and I have given you every proof you desired of my future inheritance."

"Proof, indeed! Yes—proof that you have no inheritance at all! Oh! just as though you did not know all this! Do you pretend that you did not know that your father, and your grandfather before him, had been for years past wronging another out of his property?"

Allan's blood was in arms. His father, his grandfather, accused of roguery!—their honesty impugned by an extortioner like the man before him! Foaming with rage, he exclaimed—

"How dare you, old villain, speak thus of your betters? I tell you"—and he approached him with his fist clenched—"I tell you, it is false; and that if you again dare to assert it, I will tear your tongue from your unhallowed mouth!"

"Help! help!" screamed the Jew.

But no one came, and Allan saw the moment when he might regain all he desired to obtain.

"Give me the deeds, base villain!" he exclaimed, as

ne seized him by the throat, " or I will be the death of
thee !"

The Jew's fiendish laugh, as he said, " That can I not
do, for they are in the hands of their rightful owner,"
made Allan's hand relax its grasp, while with a heavy
groan he fell, like one shot, at the feet of the usurer.

It was many hours after this scene ere Allan awoke to
perfect consciousness ; he was then in bed, both his arms
bandaged, by which he conjectured that he had been bled.
Raising himself, he put back the curtain ; a night-lamp
was burning ; there was no one in the room but his servant William, who was buried in a sound sleep.   Allan's
ideas were at first confused, and though aware that some
misfortune had befallen, or some sudden illness overtaken
him, he could not recollect anything distinctly ; but by
degrees the mists which had obscured his reason were
withdrawn, and the whole dreadful truth became present.
He perceived, that though intentionally innocent of the
result, his criminal removal of the deeds, to enable him to
raise money, had placed them in the power of his enemy,
and that virtually he was guilty of the ruin of his family,
and the stigma on his grandfather's reputation.

Hours passed on ; the servant still slept, while Allan's
soul was torn by remorse.   " I will go to my father," he
said, " I will avow all.   He can but curse me.   And what
curse can be more bitter than my own despair?"

Allan made an effort to rise, but soon found that he
was too weak to effect it, and sank back on his pillow
again, to reflect on the enormity of his conduct towards
a parent who had been only too indulgent and forbearing,
under his many acts of aggression.   He remembered the
solemn promise his father had exacted, that whatever

were his crimes (for such the chieftain designated his
thoughtless expenditure) they should always be confided
to him—and that when, in the breach of that promise,
he had sought those means for self-relief, at which, even
in the moment of commission, his soul shrunk back appalled—when he was stealthily conveying away, like a
thief, those deeds to his room—he had encountered the
venerable form of old Angus,—and the shame of that
moment became again present. He again saw the stern
and searching eye bent upon him, for though he had
assumed a tone of bravado, and even presumed to insult
the aged servant, from that hour he had felt himself a
degraded being. He foresaw that his mind must be on
the rack till he could replace those deeds; but little did he
think or imagine the abyss in which honour, reputation,
wealth, and peace, were to become engulfed by his abstraction of them. Even now it seemed a dream—a
dream too horrible to be true. Might not Isaacs have
deceived him?

At that moment the door of his chamber was opened.
It was Jarvis who entered. His step awoke the servant,
and he started up. Jarvis inquired how his master had
been. " He has slept soundly all night," replied William.
" When he awakes," continued Jarvis, " do not answer
any questions he may ask you. The surgeon says his
mind must be kept tranquil, or there will be great mischief.
If he is sensible when he awakes, you had better send for
me :" and with this admonition his friend left the room,
without even approaching his bed.

As soon as he was gone, William put some coals on
the fire, trimmed the lamp, and again settled himself to
sleep, leaving Allan to his bitter reflections. It was long
after daybreak, when, nearly choked with thirst, he asked

for drink, and having swallowed it, again closed his eyes,
as if he could, by shutting out the light, lessen the intense-
ness of his anguish.

Not for many a past year had Allan prayed with the
fervour and faith of that lonely night.   The misfortune
which had befallen him was too great for his stunned senses
to comprehend its full extent; but the heartless neglect of
his servant, who had lived with him from a boy; the luke-
warm inquiries of the man who called himself his friend,
were bitter lessons.   His high and noble-minded father,
his gentle sister, how different would have been their watch
and their care; and yet, if what Isaacs had said were indeed true, never might he hope to behold either of them
again.

" Better to know the worst," exclaimed he, mentally,
" than to grow mad on one's own fancies;" and calling
to William, he desired he would tell him how long he had
been in bed, and what had befallen him before being placed
there.   William hesitated, and Allan was proceeding, with
something of his habitual impetuosity, to insist on being
answered, when Major Jarvis again entered the room.
This time he went to the bed, took Allan's hand in his,
but at the same time placed his finger on his lip to indicate
the necessity for silence; but Allan implored Jarvis to tell
him the whole truth.   " Have I been mad," said he, " or
am I the destroyer of my race?"

" Neither," said Jarvis; " but, my dear fellow, you
must be calm — you must not —— "

" Preach calmness to others," cried Allan, as he tore
the bandages from his arm, and with all the artificial
strength given by fever, attempted to spring from his bed.
" Tell me all — all — or I will find some means of discovering it, though at the risk of life."

Jarvis, terrified at the vehemence of his manner and the wildness of his eye, promised, if he would but compose himself, to relate all he knew; and Allan, sinking back on his pillow, made signs that he was attentive.

" Terrified at your long absence," said Jarvis, " I proceeded to old Isaacs, who accused you of having tried to take his life, and confessed that, to preserve it, he had disclosed a secret which he had sworn to keep unknown."

" Go on," said Allan; " did he confide to you the nature of that disclosure ?"

" Yes," replied Jarvis; " he told me that immediately after you had left his house on the first day he refused to see us, an aged stranger called, and besought him, as he valued his own soul, to declare whether or not he was in possession of the title-deeds of the Glengary estate, and if so, for what sum he would relinquish and place them in his hands. Of course old Isaacs was too subtle to give an answer which could commit himself; but he endeavoured to extract from his simple-minded visitor on what grounds he supposed such an improbability as his being possessed of them, and who it was who would be willing to bid for them, supposing he could furnish a clue to where they might be found. The unwary man, whom I have since discovered to have been no other than Fergus the minstrel, did not hesitate to confide to old Isaacs the discovery made by your father, of the loss of these title-deeds, and the possible advantage which this loss might give a certain Mr. Muir, an impostor, who had threatened to dispossess his honoured master of his inheritance. He related, likewise, the steward's sudden seizure, and the charge he had given him, in his dying hour, to depart from the castle, and never to return till he had traced these deeds, and restored them to their rightful owner. A long life passed in faithful service had enabled the old steward, he said, to collect a considerable sum of money, which he had ordered him to expend for the release of these deeds from the custody of whoever might possess them.

" ' And why,' inquired Isaacs, ' do you think fit to regard me as their jailor ?'

" ' Why that,' replied Fergus, ' is a question I would rather not answer, because my old friend, when he charged me to get back these deeds, also charged me to preserve the honour of the family intact. But I did not apply to you without being pretty sure that I was right, though I don't wish to mention the name of one I have seen visit you within the hour.'

" ' You must leave me your address, my friend, and call again to-morrow,' was Isaacs' reply ; and anxious to be alone, to reflect on the best mode of turning this interview to advantage, he dismissed his visitor.

" Mr. Muir's professional men," continued Jarvis, " were known to Isaacs, and to Edinburgh he instantly repaired, and by degrees discovered from them that their case against Sir Norman rested on a deed of sale from your grandfather, who, when in great difficulty, sold the reversion of his estate, under a promise that, during his life, the transaction should never be made known. The purchaser's agent was the only being privy to the affair, for Sir Alexander would not confide it to his own. It was to the present Mr. Muir's father that the sale was made, who soon afterwards became, by the failure of a house in Calcutta, a beggar, and left Europe to make a second fortune. A few years after he died, and so did his agent. Both these events happened in Sir Alexander Ramsay's lifetime. The present claimant was but a child at the period of his father's death, and only within a very few years, by a search into that father's papers, became cognizant of those rights which he is now determined to prosecute to the utmost stretch of the law.   Mr. Muir considers that Sir Norman's conduct has been so offensive, that the suit has become as much a matter of pride as a struggle for property.

" ' But,' observed Isaacs, ' it is a suit which cannot stand.   A simple deed of sale without any support, and with every probability against it, will make but little way against old prejudices and established rights.   Who will believe that the title-deeds would be left with the Glengary family ?'

" ' We must,' said the agent, ' force Sir Norman to produce these deeds.   Some endorsement may have been made on them, which will establish our case.'

" ' And should there be nothing of the sort,' observed Isaacs, ' what then ?'

" ' Why, then we must rest on the truth of our case, lame as are its premises.   Mr. Muir has ample wealth, and will carry it from court to court till he gets his rights.'

" ' To get the title-deeds into your possession were a simpler process,' said Isaacs, with apparent calmness. But while he spoke he kept his eye steadfastly fixed on the man he addressed.

" ' Why, it wants no ghost to tell us that !' exclaimed the agent, with a laugh ; ' a deed of sale, with the title-deeds in hand, were tantamount to possession.'

:" ' Then why not obtain them ?   What would you give to any one who could put you on their track ?'

" ' Their own terms, were such a thing possible.'

" ' I will communicate with a friend,' replied Isaacs ; and departed satisfied with his first essay.

" The following morning brought not only Mr. Muir's agent, but his advocate, to old Isaacs' lodging.

" It is useless," continued Jarvis, " to repeat all the old usurer advances in extenuation of the act he committed, or his pretended conviction that he was acting for the benefit of the injured in parting with these deeds; for neither you nor I should believe one word of it, while we should feel certain that the 10,000*l.* he has received was his sole inducement to this treachery. An oath of secrecy was exacted from him, and his breach of it places him in some measure in our power. I have made use of it to insist on his seizing on the minstrel, and conveying him to some place where he may remain concealed, and from whence escape will be impossible."

" What is the object of this fresh crime?" faintly inquired Allan.

" I know not what you may term crime," said Jarvis, " nor why you should defend an old rascal whose folly has destroyed your family. What matters it whether the act spring from guilt or folly when the results are fatal? Do try to behave like a rational being, Allan, and bless your stars that one such idiot as old Fergus is alive in the world, to save you from all future fear of detection."

" But what shall hide from my own conscience the awful truth, that it was my cursed imprudence and base abstraction of my father's papers, which has been the real cause of his ruin?"

" Not a bit of it, Allan; how can you be so weak as not to perceive that this catastrophe must have occurred? The enemy of your house is rolling in wealth. Nothing could have prevented his gaining a verdict, sooner or later. The suit might have been a prolonged one, but what could

that have availed your father, except to involve him in a
labyrinth of debt. Believe me, Allan, it would be wiser to
think of the future, with a view to remedy some of the
evils it portends, than to dwell on the past, which is irre-
mediable."

"Why talk of the future? To me the future is a
blank; henceforth I am a beggar and a disgraced man !"

"You certainly bid fair to be both, if you indulge in
your present state of mind, and all my exertions cannot
prevent it; but I must say it is a hard case, after years of
friendship and devotion, to meet with such a return ; for I
need not tell you that your ruin will be mine. I have had
no thought of self-preservation distinct from you ; your
good or evil fortune I must share."

Allan was touched by the calm, dejected tone, in which
Jarvis spoke. Within the last few hours he had for the
first time doubted his friendship ; but habit, long dependence on his judgment, and a softness of feeling, induced
by his bodily weakness, got the better of the doubts which
solitude and reflection had raised. Putting out his hand,
he grasped Jarvis's, and soon after, exhausted by conversation and argument, sank into a deep slumber, from
which he awoke more than ever the slave of him whom
he called his friend.

Jarvis made arrangements with old Isaacs to wait two
years for the portion of the money he had advanced before
the minstrel's visit, for which Allan gave his note of hand,
and both the young men left town to join their regiment.

It has been stated that Allan's correspondence with
his family during their residence in the cottage was not
frequent. He had once, in a moment of good impulse,
entreated Sir Norman no longer to continue his allowance:

K

but his father had persisted in doing so, though its payment swallowed more than half his small income.

"Remember, Allan," said he, "that the terms debt and disgrace are in my mind synonymous, and that the honour of our family having been attacked by a foul aspersion on the dead, it behoves the living to be doubly vigilant in guarding theirs from suspicion."

But Allan, alas! was too deeply involved to be able to extricate himself. The only being aware of his difficulties always made light of them, and often, though apparently without design, induced their increase; while his victim, though sensible of the evil, had not courage to act but as he was tutored. His mind had so accustomed itself to this subjection that it at last became powerless in its own cause; thought of the future, reflection on the past, were alike painful, and both were resolutely banished.

At the period of Sir Norman's visit to London, Allan was also forced to be there, for the purpose of negotiating another loan; but he contrived that, at least to his father, his journey should wear the mask of filial and brotherly interest. The first sight of Marian converted this pretended feeling into something like reality; but the stings of conscience, each time he looked at her young and enduring form, each struggle that he witnessed for resignation under her father's deprivations, were too severe, and his visits were as rare as he could make them, without the fear of hearing some remonstrance from both of them. But Sir Norman's mind was too deeply imbued with grief to notice even the shortness and unfrequency of his son's visits, and his sister was too proud to sue for what she had imagined would be joyfully given.

His agitation on the morning Marian returned from

her first visit to the city was caused by his having, while talking to his father, approached the window, and from thence beheld the minstrel.   After that day, Allan no more visited his father or sister, and when, prior to their own departure for London, they sent to his lodging, they were told he had been suddenly ordered back to his regiment.

Something less than three years after the period of which we have been speaking, an elderly gentleman was seated at an open window of one of the houses situated on the side of the hill of Cintra.   The evening was sultry, and every now and then a flash of lightning played about the shrouds of the various vessels anchored off the bay of Lisbon.   A young girl sat at his feet; she had been reading to him; but the night had come on them so quickly, that she had been forced suddenly to resign her occupation. The book still rested on her knees, but her eyes were turned upwards to her father's face.   Silently, but not tearlessly, she watched his breathing, which seemed unusually oppressed; and as the flashes of lightning became more frequent, and illumined the apartment, she fancied that his pale features wore a look of pain and distress.

"The coming storm oppresses you, my father," said she, as she arose to open the lattice window; but not a breath of air penetrated into the apartment, while the rich perfumes from the orange-trees, and the aromatic odours of the wild thyme, served to render the overcharged atmosphere still more oppressive.

"Do not leave me, dearest," said the invalid; and in an instant Marian was at Sir Norman Ramsay's side, with one arm passed round his neck to support him as he leant forward, trying to catch a breath of fresher air. Thunder might now be heard in the distance; and it was evident that one of those awful storms with which Lisbon is often visited, was about to take place.

An hour passed, and not a drop of rain had yet fallen; but suddenly, an intense glare illumined the horizon. Marian was not sure if her father perceived it, and therefore restrained her emotion; when suddenly alarum bells were heard in every direction, and persons were observed, at each flash of lightning, to be running to and fro, as though conscious of some impending calamity. Marian looked closely at her father, and perceived that he had fallen asleep. Not for worlds would she have disturbed him by withdrawing her arm; but her suspense almost amounted to agony as she observed the blaze extend and become more lurid. Sir Norman's servant entered, and Marian, pointing with her disengaged hand to the light, whispered to him to hasten and inquire the cause. In a few moments he returned, to tell her that a vessel had most probably been struck by lightning, and that it was in flames. Heart-stricken at the idea of what her fellow-creatures were enduring, Marian continued to gaze at the terrific sight. The sparks arose in myriads to the clouds, and then descended like a shower of fire. Again the alarum bells sounded louder, and Sir Norman awoke.

"What is it?" he asked. "Where are you, my child? Are you safe, or what has happened?"

"You have been dreaming, dear father," said Marian; "but surely no dream could equal yonder dreadful reality!" And, completely overcome, she sank on her knees, and burst into tears.

Sir Norman's servant now repeated to his master the intelligence he had gained respecting the distant light,

and both father and child prayed fervently for the crew of that burning ship.

At length the light grew less intense, and then became quenched; but how many lives might have been quenched with it? Neither of those lonely watchers dared ask of each other what might be the thought of either; neither found courage to articulate; but in their very silence there was sad foreboding.

The servant had gone of his own accord to discover what had been done by the boatmen. Many of them had put to sea; and as the last effort of the flame gave out a brighter light, a raft had been seen floating towards the shore.

Daybreak found Sir Norman and his daughter still in that same apartment: the storm was over, and the glorious orb of day was rising, in all his calm and effulgent beauty, directly in front of that window whence they had a few hours before watched the light so fraught with terror and dismay, the terrific sight of which not all the beauty of that sunrise, not all the serenity of the opening day, could erase from their minds.

Marian besought her father to retire to rest; but as soon as she had conducted him to his chamber, she returned to the same spot, to weep and to pray. Not a soul, it would seem, had tasted of rest that night, for at every moment she discerned their neighbours returning from the city. But much as she desired to hear all they had learnt—anxious as she felt to discover if any of the boats had reached the raft, and how many had been saved —she felt powerless to move, or to ask these questions.

Did some mysterious foreboding whisper to Marian's heart that on the safety of that raft her future life might depend? Born in a country where superstition held sway

—nurtured among those who were its willing disciples—
the scenes of her own early life so mysterious and unfathomable—what wonder if Marian dwelt on certain
feelings till she believed them tokens of good, or warnings
of coming evil.   In the present instance there was a confusion in her ideas, whether for good or evil she knew not;
but she felt that the foregoing night would hold some
sway over her future fate.

Before Sir Norman was stirring, Marian had become
acquainted with the fact that several persons had been
saved upon a raft, whence one had been precipitated and
lost.   The vessel was a Turkish felucca, coming direct
from Tripoli, her crew mostly Turks; but one of the persons saved, though habited in an Eastern dress, was an
Englishman; the one who had perished was also said to
be of the same nation.

Towards evening, Marian was informed that the Englishman who had been saved requested admission to her
presence; and, anxious to show hospitality to a countryman, she immediately received him.   His form was noble,
and his features, though somewhat bronzed by an Asiatic
sun, bore the stamp of English birth, while his Eastern
costume gave an air of chivalrous bearing, which the dress
of his own country might not have bestowed on him.   His
countenance bore the marks of dejection and suffering,
and when he spoke, Marian fancied that his features were
not wholly unknown to her.

" What can my father have the pleasure to do for you ?"
was her first question.   " Though unequal to receiving a
stranger himself, he bids me offer you whatever hospitality
you will accept, or any other assistance you may require."

" Lady," said the stranger, " I perceive that your
recollection has not kept pace with mine.   The cursory

glance I had of you at your first visit to my father, Mr. Needham, has never been forgotten."

"Is it possible?" exclaimed Marian. "Mr. Needham's son must, indeed, be warmly welcomed by my father and myself;" and as she spoke, she held out her hand, on which the stranger pressed his lips, with an air of the deepest respect. "Let me acquaint my father with this unexpected happiness," added Marian; but Horace Needham arrested her step, and entreated that she would first listen to all he had to relate.

It was to spare Sir Norman's feelings, he said, that he had been induced to seek this interview with her. The sad forebodings which had crept over Marian's mind again became present, and, pale as death, she entreated to be told what fresh sorrow awaited them.

Horace looked at her agitated countenance till he almost lost his own self-command, and she had again to urge him to tell her the worst, ere he found voice to say, "Many of us left the burning ship; but all had not strength to reach the shore. The one who perished had been long ill; he was worn out by sorrow and sickness; accident made us acquainted; his sufferings and his self-upbraidings made me his friend. It was at my suggestion that he sought this shore—it was my promise to gain for him a pardon he dared not ask, which induced him to embark in that ill-fated vessel."

Horace paused to watch the effect of his recital, but Marian neither spoke nor moved, and he continued—"No earthly power could have long prolonged his life—no, not even a father's pity, a sister's love!" Again he paused, but this time it was to receive the death-like form of Marian in his arms. She had felt the truth, and compre-nended that Allan was the lost one.

Her swoon was long; and though Horace carried her
to an open window, and used such means as were at hand
to revive her, it was not till he had begun to fancy that
she would no more recover, that she slowly opened her
eyes. After a few moments, something like warmth returned to the fair form which he had been holding in his
arms, cold and rigid as in death. She looked at him, and
the deep sympathy with which he regarded her was sufficient evidence that she had not mistaken the misfortune
he wished to acquaint her with. To think of her father,
to lose all feeling for self in her anxiety for him, had so
long been the occupation of Marian's life, that it was at
the thoughts of his grief that she now wept.

Horace remained silent: he allowed her tears to flow
without an attempt to arrest their course. No words he
might utter could, in that heavy hour, he knew, bring
consolation; but when a tear fell on Marian's hands,
which were held in his, and she knew that tear flowed not
from her own eyes, she felt that the sympathy of at least
one heart was with her, and at length she gained courage
to inquire and listen, before proceeding to her father, to
some of the following particulars.

Horace Needham had said that accident brought him
acquainted with Allan of Glengary, but it was an accident
which not only riveted their intimacy, but turned Allan
from his path of evil to one of sincere and earnest repentance.

From an early age, travel had been the darling pursuit
of Horace Needham, and the Eastern countries his favourite
ground of search and exploit. An only child, he was his
father's idol, and his society, whenever he did enjoy it,
gave a charm to his existence; but never had the fond

father sought to restrain his son from pursuing the path which seemed necessary to his happiness. When with him he saw so much in his character to admire and be proud of, that he felt, in whatever clime fancy might lead him, honour and right feeling would be his safeguards.

On parting from his father, he had promised that this should be his last expedition to the East, and that on his return he would tax his father's hospitality for a continued residence at his country-seat. On entering Turkey, by the Danube, he had found himself benighted at the town of Semlin, and though nothing could be less inviting than the fare spread for travellers, or the beds prepared for their repose, Horace felt no repugnance to make trial of both.

The sleeping apartment to which he was conducted was not untenanted. On one of its four wretched pallets a fellow-traveller was stretched, apparently asleep, and Horace soon become convinced that the sharer of his room was in a state of delirium; his wild ravings were awful; and sleep being banished from his eyes, Horace listened with pity to the dreadful self-accusations and re-morse the wretched man was pouring forth. At length, he moved, and springing from his bed with the look of a maniac, rushed to the window with the intention, as it appeared, of jumping out; but the window, which was in the roof, was so constructed with closely-fitting iron bars, (possibly to prevent the entrance of any one from the neighbouring houses by a terrace extending along them,) that he could not effect his purpose. He then approached a small valise which was placed close to his bed; Horace distinctly saw a pistol in his hand; he sat down on his bed, still grasping it. Some words he uttered seemed as though he wished to pray; but again the delirium returned, and he proceeded with rapidity in the same strain as before.

Horace did not withdraw his eye from him for a single instant; he dared not call for assistance, fearing to render the unhappy man more desperate, and increase the danger he apprehended from the pistol; but he felt that on his calmness and presence of mind both his own and another's life might depend.

The raving ceased — the stranger evidently now prayed — the words of " Father — Marian — forgive me, and pray for my soul!" though almost whispered, were heard by the listener. In another instant he saw the pistol raised to his head.

There was no time for thought, but impulse guided Horace; with one spring he was by the unhappy man's side — his arm turned the direction of the pistol — which went off, without injury to either.

The noise of the report roused the household, and Horace, still holding the stranger in his grasp, endeavoured to assuage their fears, by declaring the report of the pistol to have been an accident. As soon as all was again still without the chamber, Horace besought the stranger to go to his bed, endeavour to compose himself, and thank God for having preserved him from the commission of the crime he meditated.

A change had come over the person he addressed; fever and delirium had passed away, and were succeeded by a state of weakness bordering on inanition. He sighed heavily, but for some hours uttered not a word. At length he fell asleep, and as Horace sat watching him, he felt convinced that the heavy sweat which now stood on his brow, though indicative of illness, must preclude any fear of an immediate return of fever. When the sleeper awoke, he cast his eyes around, and, on perceiving Horace, beckoned him to approach his bed; he took his hand, pressed it and said, in a very low tone,—"There are those who may hereafter thank you for having saved me from suicide."

Horace sent for a doctor, who pronounced the sick man to be in a very precarious state, and declared his removal quite impossible without imminent danger. For many days, Horace watched by him with unremitting care. As soon as he became well enough to converse, he entered voluntarily on his position, and confessed to Horace that for several weeks he had been meditating suicide, as the only means of saving himself from disgrace.

" My life," added he, " can bring but sorrow and shame on all connected with me; I have sinned heavily against those I most revere; their pardon I may never hope to attain. I am an outcast from society, and have been rendered all this by one whom I called friend."

Allan, for it was he who had been thus mercifully interrupted in his intended crime, continued to pour into Horace's ear the relation of his life; but as its incidents have been already related, up to the period of his father's leaving London, we shall proceed at once to that portion of it which immediately followed on his observing the minstrel standing opposite Sir Norman's lodging.

It has been said, that he rushed from the house on that occasion, regardless of his sister's voice; his object was to seek and again secure the minstrel: " But vain," said Allan, " was all search: the greater part of that day, and the whole of the following night, did I go from place to place, endeavouring to discover where he was concealed; and in despair I left London, hoping that he might not have been aware of my vicinity to him. The same round of dissipation and extravagance stained the following two years of my life, during which Jarvis appeared to be my friend. I was over head and ears in debt, and when the period approached for the payment of old Isaacs, the sale of my commission was my only resource; it was sacrificed, and I found myself still heavily in debt, and without one shilling to discharge it, or provide for myself. About this time a distant relation of Jarvis's died, which event put him into possession of a good fortune and a baronetcy, and I was weak enough to imagine that the man whom I had called friend, and to whom my purse had been ever open, and at whose instigation I had resorted to measures at which my soul shuddered, to procure large sums of money which he fully shared with me,—I say I was weak enough not to imagine that this man would choose such a moment to desert and revile me. But so it was; and without money or friends, I quitted England, where nothing short of a gaol awaited me, to seek employment in some other land. Sickness overtook me. I have been at death's door, with nought but guilt and dishonour before my eyes. I have loathed myself and all mankind, till it seemed my curse that I did not die. In my lonely wanderings, in my fevered dreams, I have beheld the minstrel's form; I have heard his voice proclaiming me accursed, till my brain became diseased, and my only object self-destruction."

Horace, it will be remembered, had been made acquainted, by his father, with the relief he had afforded Marian, and the circumstances of the Glengarys; and it seemed something like the hand of Providence which had led him to rescue from crime the son of that house.

As soon as Allan could travel with safety, Horace insisted on his accompanying him to Constantinople. At this earlier period, the Danube, which now bears on its vast surface steamers and other vessels laden with the productions of every province in Hungary, was merely traversed by the rude, half-finished rafts, navigated by the inhabitants of the district through which the rivei finds its way. These vessels, composed merely of huge beams of wood, firmly linked together by iron stanchions, never re-ascended the river, being broken up for fire-wood at the place where they discharged their cargo.

In one of these rude craft, protected from the weather merely by a small cabin raised a little above the after part of the deck, our travellers were glad to engage a passage, Allan's weakness rendering a land journey impracticable. The only sign of human habitation was the occasional mud hut of the Wallachian shepherd, built on the low marshy bank of the river. In one of these they were oftentimes glad to find protection and shelter, and to halt a day or two for Allan to recruit his strength.

Horace saw plainly that life was not long to be Allan's portion on earth; clearly he perceived that the awful fiat had gone forth, and that ere many weeks had sped, all that remained of Allan of Glengary would be, the remem-- brance of his follies, his crimes, and his repentance; and most earnestly did he seek, by every argument and en-treaty, to render this repentance sincere and availing. He would speak to him gently of his past ways, and when Allan would shrink aghast from their contempla-tion, he would point out to him that He who came to save sinners exacted no other tribute from the sinner than firm faith and true repentance.

Allan often expressed a desire that his father should know the fearful act he had been guilty of, and which led to such fatal consequences. " Could I but obtain his for-giveness," he would say, " I could better hope for mercy from above. '

As his bodily strength diminished, his senses became

more acute; and the remorse he expressed at having
subjected poor old Angus's memory to disgrace, was bitter
indeed.

They were one evening in one of these huts, unable
from Allan's weakness, to proceed. A thin partition divided their apartment from an adjoining one. Carried
away by his feelings, Allan had spoken with some of his
wonted impetuosity of language; his voice had perhaps
startled some one near them, who was willing to try if his
might also be remembered; a few chords were struck, and
then a faint and feeble tone was heard uttering some
words in the Gaelic tongue. Allan started from his recumbent position : he grasped Horace's arm as he murmured, " Save me, save me—'tis the minstrel ! "

" Be composed," returned Horace, " be patient, I
entreat you, while I go to seek this man who has so
startled you, and prove whether or not he be the person
you imagine."

" Oh, bring him not here to curse me ! " cried Allan,
as he sank back exhausted.

Horace gave him some drops of a cordial he always had
at hand, and as soon as he could leave him, proceeded in
search of the harper. On perceiving a man leaning against
the partition which separated the apartment, he went up
to him, and whispered, " Know you aught of Fergus the
minstrel ? "

The start, the agitation, and bewildered look, which
met his glance, left no doubt that Allan's recollection was
correct.

" Seek you Allan of Glengary ? " he continued; " if so,
your errand is finished; I can lead you to him; not," he
continued, " to the proud and impetuous youth you remember by that name, but to one well-nigh worn out by

suffering and remorse. Have you no peace to speak to such an one?"

"Peace!" exclaimed the minstrel; "peace to him who destroyed my only friend, and gave his memory to shame and obloquy! peace to the destroyer of his house! peace to him who ——"

A heavy noise, as of some one falling, arrested the old man, while Horace exclaimed, "He has heard all—you have killed him!"

Horace returned to the room he had quitted, to raise and restore Allan to life, who had, as he conjectured, heard all, and fallen senseless under the torture of the minstrel's words.

It was impossible for Horace to quit the unhappy sufferer that night, during which he was a prey to delirium; and when, in the morning, he fell into an uneasy doze, no one knew anything of the minstrel. He had come and he had gone, without exciting attention.

Every day that Horace watched by his friend, he became more convinced that his life was waning fast; but, at the same time, he felt assured that nothing could render calm the last moments of that erring and unhappy man, or inspire him with a Christian's hope, but the confession of his crimes, and the forgiveness of his earthly parent. Under this persuasion, he besought Allan to embark with him for Lisbon, where, through Marian's correspondence with his father, Horace knew that Sir Norman and his daughter were resident; and, at length, on condition that his arrival should not be mentioned till his father's feelings were made known to Horace, who took the whole mediation on himself, Allan suffered himself to be placed on board the vessel, the destruction of which Marian had seen reflected on the sky with feelings of such awe and such harrowing forebodings.

It was Horace who bore Allan in his arms to the raft, but who had not strength to retain him in safety there. An unfortunate movement made by the struggling crowd, anxious to save themselves, precipitated them both into the ocean, and when Horace rose to the surface, his friend was no longer in his grasp; neither could he regain the raft, but owed his safety to a floating mass which had been detached from the wreck.

It was judged better, both by Horace and by Marian, that Sir Norman should not be apprised of any part of Allan's unhappy life and degenerate conduct. He was now beyond the reach of pardon from his earthly parent, and why disturb that parent's last years by a knowledge of what could not but render those few years miserable? It had been the will of Heaven that earthly forgiveness should not be awarded to the sinner; but Horace, who spoke of his repentance, and Marian, who listened with deep interest to each proof of its fervour, could but pray that a more enduring mercy was secured to the penitent, by the one great sacrifice of Him whose death was the sinner's ransom.

Sir Norman bore the intelligence of his son's death with more fortitude than his daughter had anticipated; for the sad reverses of his own fate had subdued his feelings into a sort of drowsy passiveness.

Horace Needham had become domesticated at Cintra; his whole world seemed centred in that little spot. He had made himself so necessary to Sir Norman, that the old chieftain forgot, in his presence, that he had no son; indeed, never had he experienced from his own son the sweet and gentle offices of affection bestowed on him by Horace. There was another individual to whom his society was not less precious; but it was not till a letter was received from Mr. Needham, requesting Horace's immediate return to England, that any of them were quite sure of all they were to each other.

" Marian, my beloved, my peerless Marian, how can I leave thee?" murmured Horace, as they stood watching the starry firmament, on the morning before the vessel, in which he had taken his passage, was to sail for Falmouth; and Marian's fast-falling tears evinced that to her the separation was not less painful. " Oh, let me not depart," he continued, " without the assurance of thy love! Let us here, in the sight of Heaven, plight our troth! I cannot leave thee but as my affianced bride!"

" Think, Horace," replied Marian, " of all your father's noble conduct to me and mine. But for his beneficence, we were little removed from paupers; and is it for the . creature of his bounty to aspire to his son's hand?"

" Talk not of aspiring, thou peerless one! Say, rather, shall a proud and time-honoured chieftain's daughter think a merchant's son her equal? Ah, Marian, if thou didst but love as I do, thou wouldst know that in the bright and glorious light of that feeling, neither rank nor wealth are discernible! Love is omnipotent, or it is but a mockery of the word."

" Horace," replied Marian, " the secret of my love is no longer mine own; it stole so softly into my heart, that there was no time to be wary; and, almost before I knew it myself, its existence was known to you. In your father's hands rests its termination; whether I am to be a blessed and happy wife, or my love is to remain hid in the deepest recesses of my heart, his word can alone decide

L

Nay, look not displeased, Horace. Ask your own noble heart, if mine would be worthy to be allied with it, if that alliance were to be based on ingratitude."

" Ever right and ever perfect art thou, Marian; and in listening to these truths I feel that they but make thee more dear to me! But, dearest, why doubt my father's willingness to secure my happiness?"

" I do not doubt it, Horace. I dare not think I ought to doubt it,—for then, indeed, I should be wretched."

Horace caught the speaker to his heart, and though no plighted vows were spoken, both felt that henceforth they lived but for each other.

Little more remains to be told. The chieftain of Glengary has paid the debt of nature, but not before the stigma on his father's name had been effaced by the indefatigable and untiring exertions of our old friend Mr. Needham, the noble-minded merchant, who, from the first, suspecting treachery on the part of Mr. Muir, had persevered in his inquiries, despatching the minstrel on one expedition after another to the East, where the late Mr. Muir had died; till, at length, a deed was discovered which gave ample proof of the late chieftain's having redeemed his estate ere he executed his will. This news was brought to Cintra by Horace, who came, by his father's desire, to conduct his beloved Marian and the Glengary to their ancient home; but another revulsion of fate had been too much for the honoured chieftain. He was one among the many who find it more difficult to support the extreme of joy than to endure the bitterness of sorrow. His spirit was broken, and he calmly sank to his long rest, supported and cheered to the last by the presence and filial affection of his exemplary daughter.

* * * * *
* * * * , *

Eighteen months have elapsed since his death. The minstrel has again returned to the castle. Marian's first interview with this old and faithful servant presented a touching scene; but when first summoned to the presence of the Glengary—for Horace had, on his marriage with its heiress, assumed that distinction—how great was the minstrel's surprise to behold and recognise the traveller who had spoken with him in the lone hut on the Danube; for, wishing to assist the old man's memory, Horace had arrayed himself in the Eastern costume which he had then worn.

Once more the minstrel's harp was strung, and again the name of Glengary resounded through the castle walls.

The more happily and entirely the project of the fair Eva seemed to succeed in eliciting pen-and-ink pictures out of painted ones, the more eager did she grow that the progress of it should not flag. The second evening had already reached the accustomed hour of retirement at the moment when the last story reached its close; but, on seeing one or two of the guests show signs of departure, she seized on a beautiful design which lay immediately before her, and, as if a new thought had come to her, she exclaimed, "A Poem! we have had no poetry yet; and I have heard that Painting and Poetry are sisters, and always go together. Look! this moonlight view is poetry itself. Who will 'marry it to immortal verse?' as I have heard some poet say or sing, on a similar occasion. Oh, I know!" she continued, after a momentary pause, during which no one answered to her appeal — "I know!" and she turned to a young lady, who had just returned from

Italy, and who had lately told her many legends that she had gathered in that "sunny land." "Here," she exclaimed, "is one of those gondolas you have so often described to me—and a lover, I think, by his earnest look—and a beautiful lady up above. Why, this alone is a story, if you would but make it into rhyme. Do try!"

"I cannot invent stories, my dear Eva, as your other friends do," was the reply; "but I will repeat to you a legend I heard in one of those very gondolas, and you may fit it to your picture if you can, though it will, I am afraid, impart infinitely less illustration than it will receive."

The lady then related

LOVE'S LAST TRYST.

A ROMANCE OF VENICE.

'Tis night, and such a night as smiles.
In beauty 'neath a southern sky;
The silvery waves are hushed to rest,
And in the moonbeams slumbering lie
No cloud to dim the stainless blue,
Upon the crystal deep is thrown,
Where Venice stands in regal state,
Encircled by her glittering zone.
Amid the fairest spots of Earth,
Ye tranquil stars watch o'er below;
Never can one more lovely be
Than this ye sweetly shine on now.
Still is each sound of Life; awhile
Reposes Pleasure's wearied train,
And brooding o'er with dove-like wings,
Day-banished Silence breathes again.

Not long it reigns—the stroke is heard
Of oars, whose bright phosphoric ray

Gleams in the distance, and a bark
O'er the blue water makes its way,
Yet stealthily, as if it sought
But wakeful ears to list the song
That o'er the calm, unruffled wave,
The night-breeze gently bears along.

" 'Tis midnight's charmèd hour,
And every folded flower
Weepeth in sorrow that sweet Day hath flown,
Softly she sunk to rest,
Lulled on Night's quiet breast,
And o'er her smiles her ebon hair is thrown.
The Hours pass slowly by,
With pinions noiselessly,
On to the curtained East they sadly move,
As if they feared to break
Her slumber, or awake
The listening Echo of my whispered love.
They wait for thee, sweet one,
For thy dear smile alone
Illumes my dreary path o'er Life's dark sea ;
Rise in thy beauty, rise,
Star of these southern skies,
For weary is my way, love, without thee."

The song is o'er, and he who sang
Still lingers at the vessel's prow ;
Lofty his port, but southern suns
Have left no trace on cheek or brow
To mark him of Italia's clime ;
But through the gondolier's disguise
The Austrian Ulric stands reveal'd.
No mask but Love's keen glance defies.
Why comes he here, alone, unarm'd,
'Mid hearts that seek to work his woe ?
How will his single footstep gain
The dwelling of his direst foe ?
And yet he comes !—as seamen scorn
The dangers of the storm, and keep
Watch o'er the one bright guiding star,
That lights their pathway o'er the deep.

And who, Bianca, loving thee,
But would have risked a life's poor stars,
And felt e'en blessed were the boon
To lose it—if for thy sweet sake ?
Oft hath he stemmed the Adrian wave
To gaze upon those deep-fringed eyes,
Dark as the veil that shades their light,
And radiant as their own fair skies.
Now from Lioni's silent tower
A fairy hand puts lightly by
The lattice ; on the peaceful scene
A fond glance wanders wistfully.
'Tis she—Bianca ! —she who loves
This foe to Venice and her race,
To-morrow's dawn that gilds these towers
Will shine upon her vacant place.
A distant clime, and other tongues
Will hail her by a holier name,
And one fond glance her home shall make—
To love all climates are the same.
In very weariness or scorn,
She flings aside the gems that press
Her throbbing brow, that little needs
Their aid to make its loveliness.
Ay, loose thy richly 'broidered vest,
And throw thy mask of smiles aside,
Thy prisoned heart beats free at length
From chains the World hath forged for Pride,
Well mayst thou curse the noble blood
That flows to whelm all Life's sweet ties,
For feuds of them who sleep in death,
And one poor maid the sacrifice.

A cloud is on her brow to-night,
A nameless fear that mocks control,
Shadows the Future that had shed
Its sunniest visions o'er her soul.
Her pale, sweet face, yet paler seems,
The pearls that braid her raven hair,
Beneath the moonbeam's glittering light,
Gleam in its darkness far less fair.

Moored nearer yet the palace walls,
Once more awakes her lover's strain ;
Secure, in past security,
The signal song is heard again,
Around her slight and trembling form
She throws a mantle's sheltering fold,
Her foot has reached the postern gate,
So oft their trysting-place of old :
She paused. Perchance the ties of home,
Familiar voices, household words,
Came thronging at this parting hour
To touch the full heart's swelling chords.
Slowly she moves ; a coward eye
Hath tracked her footstep through the shade
Of the deep arch ; one moment more,
She falls beneath a ruffian's blade !
Oh ! not for thee was aimed the blow
That quenched thy young life's vital flame,
'Twas for the Austrian's bosom dealt
By him who owned a brother's name.

By a lamp's uncertain lustre, in a dungeon's narrow cell,
Where the gibes and frenzied laughter mark the spot where maniacs dwell,
Paces one whose tale of sorrow oft hath drawn the stranger's tears—
'Tis an aged man ; each midnight, through a weary length of years,
Steals he to the narrow casement—watching for his bride, they say,
And he tells the maddening story as it were but yesterday.

" Ere the vesper star had risen in the summer twilight sky,
'Neath yon tower's friendly shadow, swept my lone bark silently.
Then the cypress hushed its murmurs, and the waves their rippling sound,
'Twas to list her whispered welcome, that sweet Silence breathed around.
There I lingered, till the midnight melted into silver mist,
And the rosy hues of morning, beach and bower, and islet kiss'd.
'Mid the azure waters, Venice, throned upon her hundred isles,
Looked a bashful bride unveiling 'neath a lover's radiant smiles ;
With a timid hand withdrawing from her shrouded face the screen
That concealed her tearful beauty, thus uprose the ' Ocean Queen :'—
Venice ! let the pangs I owe thee blight thee with the woe thou'st wrought,
Let my wild curse cling about thee, that thy treachery hath bought !

May a despot's foot oppress thee, brand thee with each loathsome crime,
Graven in the brazen annals of the blood-stained book of Time!
Cycles hence, the sighs of anguish, from thy murderous hand the source,
Shall have strength to sap thy power with a stranger's withering curse!
May thy noblest blood betray thee!   Blood?   Upon my wildered brain
Comes a dream of thee, Bianca, stealing o'er my soul again.
See, the moon is bright above me; she who lives among the stars,
Comes in all her bridal beauty, smiling through my prison bars!
Lightly floats her dark hair round me;—ay, she comes to set me free!
There is blood upon her bosom, and that blood was shed for me!
What? they strike me when I clasp thee!   Fear not, love, I will not
      chide;
Long I waited through the midnight, yet thou didst not seek my side:
Nor till Morning's dawn had opened was my cup of sorrow full;
When in Death's cold grasp I found thee—mine, my lost, my beautiful.

EVENING THE THIRD.

On the company re-assembling in the library, on the third evening devoted to the Haddon Hall Revels, the Lady Eva was, as usual, duly prepared with her pictorial treasures. Holding in her fair hand the design which she wished to be next illustrated, she glanced round the gay and intellectual circle, and her eye fixed on a gentleman of whose literary abilities she had heard much, but with whom she had too slight an acquaintance not to feel timid at proffering a request. With that ready and gentle courtesy which distinguishes some few above their fellows, the gentleman anticipated her wishes, and, going up to her, remarked that the drawing she held in her hand was a masterly delineation of a wild, bold, and chivalrous scene. "Does not the principal figure in the group remind you, Lady Eva," said he, "of the pictures we have seen of Hernando Cortés?"

"I had not remarked it," she replied; "but it would gratify me particularly to hear something of that extraordinary conqueror."

The gentleman took the design from the Lady Eva's hand, saying, "I will endeavour to recollect some passages in his life, and one in particular, which connects him in my mind with this drawing."

Then, after a brief pause, he proceeded to relate—

SOME PASSAGES IN THE LIFE OF THE CONQUISTADOR.

"'They tell me that I am good for nothing; that I am a rank, profitless weed, fit only for the burning. Sancta Maria! how many brawling youths have lived to be great men, and to belie the prophecies of the grey-beards;" and the speaker, with a toss of the head which set the feather " swaling in his bonnet," smote his thigh with the palm of his hand, and laughed the clear, sonorous laugh, which youth but rarely transmits to manhood.

The laugh, sincere as it was, elicited no response from the companion of the thoughtless stripling—a pale, meek-eyed girl, who sat beside him, one small hand resting on his shoulder. It was evening—a summer evening—a summer evening in Spain. The setting sun had thrown into deepest shade the walls of old Medellin. The place in which they sat was an ivy-grown ruin, in the corner of a high-walled garden. It might once have been a private chapel: it was now a summer-house. Into the arched window-holes peeped the tall, heavy-leaved shrubs, and the languid heads of many gorgeous flowers. The still air was laden with perfume. Sultry was the twilight hour.

"Yes, they may prate," continued the youth, "and shake their heads, and look wisdom at me—a world of stern reproof in their cold, hard eyes. A fig for their prophecies! They shall see me, some day — the prophets! —if they only live long enough, a—what shall I say, sweet Marina?—a grave and venerable judge."

The young maiden could not choose but smile, as she saw the look of mock solemnity with which her friend accompanied these words, but there was something of sadness in the tones of her sweet voice, as she said — " Will you never — never, be serious — not even for my sake, dear ? — you, who have sworn to do such great things for me, to deny me, in practice, even this. A judge ! — Salamanca will be proud indeed of the plant which she reared last year. Law ! — you who are ever ready to break the law, — you to expound or administer it ! If Medellin ever glory in her son, little will be the share of honour dispensed to learned Salamanca. Our great man may be among the heroes — not among the sages of the world."

" And is't not better to be among the heroes ?" asked the youth, in an eager, and a graver tone. " You shake your head, but your eyes let the secret out. Was there ever a woman yet, who loved not the arm that strikes, better than the tongue which argues — the mailed coat of the soldier, rather than the sombre gown of the clerk ?"

" You wrong us," returned the maiden. " A true woman best loves that which most calls forth the dignity of man. And believe me, love, it is not as a scourge — as a fire-brand — that man exhibits the highest nobility of nature. If we are sometimes dazzled by brilliant acts, and clap our hands as the actors pass by, forgetful of all the sorrow — all the suffering — which has smeared, as with blood and tears, the wheels of their chariots, it is only because the weakness of humanity clings to us evermore, and being weak, we, in our erring judgments ——"

" Tut, tut !" interrupted the youth ; " if it were possible for sweet ladies of seventeen to prose with their rosy lips, I should be tempted to charge you with uttering the sagest commonplaces which have ever grated upon these ears since I did penance in the lecture-room at Salamanca. By the Virgin, such lips were never meant to preach solemnity withal ! The language of love, not of counsel, befits that

delicious mouth; and love's language, you know, sweetest,
is not always made up of words." It might have been
that there was some obscurity in this last sentence, or the
youth feared that there might be, for he attempted an
explanation; and it was a practical one.

There was a pause—there often is, after such explanations—which the girl was the first to break. "I do not
seek," she said, "to chain you down to the hall or the
cloister; but something I would do to curb your errant
propensities—to direct your aims, which are often noble,
your efforts, which are always strenuous—into one onward course, that so, steadily pursuing the path of duty,
you may in the end accomplish great things."

"Great things!—accomplish great things! I was
born to accomplish great things." He laughed, but there
was this time little sincerity in his laughter. "Yes, I
shall be very great some day; and you shall be very proud.
And little Gonzalo, too, who comes, if I mistake not, this
way—else what is the tiny figure I see through the tall
shrubs, which have now shut him quite out from us? Ah
—the fine little fellow! A brother worthy of such a sister; and he, too, shall be very proud. Yes, my boy, when
I am a great leader, you shall be one of my captains. I
will not employ you then so unworthily as now: you shall
not be a spy, but a cavalier. And what tidings have you
brought?"

The child, a fine little boy of some six years, had by
this time entered the summer-house. Running up to his
sister, he said something, but what, it was hard to divine;
partly because he was scant of breath, and partly because
his utterance was marred by a strong natural lisp. But of
the nature of the child's story there was no doubt. It had
ceased to be safe for the youth to remain longer in that

garden. The father of his beloved had returned from his accustomed afternoon ramble. It was time for the lovers to part.

" Thanks, my brave little fellow; I shall repay you some day !" and, taking the child into his arms, HER-NANDO CORTÉS kissed the cheek of GONZALO DE SAN-DOVAL. Another minute, and Hernando was on the garden wall. There was not in all Medellin one more active than he; but ancient masonry will sometimes play scurvy tricks even to nimble youths, and the garden walls of Don Sandoval were well-nigh as old as his lineage. Alas, for the young lovers! Hernando had scarcely reached the summit, ere the crumbling masonry gave way beneath his weight, and the youth fell heavily, with a mass of rubbish, on the other side. Then for awhile all was utter darkness. When the light dawned again upon him, he was lying in his father's house.

* * * Gloomy was all around : the massive stone pil-lars of that inornate church, the lofty arched roof, with its rudely-sculptured cornices, the large heavy-moulded win-dows, the simple altars, bedecked with little of the wonted finery of the faith, the dark ungainly pulpit, the long aisles, dreary at noon-tide, in the full glare of the meri-dian sun, and *how* dreary now that the few tapers, which stood upon the altars erected to the Christian's God in the new colony of Fernandina,* shed all the little radiance which struggled through the thick gloom of a starless midnight !

Gloomy was all around—more gloomy the thoughts of the lonely man, who now paced, with folded arms, those solemn aisles; now leaned, in deep meditation, against the

* Cuba.

rude altar-rails. That church was to him a sanctuary;
but at such an hour, in such a place, what wonder that
even his strong spirit should have bowed beneath the
leaden weight of despondency which sat upon his heart?
—that even he should have obstinately questioned the
value of safety, so highly priced?

He was a young man of goodly aspect, of fair proportions. Nature had been bountiful to him; and he was
now in that early summer of life, when her gifts are ever
in best condition, fresh, but with something in them, too,
of the vigour of lusty manhood. He had numbered some
twenty-seven years; and they had not been uneventful
ones. Fortune had played him some sorry tricks, but
they were mostly of his own invitation. No one, then,
thought that Hernando Cortés was his own best friend.

Another man would, in his present condition, have
appeared in most woeful plight. His hair was disordered,
his cheeks unshaven, his clothes, in many places, rent and
soiled. There was blood upon his wrists and ankles, and
he walked not without pain. But still the man who had
now a second time broken the bonds of his persecutors,
and sought refuge in that holy edifice, was of gallant
bearing and goodly aspect. Nature had been too prodigal
in her gifts for accident easily to mar and mutilate. . . . .

It was, indeed, an hour for profoundest meditation;
and even he, the man of action, whose thoughts were ever
in advance of time, whose nature it was ever to look forward, even he, in those gloomy aisles, was sunk in meditations, of which the past engrossed the greatest share.
Much pondered he upon his early years, his idle pranks at
Salamanca, his wild adventures in his native town, his first
love, his own Marina. There was sweetness there; but
not without a sting of remorse. He had been happy — so

happy. Such happiness, in after life, is not to be renewed. But what had been the end of that long dream of bliss? The old tale. And yet in heart he knew himself to be still true. Many acts of licentiousness had stained the page of his manhood; passions, strong and heady, had moved him to much wrong-doing; injuries to others, to the dignity of his own nature. The irresistible will, the fearless heart, the strenuous impulse, breaking down all barriers of right, all restraints of decency; and yet, beneath all this, there had been an under-current of purer feeling. Ever had he fondly loved the meek-eyed Marina and her lisping brother. Love! What love! To ruin, to blight, to fix a burning sorrow for ever in the heart of the loved one!

And then another image rose up before him; another young and lovely girl. One whom, in his new island home, he had courted openly, in the sight of men; one to whom he had plighted his troth; and yet time had passed over the heads of the betrothed ones, and the compact was unfulfilled. Here was another act of grievous wrong-doing. Catalina Xuarez, the much-doating, the beautiful, the true. In his prosperity he had slighted her, and now he knew the full worth of her woman's heart. A true woman — now that the toils of great peril were around him — now, she was to his aid — to rescue him; and yet beautiful as she was in her fair face, and gentle nature, and heroic truthfulness, he had not a heart to give. But justice, expediency; and then the grim face of his great enemy, Velasquez, rose up before him, and Cortés, with set teeth and clenched hands — hands still bleeding from the wounds he had received in his struggles with the cruel chains, which had fettered him on board the prison-ship — strode rapidly away from the altar. Velasquez, the Governor of

of Fernandina! how Cortés longed to meet him face to
face, and to close with him in one great struggle, neither
armed with power beyond that which Nature gives to all
her children—not as in unequal strife between governor
and vassal, but on the fair open field of manhood.   Had
not Velasquez wronged, insulted him?   And what had he
done, under such wrongs?   Nothing.   He had but conversed with others, who had their grievances to set forth ;
and had pledged himself to proceed to Hispaniola and
appeal to higher authorities ; and Velasquez called this
conspiracy—the name that coward selfishness ever gives
to the efforts of injured men to obtain for themselves
justice.   He had been beaten down—worsted for a time ;
but his hour would yet come.   " Yes," he repeated, as the
buoyancy of his nature reasserted itself, and the sunshine
of his heart burst through the surrounding gloom—" yes,
I am undermost now.   I have trodden on slippery ground ;
but courage, courage, Hernando Cortés, you have not
fulfilled your destiny yet ! . . ."

In such varied meditations as these, hour after hour
passed away, till the grey dawn of morning had succeeded
to the solemn blackness of night.   Still Cortés paced the
dreary aisle, until arrested by the sound of his own name
uttered in a low sweet voice, whilst at the same moment
he felt a light hand upon his shoulder.   " Hernando !"—
he turned round and confronted a female figure, wrapped
from head to foot in a large black mantle—" Cortés, I am
here !   Catalina is at her post beside you.   You are safe.
Listen to me, and your trials are at an end.   He knows all
—the guard is now upon the hill -- Velasquez is stirring,
but he shall not harm you—Isabella, my sweet sister, is
now at his side—she will accomplish much ; but you
must act your part boldly."

" Did I ever lose anything yet for lack of boldness ?"

" Never ; but this, remember — Velasquez will be cheated, so that he *seems* not to be cheated. He will not remove the guard, but he will be contented if you elude it. Now take this woman's mantle — I thank God that my stature is beyond that of common women. They saw me pass. They spoke to me. One man at least knew me ; he must have known that I was wending here to see you. If compelled to pass near them, with eyes on the ground and kerchief to your face, your silence will be interpreted as we would have it. Hie thee straight to Velazquez. He will not be wholly unprepared to see you. The rest I leave, Hernando, to your own strong soul."

Disguised in the woman's mantle, Cortés was about to quit the sanctuary, when a sudden thought arrested his progress; he turned round, took the hand of Catalina, and silently led her to the foot of the altar. Still holding her hand he knelt down, and in tones of the deepest solemnity exclaimed — " Holy Virgin, who now lookest down upon me and this maiden, linked hand in hand before thee, hear me, as now at the altar-foot I pledge myself never to desert her — hear me, as I solemnly vow, ere 'another moon has waned, to make her my wedded wife; and may God smite me with all human afflictions if the vow be not fulfilled !" He rose, and turning towards Catalina, said, " Such as I am, sweet one, I am yours. If you can value a heart like mine, whose freshness is lost for ever, take it. I have hesitated, for sorry is the return you must take for the gift of your virgin affections; but it is far better, Catalina, that there should be no deceit; that were a sorry stoc'. indeed to begin house-keeping upon."

The vow was kept. Within the promised time Catalina Xuarez became the wife of Hernando Cortés; and

M

Governor Velasquez honoured the bridal with his courtly presence.

* * * The last rays of the setting sun streamed through the windows of that long arched chamber, and, for a little while, the massive shadows which had covered that stirring scene, were broken by broad patches of light, falling upon the stone floor, and the solid walls, and revealing more than one strange group of revellers, who, seated at rude oaken tables, were making the vaulted roof echo with their uproarious mirth. It was a scene not of easy interpretation. The roysterers were men of all ages; judging by their countenances, of all characters; by their attire, of all classes. Some seemed to be mariners; others, the casque and the cuirass bespoke of the military profession. A few bore no exclusive stamp upon them, but in the faces of each, however varied, there was a look of eager determination, which seemed to denote a common object, a common bond of unalterable purpose.

At one end of the long vaulted gallery there was a flight of steps, leading to a narrow entrance-door, and near to this, on a raised platform, beneath an arched window, a party of men, chiefly of the military order, were gathered together, with pikes and spears in their hands, whilst a cavalier, standing upon one of the lower steps, was mustering them severally by name, and taking note of their equipments. Nor were these the only occupants of the chamber. With the rugged figures and stern features of these adventurers, were mingled the graceful forms and the sweet faces of women. . . . . On a carpet of many colours, spread out on the cold floor, near an old cabinet of carved wood, which now seemed to be used as an armoury, sat a comely dame, nursing a young infant,

and near her two ladies—the one sitting, the other standing by a window—looked forth into the outer world,
apparently intent upon some distant object. Not far from
these, in deep shadow, stood a youth, who might have
numbered some nineteen summers, of handsome countenance, and strong active figure, dressed, though with something less than the wonted ostentation, in a style becoming
a cavalier of good descent, and beside him, in eager converse, was a lady, perhaps some ten years older, whose
lineaments were like the youth's, as sister's to brother's,
but whose meek eyes, and pale sad face, told a tale of
patient sorrow, crowned with calmest resignation. At
some distance from these, near the head of a long table,
stood another cavalier, the most remarkable figure in all
the many groups, conversing with a lady of exceeding
beauty, whose sweet eyes were full of tears, whilst the
revellers beside them filled their glasses, shouted and filled
again, in all the ecstasy of half-drunken merriment. From
these turn we awhile towards the youth and his meek-eyed
sister, who stood in the shadow of the wall.

"Hear me, Gonzalo," said the latter; "and let my
words be treasured up in thy heart. Never reproach him,
my brother—never. *I* have not upbraided him ; neither
then, nor since, nor now. I come not here to blame, but
to bless. He is your friend, brother,—he is mine."

"Yours, Marina! he your friend! Hernando Cortés
your friend?"

"Yes; out of all my sufferings, the pitying Virgin,
not unmindful of my tears, not regardless of my prayers,
has helped me to derive peace undying. He is not in
effect our best friend, my brother, who makes us most
happy upon earth. 1 am contented ; be thou the same.
Cortés is thy friend. He has promised to advance thee

upon earth. Be honourable, and he will honour thee.
Thou wilt be great and glorious, for Hernando Cortés is
thy friend."

"He has promised!" returned the youth. "Alas!
Marina, what did he promise thee?"

"He was young then—rash, idle, impetuous, and
sorely tempted. He is now a man, in the lusty summer
of life, with great ends to accomplish, with a great soul
wherewith to accomplish them. What can he do without
truth? If not true to others, if not true to himself, what
but failure can crown all his efforts? Cortés is a great
man. Confide in him, and you also will be great. Your
eager longings will be satisfied, Gonzalo."

"I fear, sweet sister, that the nobility of thy nature
makes thee too hopeful of the truth and nobility of others.
But I will believe him. Yes; I will believe him, though
another now bows herself over the hand of her lord—that
hand which should have been thine, Marina."

As he spoke, the figure of Hernando Cortés was radiant with the red sun-light, which fell upon his face,
blazed upon his polished breastplate, and made a very
"flaming sword" of the bright blade, which, with point
upon the ground, he held in his left hand, whilst the lovely
woman—Catalina, his wife—bowed herself over his right,
and pressed it fondly to her lips. The face of Cortés was
that of a man who struggles against strong emotion. His
heart was touched; but he was a leader, in the presence of
his followers, on the eve of a great enterprise . . . . . .
Before them, compelled to dissemble, he retained an outward composure which had no counterpart within; and
when the last farewell was uttered, the face of Cortés was
rigid and pale as marble. . . . . He saw her depart, through
a door which opened into a small inner apartment, and as

the noisy party at the drinking-table toasted the lady of their chief, filled a beaker to the brim, and hastily swallowed its contents.

The departure of Catalina was the signal for the departure of the other women—the wives and sisters of some of the principal officers of the expedition. . . . . As one after another departed, Cortés looked anxiously around, as though eager to find himself alone with his comrades. Soon it was even as he wished—nay, not wholly—there was one woman's dress, which, in a mass of shadow, for a little time escaped his observation. When he saw that one still loitered, he turned towards a soldier beside him, put a brief question, and received an answer. He then cried aloud, " Gonzalo de Sandoval !"

The youth stepped forward and stood before Cortés. " Gonzalo," said the leader, in tones of the utmost suavity, " it grieves me to sever loving hearts, and, most of all, very young hearts; but the hour has come at which it behoves us all to think of sterner things, and I must bid you part from your beloved. Tell her that you will soon return, with hoards of gold and jewels from the New World, to claim her as your bride—bid her take one last look at the setting sun, and then, evening after evening, at this hour, to look towards the new home of her betrothed——"

" General, she is my sister !"

Cortés started; " Your sister—*Marina ?*"

" The same—she is here—she would speak with Hernando Cortés."

" Bid her come to me—nay, that were rude, indeed—I am playing the Governor somewhat early—lead me to her." The deep emotion of his heart betrayed itself beneath this assumed levity.

They had not met for years, and now that once again
they stood face to face, how changed they were! It
were hard to say which felt the most; but over his feelings the strong man had less mastery than the gentle
woman, and she was the first to speak out, in clear, un-
faltering accents.   There was something of solemnity in
the tones of her voice, as she said—"Cortés, I have come
hither not to speak of the past—the future lies before
thee, a broad and shining tract, over which I would not
cast a shadow.   Upon this great adventure thou goest
forth, with my blessing on thy head.   It is of little worth,
Hernando, but there may, in that far country, come an
hour—haply long after the moss has grown over the cross
which marks my grave—when it will be a solace to thee
to know that I have blessed thee with my whole heart,
and prayed the Virgin to smile upon thee ever.   My
brother goes with thee, Cortés—I ask thee not to befriend
him, for thou *hast* already promised to be a father to the
boy, and thou wilt find him worthy of thy tutelage; but
if I might ask a boon of thee——"

"Ask something—anything," interrupted Cortés, his
voice betraying deepest emotion—"the greater it be, the
more ready I to grant it.   Heaven knows I would do much
for thee, Marina."

"It is but a little thing," she said.   "Among strange
people—among men of different colour and different faith
—speaking another tongue, and bowing down to gods—
oh! *how* different from ours—lies thy shining career.   In
our dealings with such men, it is too common to forget
that they are fashioned of kindred clay—that they are
men and our brethren still.   I speak not, Cortés, of such
natures as thine, but there are among the adventurers,
who form thy little band of conquerors, some rude and

stormy spirits—slow to reflect, quick to act—to whom cruelty is a pastime. Men return blow for blow—cruelty will be met with cruelty—but there are those who cannot retaliate—the innocent and the helpless, who can only suffer—the women, Cortés, however little they resemble the daughters of Old Spain, remember that they are my sisters, the sisters of all the happy dames and merry maidens, who hear with pride, in thy native Medellin, of the exploits of her noblest son; and when it is in thy power, Cortés, to stretch forth the sheltering arm, and to employ the healing hand, when suffering woman looks up for aid to the leader of the white man, as to a God, remember then the last words of Marina de Sandoval, and know that she smiles upon thee, in the flesh or in the spirit, and that the mild eyes of the benignant Virgin look down upon thee in sweetest approval. Wilt thou promise?"

" As I hope for mercy ! God smite me, if I fail !"

" Enough. And now God take thee, Cortés, into his safe keeping. Farewell ! Gonzalo, I am ready."

" Yet, stay ; Marina, one word more. Have you quite forgiven. . . . ." It was too late ; she had drawn her mantle around her, let down her long black veil, and, attended by her brother, passed down the gallery without once looking back.

" Alone !" muttered Cortés; "quite—quite alone ! Now, then, for graver matters." And Cortés stood among his men—once more the great leader, inspiring, animating all. The sun had set; the revel was at an end. Even the most noisy of the roysterers now stood before their commander, cool and collected. The oath and the jest were silenced ; all remembered the great work that

they were about to do—all remembered that, ere to-morrow's sun had risen, the little fleet, which might now be
seen from the windows of that old edifice at anchor in the
bay, would be steering, with its rich freight of gallant
spirits, away from St. Jago, on its voyage to the New
World. And as Cortés now addressed his followers, now
conversed with his officers, now consulted his charts, which
had taken the place of the bowl and the flask on the old
oaken tables, a smile of triumph lit up his face ; and ever
and anon he muttered, with compressed teeth, " Not this
time under the heel of Velasquez—not this time in the
dust."

On a wretched pallet, in a small, comfortless apartment,
wanting light, wanting cleanliness, wanting every cheerful
accessory, a man lay dying, at an inn in the little sea-port
town of Palos. The ravages of sickness had not paled
his sun-burnt cheek, nor thinned his clustering chestnut
hair ; but death was written on his face most legibly—
the face of one in the full summer of life, smitten with
hopeless disease—struck down in the very flush of
triumph, the joyous pride of a great object achieved, the
heart-stirring anticipations of one who, after years of toil
and much peril in a far-off land, has returned, laden with
honour and wealth, to enjoy, in his old home, among his
own people, the harvest he has reaped so painfully abroad.
Alas ! and is this the end of Gonzalo de Sandoval ?

To die thus ; and yet not ignobly, not alone — nor
unwept, nor unhonoured. Many a group of brave soldiers,
clustered around the door-way of that little inn, or sat
in the common drinking-room, with blank faces, uttering
but few words, and those in lowest whispers ; or, haply,

after awhile, moving from their places with silent tiptoe
tread, and ever checking, with raised hand and expressive
face, the song or the shout of the careless stranger.

But twofold the honour done to the death-bed of Gonzalo de Sandoval. It is a great thing to be loved by one's
followers. It is a great thing, too, to be loved by one's
leader. And thus was he doubly honoured; for Hernando
Cortés sat by his bed-side.

From the convent of La Rabida, whither he had betaken himself on touching once again the shores of the
Old World, to rest his weary body and to refresh his o'er-
tasked mind, roused by the sad tidings of the fate of his
much-loved captain, Cortés had hurried to the inn at Palos;
and there, almost with a woman's tenderness, a woman's
zeal, he had watched and served in that dreary chamber.
. . . A great thing, indeed, to have one's pillow smoothed
by such a man ; a great thing, indeed, to have the conqueror of a world acting the nurse by one's bed-side.
Great the consolation; but the slayer of thousands could
not save one life. " Man sends forth the arrow of death :
God alone can arrest its flight. How impotent we are !"
. . . And Cortés, beside the couch of his dying friend,
bowed himself in deep humility of soul. . . .

The sick man had slept, or it was like to sleeping, for
his eyes were closed, and save ever and anon a slight movement of the one thin hand which Cortés held gently in his
own, and a sweet smile which played about his mouth, he
lay there in marble repose. His dreams, his thoughts, if
haply he were not sleeping, were very pleasant, very peaceful. The wild war-cry rang not in the ears, a sea of blood
swam not before the eyes, of the dying captain. All of
this was passed over, and other scenes floated tranquilly
before him. " Happy, happy," muttered Cortés; " the

spirit of that sweet saint, his sister, is whispering glad tidings in his ears."

It might have been so; but now the angel visitant was gone. Gonzalo opened his dim eyes, turned them upon his friend, and said, in accents low but very clear—"Waking or sleeping, I have had sweet thoughts, blessed remembrances, my general. I have been again in that old chapel, again among the tall flowers, o'er-topping me, in my father's garden—The good old man! . . . And my best of mothers! . . . My sweet sister. . . . All gone—all gone before! . . . I have been once again among them. And you, too, I have seen—the old Hernando Cortés, the gay youth, who climbed that tottering garden wall, and fell on the other side." . . .

"Gonzalo! that fall was the fall of Mexico. Then, on the sick bed, my mind shadowed forth the stirring scenes of my manhood. Then I conceived the great things which have brought me fame, wealth, everything but happiness."

"You may be happy; you must be happy; at home again; among your own people." . . .

"Oh, Gonzalo, what is Spain to me? Marina among the angels, Catalina buried in the New World, and you, my friend, my faithful companion, my brave captain—you, *thus;* you *thus,* Gonzalo!"

"A mother lives to sit under the shadow of thy great tree of honour, Cortés. The Virgin has not suffered every well-spring to be dried up in the soil of home. Think, General, of the thousands who will go forth to meet you.
. . Your old friends, your fellow-citizens. . . . How proud old Medellin is, with her namesake in the New World. Our birth-place, Medellin our mother—Medellin, your child, Corté.——"

"Say ours—what would Hernando Cortés have been without Gonzalo de Sandoval? My best of friends, bitter at such an hour is the thought that I have never done you full justice. . . . Hasty, impetuous, more ready to strike than to hear, I have wronged—*once* deeply wronged you. . . . Hast quite forgiven that hasty judgment?"

"General, for that I am more your debtor, than for all other bounties. Men err—the great and the small alike —and appearances were strong against me; but only the very great can confess an error to those who lie far below them. How doubly glorious the broad sun-light, bursting from beneath the shadow of the cloud! Never did I love Hernando Cortés, for never did I know him so well, as after that brief season of gloom, when I sat beneath the cloud of his displeasure. . . . Oh! if Marina had but lived to know how nobly you kept your promise . . . aiding, supporting me—making me all that I have been of great and prosperous, my friend."

"And that other promise. . . . I did my best—God knows I did my best," repeated the Conqueror —"At Cholula, at Mexico, Heaven knows I did not forget my promise! . . . I did not forget the sweet saint who implored me ever to be merciful to woman—that last night, how vividly even now the scene stands out before me——"

"And me—ah! yes . . . I well remember; and how, as red morning dawned, the wondering people poured down to the quay, thinking it not less than a miracle that our little fleet was standing out to sea. And Velasquez!—how I laughed to think how we had cozened him! The churl! —how blank he looked, as we communed with him from our little boat! Ah, Cortés! how the hand of God directs us! What now would have been the aspect of the New World, if Velasquez had triumphed over you?"

"What, indeed! . . . But it was not permitted to
him. I had not fulfilled my destiny then. . . . How
vividly do I remember all—how deeply do I ever bear it
stamped upon my heart, Gonzalo. In memory of that
scene, of that promise, I named the first woman over whom
I held the shield of my protection—the first whom I
saved from insult—after her, who appealed to me thus
nobly in favour of her sex—a woman, too, not all unworthy of the name she bore—one, who taught us all
that the beauty and the truth of womanhood will flower
almost as bounteously under the shadow of idols as in
the sunlight of the countenance of the Christian's God.
And Catalina, too, she was there. Poor Catalina! . . .
to think that the true and loving wife should have braved
so much, only to find her own grave; and that out of this
hallowed grave should have sprung the blackest calumny
which ever overshadowed my name! Gonzalo, Gonzalo—
when I think how much you did, at that sad time, to crush
the slander under your indignant heel, I cannot thank you
—I cannot love you too much." . . .

"And yet I did not crush it—the rank weed does
flourish still, in all its gross luxuriance. Curses on them
. . . the curses of a dying man!" And clenching his fist,
with all his remaining vigour, he threw out one of his
emaciated arms and smote the air, as though he beheld
before him one of the black-hearted slanderers of his chief.
The effort was too much for him; the strong feeling did
violence to the weakness of physical nature; and he sank
back, utterly exhausted. His hour was very nigh, ...
but not thus did he perish. Gonzalo de Sandoval died
not with curses on his lips. . . . .

Tranquilly his spirit departed—forgiving all men,
blessing all men, he turned his face towards the wall

and died.   His last words were words of peace ; and Hernando Cortés closed the eyes of his beloved captain. . . .
Honoured in life, in death was he honoured. . . . His
own followers — the best and bravest — carried the bier to
the grave, and as the last rites were performed with all
solemnity by the Friars of La Rabida, the eyes of the
Conqueror were not the only ones which glistened with
unwonted tears.

On the conclusion of the foregoing tale, a young and
enthusiastic poet, who had hitherto taken no part in the
conversation, took up two drawings which lay before him,
and which he seemed to have culled from all those which
remained unillustrated, and holding them up to the Lady
Eva, he said, " If you will let me have my choice of designs, I will, if this good company do not think me pre-
sumptuous, volunteer a share in the Birthday Revels.
These two subjects are at once so charming and yet so
totally dissimilar — the one the ideal of Romance, the other
the perfection of Reality — that their suggestive qualities
will, I feel, make up for any deficiencies in the imagination or fancy of the illustrator.   But if I am permitted to
undertake this pleasant office, you must allow me also,
in virtue of the contrasting qualities of these two lovely
designs, to unite both verse and prose in their illustration."
The offer of the young poet was gladly accepted by all
the company, and he proceeded to relate

THE SECRET OF THE FOUNTAIN.

DELMAR CASTLE was the scene of unwonted festivities.
Banquets, balls, concerts, fêtes, of every kind, followed each
other in uninterrupted succession.   Every chamber in the

spacious old mansion — once a stronghold of knightly power, now a modernized commodious residence — had its occupant. Crowds of visitors from neighbouring seats, and even from the distant metropolis, came and went, flitted to and fro, remained or departed, according to their whims, their engagements, or the proximity of their homes. The tenants on the estate and the dependants of the family were partakers, in their respective spheres, of the general joy. Happiness seemed for the time to reign absolute over this favoured spot of earth. To celebrate the completion of the eighteenth year of his only daughter, these rejoicings were given by Sir Michael Lindsay.

Beatrice was in every sense worthy of the honours paid to her. Exquisitely fair, moulded with faultless symmetry, her features delicately chiselled, and marvellously express-ive of every emotion of the soul, her eyes pure and intel-lectual, her brow ample and serene, her movements full of dignity and grace — imagination could not conceive a love-lier being. But if nature had exhausted her art in per-fecting the outward form of this noble creature, Heaven had exceeded its limit in breathing into it a spirit of unusual fineness. Under a father's tender, judicious care, her intelligence had expanded, her mind had received the highest cultivation ; and every soft and womanly feeling had been preserved untouched by the least affectation, pedantry, or conceit. A son, twelve years of age, was the only other child left to Sir Michael by a wife whom he had adored. In the lively, playful boy were centred his proud hopes of transmitting the ancient baronetcy in a direct line to posterity ; in his accomplished daughter reposed all the love that outlived in his breast his sainted lady, blended with affections of younger growth and of more flattering promise.

More than one heart fluttered during the progress of these natal festivities, at the contemplation of the beauty and gracefulness of her who was at once the divinity to whom homage was offered, and the chief dispenser and promoter of the pleasurable rites. Many anxious mothers built lofty visionary castles of future greatness for their aspiring sons, upon the illimitable expectations of fortune assigned to the young lady by their fond fancies. Meanwhile, she herself knew not of these amorous palpitations, thought not of these maternal aspirations; innocent, art-'ess, happy, she presided over her father's hospitalities with infinite cheerfulness, smiling alike on all. Yet there was one man in that throng whose approach excited in her bosom strange, undefinable sensations, whose presence oppressed her with mingled feelings of admiration, awe, and other less understood emotions. Beauchamp Marmion was one upon whom the fatal gift of genius had been bestowed, and with it all the warmth of temperament, the susceptibility, the fitfulness of exaltation and depression, which are its unfailing concomitants. Being distantly related to Sir Michael, he had spent many joyous days of his boyhood at Delmar, and had conceived a precocious passion for the "rose-bud of beauty," as he then called Miss Lindsay, and had given expression to his admiration in many of those ardent effusions which are the safety-valves through which escape the intense throbbings of the poet's heart. Beatrice had accepted his strains as so many pretty compliments to herself, more fictitious than real, without comprehending the full meaning of the glowing thoughts, and without perceiving the germs of undying love that warmed themselves into life in these inspired lays.

Four years had passed since they had rambled together

over garden and field, since he had addressed to her his
last tuneful sonnet; the sylph-like girl of fourteen had
expanded into a blooming woman—the clever minstrel
had become an illustrious poet.   His name had come to
her borne on the wings of fame; she had read his published works, and thought she could discover in them the
traces of his early feelings; she cherished the memory of
their former friendship; she dreaded the renewal of their
second intimacy.

The meeting of Beauchamp Marmion and Beatrice presented nothing to a casual observer to distinguish it from
that of any two persons of different sexes, on a similar
occasion, between whom friendship and relationship existed.   But an eye practised in the study of female diag-
nostics, might have discovered that the lady trembled
almost imperceptibly, that she lost a shade of her habitual
self-possession, that an air of colder courtesy chilled her
salutation, and that she uttered a welcome of more formal
construction than accorded with her usual free and unrestrained nature.   A keen watcher might also have noticed
that, as the greeting passed, a cloud stole over the gentleman's clear brow, that his colour sunk to a paler tone,
that his lip quivered, that his voice lost its manly firmness.

" 'Tis as I feared—she loves me not!" he mentally
exclaimed, when his reception was over—" she who has
been my genius, my inspiration, my soul—she whose face
and form wreathed themselves into every idea of beauty
that I ever expressed—she whose mind has been the heaven whence I drew all that is immortal in my thoughts
and works—she whom I dreamt of, lived for, worshipped
—she loves me not!   The puling, sentimental, frantic
rhymer is contemned, as he should be.   One of a fated
tribe, what else had I to expect, save misery?"

How strange, that that man who could, when calm and uninterested, sound the lowest depths of the human breast, unravel each intricate mystery therein concealed, and accurately translate every language of the eyes, voice, and countenance, should, when his own feelings and passions were enlisted, be more than blind, be worse than dull, be ridiculously erroneous in all his conclusions!

" Ha! 'tis clear as day! Fool that I am not to have guessed it before: she loves another—Lord Brookland. A good match—an excellent match. Rich, unthinking, riotous, the *beau idéal* of a lady's wish. What care could she have for a grub, a book-worm, a sonnet-maker, such as I ?"

Thus, giving wild scope to an imagination fertile in creating unhappiness for its possessor, and, in a fit of complete despondency, delivering himself up to what he poetically called " his destiny," Beauchamp Marmion kept as much aloof as possible from the festivities, avoided encountering Beatrice, and held communion only with his melancholy, bitter thoughts.

Meanwhile, Beatrice, unconscious of having given her former playmate the least cause of offence, and completely ignorant of the real nature of the admiration she felt for him and his writings, simply wondered at his conduct, secretly ascribed his abstracted mood and dejected manners to the influence of genius, and silently wished her birthday festivities at an end, that she might walk and talk with him, as of yore, and, peradventure, receive from him some new and graceful tribute to her charms.

Amongst the visitors at De'r ar Castle was Lord Brookland—a good-humoured, pleasant, fox-hunting, young country gentleman; the owner of no great quantity of brains, though the inheritor of large neighbouring

N

estates; a man who could boast of an excellent heart,
though not of a tender one — of a generous mind, though
not of a refined understanding. Between Sir Michael
Lindsay and the late lord a strong friendship had existed,
and they had often indulged, over their claret, in can-
vassing the probability of a future union between the heir-
apparent of the one and the only daughter of the other.
No pledge had ever been made on the subject, for both
fathers were too wise to think of promoting a marriage
that might be opposed to the wishes of the persons most
concerned; but the advantage of such an alliance for
Beatrice naturally recurred to Sir Michael's mind often
since the death of his old friend. He was resolved never
to constrain his daughter's affections, but he nevertheless
deemed the match, if it could be effected, one most de-
sirable in many respects. Lord Brookland so far acquiesced in the desires of his deceased parent and in the
wishes of Sir Michael, as to regard Miss Lindsay as the
most beautiful of created beings, next after his favourite
hunter. He believed, that being doomed, like his forefathers, to the pains of matrimony, he would not easily
find a wife who could sing a sweeter song, preside with
more affability over his convivial feasts, or attract more
admiration at a country ball, a meet, or a race-course. He
had even gone farther, and had confessed his partiality for
the young lady to Sir Michael, who referred him to her,
declaring that he could not interfere, directly or indi-
rectly, until Beatrice's inclinations were first frankly as-
certained by him who aspired to her hand.

The gaieties at Delmar Castle were drawing to a close:
the ball which was to terminate them was at its height;
the spirits of the company were exuberant. One person
only in that gay throng wore an abstracted brow, seemed

uninspired with the general mirth, glided from place to
place without evincing any emotion of pleasure—scarcely
of life. Like a mummy at an Egyptian feast, Beauchamp
Marmion appeared, regarding the hilarious crowd with
solemn gloom—among them, but not of them; dead to
the present, brooding over the past—a mockery of human
excitements. Wherever Beatrice mingled in the mazy
dance, or reclined for a moment after her fatigue, thither
would his eyes mechanically turn; but they, in truth, saw
not the graceful object which they followed—they were
engaged looking into his own breast, where everything
was dark, despairing, and teeming with dismal shadows.

The attentions paid by Lord Brookland to Beatrice
throughout this evening were remarkable. He had engaged her for almost every dance, and displayed such progress in the art of agreeable courtship as surprised all
who were cognisant of his usually blunt, unceremonious
manners. Indeed, he had convoked all his powers of
pleasing for one grand occasion, on which he had made up
his mind to settle his love affairs for life.

At the conclusion of a mazourka, Lord Brookland led
his partner to a retired seat. Having procured her some
slight refreshment, and finding his courage elevated to the
necessary pitch, he invited her to enter a convenient conservatory, to hear something " very particular" which he
had to communicate. Beatrice, wholly unsuspecting the
motive of his request, and femininely disposed to listen to
anything " very particular" from a friend, assented without an instant's hesitation. They passed into the aromatic retreat.

" Miss Lindsay," began his lordship, as soon as they
were seated—" I have your father's permission to pro-
pose--that is, to offer, I mean—pshaw! In one word,

Miss Lindsay, I think you a beautiful girl—a good girl.
I have a mind to take a wife—will you marry me? There,
now—I have said as much as if I had made a speech of
an hour's length."

While he rapidly uttered these words, he seized the
hand of the astonished Beatrice, and pressed it vehemently
to his lips.

At that moment the figure of Beauchamp Marmion
darkened the entrance of the conservatory. His eyes fell
upon the agitated girl, and lingered a few seconds, with
an expression more of sorrow than of anger. A half-
suppressed sigh escaped his lips: the figure then disappeared, unnoticed by Lord Brookland or Beatrice.

A very short time sufficed Miss Lindsay to collect her
alarmed thoughts. With dignified firmness, prompted by
that modesty and nobility which in her were innate, she
declined the honour proposed to her, and in such terms as
set the question at rest for ever. Lord Brookland and she
left the conservatory as good friends as before, though the
pretensions of the gentleman to her hand were unequivo-
cally withdrawn.

Delmar Castle had returned to its wonted peacefulness;
the bustle attending the arriving and departing of visitors
had subsided; the commotion left by yesterday's past
fête, or originating in to-day's coming festivities, was no
longer discernible. Beauchamp Marmion and a young
lady, a cousin to Beatrice, were the only guests who remained. How doubly delightful does a country seat appear after the departure of a motley crowd! How
enfranchised—how relieved from hostile invasion—how
restored to natural repose! The discordant hum of men
is succeeded by the melodious song of birds; the trampling of feet is exchanged for the sweet murmuring of

trees; the noise and rattle of society, with its conversation, suggestive of no valuable thought, is replaced by charming solitude, which speaks wisdom and true philosophy incessantly to ear and heart; the voices of passion, of envy, of malice, of paltry ambition, are hushed, and in their stead, love—fresh, genial, all-pervading love—breathes from field, and plant, and flower, and bird, and beast.

Beauchamp Marmion had consented, after much persuasion from Sir Michael, to prolong his stay for a little His pride and his reason counselled him to go, but his destiny and his heart urged him to remain. He contemned himself for his weakness, in hovering around the light which had vitally seared him, yet he could not summon resolution enough to plunge from it into unfathomable darkness. Retracing those steps, which in happier days he had taken with her through dell and glade, he fed his melancholy to repletion; and then, in the secrecy of his chamber, relieved his breast by venting his tribulations in wild and agonised verses.

Delmar Castle, like many old seats which have undergone successive modernisations, presented, both in itself and the buildings attached to it, a medley of all the styles of architecture now extant. Egyptian, Greek, Hindoo, Italian, Gothic, Moorish—there were specimens of all— and some so mixed and confounded, that they literally can be described only as the composite.

One of the curiosities of the castle was a reservoir of water, which went by the name of "The Magic Fountain." The copious stream of a rivulet had been conducted with much art and taste under a high and magnificent arch, and thence caused to form a beautiful cascade, by falling into a tank of large dimensions. The mysterious way in which the architect had contrived to let the superfluous waters escape, so that the basin, though ever receiving, never overflowed, gave rise to its name.

The Magic Fountain was a favourite retreat of Beatrice, as well for its cool shade and convenient bowers as for the ideas of romance which somehow were associated with its locality. Thither she and her cousin, Caroline, repaired to sing, and chat, and read away a lovely evening. Seating themselves on a flight of marble steps that led from a terrace down to the aqueduct, they indulged for some time in sweet retrospects and bright anticipations becoming their youth, their beauty, and their innocence. Their confidences were exchanged, charily at first, and afterwards less reservedly. Yet still each had a little secret lurking in a corner not yet unfolded—a secret that she could not unbosom—a secret that perhaps should die with her unrevealed. Fearful lest her tongue might utter that which should be left unsaid, Beatrice seized her mandoline, of which instrument she was a proficient, and ran her taper fingers along the chords. The strains extracted were for awhile fantastical, but soon they settled into a pretty simple melody, to which her voice kept concord. With particular sweetness and expression she sang and played the following

Serenade.

"WAKE, maiden, wake! Rise, beauty's sun,
 And at thy lattice high appear!
The sky a sable pall hath on,
 In mourning for thy absence here.
Arise; and with thy peerless sight,
Dispel the gloom of sorrowing night!

" The winds that but a little past
   Breathed tones of love when thou didst hear,
Now howl in grief—each deep-drawn blast
   Bewailing thy sad absence here.
Up—up, then ! one kind look or tone
Will change to love their savage moan.

" Appear—appear, blest sun ! and light
   All heaven and earth with joy again,
Lest nature, grieved, should turn to blight,
   And chaos recommence again.
Appear, my love—appear ! and fill
With bliss thine ardent minstrel still.

" Arise ! and with thy peerless light
   Dispel the gloom of sorrowing night ! "

Beatrice's cheeks were suffused with blushes, her eyes
sparkled with animation, her whole being glowed with enthusiasm. Caroline, though no alchemist, could not avoid
discovering that there was something in this song more
than the words imported, something that touched the
tenderest chords of her young cousin's heart. With femi-
nine tact, she refrained from noticing Beatrice's emotion,
and merely exclaimed,—

" What a charming air ! I don't think I ever heard it
before."

" I should think not; it is by an unknown composer,"
replied Beatrice, with a faint smile—" that is, the music,
I mean," she added, correcting herself.

" But the words—are they too, by the Unknown ?"
demanded Caroline, curiosity having urged her to put the
question in a direct shape.

" Unknown !—no !" answered Miss Lindsay, kindling
into emphasis. " But come, I have a book of beautiful
poetry with me ; let us sit by the fountain and read."

As she spoke, she laid down her guitar, and leading

Caroline by the hand to the marble bench beside the fountain, the two cousins seated themselves, and began to peruse a dainty volume, which Beatrice took from her reticule. Page after page was recited, the last being ever pronounced yet more exquisite than its predecessors. The poems were short, and written at various times, under divers shades of feeling, and on many different topics. One deep vein, however, ran throughout them—the vein of early, pure, requited love.

Beatrice was the reader. She had evidently learnt the pieces by heart ; and she threw so much natural eloquence and passion into them, that they came to the ear of Caroline like strains of inspiration—like music really divine.

" Ah ! you have not heard my favourite yet," broke in Beatrice, exultingly, as she interrupted her cousin's exclamations of delight. " Listen to this !" she cried, springing to her feet, and preparing to give the verse the benefit of her impassioned elocution. Then, standing before her entranced cousin, she read, or rather recited,

The Poet's Bride.

" THE Poet's Bride—oh, happy girl ! well mayest thou look so proud,
And walk with such majestic step among the envying crowd ;
The empress seated on her throne—the goddess in her shrine —
Commands not half the worship and the glory that is thine.

What kingly bridegroom ever clothed his regal one in rare
And gorgeous robes of beauty, such as those which thou dost wear ?
What amorous god did e'er bedeck his heavenly queen above
With gems immortal such as those the Poet gives his love ?

Oh no ! the robes the Poet weaves are wrought of threads of light,
Are dyed in fancy's rosiest shade of colour — soft and bright ;
The gems he gives are brilliant stars, whose lustre ne'er will dim—
Alike beyond the hand of theft, or fashion's varying whim.

1 he flowers he weaves around thy brow are of unfading bloom ,
From time they gain a lovelier blush, a costliei perfume.
The golden braid and silk he gives, to mingle with thy hair,
Are bright beams conquer'd from the sun, and chain'd for ever there.

From heaven he wins its softest, purest, and brightest blue ;
To give it to thy witching eyes, to tinge their modest hue ;
The quickest lightnings are impress'd, in fiercest hour and wild,
Are tamed, and gently taught to play among thy glances mild.

At morn the virgin snow he takes from mounts of fearful height,
To give unto thy neck and breast an all-surpassing white ;
While sweet Aurora of her blush is half despoil'd, thy brow
And cheek of beauty to enrich with ever-chast'ning glow.

The voice of rills, the bee's sweet hum, the music of the spheres,
Are brought to murmur on thy tongue, which ravisheth all ears ;
And gentlest zephyrs, as they play th' Æolian harp along,
Are ta'en, and hush'd to sleep, to wake in thy harmonious song.

Then walk in conscious dignity — oh happy, happy Bride !
Thou art the Poet's only love, his glory and his pride !
Nor empress on her purple throne, nor goddess in her shrine,
Can boast one half the dazzling fame and glory that is thine."

By the time Beatrice had concluded the poem, she was
nearly overcome by her emotions. Caroline likewise was
much moved. The moment for entire and perfect confidence between the two girls had arrived.

" Oh, Beatrice ! you love this poet ?" was the first
startling question that rose to Caroline's lips.

" I do," was the simple reply.

" And he is——"

" Beauchamp Marmion."

" He ?—and the writer of the Serenade ?"

" The same. He wrote it for me, four years ago this
very night. I have set it to a little tune of my own composition."

" And you would be a poet's bride ?"

" Rather that than queen of the universe."

A loud merry laugh pealed in the ears of the affrighted ladies, and brought the interesting conversation to an abrupt termination. Appalled, they turned, and perceived the delighted face of the young heir of Delmar, who had approached them unnoticed, and who, from behind an adjacent tree, had distinctly heard the whole secret of his sister's heart.

Ere they could devise any expedient to stop his tongue, the boy had scampered off, shouting and dancing at the trick he had played, and determined to let all the world know that Sister Beatrice was to be a poet's bride.

Marston Lindsay was an intelligent, high-spirited boy, a favourite with every one, somewhat of a pet, and excessively fond of " harmless mischief." He loved his sister better than all the world beside, and would have suffered martyrdom rather than seriously injure her by word or deed. But to banter her, or make her blush, was his greatest pleasure. Now, he believed himself richer than Crœsus, for he was in possession of a treasure : how to get rid of it, was what puzzled him ; how to exchange it for the greatest quantity of fun, engrossed his imagination. Poor child ! he little knew what it is to sport with a young maiden's first declaration of love ; he little understood the meaning of the confession he had overheard ; his was the gamesomeness and innocence of twelve years.

With perversity of judgment, to which ardent, proud, over-susceptible minds are unfortunately prone on matters touching their own affections, Beauchamp Marmion had, during his visit to Delmar Castle, misconstrued every word, look, and tone of Beatrice. He had worked himself into the conviction that she had forgotten their early loves, and cared not for him beyond a mere acquaintance; he believed that he had irrefragable proof of her engagement to another; he regarded their eternal separation as sealed; he vowed that, though his heart should break, he would never let her hear a sentence of reproach from his lips. But the torture of daily beholding the idol he worshipped, and yet of maintaining a rigid silence in his adoration, was beyond his strength; the task became insupportable; he resolved to leave Delmar without delay. Returning from a long sombre walk, and deep in meditation on his blighted hopes and miserable fate, he was suddenly arrested by Marston, who, glowing with excitement, and almost out of breath with running, whispered joyously in his ear, —

" Oh, I have such a secret to tell you about Beatrice ! We will have such quizzing of her !"

Beauchamp trembled violently, and grew ghastly pale; he attempted, but could not utter a syllable. The boy continued—

" She's going to be a bride—a poet's bride—ha, ha, ha ! I heard her say it myself, just now, to Cousin Caroline. Do come and let us tease her about it !"

Beauchamp leant against a tree for support. He felt stupified, under the influence of a dream. He was recalled to his senses by the boy, who said—

" Are *you* a poet ?"

The question passed through every fibre of Beauchamp's frame like an electric shock. His suspicions and his despair yielded to the potency of that simple question.

" Why do you ask, Marston ?" he, after a pause, articulated.

" Why, because, if you are, and that you have written the book of poetry, you are the very person I heard her

say she loved. Now I think of it, your name was mentioned. But, come — do let us go back to the Magic
Fountain, and torment Beatrice! She will blush so! We
will have rare sport!"

The boy rattled on. Beauchamp learnt what gratified
his wildest wish, what almost surpassed his credence.
Having enjoined the most inviolable secrecy to Marston,
they returned towards the Castle. The dark cloud had
entirely cleared away from the brow of the poet. That
night the courteous moon and accommodating stars were
witnesses to lengthy explanations, to repeated vows of
mutual passion, to eloquent protestations of eternal love,
and to the formal registration in Hymen's book of two
beings who were resolved to be made one with the
shortest possible delay consistent with duty and propriety.

Beauchamp Marmion prolonged his visit at Delmar for
several weeks; the reserved misanthrope became the soul
of domestic joyousness; the sarcastic railer at all woman-
kind was changed into the devout believer in the perfecti-
bility of one; the desponding lover was turned into a
thrice happy betrothed.   A poem which he had written
under the paroxysms of his late insanity, and into which
he had thrown the concentrated gall of his diseased mind
— painting woman as a fiend, and representing himself as
the lacerated victim of her black arts — caused him to
laugh immoderately when he thought of it.   The irony,
the reproach, the invective, the denunciations, launched by
him upon the whole sex, now appeared so exaggerated, so
grossly unmeasured, that he resolved to commit the mad
effusion to the flames.   Before doing so, however, he be-
thought him of showing the manuscript to Beatrice, to
prove to her from what a state of frenzy she had rescued
him.

Beatrice read the composition, shuddered, wept, thrilled
with admiration —
" Burn that !" she exclaimed —"that!   Why it's a
master-piece—there 's genius in every line—lightning in
every thought; there never was —there never will be—so
intense, so magnificent a poem!   If you love me, you
must publish it, without a word of alteration."
     With the unhesitating compliance of an affianced one,
Beauchamp packed off the poem to his publisher.   The
critics ratified the opinion given by Beatrice: the author
was pronounced to be the greatest of living geniuses, and
the most injured of men; and while the world was bewailing him as one reduced to a shattered wreck by a heartless
female fiend, he was enjoying the best of good cheer, and
anticipating the delights of paradise with her who was the
faithful angel of his love and life.
     Twelve months rolled on from the day when Marston
overheard the confession at the Magic Fountain.
     Within a tastefully appointed dressing-room a lady sat,
motionless, entranced, rapt in beatific visions.   She was ap-
parelled in rich but simple robes, and her unadorned beauty
shone resplendent in its own lustre.   Her eyes were kindled
with happiness, her cheek was glowing with content, her
form was dilated with pride.
     Her tiny feet resting on an embroidered cushion, and
her marvellously small hands reposing in her lap, she appeared an exquisite model for a sculptor.   But on what
were her eyes fixed? where was her wandering mind?
They were gazing into the profundity of the future.   They
were contemplating splendid triumphs, unheard-of glories,
crowns of immortal laurels, pageants, trophies, honours
greater than ever before were dreamt of — brighter than
ever could be realized.   Let us not interrupt her delicious

trance—let us not break the spell of enchantment which
envelopes her—let us not dissipate the illusion in which
she revels: the realms of imagination are her own, for she
is young, lovely, enthusiastic ; she has reached the pinnacle
of her ambition—she is the wife of Beauchamp Marmion
—she is the Poet's Bride !

The best of all good things is a good example, for it is
the maker and multiplier of good.   That which was set by
the volunteer relater of the foregoing tale was followed, on
its conclusion, by a lady whose distinguished literary position, as *the* Royal Historian *par excellence*, might well
have entitled her to set an example on the present occasion,
rather than to follow one.   "I am not an adept at impro-
visation," said she, "but there is a subject, of which this
beautiful drawing reminds me, that might inspire the
darkest imagination, and awaken the drowsiest fancy.
But you must allow me to treat of it in 'numerous verse,'
for plain prose cannot reach 'the height of my great
argument.' "

So saying, the accomplished Historian of the Queens
of England proceeded to sing—

QUEEN MARY'S WELCOME.

O'ER Leven's dark tow'r the young May moon has risen,
And our Queen, our bright MARY, has 'scaped from her prison.
Good speed to the shallop, that bears o'er the wave
The fortunes of Scotland, the fair and the brave.
She raises the signal — her gold-broider'd veil,
With its border of crimson, it floats to the gale,
And gleams in the moonbeam, all glorious to see
Our Queen, our own MARY !   Once more she is **free** !
We see her, we know her ; and there, by her side,
Stands the gallant young stripling, her champion and **guide** :

Oh! Willie the landless, the orphan,* shall win
Prouder name by this deed, than the lords of his kin.

" Though traitors have broken their faith and her laws,
Our Queen hath good friends still to fight in her cause ;
Ay, men pure and stainless, who never have sold
The honour of Scotland for England's base gold.
Oh, many 's the vigil we've kept for her sake
On this storm-beaten rock, that o'erlooks the broad lake,
Till practised through darkness and mist to descry
Every object, that varied its surface, flit by.
Long months we have watched for this moment in vain,
And each night found us still at our eyrie again.
How our hearts throbbed and fluttered with eager delight,
When we first marked the shallop unmoored for her flight.
As it glided the castle's dark shadow beneath,
Every pulse was suspended—we scarce drew a breath
Till we saw it, still trembling 'twixt hope, fear, and doubt,
O'er the moonlighted waters shoot vent'rously out.
But the peril is over ! she springs to the shore—
She is Queen of the true men of Scotland once more!"

They gather around her, that stout-hearted band,
They kneel at her feet, and they kiss her fair hand ;
But brief are their greetings ; 'tis death to delay ;
The fleet steeds stand ready : the word is—" Away !"

Queen MARY has mounted ; a blush on her face,
As they murmur of " beauty and womanly grace ;"

---

* Willie Douglas, commonly called Willie the Orphan, or Little
Douglas, was a young cadet of the noble house of Lochleven, brought
up as a page in the castle. When his cousin, the gallant George
Douglas, was banished from Lochleven by his mother, for contriving
the former ineffectual escape of Queen Mary, with whom he was passionately in love, Little Willie succeeded to his trust, and, although
only sixteen, successfully completed the undertaking. Many interesting
particulars of this brave boy are to be found throughout the Letters of
Mary Queen of Scots. (See second edition, lately published by Colburn.)
Queen Mary did not forget her obligations to Willie at the hour of her
death ; his name)ccurs in the will she wrote on the night before her
execution.

For soft as the moonlight that kisses her brow,
Or the plume that waves o'er it, her bearing is now;
Yet no daring moss-trooper that scours Ettrick side,
More firmly can sit, or more fearlessly ride.
Like a bird just escaped from its cage, in her glee,
She feels the bold spirit that gladdens the free;
One touch to her courser, and off like the wind,
She leaves mountains and woodlands and waters behind;
And she proudly looks back to her friends with a smile,
As she dashes the first through the rocky defile.

" Nay, forward, dear Lady, the race is for life;
Push onward amain, through the fair plains of Fife;
We must pause not for breath, nor to tighten a girth,
Till we've won the steep bank of the wide-rolling Firth.
Then hey for the ferry—St. Margaret to speed!
May the boatmen be ready and true at our need."
They have crossed the wild waters, and there, on the strand,
Fair escort and tried, the brave Livingstones stand;
And the Hamiltons, foremost in courage and zeal,
Pour down to the muster from bonny Kinneil.
Already an army sweet MARY commands,
Who'll avenge her, or die with the arms in their hands;
And brightly the Monarch has smiled through her tears,
As she bows to her yeomen, and welcomes her peers,
While they gaze on her beauty; and vow " 'tis a cause
To win cowards to fight for true glory's applause."
Now, gallant Lord Seaton, lead on to the west,
For the Queen comes to Niddry this day as thy guest;
Brief warning hast thou to prepare royal cheer,
To shoot the wild moor-fowl, or slay the red deer;
Yet fling wide thy portals, and blithe will she be,
Though rude be the fare, to take breakfast with thee.

Ah, grey roofless castle, how changed is the scene
In thy desolate halls, and thy courts lone and green,
Since thy lord knelt in homage to welcome his Queen,
And they rang with the shouts of the loyal array
Who feasted with Seaton and MARY that day,
While gaily the strains of the minstrels arose—
" Here's a health to Queen MARY! and death to her foes!"

At the conclusion of the foregoing poem, a young writer, whose *forte* is the reflective and meditative rather than the stirring and imaginative, signified his willingness to contribute his share towards the Revels of the evening, provided the company would accept, in place of an illustrative tale, the result of those reflections and associations which had been called forth in his mind and memory by the contemplation of a design, the profound *repose* of which seemed, he said, to put to flight all thought of movement and action, and leave no room for anything but the brooding image

" Of those lone walls and solitary cells
Where heavenly pensive Contemplation dwells,
And ever-musing Melancholy reigns."

The offer was gladly hailed by the Lady Eva, if only for the variety it would give to the proceedings of that evening, which it was determined should close with the following Reflections on

THE ABBEY IN RUINS.

" There is a temple in ruin stands,
Fashioned by long-forgotten hands.
*   *   *   *   *   *
*   *   *   *   *   *
Out upon time ! it will leave no more
Of the things to come than the things before !
Out upon time! who for ever will leave
But enough of the past for the future to grieve
O'er that which hath been, and o'er that which must be.
What we have seen, our sons shall see ;
Remnants of things that have passed away,
Fragments of stone rear'd by creatures of clay."

BYRON.

O

POETRY accommodates the shows of things to the desires of the mind, and as these desires are infinitely various, so are the forms of beauty into which the genius of poetry moulds the thoughts of the heart. Where is the feeling heart of man or woman that will not, in certain moods, acknowledge the romantic, melancholy beauty of Byron's complaint of Time? Who does not yearn over departed memories, when he looks upon a magnificent ruin, nor wish he could unlock the heart of its mystery, and live in the spirit of the time when as yet it was no ruin, but the scene of life and emotion—of battle—strife, perhaps, or of love's soft persuadings, or deepest policy, or high resolves, or (highest, holiest of all!) of religious strivings—meek aspiration, lone endeavour, looking through the gloomy gates of death to the joys of heaven and the ever-lasting song of angels?

Yes, such are often the speculations of an ardent, contemplative curiosity, plunging into the far and shadowy depths of time, and reproaching the destroyer that he has left so little.

But, again, the mind sets out upon a different flight; and at first hovering o'er the crumbling remains of departed strength and magnificence, subsides at length into calm and not unpleasing contemplation of the work which time has done, and gradually arrives at a kind of worship of the dim magnificence of ruin, acknowledging that there is a Providence even in decay; which, while it sweeps away much that is too hateful for prolonged existence, bequeaths to us bright dreams of the past, and makes room for the healthful exercise of head and hand in every successive generation of men.

Hail! thou superb relique of the middle ages—the abbey of the olden times, the castle and the church in one; the

abode of the learning and policy of the period, and not unfrequently of the stoutest hearts that rushed to battle as to
a banquet—of the strongest hands that wielded the ponderous lance as it were but a riding-wand, or the huge
sword that cut through plate armour as if it were but a
woollen doublet! Hail, old abbey! magnificent even now,
in thy stern, stony grandeur, an image of enormous power!
Beautiful, too, in the graceful shafts and delicate tracery
of the windows, presenting images of the elevation and
piety which graced the barbarism of the time, and often
checked the ruthless hand of the bold and cruel. See how
the light streams through, like a gleam from heaven, upon
the stern monument of human strength, and of the short-
lived existence of it.

" Fragments of stone rear'd by creatures of clay."

Yes, " clay "—as to their mortal bodies, which have
long ago crumbled into dust and ashes! But the spirit
which was in them, wherever be now its abode, or what-
soever its mode of existence, did its work in its time, and
has not perished; but survives, not only in history and in
tradition, but in its effects. We are inheritors, not' only
of the names and the possessions, but of the spirit of our
fathers; and though they have all undergone changes, yet
survives it in pure prosaic matters of fact as much as the
antique works of men's hands, and more than they. Time
rolls his ceaseless course, and decay and reproduction proceed in their everlasting round; but as the leaves of this
year are the nourishment of the trees of future years,
which in their turn produce more leaves, so do the thoughts
and deeds of men, which lie still perhaps for ages, yet serve
their office as the material out of which future thoughts
and deeds are matured.

" Time rolls his ceaseless course.   The race of yore,
    Who danced our infancy upon their knee,
  And told our marvelling boyhood legends store,
      Of their strange ventures happ'd by land or sea.
  How are they blotted from the things that be !
  How few, all weak and withered, of their force,
    Wait on the verge of dark eternity ;
  Like stranded wrecks, the tide returning hoarse,
To sweep them from our sight ! Time rolls his ceaseless course."

But the legends do not altogether die, which have been
poured into the ears of our marvelling boyhood.   True,
they do not survive, as in the mind of the wondrous Wizard
of the North, who wrote those noble lines; but in other
forms they still live, and move, and have their being, and
will some day leap up into obvious life, after the sordid
bustle and mechanical clamour of this present time shall
have passed away.

The half-ecclesiastical, half-military strongholds of the
middle ages, were frequently built by the side of deep
waters which laved their walls.   Some say this was for the
convenience of fish, which has been, time out of mind, a
more religious kind of eating than flesh, and therefore a
special convenience to monks.   Whether fish generally
appeared upon the tables of lordly abbots for the special
uses of fasting, must be left to the decision of antiquaries.
Even tradition is prone to scandal, and therefore we must
not too readily yield to irreverent suspicions, which are
sometimes indulged in concerning the social habits of religious orders in the olden time.   Monks were fat in those
days, and some of them were certainly the best judges then
extant of a good dinner, and the way to cook it.   But
it is to be remembered, that a life of peace and content-
ment, for which religious retirement is the best security,
will cause the frame of a man to swell into obesity, inde-

pendently of good living; and if the monks were the most
learned men of their day in culinary science, the same
thing was to be said in respect to all other branches of
recondite knowledge. What would have become of the
classics or the sciences, of Greek or of gastronomy, without
the help of the monks, during the ages of feudalism and
chivalry, it were hard to conjecture. If the spread of
knowledge have overthrown the monasteries, it is but
another instance to which we may apply the illustration of
the bird that died by a shaft feathered from its own wing.
Perhaps it may be contended, that in the case before us
the owl should be taken for the illustration rather than
the eagle. It may be so; yet, with all their vices, it is
true that the monasteries preserved and kept alive, after
their own peculiar fashion, the learning and the arts,
which otherwise (so far as appears on the face of human
affairs) might have perished for ever.

However, there is but too much reason to believe, that
not alone for the convenience of replenishing their larders
with piscine food, were these edifices constructed by the
margin of deep waters. The military advantage was manifest. It was almost a security from attack on tne sides of
the building which could only be approached by boats,
and was often a means of escape under cover of darkness,
and with muffled oars. No sentinel could challenge upon
the watery path, and the opposite shore might be one of
safety. Happy, however, it had been if this were all; but,
alas! there were darker and more terrible uses of the con-
tiguous lake, than those which belong to the exigencies of
war and siege. The dark waters formed a capacious and
an ever-ready grave, to which many a wretch was hurried,
of whose departure to the shadowy shore of another world,
the existing world, beyond the stern abbey walls, know

nothing. The convent bell noted not their fate to the passing wind. The judicial sentence was passed in the secret council chamber, and then came the fatal *oubliette*, and the dark wave beneath closed upon the victim for ever. Awful are these dread reminiscences of the deep, dark dungeon, the secret way to the chamber of trial, so frequently, also, the chamber of torture; and then the horrid death and unhallowed burial of the *oubliette!* Thank Heaven! such things are now but memories. From *that kind* of cruelty and injustice the condition of civilized mankind is now free.

The stern old walls of the abbey are slowly yielding to the decay of time, while moss and lichen cover the rude traces of ruin with their softness, and wild flowers wave, in short-lived beauty, in the crevices of the mouldering stone. But other traces of the past are there which appal the sight. The lake yields up its dead. The very waters change their place in the long round of revolving years, and the receding tide reveals the story of long-forgotten tyrannies and murders. Where be the hands that did these deeds, or they that grasped, in helpless fury, the sword which the waters have now abandoned? Sad record of a miserable time! The dungeon-stone, with its ponderous key, is there. Where be they whose eyes it shut out from the world's light—whose groans it hid from the world's knowledge? Horrible thought! More terrible than death was that lingering existence in a living grave, tortured with thinking of all that might be without, and finding nothing but despair within. How long it must have seemed to wait for death!

But *that*, at all events, was sure. It might be waited for long, but it would not be waited for in vain. Lo! these are the records of the inevitable fate of man. These

skulls are the most awful of the ruins which we contemplate. What are decaying walls? Such works as man
hath done, man may do again. But here is ruin indeed,
and who shall pretend to rebuild it, or its likeness?

> " Look on its broken arch, its ruined wall,
> Its chambers desolate, and portals foul:
> Yes, this was once Ambition's airy hall,
> The dome of Thought, the palace of the soul:
> Behold, through each lack-lustre, eyeless hole,
> The gay recess of Wisdom and of Wit,
> And Passion's host that never brooked control;
> Can all saint, sage, or sophist ever writ
> People this lonely tower, this tenement refit?"

These, indeed, are sad and solemn relics of the deeds
and of the actors of them, who have long ago been swept
away " adown the gulf of time." Fearful relics! But let
us not, after all, while admitting and detesting the horrors
of feudal tyranny, judge even these times too harshly.
The victims of the tyrannies to which allusion has been
made, were *generally* men of turbulence and ambition,
who would themselves have been playing the part of
tyrants over others, if they had not been the victims of
tyranny themselves. Their lives were an alternation of
conquest or of suffering, and with that they had laid their
account. And though the ecclesiastical strongholds were
often the scenes of cruelty and vengeance of their own,
yet they, too, were the places of refuge, and the only
available places of refuge, from the blind and headlong
rage of infuriate princes and nobles, whose cruelty knew
no limit, and whose power had scarcely any check, save
that which was interposed by ecclesiastical authority and
privilege. The sanguinary lord might pursue his vassal to
the death, or wreak what vengeance his aroused passion

might dictate upon the rival he had overcome, unless the convent opened its gates, beyond which the rude foot of brutal force dared not follow. There was in this way provided, on many occasions, if not always, a home of peace amid the terrors of feudal war and persecution.

Again, we are to remember that, along with these terrors and these tyrannies, there was also a protection for the common people. They belonged to their lord; they fought for him, and were fed by him, so long as the land gave enough of food for all. The tyranny of the feudal lord has been swept away, but another tyranny has succeeded—that of circumstances and of necessity. And the new tyranny spares the ambitious, adventurous, and turbulent few, while it falls with strong and stern hand upon the many. The feudal lord may no longer compel a man to the wars, but neither is the owner of great possessions bound to share them with the people. They have now a lord who is called Necessity; and though they have theoretical and legal freedom, yet Necessity commands them to dig in the deep mine far from the light of day, or to labour at the loom, or to enlist in the factory army, and to submit to the drill and discipline of the spinning-jenny, where the sound of the bell which summons them to work is quite as peremptory as the roll of the drum on military service. True, they may disregard it without fear of the halberts or the lash, but not without fear of "destitution," which is no less sharp a punishment. In short, society, with all the progress it has made from the institutions and habits of the middle ages, has, for so far only, escaped from one kind of evil to another. The achievement of a condition of society in which the multitude shall escape from the tyranny of the more powerful few, and yet have the benefit of protection, and a right to share in whatever the land to which they belong produces, is yet a *desideratum* in the world's history, and perhaps will be till the *millennium*. It is much easier to effect changes than to make sure of improvements. Not that we should therefore be deterred from constantly trying to improve; but if we are wise, we shall neither indulge in indiscriminate scorn of the errors of antiquity, nor in the vanity of complete satisfaction with what we may conceive to be our own vastly improved methods of managing the affairs of mankind.

As for the monks, it were indeed easy enough to repeat the charges which have been justly made against the *abuses* of their establishments; nor is it to be doubted that superstition and laziness were in the monastic ages very common characteristics of the lives of these secluded worthies.

But we should also bear in mind that these establishments did not always and altogether consist of abuses. At all times, but especially in periods when violence and war disturb society, and mar the fair face of earth, it is natural that certain portions of men should associate for the sake of peace and piety. It is natural that they should endeavour to find some kind of refuge, not merely from personal danger, but from "the shock of accident," and the perpetual disturbance of ordinary life.

> " What other yearning was the master tie
> Of the monastic brotherhood, upon rock
> Aërial, or in green, secluded vale,
> One after one, collected from afar—
> An undissolving fellowship ? What but this—
> The universal instinct of repose,
> The longing for confirmed tranquillity,
> Inward and outward ; humble yet sublime ;
> *The life where hope and memory are as one .*

> Earth quiet and unchanged ; the human soul
> Consistent in self-rule ; and heaven reveal'd
> To meditation in that quietness !
> Such was their scheme : thrice happy he who gained
> The end proposed !   And, though the same were missed
> By multitudes, perhaps obtained by none,
> They, *for the attempt*, and for the pains employed,
> Do in my present censure stand redeemed
> From the unqualified disdain that once
> Would have been cast upon them by my voice
> Delivering her decisions from the seat
> Of forward youth, that scruples not to solve
> Doubts, and determine questions, by the rules
> Of inexperienced judgment, ever prone
> To overweening faith ; and is inflamed
> By courage, to demand from real life
> The test of act and suffering, to provoke
> Hostility—how dreadful when it comes,
> Whether affliction be the foe, or guilt."

So sings Wordsworth, the prince of meditative philosophers, though some persons find a difficulty in discovering
liveliness in his poetry.   Yet, speaking (or singing) upon
this very subject—that is, the desire of the human heart
for peace—few will deny the extraordinary energy of his
verse :—

> " ———— Not alone
> Dread of the persecuting sword, remorse,
> Wrongs unredressed, or insults unavenged
> And unavengable, defeated pride,
> Prosperity subverted, maddening want,
> Friendship betrayed, affection unreturned,
> Love with despair, or grief in agony ;—
> Not always from intolerable pangs
> He fled, but compassed round by pleasure, sighed
> For independent happiness, craving PEACE,
> The central feeling of all happiness."

Farewell, then, thou beautiful ruin of the olden time
of religious brotherhood.   Doubtless thou hadst thy scenes

of woe and of terror, the emblems of which lie scattered round. But let us believe that thy main purpose was that of peace, of a shelter from the storms, or from the satiety of the world, and of calm devotedness to the hopes of another and a better.

FOURTH EVENING.

As the company assembled in the library on the fourth evening of the Lady Eva's Birthday Revels, they found her looking, even more anxiously than usual, for the arrival of her guests — for, at these literary meetings, she had now grown to regard the guests as hers, for the time being. On this occasion, however, it seemed that she looked for some one of those guests in particular; and *which* of them it was, became evident on the entrance of a writer of a popular novel, the title of which pointed at one of the most celebrated of those historical localities, our Royal Palaces.

"Ah!" she exclaimed, as the writer in question entered the library, "I thought you would never come! Look at this beautiful picture — an Astrologer among his books. I do not very well know what astrologers are; very learned and very clever people, I have heard; and very wise in foretelling what *will* happen before it *does* happen. Is it not so? Now, then, I will be an astrologer, and will predict the pleasure you will afford to all this good company, and to me in particular, if you will only tell us a story about this picture, as full of pleasant mystery as that 'prophecy fulfilled,' which, I remember, kept me wide awake all night after I read it."

The request of the Lady Eva was complied with as frankly and promptly as it was made, and the company listened with marked attention to

THE ASTROLOGER.

" BEAR me on that blood track !" gasped convulsively Count Christofle, vainly and feebly struggling with his comrades in arms, who were carrying their wounded friend from the field of Roras. "Bear me to her !" he again indistinctly murmured ; " let me but die at her feet — rather, let her trample me to death ; my arm it was that drew her blood !" He fainted, and was being slowly borne to the rear by his officers, when the foe, led on by the father of the wounded lady, roused to fury and exasperation at what the former conceived to be a deliberate act of unmanliness, and only to be atoned for by the heart's blood of her dastardly assailant, pressed forward with resistless force, and broke the devoted band of the Albigenses. Dispirited by the fall of their leader, they gave way.

The extraordinary appearance of the Lady Ludovica on the field of slaughter had taken the party of her father by surprise, and none more so than himself. At that moment the combat between the troops of the Duke of Savoy and those of the Protestants was at its hottest. The battleground was now, owing to the giving way of the Duke's army, a meadow, at the foot of a fort in which the lady had, unknown to her father, secreted herself with one of her maids, to behold the varying fortunes of the fight, and

from its embattled height pour out fervent prayers to
Heaven for success to the avengers of the holy Romar.
apostolic church. The fortunes of the day had varied ; at
last the forces of heresy, which, though inferior to their
adversaries in number, seemed united, and, led on by a
youth, absolutely drove in those of the champions of the
church. The quick eye of filial instinct perceived that her
father was wounded; his head bent over his horse's neck
in an unequal conflict with his younger opponent; and,
unable to restrain herself, she rushed from the tower down
the steep ravine, the brink of which, when calm, she had
trembled to approach. Pushing her way amid pikemen
and archers, she threw herself before her father, and the
next moment received a sword-cut on her ivory shoulder,
from the falchion of the leader of the adverse army, at that
time in personal encounter with her parent.

The life of the latter was undoubtedly saved by his
daughter's sudden intervention, for though her person was
unseen when the blow was aimed, it was not brought fully
home before the fire-flashing eyes of the striker were involuntarily widened by the unlooked-for vision between
him and his intended victim : and by the instinct of true
valour, ere a thought could take birth in his brain, his
arm became flaccid and aimless ; the weapon in his hand,
missing the duke, glided on, rather than smote, the bust
of the lady. From a fearful gash gushed the ruddy life-
stream over her beauteous shoulders, staining the white
robes that enveloped her figure, and trickling on the path
up which she was carried. Count Christofle's failing
vision was not insensible to the revolting spectacle. Horror
and disgust overpowered the instinct of self-preservation ;
and had he not sunk under wounds in .all parts of his
person, he had resisted the succour and protection of his

soldiers, and had thrown himself from very shame on the soil stained with her blood. His eye had met hers but for a moment—it was a cruel one—too late to avert the act that would abase him for ever—too late to check the fatal blow. What man could forget the scornful glance of a woman against whom his hand had been raised? From that moment, until some hours afterwards, the smart of his wounds was unfelt. Count Christofle, insensible in the arms of his faithful guards, saw them not all cut to pieces in defending his helpless person from outrage—nor beheld the savage glee with which his capture was regarded by the victors. Halberds and battle-axes were raised for severing him limb from limb on the instant; and more than one impatiently claimed the honour of carrying on his pike the heretic's head to the Duke of Savoy, as the most acceptable present that could be made.

The axe was raised, and would have fallen, but for the suggestion of the grimmest and most relentless of the persecutors of the reformed, Captain Mario, who, acting under the orders of the Marquis de Pianesse, had directed his soldiers, under pain of being shot as mutineers, to exterminate every Protestant in the district of Roras, "from the oldest to the youngest amongst the males; from the pregnant female to the sucking child." These horrid commands were obeyed by none of his papist soldiers with more zeal and cheerfulness than by one Irish Catholic regiment. "Drag the heretic to the tower of Mount Capulet," they cried; "and, if possible, we will prolong his life, that he may suffer the tortures of the rack, and that it may ebb slowly, in excess of agony!"

This brutal thought was received with cheers; additional punishment to a brother mortal who refuses to substitute the word of an Italian pope for the word of Christ nimself, was, in the mind of these adherents of the former, an additional claim for the favour of the latter. By this mode of reasoning was Piedmont sought to be depopulated; stimulated and confirmed by the bull of Pope Innocent the Eighth, dated 1487, and that of Pope John the Twenty-second, dated Avignon, 1332, expressly exhorting "all Catholics to extirpate heretics wherever they exist, as well as to absolve all Catholics from censure in breaking faith with one, let the pledge be of the most solemn nature soever."

Count Christofle was therefore dragged up the rugged rock to the tower, and cast into a noisome dungeon. The Duke of Savoy received the intelligence of his enemy's capture with exultation. His highness enjoyed the distinction of being the most bloodthirsty of the *holy* Catholic army employed in the murderous commission issued by the head of his church. He boasted of having impaled alive, and burnt, and hewn in pieces, more men and women and children than any of the generals embarked in this frantic service. These tortures and persecutions failed, however, to convince the simple mountaineers that Catholicism was the only true type on earth of the mild church of Christ, whose law *is* "peace on earth and good will to all men." However their want of perception might be wondered at, its consequences were unflinchingly prosecuted. This devoted people, driven from their mountain homes, their farms, and villages, by the emissaries of eight successive popes, had, in a moment of desperation, bound themselves together, as a last resource, into a legion; resolved to die at once with arms in their hands, rather than be seized singly for the stake and the gibbet. Their once smiling happy valley was now a scathed desert, blackened ruins only marking what had existed, ere conflagration and the sword had laid waste and depopulated one of the fairest portions of God's earth.

The young chief, under whose command they had sworn to range themselves, could boast of no high birth, had no support from alliances, and of territorial influence possessed not an acre. But his father was their valued pastor, and was a good man; his flock thought him the best man living. What genealogical distinction could be prouder? Purity of conduct, almost bashful modesty, bravery united with prudence, the good word of the young and the smiles of the old, were his reward. He had distinguished himself early for these qualities under Janavel, Laurens, and Benet, and was bequeathed to his little band by the former redoubtable Swiss patriot, as the richest legacy he could leave them. Under him, the villagers of Lucerne, Bubiane, and Bargis, had attacked a force five times their number, posted at the foot of Mount Capulet, under the command of the Duke of Savoy.

Covered with wounds, Count Christofle was laid upon a pallet; the refined cruelty of the man into whose power he had fallen, seeking through surgical aid to revive his strength, and render his nerves more susceptible to the agonies of the torture. Fully aware that on his recovery from his wounds,—if he ever should recover, which he had no reason to desire,—he had nothing to expect but a miserable end at the hands of the Duke, the assiduities of a medical attendant greatly astonished the sufferer.

He noticed that the Doctor placed a constraint upon himself, and spoke but little; never more than was necessary for acquiring a knowledge of the progress of his patient. He avoided his eye, and at every confession of amendment showed an uneasy aspect, and tokens of an unaccountable reservation of feeling which he would fain

P

disguise; but the Count's interest—nay, respect—for his medical attendant, involuntarily rose at these mysterious indications ; a weaker man had been alarmed at them.

One day, seeing that Dr. Hersheim was alone in his room, the nurse who invariably accompanied him being dismissed on some errand, the Count raised himself in his bed, and put a question he had long desired to ask, whilst the burning blush of shame that rose on his cheeks implied the miserable sense of abasement which accompanied the inquiry.

"Dr. Hersheim," faltered the Count, "in what state is the Lady Ludovica ?"

" Lady——," scarcely articulated Dr. Hersheim ; relieving his embarrassment by pretended inattention to his querist.

"The Lady Ludovica—yes ; I could not have been deceived ; though but for a second did her beauteous face flash before my eyes."

This was true ; for the lady had thrown her arms upwards to her father's neck, as he sunk from his horse before two terrific strokes on his cuirass and helmet from the Count's two-handed sword.

Dr. Hersheim regarded his patient for some time in silence—a cause for hate struggling with a generous nature, and its offspring compassion. The nurse re-entered; he seemed relieved by this interruption to further conversation, and in a few minutes more the prisoner was left alone.

No opportunity arrived for some days to renew the inquiry, though it was on the Count's tongue whenever any movement of the nurse betokened a temporary retreat from the bed on which he lay. He thought that Dr. Hersheim was aware of his desire to repeat the inquiry, and avoided its recurrence by watchfully retaining a third person at his elbow. Yet how, pondered he, could the doctor have dived into his thoughts, and imagine cause for embarrassment on the part of the inquirer, unless motives for shrinking from naming the lady existed in himself also? Surmises, uneasy, because undefined, floated in his brain that evening, and made the still hours of the solitary night more cold and disheartening.

Another slept uneasily in the fort that night. Was it the Lady Ludovica? No; it was the young disciple of Æsculapius himself. He had, for the care and treatment of his patient, a double set of instructions—two-fold, yet how contrary! One originating in cruelty, thirsting for revenge, and another in woman's tenderness to the stricken, in which her own wrongs are ever forgotten. Unhappily for his peace of mind, the channel and instrument of these instructions was far from being impassive for the secret purposes of either party. The Lady Ludovica was acquainted with her father's implacable temper, and the terrible ordeal destined for his gallant captive on return of convalescence, and knew that this savage parent had resolved he should undergo, prior to the exhaustion of strength and extinction of life, under its excruciating torments. She was a lady of high spirit, great beauty, and of that command of temper which irresistibly sways all minds within the sphere in which their possessor moves. The young Genevese doctor worshipped the high-born beauty from a humble distance, but his adoration was from his very heart. He would not repress the self-exaltation of his devotion; but he knew its object to be as remote from his destinies as the bright morning-star, shooting her gentle radiance through the mists of receding night.

At the end of a month the Count was able to walk in

a corridor adjoining his cell, a much superior apartment to his first lodging within these walls. To his astonishment, a tall female, with a single attendant, **entered** the corridor from a small portal, which was instantly closed after them. She advanced up the passage, only lighted from narrow gratings in the thick stone walls. Count Christofle drew back before her stately form, the upper portion of which was enveloped in a cloak, which, thrown over the head, and held together by her left hand, would have precluded any glimpse of her face, even had sufficient light from the gratings allowed it.

He retreated to his cell, at the door of which he perceived the muffled female pause, as it were, hesitating to enter. She entered not, but stood immovable for some minutes before him. Silence was not broken by either party. The lady turned round, was the next moment plunged in the gloom of the corridor, and, before Count Christofle could recover from his amazement, and grope his way towards the quarter where she had disappeared, the small door was closed with a dull firm clang, which told, as far as sound could indicate, of the hopelessness of escape, save possessed of the means of working its ponderous lock of six well-sprung bolts.

He now regretted his want of courage to address the figure, of whose identity he remained uncertain. Some one was surely interested in his fate. Save from his medical attendant, no word of comfort had been uttered during his melancholy incarceration. The few words of kindness dropt from the latter were treasured for days after they fell from the amiable Doctor's lips. Their remembrance, and the scanty segments of sunshine that for a brief period of the day speckled the cold stone wall of his cell, formed the sole materials for cheerfulness.

Beyond these, he had nothing to expect until the gates of heaven should pour a flood of celestial brightness upon his soul, and give to his spirit above the rest denied to it on earth. He was, however, seized with a shivering fit during the night, and on the approach of daylight was in a state of high nervous fever.

By Dr. Hersheim's manner it was evident that a change in the bodily health of the Count was anticipated. The Doctor was earlier than usual in his attendance, and from the moment of his entrance to that of his departure, his eye never ceased regarding his patient uneasily. For the next few days he was weaker than he had been since his imprisonment. On the fourth from the day of the visit of the veiled figure, the Doctor, in a tone of indifference and ill-dissembled reluctance at being made the medium of communication, informed him that a religious lady, a Sister of Charity, who wished to speak to him on points connected with the salvation of his soul, would be in his apartment the following morning.

" Will not the bigots let me die in peace ? To listen for a moment to one of them is a compromise of my constancy to the cause for which they persecute unto death. Spare me, Doctor !"

The Doctor seemed touched by the energy of his appeal, and was about to shape the request more persuasively, when the Count seized his arm, and with grinding teeth, and every muscle of his attenuated frame knit, with an effort which a sense of utter hopelessness alone could have endowed the prostrated youth, he almost shrieked in the former's face :

" Doctor ! you have practised upon me. If I am to die by poison, why is it slow and tormenting ? I once thought I had a friend in you. Oh, my God! how have I been deceived!"

Doctor Hersheim rose from the bed on which he was sitting. Successful as he had hitherto been in concealing his sympathies and sentiments, this direct attack on his uprightness and humanity overcame his discretion, and he exclaimed:—

" Poison thee, brave youth! That end would have been too happy a one in the eyes of the powers that control both thee and me; and a destiny to be envied by all who are at their mercy."

"Then why am I thus thrown back from the hour I took that potion from thy hands, and was persuaded by thee to be nearly bled to death?" he muttered, in bitter and disdainful accents.

" To deprive thy energies, from waste or pain's endurance, from giving thee further being in the world. Wouldst thou have executioners draw drop by drop thy blood; or wouldst thou yield it me for lengthened life? Wouldst have it prolonged at the behest of an angel, or shortened by a——" fiend, the excited Doctor would have said, but aware that too much had fallen from him, he checked himself.

" An angel!" murmured the exhausted prisoner, unconscious of the Doctor's emotion.

" That angel thou shalt see this night," exclaimed Dr. Hersheim, unable to veil his kindly feelings towards a tyrant's helpless victim, though that victim had acquired an interest, by his sufferings and his impending fate, in a bosom in which he had for many years prayed to have but the humblest place.

Count Christofle, supposing it was to the angelic attributes·of a devoted Sister of Charity that his doctor alluded, shook his head slowly, to mark how greatly he desired to be spared her visit, then sunk on his pillow.

He was visited next morning by Dr. Hersheim, who, whilst informing him of the approach of the holy Sister of Charity, appeared desirous of adding something, but checked himself. A few moments after his departure, a female in the garb of a Sister of that holy order which aspires to earn, by ceaseless watchings round the bed of pain, the rewards promised by God to those who "visit the sick and fatherless in affliction," entered the apartment. Her face was concealed by a veil worn under the white coif, which is the distinguishing mark of the Sisters, but that her eyes were large and expressive he could plainly perceive. In a collected and firm tone she at once told him that her object in paying a visit to the greatest foe of her church was to offer him pardon from the Duke, as well as absolution from the Archbishop of Arun, if he would renounce heresy, and bid his brethren do likewise. With warmth and energy she painted the beauty of unity, and the duty of obedience to God's priesthood in his church, the torments in the next world awaiting rebellion against its canons, and the duty of their holy head, the Pope, in this, to exterminate contemners of his ordinances. The church had never a more persuasive and eloquent missionary, or one who clothed its dogmas more attractively.

The Count, raising his head upon his hand, leaned forward from his pillow as respectfully as his weakness would permit; but his anxiety was, not to hear her eloquent sophistry, or to allow himself to be entranced with the beautiful garb in which subtlety and enthusiasm were dressing errors, but to imprint upon his own mind the faint outlines of feature partly visible through the veil, that he might beguile his solitary hours at her departure, with painting, by the aid of imagination, a countenance worthy of them.

During her discourse, she paused several times, as if expecting a reply; but the Count had no wish to interrupt his earnest counsellor, who rose to depart, after bidding him weigh well the words she had spoken.

The next day the lady came again, as before attended by a Sister of the same order, who stood apart during the interview, and whom the Count desired to be seated in vain. At the close of this interview, the lady spoke more rapidly, and he thought with some show of mortification at her want of success, for he still preserved silence: the sweet sound of woman's voice, apart from the subject that evoked it, reminded him too much of the world he had quitted, of happier hours never to return, and was too entrancing to permit him to interrupt its enchantment.

At parting the supposed Sister left a book in his hands, with earnest injunctions to read it in a right mind. He found it to be a defence of the papal faith, by Bellarmine. He had seen this book frequently, and heard its sophistry exposed. He resolved to put on paper all that he recollected of the arguments of the most learned of the Reformers of the age a century before the one in which he lived, as well as of those who had been the light of the primitive church of the Waldenses.

To learned refutations of modern errors engrafted upon the church by her hierarchy, the Count added confutations of the charges against his brethren, extorted by their behaviour, from the lips of those who would fain be their persecutors. He bade his fair spiritual adviser remember that a high authority in her church, Jacob de Riberia, confessed, " that the Albigenses taught their children, yea, even their daughters, the epistles and gospels, and that he had heard a plain countryman repeat the book of Job, and divers others that could perfectly repeat the whole New Testament." He reminded her that a friend of the Duke of Savoy, the Bishop of Cavaillon, appointed a monk to dispute with them, but that he returned and declared "that he had not so much profited in his whole life in the Scriptures as he had done in those few days of his conference with the Waldenses." The Count continued at his new employment on behalf of the faith he inherited from his fathers, which he had hitherto only defended with his sword. At times he sunk from exhaustion, at others he seemed supported in his work of devotion with supernatural aid; words from the source of truth flowing unceasingly over his page.

At length the visitant, bent upon the conversion of a soul from perdition, was again in his prison-room; and the pages he had written were respectfully presented to her at the close of a more impassioned address than he had yet heard from beneath the closely-veiled coif; but its wearer recoiled from them as from a poisonous serpent, after hearing from their writer the nature of their contents.

"I came to save thy life on earth, and thy soul in eternity," she said; "thou meetest my intercession with contumacious persistence in error. The Lord have mercy on thee!"

Here she was overcome with emotion, and Count Christofle, alarmed lest she should fall from the miserable seat that supported her by his bed-side, stretched out his arm. Rising at the same moment, her veil caught his hand, and disclosed the noble features of the Lady Ludovica, under the stiff linen coif of a Sister of Charity.

There was more than religious interest in the brilliancy of her dark hazel eye and flushed cheek. Solitude and reflection had engraven the momentary vision of the lady of the battle-field upon his memory. These, at the raising of the veil, flashed so vividly over his mind, that, uttering a wild cry, he fell back on his pallet and fainted.

The lady, darting a frightened glance at his pale, insensible countenance, directed her attendant to call instantly Dr. Hersheim, who had remained in the corridor; her hand involuntarily clasping that of the prisoner by an impulse consistent in any one with consciousness of having endangered the life of a fellow-creature, as well as, perhaps, with feelings which to herself she would refuse to acknowledge.

The Doctor started at beholding the noble lady bending over the person of his patient, her face marked with expressions so at variance with the proud majesty that awed the loftiest peers and the most stately dames of the Court of Savoy. He was by the bed-side, in her presence, ere he was perceived; when, gracefully rising, without betraying any surprise or annoyance at the discovery of her position, the lady quitted the room.

The Doctor, perceiving the closely-written pages which were lying on the bed, where they had dropped from the Count's hands, shrugged his shoulders, half repented of his indulgence to his patient, and proceeded to restore him. This was not effected so quickly as he expected. Reaction from strong emotion is slow in a weakened frame.

Under a change of treatment, his strength altogether recovered, for nature was no longer tampered with. Having one morning, with a bitter smile, expressed his wonder to Dr. Hersheim at the Duke of Savoy's delay of the gratification of his revenge, now that his victim was ripe for the slaughter, the former, with a warmth and frankness never before evinced, took both his hands in his, and bade him from that moment consider that he was his friend.

"Pardon me," replied the Count, with the spirit which returning health had restored to him; "the relentless persecutor of the humble followers of the gospel, and myself, can have no mutual friends; and as long as I am a prisoner only for being a humble soldier of the latter, the minions of the former and myself are sworn foes."

"For your distrust I will not censure you; but the day may speedily arrive when you may find a difficulty in pardoning yourself for it."

With these mysterious words, the Doctor prepared to take his leave.

"When shall I see you again?—have I still the privilege of being on your sick list? Though I hold our friendship but conditional, I would not exchange willingly my doctor for a turnkey," said the Count, perceiving his motion towards the door.

"This evening, I will return. Do not prepare yourself for repose. It may be late, but you shall see me," said the Doctor, in a firm tone and assuring manner

That evening, Count Christofle, conducted beyond the ramparts by Hersheim, quitted the Tower of Capulet by a path well known to him, over the mountains, to Aix in Dauphiné, and rested there three days, to cheer the spirits of some devoted refugees, who forgot their own danger in joy at beholding their leader alive and at liberty. He then repassed the mountain, skirting one of the Alps, by Villar and Bobi, named Pelaa de Geanvet. With not more than twenty men, he surprised Lucernette, a village near Lucerne, and killed many of the Duke's army. A thousand troops were instantly roused to arms, but Christofle and his band cut their way through this surrounding force without losing a man.

Sick at heart with all he heard, and despairing of brighter days for his countrymen, he resolved to enter the service of the great champion of Protestantism, Gustavus Adolphus; and communicating his views to an officer of that prince, who was then in Piedmont, encouraging the Protestants in their resistance of Catholic tyranny, was entreated by that gentleman to repair immediately to Stockholm.

In the wars of the King of Sweden, Count Christofle maintained his justly acquired reputation, and towards the close of three years from the period of escaping from the Tower of Mount Capulet, had amassed a sum large enough to carry into effect a long-cherished plan of transporting himself and a select band of adventurers to the newly-planted colony of Delaware, in North America, whither many Swedes and Saxons had already repaired. Instead of embarking from the Swedish ports, the place of rendez-vous fixed on was Trieste, a ship being there placed at their disposal. Count Christofle passed through Germany; found most of his party already at Trieste, but learnt that two of their number were at Malta, with an assorted cargo of the productions of the Levant, which would prove highly valuable at their place of final destination.

Whilst his brother adventurers were busily engaged embarking the goods that were to yield them this profit, Christofle traversed every part of the island, so long the stronghold of the intrepid military monks of the Christian faith, and the bulwark against the westward progress of Moslem invasion.

He found every one full of the praise of a wonderful

Astrologer, who not only responded to his querist correctly, and foretold the domestic incidents of every man's
future life, but presented individuals to each other who
were dwelling a thousand miles apart. The Count was no
exception to his cotemporaries in entertaining an universal
belief in auguries disclosed by the disciples of astral science. He found that the Astrologer was reported to have
been once a physician, who, from a disappointment in love,
had betaken himself to the occult studies, in which he had
become such a master as to be consulted from all parts of
Christendom.

To this Astrologer he resolved to repair, in order to
learn all he could about the powerful lady who, he doubted
not, had saved his life—whether the merit he attributed
to her was her due, and whether she had been induced to
influence her father to abate his rigour against his Protestant subjects,—and if so, whether from a conviction of the
abuses introduced into the church of Rome, or from kindness for him. This last reason embodied illusions too
flattering not to be cherished, groundless and visionary as
he in calmer moments was obliged to confess them to be.

The Astrologer had resided two years at Malta, under
the especial patronage of its knights, and three years had
elapsed on the very day of the Count's visit to him, since
the nocturnal flight of the latter from the Tower of Mount
Capulet. The Astrologer's abode was in the chapter-house
of a decayed hospital, or institution of these military
monks. Its octagonal form contributed greatly to the
picturesque aspect of its internal architecture, which was
not a little heightened by the grotesque objects that met
the eye on all sides. Every bird, beast, and fish, whose
shape outrages nature's harmony, or disgusts by its dis-
tasteful features, was found hung in mid-air, in varying

attitudes, from the roof to the floor of the chapter-house, ranged round the central column of the crypt. The form of the apartment much aided the effect of its contents; for nowhere could the eye rest amid the bewilderment of objects.

The man of destiny was tall, stately, and venerable; a long beard fell on his breast, and his eyes were deeply sunk in his head; he was enveloped in a rich green mantle deeply edged with sable, a cap of the latter material covering his head. At the Count's entry, the Astrologer was seated before a table covered with horoscopes and planetary types for the calculations of nativities. After raising his head in the direction where the former stood, he started backwards, but immediately recovering his wonted composure, dexterously, though gracefully, drew his mantle more closely around him, and by a scarcely perceptible motion, pulled his cap over his forehead, so as more completely to shade the upper part of his face. He waved silence to his visitor, but put out his hand to receive the paper on which the hour of his birth was written, as well as the questions to be propounded, which the former, knowing the regulated forms exacted by these mysterious personages, had duly prepared. On it was written—"Date of my birth, 16 May, 1630, at 5 m. past 6 in the evening—Was Lady Ludovica, daughter of the Duke of Savoy, the contriver of my escape from the Tower of Mount Capulet?—What is her employment at this moment? and upon whom and what does she most think?"

The Astrologer held this paper so long in his hands, that Count Christofle imagined it had been written unintelligibly, and was about to offer verbal explanation, when the former betrayed so much agitation of manner, that he feared to approach or disturb him. After a visible effort to recover himself, the sage, in a voice the Count thought he had often heard before, desired him to stand outside of two circles drawn on the floor. Flanking them, due north and south, were two large globes, and in the centre was a sarcophagus from the pyramids, carved on every side with the mystic cabala of the Magi of Egypt. The twelve signs of the zodiac were drawn between the outer and inner circles. The Astrologer waved his wand round its centre, occasionally pointing it towards Sagittarius, and gazing intently upon the contents of the sarcophagus, from which a grateful perfume was dispensing itself around. Sagittarius was the sign under which the nativity of his questioner was cast.

After some moments spent in cabalistic invocations to strange sounding names, which he could not catch, the Astrologer, in a solemn voice, said—" Thou art governed by the first lord of the triplicity of the tenth house, and wilt be fortunate, and arrive at honour. Thou hast been constant and devoted, and the cause thou hast fought for with thy blood shall triumph in the face of heaven. In the west shall arise a mighty nation, sprung from England, the cradle of the religion 'whose worship,' as the service of the church saith, 'is perfect freedom,' where tyranny and persecution for conscience sake shall not so much as be heard of in the length and breadth of its beautiful land. The country which shall send forth these children of light will be the beacon of thy faith, the soil where God shall be worshipped in spirit, and where no man maketh his fellow afraid. But in combating Antichrist, thou must enlist Charity, the sister of Truth; learning and an instructed mind will convert more than the sword."

The Count showed signs of impatience, which the Astrologer perceived; and after some further remarks upon

the positions of the planets in conjunction with his nativity
sign, he regarded him so intently, whilst his hand, still
holding the wand, passed to and fro before his forehead,
that the Count felt a sensation altogether different from
any he had yet experienced.   The atmosphere before him
over the sarcophagus became a luminous medium.   Gradually thin vapoury clouds floated before the centre of the
luminous atmosphere, thickening and becoming more
opaque, as, dispelling themselves, they diminished the relief of the grotesque intercepting objects.   Behind deep
volumes of cloud was silvery moonlight: the planet itself
was seen in unclouded loveliness, its cold rays fading on
the form of a lady, who, as far as he was able to discern
through the clouded foreground, was bending over a volume.   Whilst the clouds gradually fell away to the right
and the left, the bright moon above her made clearly
visible the features, shape, and dress of this lady, whose
slender neck, finely-moulded head, and magnificent bust,
as they thus slowly developed themselves, could leave no
doubt of their possessor.

Count Christofle breathed fast.   His question was
answered!   The recumbent lady before him in the pale
moonbeams was the angel that loosened his bonds and
delivered him from a shameful death.   Deep and solemn
were the commencing incantations of the commanding
genius of this mystic revelation; but they assumed a
louder and more authoritative tone as the vision became
more distinct; and as the lady turned over a leaf without
raising her eyes, his voice became awfully sonorous, its
triumphant tone communicating a corresponding thrill of
exultation to his enraptured client, who was also wrought
up to a state of excitement that would have prostrated him
before the figure, but for a power unseen that kept him

anding spell-bound where he was With the softest
ove of her transparent hand, the page was turned, and
the same moment a ray of crystal light fell on the
athery leaf of her phantom volume. The eyes of Chris-
fle read his own words written by his own hand in the
ison tower; the pages under the intent meditation of
e beautiful spirit before him were the same he had
aced in her corporeal hands, and had seen left, con-
mned, on the floor of his cell, up to the last hour of his
tention, for he had not had the heart to remove them. A
m passed over his eyes, and the next moment all traces
' the vision were fled. Instead of a bright celestial atmo-
here, in the serene depths of which he had been existing
r a period measurable by no method of time, an alligator
as swinging before his eyes between two stuffed owls;
id the Astrologer was standing outside of the zodiac on
e floor.

"Thou art satisfied, gallant youth," murmured the
strologer; "I know thou art. Set forth on thy journey.
iou hast no more to ask of the devoted disciple of Cor-
lius Agrippa ? "

" I would know tidings of an old friend who, next to
ir whom thou hast made visible to my eyes by thy art,
aims my honour and service."

" I know whom thou meanest. Regard him also,"
claimed the Astrologer, moving behind the column of
e crypt; and Count Christofle the next moment beheld
r. Hersheim, in the same dress in which he visited him
prison. He would have thrown himself into his arms
id embraced him; but immediately a glare of blue flame,
llowed by a thick sulphureous vapour, passed between
e Doctor and himself, and from it came these words—
In three days thou shalt see me again !" In another

Q

moment the Astrologer's cap of sable towered above his
implements and spheres, and the Count was recoiling from
the column, rubbing his shoulder after a hard bruise, to
which his anxiety to embrace his prison doctor had sub
jected him. Shortly after, the Count found himself in
broad daylight, outside the chapter-house.

The revelations involved in the vision he had jus
beheld were not to be slighted. Count Christofle instantly
resolved to repair to Lucerne, and satisfy himself of thei
verity. If so, what an alteration might not the change o
religious opinion in the daughter make upon the council
of the father. Could it be possible that he was to be instru
mental in working a change on which the lives of thousand
must depend ? He decided to leave Malta by a vessel now
in the harbour, bound for Genoa, and rejoin his friends a
Gibraltar, on his return from Lucerne, where he induced
them to believe pressing business demanded his presence

He took ship next day, and landed in Sicily on the
third, when the first person who greeted him on shore was
Dr. Hersheim. The crowd on the quay was great. The
various costumes of the motley population of this island
with those of the soldiery of a dozen different powers
always touching there on their passage from the Levantine
States, distracted his attention for some minutes. He had
grasped his good friend's hands, and received a salute on
both the cheeks, after the manner of his countrymen ; the
embrace was warm and human ; he felt it the harbinger
of a renewal of associations with the land of his birth ; yet
he could not entirely overcome a sensation of awe and
astonishment, amounting even to distrust of his senses, as
he beheld the form phased so preternaturally to them but
a few hours previously, in the chapter-house at Malta
His quickened susceptibility for aerial revelation now

pictured, under the crimson and green scarf of a Neapolitan fish-wife, the Madonna of the Capella Sistina — the
realisation of majestic womanhood, of that tremendous
genius and grand moral being, Michael Angelo. And, as
the features under his gaze relaxed from spiritual to
mundane perfection, he could have sworn that the visitant
of his prison cell, the eloquent and beautiful Sister of
Charity, was before him. In his delirium of joy and
astonishment, he turned to his friend, who was but a few
moments before cordially welcoming him to a strange land.
He was not there, nor to be found amid the crowd, nor
could any one say that such a person had been seen. He
believed himself still to be under the influence of enchantment, and was now more than ever anxious to find himself
in Lucerne.

He landed at Genoa; and he there heard that the
inhabitants of the numerous towns and villages who held
fast to the simple faith of their fathers still groaned under
oppression.

On the second day of his arrival, news came that this
persecution had ceased altogether, by order of the Duke
of Savoy, on the very day that Count Christofle had
consulted the wondrous Astrologer at Malta; and the
story in Genoa ran, that a sudden conversion of the Duke's
only daughter was the cause of this unlooked-for clemency.
She was found one morning by her maids, it was said,
reclining on her couch, so deeply engaged in perusing
some sheets of manuscript before her as to be insensible to
their approach, and they found that she had not disrobed,
nor had sought slumber during the night; nay, that
without a pause for the daily arrangement of the toilette,
she had sought her father in his bed-chamber, and after
falling on her knees, and praying to Heaven for strength

to endure the consequences of the course she was about to take, had declared to him that she would quit his palace, repair to England, and incite the Lord Protector of that Commonwealth (then regarded as the head of the Protestant interest in Europe) to make war upon his principality unless persecution throughout it entirely ceased. The Duke, who was ever influenced by the masculine mind of his child, promised all she desired ; and the latter refused to take meat or drink, or change her disordered apparel, until orders were despatched to publish the amnesty throughout the valleys of Piedmont. To this intelligence was added, that the writings which had ultimately wrought such a joyful amelioration in the condition of his countrymen had been found in a cell from which an heretic prisoner had escaped some three years previous, and which had been from that time unoccupied.

Arrived at Lucerne, he had the happiness of finding all he had heard at Genoa perfectly true, and of receiving the highest reward a son can take from the hands of a parent—the blessing of his aged father, to whom alone he imparted his share in restoring the peace of the valley.

The words of the Astrologer still rung in his ears, promising him success and good fortune in all his undertakings. He resolved not to be distrustful of the augury, already in part so wonderfully realised, but go forward to the New World with the companions he had engaged to join. This resolution was no sooner taken, than a message by one of the chamberlains of Lady Ludovica invited him to her presence, with an intimation that her influence with her father was at his command, to obtain any post of honour, advantage, or privilege, he might desire. The terms of the invitation left no doubt of the anxiety of his fair and distinguished convert to see him. Men possessed of a less susceptible mind would have rushed exultingly to so flattering and propitious an interview, but the Count recoiled therefrom, instantly resolving not to retard his departure from Europe a single day. His hand had smitten the form of this lady: and his eyes could never again knowingly meet hers; though her kindness towards him assured him that her forgiveness was sincere, his ears could not endure to hear her lips pronounce it; his manliness would receive a shock therefrom, and all the purpose of his existence be paralyzed, by the abasement of that moment.

To carry out the prediction of the Astrologer, he fled the patronage of his sovereign's daughter, all-powerful as he knew her to be. The lady was astonished at this disdain of her favour, and sent to the Astrologer, in Malta, to learn its cause. He declared—"that the destinies of both the Count and herself forbade another interview in this world; and that, having accomplished her glorious work of pacification, her own end was nigh." Had the Count and herself, he said, met after the wonderful effect produced on her mind by the former's written pages, their feelings would have been too deeply interested in each other to have parted; and the impossibility of their union, and her own short space of life, must have lessened the power of the former to accomplish the great cause to which she would die a martyr. This noble lady expired shortly afterwards, from poison administered by a villain, in hopes of finding favour with Rome. So was fulfilled, to the letter, the prediction of the Astrologer.

––––––––––

NEAR to the Lady Eva was seated a venerable diplomatist, who had known her from her cradle, and felt for her all the tender attachment of a father. When the foregoing tale was concluded, the Lady Eva arose, but paused, as if in doubt whether she might venture to solicit this dear old friend to assist her project; at length, conquering her feeling of shyness, she glided gently behind the Baron's chair, and affectionately resting both her beautiful arms on his shoulders, held before him a drawing representing an Italian landscape, with a marble fountain, and a guitar lying on the steps leading to it.

As the graceful Eva bent forward, her rich and luxuriant ringlets softly caressed the furrowed cheeks of the old Diplomatist, whilst she whispered—"Will it tax your indulgent goodness too much to fulfil my request?" And here let us observe, that the Baron's appearance did truly embody the very ideal of "indulgent goodness." His silver hair partly shaded a forehead replete with wisdom and profound observation, whilst the expression of his eyes and mouth was so redolent of sweet benevolence, that he never failed to awaken confidence in the pure and young. Often, indeed, had he been heard to say, that the brightest pages he had learned in the history of the human heart were from the outpourings of young and unsophisticated minds.

Fondly pressing the Lady Eva's tiny hand in his, he said, "Dear child, I am too old to weave the web of fiction; but, strange to say, this print evokes in my memory some scenes of days long gone by; and often have you reminded me of the interesting girl who was the heroine of that tale."

Then sighing, as he fondly gazed on Eva's speaking countenance, he added, " You are fair and good as she was, sweet maiden. May you enjoy a happier destiny !"

The Baron then proceeded to relate the story of

THE GUARDIAN ANGEL.

In the opening of the spring of 1829, when Paris, by its gaieties and fêtes, was attracting and enthralling the natives of every part of Europe, the young and noble diplomatist, the Marquis de Querancy, was suddenly ordered to proceed without delay to Naples, with important despatches. To any other Frenchman, such an order at that moment would have conveyed inexpressible annoyance. But even Paris had failed to rekindle one throb of pleasure in the mind of De Querancy. All things seemed to him tasteless and hollow in the most brilliant salons he frequented. Did a murmur of applause direct his attention to any new beauty among the many syrens of the day, his calm and passionless countenance reflected neither emotion nor admiration. In such a temper of mind, it could be no grief to him to leave Paris; and having but a few hours to prepare for his journey, he determined not even to make a single visit of adieu, except to a young Englishman, Clarence Russell, with whom he had travelled in the East, where they had become intimate, and much attached to each other. Clarence Russell, like the generality of his countrymen, ever desirous of change of scene, proposed, on the spur of the moment, to accompany him to Naples, an offer which was gladly accepted by De Querancy, and the two friends left Paris together.

It had been the Marquis de Querancy's intention to travel day and night till they reached Naples, but when they came within sight of the Eternal City, Clarence Russell mentioned, for the first time, that he had never seen Rome. "Of course, my dear Arthur," he added, "you will indulge me by remaining here one night? I

care only to visit St. Peter's in the morning, and will be
ready to start immediately after." De Querancy felt it
would be too churlish to refuse his friend so natural a
desire, but it was with a heavy sigh that he consented to
it.   Alas ! Rome, the mighty sepulchre of the martyred
saints, the great and the wise of yore, was also the sepulchre of all the Marquis's earthly hopes.

When the friends drove up to Cerny's well-known
hotel, Piazza di Spayna, it was about four o'clock in the
afternoon, and having ordered dinner for seven, they
sauntered forth in that listless way usual to travellers who
want to kill time in the interim due for the preparation of
meals.   Wrapt up in his own sad thoughts, De Querancy
followed Clarence Russell whichever road he chose to lead.
After walking some time, the latter called his friend's
attention to a neighbouring height, crowned with those
glorious pine-trees so peculiar to Rome, expressing a wish
to reach the spot on which they grew, and they found
themselves in the Pamphili Doria gardens.

It was about the middle of April ; some gentle showers
had fallen in the early part of the day, as if to refresh the
verdure, and bring forth a thousand balmy odours.   Who
has ever visited Rome without lingering with delight in
the shades of Pamphili Doria ?   There the pine-trees
reign supreme in their melancholy ; the Parma violets
grow wild ; and the grass is peculiarly enamelled at this
season with anemones ;— in short, there is a wild romance
about these haunts that well becomes the Eternal City.

Clarence Russell proposed to rest awhile on the marble
steps of a beautiful fountain, admirably situated under a
natural arch of noble trees, and where a cascade seemed
to pour forth showers of diamonds, its waters sparkling
under the bright rays of an Italian sun.   De Querancy

approached this fountain slowly, his eyes fixed on the ground. Unhappy man ! Blindfold he could have led the way. On the last step there was a guitar, with a white ribbon attached to it. Clarence Russell, passionately fond of music, snatched it up, and began singing that well-known Neapolitan melody—

"Ah, che soffrir mi resta!"*

Often and often had De Querancy heard that air sung in various salons in Europe; but when at this moment, and on this spot, it burst upon his ear, all the long pent-up emotions of anguish broke forth, and, gasping for breath, he hid his face in his hands, and wept like a child !

Clarence, startled and amazed, ceased singing, and placing his hand on his friend's shoulder, exclaimed, "Good God! my dear Arthur, what can move you thus ? Far be it from me to surprise a confidence from any one ; but I have more than once felt the relief which springs from sympathy and friendship. Say, Arthur, shall I leave you alone, or will you confide your grief to one who has long watched, with affectionate anxiety, the settled sadness which pervades your every action ?"

"Clarence," replied Arthur, "well do I know your frank and manly character, and that a mind like yours will pity rather than ridicule my weakness. I will, there-fore, as you desire it, try to give you an insight into my chequered life, nor attempt to palliate the faults and errors which have tended to cast an irreparable blight over my whole existence."

Clarence warmly pressed his friend's hand, and Arthur began :—" My father perished on the scaffold during the fury of the Revolution, a martyr to his religious and politica

* Written by Prince Pignatelli, the night previous to his execution.

creed. He left an inconsolable widow, wholly devoted to his memory, and who clung to life only to fulfil his dying injunction to educate me, their only child, in those loyal sentiments for which he had died. All my nearest relations trod the same path of duty, serving the cause of legitimacy to the last, either in the wars of La Vendée, or in upholding their followers while struggling in manifold ways against those monsters of iniquity who have cast an eternal blot on the fair pages of French history. To these fatal remembrances, and also to the wild Breton legends — to which I listened in childhood with pleasing dread — do I trace that melancholy so unusual to my countrymen, which, even in those times, affected my mind. How shall I describe to you all the tenderness of my mother — that best of women — who, during the emigration, denied herself every extra comfort to bestow on me an enlightened education, and grant me every indulgence my young mind could anticipate?

"On the restoration of the Bourbons, we left Bath, the retreat chosen by my mother during our exile from France, and returned to the home of my ancestors — an old French château, near Nantes. I became naturally anxious to see something of the world, but delayed expressing my earnest wishes from filial piety to that revered parent, who rested her whole happiness in me. My fortune being nowise proportioned to the nobility of my birth, the army or the navy were the careers I sighed for ; but when I merely glanced at these projects, a pang of anguish disturbed the sweet serenity of my mother's still handsome countenance. 'I had anxiously prayed, my Arthur,' she exclaimed, 'that you might not choose the military career, for it has been ever fatal to all of your name. Think not, my son, that I thus oppose your wishes to

satisfy my selfish love; I feel that the dull life you lead
in these remote parts is unfit for one of your character
and age. I only wish to aid your choice. Few careers
are more promising than diplomacy; and I have some
interest at the present moment with our ambassador at
Rome, who is one of your lamented father's oldest friends.
I should be proud to see you introduced into society under
his tutelar care. He was ever my type of all that wins
and commands respect in the aristocracy. Most truly did
Madame de Staël describe the Duc de L. M. as " *the first
gentleman of France.*" '

" I renounced, with much regret, my military plans,
but felt amply compensated in sacrificing my wishes to
those of this admirable mother. To an Englishman, this
entire submission to a parent may appear overstrained;
for, on reaching manhood, your first impulse is total
emancipation from home, and the shackles of womanly
influence. With us, the holy ties of gratitude bind us all
our lives to the will of her who gave us birth. Hence the
great moral influence women exercise throughout France.
To woman's gentle sway may be attributed the intimacy
kept up through life in French families, which you have
often pronounced so patriarchal, while you lamented that
it was rarely, if ever, to be found in England.

" On my coming of age, my mother wrote to ask the
Duc de L. M. to have me appointed to the French embassy
at Rome; and by return of post he answered, with his
usual gracious kindness, that the son of his ever-lamented
friend should find in him a second father.

" I think it worth mentioning a strange incident, which
happened the day before I left home — unheeded at the
time, but which has since proved a foreshadowing of my
future fate.

" Among our tenants was an old peasant, called Dame

Marguerite, supposed by the surrounding peasantry, who, in Brittany, are most superstitious, to have the gift of second sight. She was grandmother to my nurse, had received a superior sort of education for her rank in her life, and had often attracted me in childhood by her love of fairy stories. I always entertained a kindly feeling towards the aged sybil, so I turned into her cottage to take leave of her; and remembering the supernatural gifts attributed to her, (though incredulous to their reality,) begged Dame Marguerite to tell me my fortune, and held out my hand to her, that she might peruse the lines therein, according to custom.

"The aged woman gazed on me long and sorrowfully; then bid me remain in ignorance, 'For,' added she, in her wonted figurative mode of expression, 'the traveller should set forth with a light heart, not to faint on the way.'

"I then insisted on her explaining the mysterious sense of her allusion.

"'Woe to me,' said Dame Marguerite, in her low but impressive voice, 'for I look on the last scion of the time-honoured house of Querancy! To you, also, the month of April will be fatal! Shun women and music.'

"I chid my venerable soothsayer for her evil omens. The warning concerning April was natural enough, for in that month my father was guillotined; but as to the two latter prohibitions, I told Dame Marguerite that without them life was little worth.

"I never mentioned this anecdote to my mother, who behaved on this trying occasion—her first separation for a lengthened period from me—with her wonted fortitude; not a murmur escaped her lips; but to offer up prayers in her lonely retreat for her child's happiness, was henceforth her sole vocation on earth.

"I arrived at Rome on the 20th of April, 1817. It

was the residence of all others most suited to my pursuits, for I was born an innate artist. The embassy was a home to me in every sense; the general society delightful; but ere long, one house became my chosen resort in preference to all others. This was the Villa Manno, the residence of Uberto Manno, the most remarkable person in Rome at that epoch.

" This eminent artist — Roman by birth, painter by profession — was the honoured guest of the great and the talented of all countries. The fine arts were hereditary in his family. Uberto Manno's racy wit and pungent satire charmed alike his friends and terrified his enemies; his rapid conceptions, and graphic pencil, raised him to a proud eminence among his brother artists. To these he was courteous and generous in the extreme, his purse and advice ever liberally given ; but to the great and noble he could, at times, assume a haughtiness of demeanour which became well his democratic principles, if their talents or conduct equalled not their worldly advantages. All the softer shades of Manno's character shone forth in his intense love for his only child, Virginia ; her mother had died in giving her birth. It is well-nigh impossible to do justice to the endearing charms of this angelic being. Her features were pure as those of the first blonde virgins of Raphael ; her figure light ; her step elastic as a sylphid's ; her long swan-like throat inclined rather forward, as if the gentle maiden bent under the constant admiration she called forth from each passing observer. To Uberto's deep regret, she possessed not the family talent of paint-ing, but her talents for music were surpassingly great. When at the piano, singing hymns to the Virgin, she seemed the personification of a St. Cecilia ; and yet was most touching when singing to the guitar that same air

which so powerfully affected me just now.—A ravishing
mixture of saint and of sylphid ; sometimes she looked too
ideal-like for human love; and then, the moment after,
would enchant one by dancing the saltarella in the Roman
costume, with the buoyant joyfulness so peculiar to her
sweet self.

" At the end of May, Rome is quite deserted, for the
malaria reigns in all its loathsome vigour, and few care to
brave this infectious malady ; for me, spell-bound by the
attractions of the Manno villa, I remained the whole summer. Too brief were the hours, the days, I passed with
Uberto Manno and his daughter, devoted to the cultivation
of the arts, and under all the illusions of a first love.
How often, during the great heats, have we sat on these
very steps, sketching, or reading the great poets of France
and Italy alternately aloud, or listening to Virginia's
seraph voice, accompanied by her favourite guitar ! The
only alloy to the rapturous existence I enjoyed, was the
remembrance of all my mother's inveterate prejudices to
my marrying one beneath me in birth ; this prevented me
at once telling my hopes and fears to Uberto, for I dared
to hope that my presence was not indifferent to his fair
daughter. Also, I had heard the painter declare that he
would never consent to Virginia's marrying out of her own
sphere ; and I had reason to know that more than one
Italian noble had vainly tried to win her hand; but, full
of sanguine hope, the best dower of the young, I thought
time and constancy would level every obstacle, when a new
addition to Manno's family circle changed its aspect
entirely.

" The new comer was Uberto's nephew, Antonio Carelli.
He was an orphan adopted by Manno, and his most promising scholar. His uncle had often mentioned his talents

with pride, so I was fully prepared to regard him as a friend; but at our first interview, after one keen glance of his fiery eye round our daily group, I felt we were henceforth rivals and enemies. Antonio was an ardent republican, impetuous in every impulse. As a Frenchman, he hated me; as a rival, he defied me in his inward soul! Madly jealous of the admission of a stranger into his cousin's intimacy, whom he loved with all the fiery passion of a southern, he was ever on the watch, by means fair or foul, to find an opportunity to exclude me from a society so replete with bliss to us both.

" Virginia was of too soft a nature to repulse any one, still less Antonio, whom she had regarded as a brother from her cradle. She submitted, with gentle patience, to the insolent sarcasms, and various inuendoes he daily poured into her ear, and would, when I was tasked by the young Italian beyond endurance, turn on me her dove-like eyes, as if to implore forbearance for her sake.

" Fluctuating between my growing attachment to Virginia and the certainty of my mother's displeasure, I continued undecided how to shape my course, and felt truly miserable. One morning, on entering Uberto's studio, Virginia passed by me rapidly, but I had time to see that she was much agitated, and in tears. I found her father, brush in hand, pacing the room in a disordered manner, and speaking with vehemence to Antonio Carelli, who, on my appearance, left the studio, but cast on me, meanwhile, a withering look of hatred and triumph.

" ' Marquis de Querancy,' exclaimed Uberto Manno, fixing on me his eagle eye, as if to read my inmost thoughts, ' you behold in me a most unhappy parent! For the first time my child dares to disobey me, in opposing herself to the fond scheme of my life, to see her united

to Antonio Carelli, my best and most promising scholar
that my works, my family relics, might be bequeathed to
the two dearest objects I have on earth.'

"I was stunned with this unforeseen disclosure. On
recovering myself, my first impulse was intense joy at
Virginia's open repugnance to a union with her cousin ;
and forgetting all things in my love for her, I would have
implored her father to bestow her hand on me, as the
dearest boon life could afford, but I detected a lurking
sneer on Uberto's lips, as he awaited my answer. I fancied, that, instigated by my wily rival, Uberto only sought
to provoke the offer of my hand and fortunes, to reject
both with scorn. Ancestral pride resumed its sway, and
hiding my deep emotion, I merely uttered some commonplace phrases about offering my best wishes for his and his
daughter's happiness. I left the Villa Manno for the first
time dejected, resolving to absent myself from it for a
time, and yet watch, unseen, if Virginia became too easily
amenable to her father's wishes. An excellent opportunity
occurred to me to follow up this plan, and give the irri-
tated artist time to cool over his first resentment at my
thus crossing his favourite scheme.

"My mother wrote to me at this time, to desire me to
enact the part of cicerone to the noble family of De Gos-
son, neighbours of ours in Brittany. As winter was fast
approaching, they proposed to me to devote the last days
of autumn in visiting the most celebrated spots in the
environs of Rome, such as Albano, Tivoli, &c. I agreed
willingly, for I sought distraction of any kind, and was
pleased at having social duties forced upon me.

"In the De Gossons' society I met, for the first time,
the beautiful Countess Zamoysky, a Pole. And here I
must dwell at some length on this woman, who, by her

dazzling beauty and treacherous arts, exerted such a fatal influence in separating me for ever from the only woman I truly loved.

"Painters have vainly tried to reproduce the perfect loveliness of Madame Zamoysky's features. Her glorious black eyes; her luxuriant dark hair, braided on her high and intellectual forehead; the perfect oval of her face; the rich tints of her complexion, are to be found only in Raphael's Madonna della Seggiola,* or in Domenichino's Sybil in the Capitol; then her figure was like the Diane Chasseresse, so truly proud and commanding in every aspect—in every gesture. She was the admired of all, but loved by none. Public report described her as accepting universal homage as her due; but perfectly passionless, and of spotless reputation, though united to a man much her senior in years, and wholly unworthy of her. The Count Zamoysky was a mean, cringing courtier, making poor attempts at wit, and gladly sheltering his nonentity under the shadow of his wife's celebrity, to frequent every house open to society, where otherwise he would have been voted an intolerable bore.

"A young Russian princr at the time insinuated to me, that the lovely Pole had more than once taken pleasure in drawing on young and inexperienced men, to study the intensity of their youthful adoration for her charms, and when they dared to claim the reward due to their devotion, rejected them with scorn and derision; but this I listened to as the calumny that too often attacks women of superior beauty, shielded by equal virtue. My own heart filled with the image of Virginia, I feared not to indulge in all the gratification I derived from Madame Zamoysky's various talents and fascinating manners.

* At the Palais Pitti, in Florence.

R

"Towards the winter, foreigners began to pour into Rome from all sides. The carnival promised to be unusually brilliant; and at every fête Madame Zamoysky was the magnet of attraction—the cynosure of all eyes.

"She attended regularly Uberto Manno's Monday evenings, where the fair Virginia presided, and did the honours of her father's house with matchless grace. These soirées were delightful, for there, mixed with the most eminent artists of all countries, was to be seen, in turn, each illustrious traveller passing through Rome. In return, Uberto Manno and his daughter were invited to all the embassies and best houses then open in Rome. The painter accepted these invitations, not from a wish to soar above his equals in rank, but as a tribute paid to the divine art, of which he was the most ardent votary.

"On my return from our excursions in the environs, I remarked, in my morning visits to Uberto, that Virginia was no longer to be seen in his studio; so I was obliged to defer, till the next Monday evening, my purpose of learning, from her own lips, her reasons for rejecting Carelli's love. Her answer, I was resolved, should decide my future course. Dancing and music were equally resorted to at Manno's soirées. During a waltz with Virginia, I ventured to allude to her sorrow, which I had involuntarily witnessed, also her unusual absence from her father's studio; and told her how painful both these circumstances had been to me. A bright blush suffused her cheek, and her little hand trembled in mine, seeming to bid me hope my affection was returned, when Carelli suddenly interrupted us by claiming Virginia's hand for the saltarella, just asked for at the express desire of Madame Zamoysky, who, leaning on the young painter's arm, said she would take no refusal. The whole assembly made way in the centre of the room for the youthful couple, who performed their native dance with grace and vivacity. Never did Virginia look to more advantage than on that night, dressed in virgin white, as was her invariable custom, her beautiful blonde hair richly plaited round her head, her soft blue eyes downcast, as if unwilling to encounter the general gaze of admiration her dancing called forth.

" 'Does not Virginia remind you,' said Madame Za moysky, 'of those graceful dancing figures on the Etruscan vases?' Then, following my eyes, jealously riveted on Virginia's every movement, she continued, ' How admirably they contrast at this moment ! Behold Carelli's manly figure, seeming to uphold the aërial nymph-like form which now clings to him for support — now turns away in affected coyness. What a pity,' added she, as if thinking aloud, ' that her mind is not as candid as her angelic countenance would seem to denote, and that, by an unpardonable spirit of coquetry, she persists in distressing her doting father and devoted lover.'.

" I asked, abruptly, if their engagement had been long known ?

" ' When I was here last winter,' answered Madame Zamoysky, 'Carelli, who is a great *protégé* of mine, informed me of their mutual attachment, and that their youth alone retarded their marriage. But he now tells me, that on his late return from Russia, he found Virginia altered, and capricious in the extreme ; but he knows that it is only to put his love to the test, for that her heart is his, and his only.'

" Knowing that she must soon hear it from others, I frankly avowed to Madame Zamoysky my unabated love for Virginia, assuring her, at the same time, how totally

unconscious I was till now of her previous attachment to
her cousin.

" I left Manno's house without attempting to resume
my broken conversation with Virginia, for the mere suspicion of her having trifled with my feelings wounded me
to the soul; and besides, Carelli never left her side for the
rest of the evening.

" The next day, when I calmly reflected on the past, I
called reason to my aid, and ended in convincing myself
that, to my sorrow, I had mistaken Virginia's endearing
sweetness of countenance and manners for a warmer feeling. I could not bear to suppose so guileless a being
could voluntarily inflict the pangs I felt; then I thought
on Carelli, and pride came to my aid. Was I, the son of
one of the noblest houses in Brittany, to dispute Virginia's
heart, inch by inch, with a low-born artist, and by so doing
incur the lasting displeasure of my beloved mother? No
—never! I would strive to forget Virginia, whose greatest
charm, in my eyes, was gone, for I had hoped to win
a virgin heart. I thought, with gratified pride, on the
unfeigned sympathy shown me by Madame Zamoysky,
and sought her society more than ever. How it humbles
me, Clarence, to show myself to you, whom I so honour
and esteem, in such a despicable light! Yet such was my
miserable infatuation for Madame Zamoysky, that it hurried me on, step by step, to the renouncing of a pearl
without price—to be ensnared by the specious wiles of
one, who, like the ignis fatuus, beguiles the benighted
traveller but to lead him to destruction.

" One of Madame Zamoysky's greatest attractions in
my eyes, was the respectful admiration she testified for
my mother, from the various details she had learnt from
the De Gossons. How she won me by dwelling with

e.oquence on the sorrow the disparaging union of her only son would give her! Then, if in our walks to the galleries, or during our musical repetitions, the theme of love was mentioned, how glowing were her thoughts on that subject, how touchingly she would deplore the misery of conjugal life unblessed by mutual sympathies! At such moments as these, I thought her the most interesting of her sex, and felt proudly happy that this lovely woman should thus single me out from the crowd of admirers watching for a smile, to impart to me alone her hidden sorrows, ever carefully veiled from the public eye by a haughty reserve.

"The winter passed most rapidly. I now no longer frequented the Villa Manno in the morning; and when I met Virginia, which was but seldom, at the different balls and parties, her manner was frigidly cold. A bare recognition passed between us. This I ascribed to her entire return of Carelli's affection.

"One evening, at Madame Zamoysky's house, tableaux were proposed. The most successful were, Virginia as a Virgin of Carlo Dolci, and the Countess Zamoysky as the Sybil of Domenichino. This latter tableau caused enthusiastic admiration. Manno and Carelli were the directors of the whole. When the tableaux were over, Carelli approached Madame Zamoysky, exclaiming with transport— 'You were indeed an object to bow down before and worship, as the ideal of beauty, and a new source of inspiration to us artists!'

"Indignant at the presumption of the young artist thus openly expressing his admiration to the fair Countess, I drew her arm through mine, and left the spot where Carelli stood.

"'You are wrong, Querancy,' said she, as if reading

my thoughts, ' to blame us women for listening graciously to the artists' praise. Their homage is sincere — solely prompted by the love of their art; and then,' added she, in a soft murmur, ' I do feel a grateful triumph, if, for one night only, the Sybil has effaced the Virgin.'

" I gazed on the fair Countess at these words ; and, as she stood, her lustrous eyes raised towards mine in all their radiant beauty, I must have been more than human not to yield to the rapturous triumph of that hour.　I led her out on the moonlit terrace, and, for the first time, breathed words of passionate love into her ear.　She listened, and checked me not, and I thought a tear fell on my hand.　When I paused for an answer, she recovered her usual composure, and told me that another time she would chide me for my folly, but in so bewitching a manner that I could have wished to be reproved for ever by so lovely a monitress.　Her husband called her in, to speak to some guest who was leaving the assembly, and thus we parted for several days.

" I called repeatedly at her house, but was invariably answered that the Countess was too indisposed to receive.

" During this interval, I had a conversation with Uberto Manno, which stung me to the quick.　Latterly, he had resumed, whenever we met, his old familiarity— doubtless, no longer finding in me an obstacle to his matrimonial plans for his daughter.　Madame Zamoysky was the subject of conversation among the visitors present. On leaving the house where we had met, he followed me to the door, and, in a whisper, complimented me on the miracle I had effected, in touching the heart of one as dazzling in her beauty as she had been hitherto invulnerable in her virtue.　I writhed under the hidden satire of the father of Virginia, and this within the hearing of

Carelli. A fearful doubt flashed across my mind. Was I, too, to be one of the many dupes formerly alluded to by a friend? I resolved to demand an interview of Madame Zamoysky, and probe her very heart. I wrote, accordingly, a most emphatic letter, imploring her, if I had not loved in vain, to wear, on the following Tuesday, a nosegay of white camelias, which I should offer to her on that day. Should she not grant my supplication, I resolved instantly to leave Rome, and endeavour to forget one who had led me to believe that my fondest hopes were about to be realized.

" I named Tuesday, for that day had been proposed previously by Madame Zamoysky, as a sort of farewell party to her immediate circle of friends in Rome. The remaining days that preceded the one so fraught with interest to me were spent in a state of feverish excitement; my whole destiny seemed, by the agony of suspense I endured, to be summed up in that one day.

" Tuesday at length arrived, and a more beautiful day never gladdened the opening spring. Though early in April, the weather was warm enough to allow the repast to be laid out on the grass, just within sight of this spot where we now sit. All the details of the pic-nic were organized by the Count Zamoysky, who, in such matters, enjoyed an undisputed supremacy.

" I watched, meanwhile, with torturing anxiety, each carriage that arrived, till the object of my solicitude, Madame Zamoysky, appeared in her all-surpassing loveliness, carrying in her hand the nosegay of camelias already mentioned. When I approached, she received me with her brightest smiles, and allowed me to pick from her nosegay a bud, which I proudly wore near my heart for the rest of that eventful day.

" Never did this fair enchantress exert to greater advantage her powers of captivation. Judge of the rapture
of my soul, to feel that all these blandishments were exerted for me, and me only.

" The weather seemed to exhilarate the spirits of all
present; the women were beautiful, the men all animation.
Additional zest was given to the pic-nic by the unlooked-
for apparition of a band of strolling Hungarian gipsies in
their fanciful costume; and many youthful couples were
to be seen eagerly inquiring from them of their future
destiny. Only late in the afternoon, Uberto Manno and
his daughter joined our party. Carelli hastened to her
side, with the tender eagerness of an affianced lover. A
young Russian tenor had just been singing his national
airs to the guitar, and a general wish was expressed that
Virginia should favour us with a song. She appeared
much distressed at the request, and said, she feared her
voice would fail her. But Carelli besought her to try only
one verse of ' Ah, che soffrir !' which was ever her song of
predilection. Was it my fancy ? As she turned to reply,
her dark blue eyes met mine, and I thought I read in them
reproach, and deep anguish. Her father hastily whispered to her, and instantly Virginia made an effort to sing.
She murmured, rather than sung, the touching complaint
of the Neapolitan poet ; but so heartfelt was the expression she gave, that each breath was hushed to catch the
low tones of her seraphic voice. She soon paused, and,
with artless grace, begged of Madame Zamoysky to finish
the verses, adding, that she would do more justice to the
composition than was in her power to effect. Then, com-
plaining of the damp of the evening, she rose to return
home, followed by her father and Carelli.

" A fast ebbing tide of pure and happy recollections

rushed through my memory, as I watched that fairy form
vanish in the distance; for I looked for the last time on
her, who will be to me, while life lasts, ' the day-star of
memory.'

" The Countess Zamoysky roused me from my reverie
by the impassioned fervour with which she sang. She
electrified all present. Virginia was forgotten in the enthusiasm of applause bestowed on the lovely virtuoso.

" At that moment one of the gipsies renewed her
whining importunities to tell me my fortune. A pang
shot across my heart, for she made a long-forgotten chord
vibrate in my memory—the predictions of Dame Marguerite,
apparently about to be fulfilled.

" Was not the month of April fatal to me and mine ?
Was not my whole soul enslaved by woman's charms —
enhanced by music's softest strains ?

" It had been agreed upon that the same party should
meet again in the evening at Madame Zamoysky's house.
Manno and his daughter did not come, but Carelli did;
and I observed that he talked long and earnestly to the fair
Countess. I vainly strove to speak to her a moment in
private; though I had never witnessed her whole demeanour more soft and yielding, still I fancied she avoided
giving me an opportunity to speak to her alone.

" I remembered that the Count Zamoysky was engaged to play whilst at the Russian embassy, and would
certainly not return home before two in the morning. I
therefore determined on creating an opportunity to solve
all my doubts respecting Madame Zamoysky's sentiments.

" At eleven, the company began to leave, and I
feigned to leave also; but, thoroughly acquainted with
every issue of the apartment, on finding myself alone in

the last drawing-room, I turned into a door on the left that led into the library, and which, I was aware, opened into Madame Zamoysky's boudoir. The library was lit by a single lamp. I was just enabled to find my way to the window, where I hastily concealed myself behind the thick damask curtains, in the deep embrasure of the window common to old Roman palaces. From it I could watch unseen whatever passed in the great receiving room, the windows of which were exactly opposite, and left open on the terrace. Thus I should be enabled, on seeing the last guest depart, to emerge from my retreat, and obtain the interview I so ardently sought.

" Soon after, I beheld the Countess alone; she remained wrapt in thought for a short time, her beautiful head resting on her arm, supported by the piano. She then drew from her bosom a small note, and, on perusing the contents, an air of soft regret subdued the brilliancy of her dazzling beauty. Might it not have been my letter she was reading, and perhaps despising me for the timid diffidence that restrained me from pouring forth my vows of passionate love at her feet?

" She roused herself, and, tearing the letter with a haughty air that became her well, left the room. The lights were all extinguished; the clock struck twelve— each stroke resounded on my beating heart. I listened to the retiring steps of the servants—then all was silent.

" I soon after heard distinctly the Countess's voice in the adjoining boudoir, dismissing her maid, and telling her that she would write till the Count's return home.

" Then only I ventured to leave my retreat, when, to my utter consternation, I heard a carriage roll into the court, and Monsieur Zamoysky's voice in the outer room, already described. Thus all retreat was cut off. He entered the library, giving me barely time to screen myself again from view, and in the perturbation of this crisis I upset a flower-stand, actually placed in the window where I stood.

" Zamoysky, guided by the noise, walked straight up to the window, and tore the curtains open. His wife, equally attracted by the same noise, entered from her own door, and found me face to face with her husband!

" The Count demanded of me what was my purpose in being thus suspiciously concealed in the vicinity of his wife's apartment at this hour of the night, and if he was to conclude it was with her consent.

" This demand gave Madame Zamoysky time to recover herself; and with admirable presence of mind, and all the dignity of offended virtue that conscious innocence ought alone to impart, she addressed herself to me, saying she defied me, by word or deed on her part, to exonerate myself from the outrage I had offered her, in thus invading the sanctity of her privacy; and then added, with galling irony, that it was a well-known weakness of Monsieur de Querancy's, to imagine his love acceptable where it was wholly unrequited. She then implored of Monsieur Zamoysky to forgive my youthful presumption, more to be pitied than resented, and retired into her apartment.

" While she still spoke, the veil which had hitherto obscured my blinded intellect had fallen for ever! Her beauty seemed to me abhorrent, since it was but the mask of a soul stained with perfidy of the darkest dye. That voice, which a few hours before I had compared to a syren's, sounded harsh and discordant, from the utterance of premeditated falsehood.

" Powerless—for there is no vengeance to be wreaked on a woman—maddened, and reckless, life appeared to

me an intolerable burthen. Gladly would I have offered
a defenceless breast to the weapon of an injured husband.
Animated by this feeling, I scorned all subterfuge, and
declared to the Count Zamoysky that I came there resolved not to leave an art untried to seduce his wife from
the path of conjugal duty, and therefore awaited his
wishes, to give every satisfaction to his offended honour.

"He sternly interrupted me by saying, 'Is it not
enough, sir, that your audacious presumption has exposed
a blameless wife to the comments of my servants, without
incurring further publicity and scandal to her fair fame
by a duel? Her wishes are ever my law. I merely request your absence from Rome for a time, and trust, for
the future, you will refrain from measuring a virtuous
woman's high sense of duty by the laxity of yours!'

"Struck dumb by such an odious combination of
treachery and meanness, I fled from the house, like one
pursued by avenging furies. I returned to the embassy,
and, late as it was, demanded an audience of the Duc
de L. M. After briefly relating my miserable discom-
fiture, I appealed to his paternal kindness to help me to
leave this now hateful city, and, if possible, enable me to
hide my cruel disappointments by some far distant
diplomatic appointment.

"The Duc de L. M. soothed my youthful anguish
with fatherly kindness, then wrote on the moment a letter
to the minister of foreign affairs, in Paris, begging of him
to forward my wishes. This done, I ordered post-horses,
and before daylight was on my way to France.

"Bitter were the reflections that tormented me on my
cheerless road home, which same road, but a year before,
I had travelled buoyant with the exhilarating visions of
early youth. But the deepest sorrow I felt was, to have

become an object of contempt to Virginia, and ridicule to the sarcastic Uberto Manno.

" Fortune favoured me so far, that I was enabled to effect an exchange with a brother diplomate, who was to have started within a few days for Rio Janeiro, but who gladly consented to take my vacant post at Rome.

" I had but one day to devote to my poor mother. Our meeting was a sad one, for she was painfully alarmed by the alteration of my whole appearance. In reply to her tender inquiries, I merely glanced at an unfortunate attachment to one already engaged; for I cared not to sully her pure mind by the fulsome tale of Madame Zamoysky's heartless coquetry; nor until this day have these details ever passed my lips. My mother saw me so firmly bent on trying to divert my cares by total change of scene, that she encouraged the idea; and thus I left my home for the second time, and joined at l'Orient a schooner bound for America.

" I spent nearly two years in the Brazils. When free from my diplomatic duties, I made long excursions into the interior parts, and occupied myself principally with botanical researches, for which I have a decided taste. I loved to explore those sublime solitudes, and reflect on the overthrow of such mighty empires to fulfil the inscrutable decrees of Providence! Among these great wrecks of the past, I tried to forget my pigmy sorrows, and sought oblivion of the hard lesson taught my wounded heart by the hollow arts of European civilisation.

" Towards the second spring of my stay in the Brazils, I joined a large party of travellers bound to the northern parts. On the third day after our departure from Rio Janeiro, my attention was arrested by an Italian artist relating the consternation he had witnessed at Rome, occasioned by the suicide of a most promising young brother artist, Antonio Carelli. Inexpressibly shocked at this news, I eagerly asked the Italian for further details.

" ' It appears,' he replied, ' that at the last exposition of modern paintings in Rome, his picture of ' The Guardian Angel ' was pronounced unanimously to be the finest production of the times. It created tenfold interest from the well-known fact, that his source of inspiration was his affianced bride, the lovely Virginia Manno. Favoured in love and by the arts, his rash act of self-destruction will ever remain a mystery. The day after his triumph, he was found dead in his studio ! His unhappy cousin, overcome by this fatal blow, has retired for a time, to give vent to her grief, in the convent on Monte Pincio, at Rome.'

" What a succession of thoughts and projects whirled through my brain on hearing of this unforeseen event ! But one idea was all absorbing — Virginia was again free ; and my first, my unforgotten love, might still be mine ! Carelli's untimely end led me to conclude that Virginia had not repaid his love. Like me, might she not have been the victim of Carelli's arts, prompted by the Countess Zamoysky ?

" My resolution was soon taken ; once more restored to hope, all future obstacles seemed easy to overcome. Instead of prosecuting this journey, I would return to Europe by a ship which was to sail the following week.

" I pleaded urgent business to excuse my abrupt departure from my fellow-travellers ; and having obtained astrong mule, resolved not to delay a moment till I could reach some public conveyance to take me back to Rio Janeiro.

" The sky was dark and lowering ; a low wind clearly

indicated the coming storm. All my companions endeavoured to turn me from braving alone in the forests the
coming tempest. Their friendly advice was lost on my
unwilling ears. They knew not of the fair prize which
would have tempted me to encounter far greater dangers
We parted company, and I rode on like one impelled by
irresistible fate. The storm raged about me with terrific
fury. My faltering mule, blinded by a vivid flash of
forked lightning, came down on its knees, and threw me
on some fragments of broken pillars, where I lay a senseless heap amid the fury of the elements.

" I afterwards learnt that I was found by a Jew pedlar
merchant returning to his home, a sort of place of way-
fare to benighted travellers in those solitary parts. Like
the good Samaritan, he picked me up, laid me across his
mule, and conveyed me to his home.

" On recovering my senses, my first question was to
inquire the day of the month, on account of the vessel
sailing for Europe. My host told me it was the first of
April. I shuddered; for again Dame Marguerite's warnings arose before me. I was seized with a burning fever,
from the wet to which I had been exposed, and soon after
became delirious, as I was afterwards told by this most
hospitable Hebrew. I lay stretched on a bed of sickness
for six weeks. My host had a good deal of medical knowledge, and to his care—but, above all, to my youth and
vigorous constitution—I owed my recovery.

" This deplorable accident retarded my return to
Europe for four months; at last, after an unfavourable
passage, I landed at Havre. My first impulse was to ask
for a newspaper; judge of my despair on reading, that
the daughter of the celebrated Uberto Manno had taken
the irrevocable monastic vows, at the convent of the Monte

Pincio, at Rome. Had it not been for the cruel mischance that delayed my return, I might have been in time to dissuade Virginia from her fatal resolution. Bereft of my last hope of happiness on earth, I sought my mother's counsels. She recommended me more than ever to pursue my career. I obtained a special mission to the East, where I first met you, my valued friend. I have declined promotion, not to be tied to one particular spot; and thus I intend to lead the life of a wanderer, tasting of every excitement in turn. But, alas! to you I confide that 'the heart—the heart is lonely still!' Its last throb will be for the loved one immured for ever in yon dark convent walls!"

The friends rose to leave the gardens, when, again attracted by the form and workmanship of the guitar, already mentioned, De Querancy examined it more closely, and observed engraved on it the initials "V. M., 1817."

Struck by this mysterious coincidence, he proposed to Clarence to obtain, if possible, further information on the subject, by inquiring at the Villa Pamphili Doria to whom this instrument belonged.

While he was speaking, a young girl ran up to them, claiming the guitar, saying, that she had been playing on it at the fountain, but having run home to attend her sick grandmother, she had been detained longer than she had expected.

De Querancy asked her her name. She replied, "Virginia Cecchini." On hearing this name, he bid her lead them at once to her relation—for such he remembered to have been the name of Virginia Manno's old nurse, whom she loved and regarded as a second mother. As they entered the room into which the young Italian introduced them, they found an elderly female spinning, evidently

suffering from the wasting effects of the malaria. On
seeing De Querancy, Camilla Cecchini uttered an exclamation of surprise, not unmixed with ·pleasure. She
greeted him as an old acquaintance, and said, " Ah, signor, I little thought I should ever have had the honour of
receiving you! Sad, sad events have taken place since
last we met!" (And tears rolled down her face as she
spoke.) " I see the purport of your visit," she added,
looking at the guitar De Querancy still held in his hand ;
" you must have already recognised it as belonging once
to my dear young mistress, and wonder, doubtless, how it
came into my humble possession." De Querancy bowed
assent, and she spoke as follows :—

" It was in 1818 that you left Rome, if I remember
well. Soon after that time, my poor child (as the Sig-
norina Manno ι. lowed me to call her) grew paler and
more sorrowful every day. We all concluded that this
deep grief was caused by her father's immovable resolution
to unite her to her cousin Antonio Carelli, who vainly
tried, by tenderness and violence in turn, to win her to
listen to his love. She sought relief to her cares in the
fulfilment of her pious and charitable duties, which obtained for her the touching surname of ' the Guardian
Angel.' It was this inspired her lover with his *chef-
d'œuvre*—since his death given to the nuns of Monte
Pincio. My dear mistress's only solace was to sit for
hours alone in her room, singing to the guitar. One evening she was thus employed, singing her favourite air,

' Ah, che soffrir mi resta !'

when Carelli surprised her, and I heard him in bitter tones
reproach her for her inexorable cruelty to him, and unavailing regrets for the worthless stranger.

s

" For the only time in her life, I believe, Virginia was roused to anger. She told him, with dignity, that it was ungenerous to persecute one who had never for a moment deceived him; that solely from obedience to her father she would accompany him to the altar, since he persisted in claiming an unwilling bride. ' Heartless one!' he exclaimed, ' then be the results of this declaration on your head!' And he rushed from her presence. A few hours afterwards he committed the dark deed which has con · signed his family to eternal sorrow.

" My young mistress, on that day of dreadful memory, attended, as usual, morning mass at the Convent of Monte Pincio, where she was loved as a daughter by all the good nuns. When I told her the fatal catastrophe, she was horror-struck, and accused herself of being the cause of Carelli's untimely end. Vainly I strove to console her; she bid me leave her, to find comfort in solitude and prayer, for she dared not return home and face her father's anguish! She judged rightly. Uberto Manno declared he would never forgive her in the first ebullition of his fiery passion. This was, unfortunately, repeated to his gentle child; and, heart-broken with remorse, she dedicated herself to a holy life of penance, in the hopes of atoning for her involuntary share in her cousin's death. Too late, Uberto Manno demanded the return home of his only child. He was made aware of her vow; he mourned, but dared not oppose it. After her taking the habit, he left Rome, and, I hear, seeks to forget the downfall of all his fondest hopes, in distant travels to the Eastern courts, where he is received with the royal hospitality due to his splendid talents.

" The day before my dear child pronounced the irrevocable vows, she called me into her cell, and holding to

me yon guitar, she said, 'My good Camilla, I love you as
a mother; therefore I wish to bequeath to you and yours
a remembrance of me, and one of the things dearest to me
on earth. Henceforth my voice shall only sing the prai es
of the Most High! Nor,' added she, in a low whisper,
'could I look on this guitar without my memory strayi g
back to earthly remembrances far too tender. Teach, y
Camilla, your granddaughter, and my godchild, to sing to
it the songs I loved best.' And as a relic have I treasured
ever since that guitar, which, for the first time to-day,
was taken out of my room by my grandchild to the
fountain.

" The Manno villa is now a deserted mansion. Though
made independent for the rest of my days by the bounty
of Uberto Manno, I consented to take charge of this villa,
in the absence of the Prince Pamphili Doria, hoping to
derive benefit to my health from its elevated situation."

De Querancy thanked her warmly for all the details
she had given, and rose to leave, when she beckoned him
back, and whispered, " To-morrow is Easter Sunday; *she*
will sing at high mass!"

The next morning Clarence went to St. Peter's, and
De Querancy attended high mass at the chapel of the
French convent of Monte Pincio. Strangers are admitted,
for the nuns who sing are entirely concealed by a thick
curtain, which screens them from public gaze.

When the friends again met to proceed on their
journey, De Querancy appeared wonderfully calm, and in
the evening ot that day he voluntarily spoke of his sensations in the convent. "Wildly," said he, "did my
heart beat, when the solemn silence of prayer was broken
by the unforgotten seraphic voice of my lost Virginia !

" The subject chosen, sung in Latin, signified, ' The

Lamb has redeemed his sheep ; Christ, who was innocent,
has reconciled sinners to his Father.' How render the
convincing truth, the ineffable expression, the inspired
singer gave to these sublime words ? She infused into all
present the glad tidings of mercy and hope. For me, my
head buried in my hands, I knelt motionless, drinking
in each sound of that loved voice! When high mass
was over, I remained alone in the chapel, overwhelmed
with an intense feeling of solitude ; it seemed as if I
had enjoyed a foretaste of heaven, but to feel still more
my exile on earth. As I once more raised my dejected
head, the bright rays of the noonday sun attracted my
eyes to a picture on the side of the chapel ; there I beheld
Carelli's beautiful conception of the Guardian Angel.
There stood Virginia, arrayed in flowing robes of white ;
her fair hair, as if gently supported by the wind, formed
a crown of golden glories round her angelic head ; her
azure eyes, beaming with a soft, but all-penetrating gaze,
seemed to search the depths of my desponding soul ;
whilst her parted lips, and hand raised towards heaven,
indicated that permanent rest was only to be found there.
The kneeling Christian, clinging to her gown, his dark
brow resplendent with genius, yet marked by doubt and
grief, was a most faithful portrait of the unfortunate
Carelli. Long—long did I dwell on this sublime picture,
and as I did so, a holy calm entered my troubled soul ;
I felt invigorated with new and healthy ideas ; I knelt
before this image of spotless purity—touching victim of
the unruly passions of men—and vowed to lead, henceforth, a life more worthy of the love she had felt for me,
by forgetting my own selfish sorrows in helping to assuage
those of my fellow-creatures.

" Before leaving the convent, I wrote to request of the

abbess to allow me to have a miniature copy of the *chef d'œuvre* in their possession, and begged to offer a donation to the orphan asylum belonging to them. My two demands were graciously received. I thus learnt that sister Virginia had the orphan asylum under her special care; she was described to me as a perfect saint on earth — so rigorous in her austerities, (though apparently delicate,) so indefatigable in her admirable charity to all. How my hand shook as I wrote my name in the book, with the exact date, among the various benefactors of the convent. I breathed a fervent prayer that my name might be read, at some future time, by the ' saint-like' Virginia, and—oh, blessed thought!—she would, perchance, rejoice in her holy influence over me."

The sequel of this touching narrative was made known to me by Clarence, after his friend the Marquis de Querancy's death, which occurred in 1832.

" Great," said he, " was the change wrought in my noble friend the Marquis de Querancy, dating from the time of his visit to the convent of Monte Pincio. No longer yielding to that mournful apathy which had so long lulled the bright faculties of his powerful understanding, he seemed upheld by some secret impulse, which led him onwards, unerringly, to every ennobling pursuit.

" After having concluded most satisfactorily his diplomatic mission to the court of Naples, he returned to Paris, and soon afterwards spoke, for the first time, in the Chamber of Peers. All present were filled with respectful ad-miration at the sentiments he professed on that occasion ; his unaffected piety, fervent patriotism, and extended views of benevolence, were worthy of the disciple of Chateaubriand, and portrayed with the vivid eloquence of .Berryer

" Frugally simple in his person and tastes, he devoted his fortune to every laudable purpose, and by his personal exertions improved inconceivably the country and peasantry surrounding his estates in Brittany.

" One of the traits I admired most in my lamented friend was, that though perfectly insensible to the charms of the fairer sex, he never affected cynicism or contempt towards the follies of other young men, and thus won over more than one from the paths of vice, by the encouraging example afforded by his own exemplary life.

" In 1830, when the elder branch of the Bourbons were expelled from the throne of France, faithful to the political creed of his ancestors, he protested against and declined to serve the newly-elected King of the French ; and hoping for better times, he vowed unalterable fidelity to the youthful Henri de Bordeaux, that innocent victim of the faults of his forefathers.

" In the year 1832, when the cholera raged so fearfully in Paris, the Marquis de Querancy, who was there at the time, instead of flying the fatal contagion, thanked Heaven that he had found a vast arena, wherein to exercise the all-engrossing charity which animated his whole being.

" He is known to have emulated, and shared to the utmost extent, the untiring zeal and holy labours of the poorest Catholic priest at this dread era in the annals of human sufferings. Like them, filled with holy abnegation of self, he was ever to be found at the pallet of the plague-stricken ; his immense charity and heroic courage are recorded but by the all-seeing eye of God.

" At last, worn out and exhausted by mental and bodily fatigue, my poor friend was afflicted by a pulmonary complaint, which the faculty at once declared to be beyond all human remedies. His mother came up to Paris to attend his dying moments, and I found her worthy of the tender veneration her son had always entertained for her.

" Most grateful was I to be thus enabled to share, if not to alleviate, the sorrow of this heart-stricken mother.

" On the evening of his death, De Querancy profited by his mother's absence from the sick-room to speak to me in private.

" So emaciated was my poor friend by illness, that it would have been difficult to recognise in him the once so admired Arthur de Querancy. But a higher, holier beauty now adorned his head; it was the calm serenity imparted by the high faith of the dying Christian.

" ' Is it not singular, dear Clarence,' said he, ' that Dame Marguerite should have prophesied so true, for to-day is my birth-day, the 20th of April! But I die most happy, for I have borne my cross,' said he, looking mournfully on the miniature of the Guardian Angel, which never left him. ' Think you not, Clarence, that I am now more worthy of the pure love of my Guardian Angel ?'

" As he yet spoke, his mother approached the bed-side, and offered him the calming draught she had left him to prepare.

" De Querancy bent gently forward to accept it, and in this dying effort breathed his last sigh on that fond maternal bosom, whence he had derived the first sustenance of life."

At the conclusion of the foregoing tale, a gentleman, in whose mien and bearing there was something which bespoke the gallant profession to which his life had been devoted, and whose bronzed complexion showed evidently that he had stood the brunt of "the battle and the breeze," took up from the table at which he was sitting an exquisite design of a dismantled ship under severe stress of weather, and, addressing the Lady Eva, said, " If you will let me tell you a simple tale of the sea, of which this drawing reminds me, it may serve, rude though it be, to afford time for others to prepare something more worthy the occasion on which we are met together—an occasion which it would grieve me not to be allowed to assist in cele-brating."

The offer was gladly greeted by Lady Eva and all the company, and the gallant veteran proceeded to relate

THE NUBIAN SLAVE.

" Mislike me not for my complexion ;
  I wear the shadowy livery of the sun,
  To whom I am near neighbour."
                              SHAKSPEARE.

OVER a parched and arid desert a train of captives painfully pursued their way.   The air was heavy with intense heat.   The sun, whose outline was obscured by the hazy atmosphere, seemed to communicate to the vast surface of heaven his own burning and blinding power. A pale and sickly hue of yellow coloured the whole scene. It gave to sky and desert the same scorched aspect, and from its universal and intolerable glare was infinitely more dreadful than the fierce brilliance of an unclouded noon. The sand, level, and to the eye boundless, had a hard and polished surface, which presented an image of frightful sterility. That saffron light cast no shadow on the earth. The fainting traveller looked in vain for the reflection of his form. There was no shade, no air. Around, below, above, heat was present, as if it were concentrated into a palpable substance, resting heavily on the head, weighing down the limbs, oppressing and suffocating perspiration.

To rest was to perish. The captives, with languid steps and throbbing temples, moved on, animated by the prospect of moistening their parched lips, as the guide indicated that wells were at hand. "Water! water!" was repeated in many dialects of Africa, one desire, in a dozen languages, and by hundreds of voices, — "Water, water, or we die!"

Old Haloo, the chief of the band, whose life had been passed in the traffic of slaves, looked on the fainting throng, as if to calculate how much longer nature could support existence. He took a skin from his camel's back, drank himself, and wetted the mouth of the beast. His prisoners waited with expectation. "Oh, water," muttered he; "if you want water, you must move more quickly." He menaced those who seemed most eager for relief with a heavy scourge. He was understood, and the unhappy beings endeavoured to quicken their pace.

The train was numerous. Most of the captives were young, some mere children, others rising into youth, others approaching husty maturity. Those who carried on the traffic in human life understood their trade. The young were sooner tamed and more docile to command. More died, it is true, but they cost little, either to take or to keep. They did not attempt to escape, so there was something saved in fetters. A ship would carry twice or thrice as many of them as of full-grown beings; and if they were judiciously chosen, they sold well.

In this band there were almost as many girls as lads and men. With few exceptions, all were unconfined. There was no fear of their attempting to escape upon the Desert. Their homes were hundreds of miles away. Around the neck of each was a bag, containing roasted maize. This was the sole provision for their journey. Each carried a supply for several days. They received water only at the appointed resting-places, which were often at the distance of a long and weary day's travel. They were driven forward like a herd of cattle, kept from straying by natural instinct. When they approached a habitable country, they were bound together in gangs, to prevent any from deserting. In this mode they were hurried to the sea-shore, to be borne across the Atlantic, and commence their life of slavery.

But now they thought not of the future. They had but one wish; they believed that they should be happy if they could but satisfy the thirst which consumed them. Panting, and with swollen tongue protruding from the mouth, they pressed on, repeating the one word that animated them to exertion. Some, unable to endure their agony longer, fell. They were left to perish on the burning sand. In the Desert life was cheaper than water.

The horrors of that day drew to a close at last. In the distance, the guides who had advanced were seen filling skins and vessels from the well. A cry of joy resounded through the train. The single camel of the expedition stretched forth his long neck, and quickened his pace, while his large lips trembled with desire. As the resting-place was reached, the sun went down, and water and shade were attained together. The younger captives forgot everything in the exquisite sense of relief and delight they experienced. When their wants were relieved they were careless of the future, and sank to rest beneath the large palms, which, at the edge of the Desert, gave promise of a more fruitful country.

One man alone had performed that day's march with fetters to his wrists, and a thick rope attached to his ankles. He had been brought from a province of Nubia, where the White River watered the sultry plains, and tall mountains cast on them a grateful shade. A tribe of the Desert had invaded his village, burnt the dwellings to the ground, and made him prisoner. He had struggled desperately, but in vain; though well had he maintained his reputation for courage, and justified the confidence reposed in him. Three of the savages fell by his hand; at last, he was only overpowered by numbers. Bound hand and foot, he had been transferred from one tribe to another, till he formed part of the band destined for the sea-coast. This man was prized by Old Haloo, for his youth, large frame, and prodigious strength. No labour seemed to tire him, no punishment to subdue his spirit. He never complained. He took food and water when offered him, but he never asked for either, and, unlike the other captives, he disdained to carry provision for his journey. He was considered of too much value to be neglected, and so was supplied with sufficient nourishment to support life. He had more than once endeavoured to escape, and was now so fettered, that no struggles could avail him. At night, he was securely tied to several of the other prisoners.

When the well was reached, this man had thrown himself to the ground and closed his eyes. Water was paraded before him, but he did not heed it. He did not stretch forth his hand for one draught of that precious fluid which the herd of captives sought so eagerly.

All were first served, and then were taken to him a few drops of water, sufficient to support life, but not to quench thirst. This was gratuitous torture, for the element was now abundant. When the vessel was offered to him, he struck it to the ground, and dealt a heavy blow to the slave who bore it. His outcries brought Old Haloo to the spot. He was enraged, but did not wish to lose the hundred dollars which he knew he should receive for so valuable a prize on the coast, and a larger supply was brought. The Nubian drank it, and ate some grains of maize. He next received the punishment of the scourge, ordered him for his disobedience, without a word, and appeared easily to fall asleep.

There are people who hold that the colour of the skin affects the rights of humanity. They hear of an African's stripes and chains with indifference, for he has thick lips and woolly hair. He is not of the Caucasian race; perhaps, even, he may have little sense of physical pain. Why should they care for agonies that cannot be told told in a civilized tongue! Freedom was made for the white skin, slavery for the coloured. Thus is God's creation abused. Never does he give life but for enjoyment. Man makes the existence of his fellow one scene of wretchedness and torture.

No one could pierce into the thoughts of the Nubian that night, or tell the pains of his body, the misery of his spirit. He lay still, but he did not rest. Sometimes a low groan escaped him, which he sought to suppress, as unworthy his fortitude. His bonds had fretted him, and now he could gain no relief from their pressure. To him, of all the band, that night brought no relief. He longed for the dawning of day, though with it his sufferings would re-commence; the rest and silence of night he found more intolerable than the toils and action of the day.

In his village home some scattered light of Christian truth had reached him. He had gathered that one God reigned in heaven, and that love and justice were his attributes. Often were his fettered hands raised to the sky. Was his muttered prayer for deliverance, or for vengeance? He must have thought the answer long delayed. Yet it did not seem that hope deserted him. His fellow-captives sometimes saw him on his knees, and they attributed his surprising resolution and untiring strength to the supernatural aid he received in those moments from the Deity he worshipped.

Twelve days more of privation and of fatigue to fainting, brought that band, in diminished numbers, to the shore. The discipline that tames the lion and the tiger—hunger and weariness—had made them obedient to the slightest gesture of their drivers. They were weak in body, but yet weaker in spirit. They humbly entered the boats, though the raging surf threatened their destruction, and were conveyed on board the vessel anchored in the distance. The Nubian went with the rest, for he was now incapable of resistance. If these poor creatures had any thought, they must have wondered for what end irons were riveted to their limbs, when they of themselves were almost incapable of moving them. They were stowed thickly in the hold, without light and without air. The slave-decks were ready, the schooner sank deep in the water with her cargo of flesh and blood, and the anchor was raised.

Fair, but roughly, blew the breeze. The vessel rose to the swell, and gallantly flew over the waters to the west. Night and day the ship rolled onwards, no pause in her

motion for an instant, no abatement of the heaving of the
waters. Frightful were the groans and shrieks of the
captives. " 'Tis no matter," said the captain ; " they are
safe. No escape here." He was wrong. The escapes
were numerous. Each morning the dead were separated
from the living — not before. Those who were not on the
watch, yet heard in their berths below the sullen plash in
the waters which sounded the funeral knell of the victims.

It was horrible to see the shoal of sharks which followed that ship. They seemed, like the rolling waters, to
know no rest. They knew their prey was in that vessel,
and they never forsook it. Often, in the day they were
not seen. They knew their time, and they observed it
regularly. Long before the sun rose, these monsters, in
the earliest dawn of light, were observed moving on the
surface of the water, opening their huge jaws, springing
over each other, touching the sides of the ship, as if they
smelt their prey through the planks, and manifesting the
most furious eagerness to obtain it.

The captain was naturally more careless than cruel.
When matters went well, he was good-humoured enough ;
but when crossed, he lost all control over himself, and his
bad passions blazed forth with irrestrainable fury. In his
wrath he was a perfect fiend. The slave-trade brought
him wealth, and he was indifferent about the rest. There
are many characters like his in the world, though not all
are exposed to the same temptation, who suffer themselves
to be guided by events, without a thought for the consequences. He had no interest in his cargo, but he felt a
pride, as he expressed it, in landing it in good order. He
had amassed wealth, for his schooner was a smart thing,
and had distanced many an English cruiser. She had so
good a look about her, too, that she was not often sus-

pected, and besides the traffic in slaves, the captain did
something in ivory, and other commodities. He was
British born, and had been bred to the sea, but had
lived a free life in the West Indies. For the last ten
years he had said, " A few more trips, and I will give over
this trade ;" but the temptation was too strong for him.
The profits of a run from Africa to the Brazils or Cuba
were enormous, and he was so well known, and had so
great a reputation for dexterity and success, that he had
abundance of commissions offered him. No one, it was
found, made the passage so quick, or brought home so full
a cargo. As for the guilt of his occupation, that troubled
not him. When his wife remonstrated, he shook a bag of
gold in her ear. " Negroes, hey," said he, after a successful voyage, " pooh, pooh ! My trade is in gold dust,
nothing else." This man was as fond of his family as
one of his rugged nature could be, and for his sole child,
a girl, he hoarded the wealth made by his perilous and
criminal voyages.

His present cargo had been reduced in strength beyond
the safe limit. Their wretched confinement, coming immediately after their dreadful journey, had produced a
malignant fever among them, and the mortality was so
great that it seemed likely the captain would have but a
scanty complement to land. This soured his temper, and
when some of the crew fell sick, and he had scarcely hands
enough to work the vessel, he fretted like an enraged
brute. He had but one consolation. The voyage promised to be unusually rapid. He was bound for the
Havannah, and though he had lost a third of the slaves
on board, he congratulated himself on being within three
or four days' sail of port. A new mortification awaited
him.

The wind changed, and with the change his glass fell. He saw certain indications of stormy weather, and prepared to meet it, cursing the mischance which deprived him of half-a-dozen stout hands. Thick clouds gathered, but at night the wind went down with the sun. In the morning it increased to a gale, and, as if to complete his ill-luck, a fine brig was seen in the distance with the Union Jack flying at her mast-head. She was an English cruiser, that was quite clear; and it was soon evident that she had suspicions of the schooner, and was crowding all sail the gale would allow her to carry in pursuit. The captain's mind was made up to run for it. He hoisted canvass till the schooner's mast groaned with the press, and adopted every resource of experienced seamanship to baffle his pursuer. He resolutely disregarded all signals. He believed that he could hold his distance till night, and in the darkness he did not doubt he could escape. But it soon appeared that the cruiser was the better sailer, and that her commander, heavy as the gale was, did not fear to put her sailing qualities to the proof. By noon, the distance was greatly lessened, and the captain saw that the guns of his enemy would be brought to bear upon him long before night.

His position was desperate, and he determined to try an expedient which he had more than once before found successful. A raft was rudely constructed of some spare spars; to this were lashed half-a-dozen of the captives. Their entreaties were no more regarded than the whistling of the wind. As a wave advanced, the raft was lowered to its surface. The result was watched by the crew of the slaver with breathless suspense. The captain calculated rightly on the humanity of the English commander. The height of the sea was disregarded — a boat was lowered from the brig; the chase was for a moment slighted, in anxiety to save the wretched beings whom the waves threatened each instant to engulph. They were safely got on board, but not until the distance between the two vessels was perceptibly increased. Three several times was the same plan tried with the like success. At evening the schooner was still beyond the range of her pursuer's guns.

Still the gale increased; the sky was obscured by pitchy clouds, and the schooner plunged madly through the darkness. Tremendous squalls of wind and hail swept the decks; one fearful sea, breaking over the bows, carried away part of her bulwarks. Every inch of canvass was taken in, but not before two seamen had been carried from the yards with the sail they were reefing. The long swollen waves strained the vessel fearfully, as she scudded under bare poles. At one moment she rose on the crest of a mountain of water, and at the next plunged down into the black gulph which seemed yawning to swallow her up.

It is a horrible thing when the bad passions of man mingle with the wrath of the elements — when the lightning's flash is answered with a sharp curse, and the awful peal of thunder with a blaspheming laugh. So it was in that night of storm. The captain, infuriated by the events of the day, raved on the deck like a maniac. He stood by the helm with clenched teeth. In the darkness of night his eyes flashed fire. There was murder in every glance.

Suddenly a wild uproar rose from below, a clanking of chains, and a rush against the slave-decks and bulk-headings, which made the stout timbers of the schooner quiver. The captives, feeble as they were, had become possessed with the strength of madness, as they felt the waters rising round them. The ship had sprung a leak.

T

and the sea rushed in through the gaping seam. The
desperate slaves, banded together, rushed against the par-
titions which confined them, or trampling down the
weakest, made a platform of their bodies, and beat their
fetters against the decks above them.

The seamen, worn out at the pumps, left them. The
ship, they said, wanted lightening.

The captain laughed devilishly as he caught their
words. "Ha! ha!" he raved, "we'll lighten the ship
and quiet those noisy fellows down here together. Now
run out a plank there: so, so. There shall be a clean
ship, if we're caught at last."

The slaves were ordered up on deck by half-dozens.
They complied with alacrity, believing that they should be
saved from the waters that rose around them, reaching
now almost to the necks of those who were stowed lowest.
They came, to meet a more certain and speedy death. The
captain's hoarse voice was heard above the howling of the
storm : "If they resist, kill them, and throw their bodies
overboard." All shared the same fate ; there was no distinction of sex or age. Most fled from the gleaming steel
to the raging waters. That wild scene of massacre is too
horrid for mortal view.

* * * * * *

With the last batch came the Nubian, worn almost to
a skeleton, yet with some portion of his vigour remaining.
He obeyed the order, and came on deck. He had heard
the screams of those who ascended before him, and at a
glance saw his intended fate. A plank stretched to the
sea; he must tread it, or be cut down by the cutlasses of
the merciless men around him. He advanced firmly and
unresistingly to the plank. As his foot touched it, and
the armed men were off their guard, he turned, and his

eyes met those of the captain, glaring with the fury of a
tiger, about to spring upon his prey. The glance exchanged
was momentary, but of terrible import. It spoke the
mortal hatred and defiance of deadly foes. The captain
raised his arm to strike. The Nubian sprang aside, struck
with his fettered arm a sailor who opposed him, into the
sea, and leaping forward, agilely ascended the foremast,
clinging to portions of the rigging. With a fierce oath,
the captain called for a musket; he raised it to fire. At
that instant the clouds opened, and his aim was dazzled by
a stream of lightning, which, illuminating for an instant
all the scene, showed the Nubian clinging to the mast, yet
shaking his chains in defiance at his enemy—the blood-
stained deck, the dimmed cutlasses, the black waves, and
here and there a human form, tossing up its hands in wild
despair above its head, ere it sank for ever in the depths
of ocean. The rage of the elements was hushed for a
moment, as in awe, but as the thunder rolled away, a terrific storm-gust made the ship groan fearfully; another,
and the foremast, snapping near the waist, fell with a
tremendous crash into the boiling sea.

In the morning, the schooner lay like a log upon the
water. But her pursuer was nowhere to be seen, and she
reached port in safety. Of her captives, not one remained.
When the blood-stains were scraped from the deck, all
trace of the massacre was lost.

Through the night the Nubian clung to the mast.
Despite of his chained hands, he lashed part of the rigging
around him, and kept himself above the sea. When day
broke, he raised his head, but he could see only the moun-
tainous waters rising on every side. As the long waves
swept by, he could discern the heads of sunken rocks above
the trough in which he rolled. A few sea-birds flew above

him, as if awaiting the moment when life should be extinct,
to dart upon his body. These signs assured him that land
was near, though he despaired of reaching it. He was
saved beyond hope.

A maiden, in the first blush of youth, and bright and
beautiful as morning, looked from the topmost window of
her dwelling on the northern shore of Jamaica. She was
watchful, for her father was at sea, and she had been
taught to dread the fatal fury of the tempest, as she
dreaded the hurricane which sometimes swept the shore of
produce and of life. She perceived a speck on the distant
waters, though hardly could she discern a living form.
Issuing from her dwelling, she hastened to the beach, and
offered a reward to the fishers who would venture forth
and make for that fragment of a wreck—a father, she
said, might be clinging to it in agony. A stout boat was
manned; it returned with the senseless Nubian. He had
fainted when taken from the mast. The young girl had
him conveyed to her house; there he was tended during
a delirious fever. His language was not understood; but
the visions that distracted his mind could be gathered from
his gestures. He shrank appalled from the frightful
images terror had stamped upon his brain, or with raised
hands seemed to call down maledictions from Heaven upon
the authors of the guilty scenes that were ever present to
his fancy.

His treatment was kind and merciful. A great reproach
had just been removed from the English name. The truth,
long since recognised, that all men were brothers of one
great family, was now practically acted on. Property in
man was abolished in all our possessions; a coloured skin
was no longer thought unfit for freedom or deemed a bar
to the immortality of heaven.

In the gentle breast of this young maiden a peculiar
interest had been awakened for the African race. She
had been taught that a long arrear of justice and benevolence was due to them for the wrongs they had suffered,
and her heart, filled with pure and kind feeling, gladly
received lessons which made the exercise of its gracious
tendencies a duty. A minister of the English church had
settled in the neighbourhood of her dwelling. He had left
home, ambitious hopes, the pleasures of society, the chance
of distinction and wealth, to take up his abode in this
retired district, that he might gather the despised negroes
into a church, and prepare them for freedom. In the long
intervals of her father's absence, the sweet girl found in
this good man a friend and instructor. Delighted with
the child-like and artless simplicity of her nature, he
watched over her education, and taught her the graces of
polished life. He was glad that she had rescued the ship-
wrecked Nubian, and now attended to him ; for he believed
that all the virtues required exercise, and that they
flourish best when their blossom is left to ripen into
fruit.

The name of this young girl was Mary Langley.
She was a child when her mother died, and as she saw
her father so seldom, her disposition had been much left
to the guidance of Nature. She grew up with the untrained beauty of the plants that made her home a garden.
In her heart, the love and charities of her faith had
flourished in the wilder luxuriance for being untrained.
When her father saw her, he was satisfied with her
lovely and blooming appearance. Though now rising
into womanhood, he would still treat her as a child,
would take her up in his rough arms as he did in her
infancy, and let her silky brown tresses flow on his breast,

while her graceful arms embraced his neck, and he decked her out with trinkets. He could not understand all the tenderness of her character, nor make out why she was sometimes sad when he was boisterous in mirth. He saw in her only the innocence and endearments of childhood. Sometimes she would laughingly try to make him share her feelings. He listened as men do who hear mysteries of which they can make nothing, so he interrupted her by telling her what a fortune she would have when she was a woman. Yet these two beings, so opposite in sentiment and disposition, loved each other fondly. Nature had linked them together with those mysterious bonds of affection which triumph over time, separation, and death. If her father did not soon return, the maiden was to join him at a port in South America.

The Nubian recovered, but it was evident that he had suffered much; his manner was dejected and reserved, and sometimes it seemed that the visions of his delirium returned, for a convulsive movement, momentary but frightful, passed over his usually rigid features. He appeared not wholly ignorant of Christianity, for he recognised a gold cross which Mary wore about her neck, and devoutly kissed it as the emblem of salvation. On the past he was silent; a nurse, who had recognised some words he had spoken in his fever, addressed him in the same tongue, but he remained mute. He made rapid progress, however, in acquiring some knowledge of English. When he spoke in that language, he said he had been dragged from his home, and wrecked on his passage. He would say no more.

His gratitude to the young girl who had saved him seemed boundless; he recognised her as the preserver of his life, and was willing to devote himself to her service.

Her care in his recovery, her kind tones, her beaming smile when she met him, penetrated his heart with a sense of her goodness. His large frame remained motionless while she addressed him, his full and expressive eyes alone spoke his emotion, and betrayed the eagerness with which he sought to comprehend her meaning, when he only partially understood her words. He seemed to know her wishes by intuition, and to take delight in studying and gratifying her tastes. Her garden, under his care, was beautifully kept. The spot was richly favoured by nature, it was open to the cool winds, and shaded from the fierce heats by hills, and plantations of cocoas and tamarinds. All the choice and varied vegetation of the fertile soil assumed, under his hands, the most luxuriant growth and beautiful arrangement. There was no toil to which he seemed unequal. Once Mary expressed a wish for a shaded walk, the Nubian knew no rest until the appointed space was planted with young trees of the choicest kinds.

When abroad, an antelope and an elephant could scarcely have presented a greater contrast than these two beings. Mary was only just rising into womanhood, though in that ardent clime nature brings the human form, as she does all other things, to maturity earlier than in colder regions. For her height, her shape was exquisitely delicate,—only beginning to acquire that smooth roundness which indicates the ripening of the child into the maiden. All her motions were full of airy joyousness; she had been subjected to none of the discipline of schools, and loved to let the evening air sweep her tresses from her face, and to play amid the wild luxuriance and beautiful solitudes of her home, with the delights that Nature presented to her. The Nubian's massive frame was firmly knit; he had just entered into the period of vigorous manhood; his motions were grave, slow, and measured. When the young girl was revelling in the soft cool air, that blew from the ocean at evening, he remained standing motionless, like a colossal statue, with his hands crossed upon his breast, and his eyes to the earth. They seemed personifications of grace and power met in amity. Hers was the will to devise, his the strength to execute.

The Nubian was attentive to the offices of the church, and had been formally baptized by the name of Christian. The good minister, regretting to see his time passed in a way that could be little useful to him, mentioned in his hearing, that labour was greatly wanted at a neighbouring plantation, and that, in the present scarcity of hands, strength and industry were equal to a fortune. He had not calculated wrongly on the Nubian's quickness—the next morning he was gone. The young girl pouted a little for his loss, but the minister showed her how much better a life of toil would be for Christian, by which he might realize an independence, than a life of profitless servitude. She was convinced, and yielded.

The Nubian's proffered service was readily accepted. He toiled with unremitting energy, and was speedily noticed as a prosperous man. His savings were large, and were prudently invested. He soon saw that in this country wealth was power, and power he coveted, to realize the projects which now began to shape themselves in his soul.

He saw the gentle Mary but once in the week,—he knelt with her in the house of prayer. When the service was ended, he stood beyond the church porch, tranquil and motionless, to wait her words. His answers to her questions were brief, yet, it seemed, nothing of what she said was lost to him. He appeared impassible and motionless, but each accent of her tongue was treasured up in his heart. For her he often obtained the choicest fiuit, the finest mangoes, the largest cocoas; sometimes too, rare shells and beautiful plants. These offerings were delivered to her attendants without a word. He departed as swiftly and as silently as he came.

A sorrow, which no care could remove, clouded the brow of the sweet girl. Her father wrote to her of crosses and misfortunes, which rendered it impossible for him to come to the island. Months after those notices of disaster came word that she should quit her home in a vessel which would call for her, and join him at Rio Janeiro. He intended, he said, finally to settle at Jamaica, but he had arrangements to make first, and he could not bear longer to be deprived of the delight of seeing his dear daughter. She who had been born on this spot was loth to leave the flowers she had tended with so much care,—the domestics who had grown so fond of her,—the dear minister who had been her friend from childhood; she loved them all, yet her heart told her the faithful Christian would suffer from her absence the most. When she took leave of him, he remained mute and still, as though he had no power of motion; but he lost not a word of her parting instructions. She would write often, she said, to the good minister. His eye glistened with delight as she added, "And sometimes to you too, Christian, for I shall never cease to take an interest in your welfare." He made no answer, but kneeling, raised her hand to his lips. His gesture was full of devotion and love; he seemed to be performing an act of adoration; when he rose, he bent his head upon his breast and left her.

There are breaks in real life, which its historian does but imitate when he passes over months or years with little comment. Not that preparations for great events

are not in progress, but that the movement is so slow and
gradual, and often so hidden from human view, that its
progress cannot be traced day by day. When Etna volleys
forth its flame and lava, we note the awful progress of
destruction with fear and wonder, and chronicle its minutest
effects. But we think nothing of the mountain while it
remains in repose, though in its quietude a powerful
agency is working in its breast, and each hour it gathers
force and materials for a new explosion.

Four years passed by, and then a letter was received
from Mary, announcing her speedy arrival. Her father
would follow; she came first to prepare his reception.

In this interval the Nubian prospered beyond all expectation. By his unceasing labour he had amassed
wealth, which the diminished value of land enabled him
to lay out to excellent advantage. When the foundation of
his fortune was thus laid, his progress was rapid, for on
himself he spent nothing. A fortunate speculation proved
his shrewdness. He foresaw the failure of the next year's
sugar-crop, and bought extensively at a low price; the
result justified his expectations. He cleared an enormous
profit by the transaction, and at once established himself
both as a merchant and a planter. His estates were
thenceforth prudently managed. He was a kind but vigilant master, and soon acquired all the details of commerce.
He still maintained his reserve of manner, but with that
few persons troubled themselves; they were content to
know that he was prosperous and wealthy.

When Miss Langley arrived, he was the first to welcome her. To her his fortunes had made no change in
his manner; he was still humble and submissive in her
presence as when he first devoted himself to her service.
She found her home more beautiful than she left it, for the

Nubian had been unceasing in his care to heighten the
charms of the spot; nothing had been omitted that could
gratify her taste, or minister to her convenience. He had
made that sheltered dell a paradise of nature, having collected in it whatever was most rare and beautiful in that
beautiful clime. When, after her first burst of pleasure at
the improvement she saw around, she remonstrated at the
expense that must have been incurred, the Nubian intimated, in a quiet though sufficiently expressive manner,
that he regarded her as his mistress still, and held himself
indebted to her for all that he possessed. Mary was
touched by gratitude so fervent and unusual; she allowed
the Nubian to pursue that course from which he seemed
to derive most pleasure, and he was thankful to her for
this compliance with his wishes. Each morning he sent
to her some token of his remembrance, trifling, but sufficient as a tribute of homage. To him this seemed an
acknowledgment that his life was due to her, as a single
prayer in the morning consecrates us to the service of
Heaven through the day. He saw her but once a-week,
on the Sabbath, as before; and he still waited, with crossed
arms, beyond the porch, for her to address him. Sometimes he escorted her home, and walked with her through
the beautifully shaded paths he had helped to form. Custom easily reconciles us to outward appearance. Mary no
longer thought of the colour of his skin; she conversed
with him, as she did with the minister, and regarded him
as almost a dear friend. She was pleased with his penetrating remarks; and on his side he was never wearied of
hearing Mary's descriptions of the various lands she had
visited. Her voice was, in his ear, sweeter harmony than
music could ever form. He never ventured to speak of

her personal appearance, yet he thought, and with truth, that she had become more lovely during her absence.

Mary was at this time one-and-twenty. Born of English parents, her skin had been purely fair, but it had been tinged by the sun, so that it had now always that shade of beautiful and healthy red which we observe with admiration colours the face and bust of a blonde, when exertion or excitement makes the blood dance with quicker motion through the veins. From contrast with this hue of her complexion, her eyes appeared of a deeper and purer blue, and to float in more brilliant lustre. Her bright hair hung in curling masses down her face, framing the sweet profile, which looked forth in gay playfulness. She had become more thoughtful, but not less innocent. Her travel had taught her more of the world's crimes, but had not fixed one stain upon her heart.

The morning was bright, when a ship was perceived in the distance. Langley had at length arrived to commence his life of calm tranquillity. The news ran over the neighbourhood, and the surrounding residents came down to the beach to welcome the voyager,—the Nubian with the rest. Mary was caught in her father's embrace as he stepped from the beach. Her companionship had smoothed the natural roughness of his disposition. He returned kind greetings to all who met him, clasping the good minister warmly by the hand. Mary turned to introduce the Nubian, but he was nowhere to be seen. She was vexed at this, for she wished to present him to her father at a favourable moment, when he would perceive the estimation in which the fortunate Christian was held. She knew his general dislike and contempt of coloured people, and for that reason had not said a word to him of Chris

tiac's rescue from the sea by her means. She preferred
that her father should first view him prosperous, before he
was told of his destitution some years previously.

From that day the Nubian was absent for weeks. At
his dwelling it was told that he had been called by urgent
business to Kingston, the capital of the island.

It seems that in the soil of human hearts there is none
so barren that some precious quality will not take root in
it, which, if watered and nourished, may change the constitution of a bad nature. The poets have feigned that
this principle of fertility pervades all nature, and have
told that the toad, ugly and venomous,

" Bears yet a precious jewel in his head."

In Langley's soul this jewel was his love of his daughter.
What to him seemed folly in others, was holy and blessed
in her. By constantly sharing in her pure thoughts, he
learned at last to comprehend them, and perceive their
beauty. Imperceptibly, he learned to delight in her innocent pursuits. At first, when she told him of her schemes
of charity, and would make him share them, he complied,
from a vague feeling of curiosity, or to gratify her humour;
but afterwards, from the strong force of sympathy, her
purity attracted his mind nearer to her own. As spirits
of darkness flee from the presence of light, he found himself, when with Mary, another person, his bad thoughts
flying from him, as the dark visions of Saul rolled from
his soul at the sound of David's harp. This change had
been long in progress, unknown to himself. He felt himself another and a better man, though he could scarcely
discover the agency of his improvement. Let no one say
that the attraction of goodness is weak. It is more powerful in commanding homage and respect than any other

quality of humanity. We recognise it at once—we bow down before it—we feel irresistibly attracted to imitate what we admire. If gross passions prevail over its sweet influence, we yet never cease to regret the fatuity that has lost us heaven for earth. If we dare to deny its supreme excellence with our lips, we acknowledge it with our hearts. We are infidels only outwardly. The world may refuse to bend its knee, but it never can refuse the worship of its soul.

In his calmer and secluded hours, with Mary as his guardian angel always near him, the conversion of Langley went on. He experienced a felicity he never knew before. He had been used to consider the clergyman a fanatic; he now regarded him as a sober and a sensible man. People having only a partial acquaintance with the world, are apt to mistake sentiment for character. The two are wholly apart from each other. Langley was as bold, as adventurous, as active, as ever he was, but his energies were now turned into a new channel. He became an ardent experimentalist on the qualities of soils; he invented improvements in crushing-mills; and, in short, brought into the life and occupations of a planter all the industry and resources which had distinguished him in another career. He learned to take an interest in Mary's flowers, and her schools for poor children, and talked of building a church after his own design. But in the midst of this new and happy life he never looked back.

He sat one evening, in company with the good minister, engaged in cheerful chat. Mary had just finished an exquisite little air. The wax-lights brightly illuminated the large and lofty apartment, rendered cool by the evening air stealing in through the closed jalousies. The minister was not one of those austere spirits who dislike

whatever savours of gaiety and enjoyment. The soul, he
neld, resembled wax in this—that an impression was
often most surely and lastingly stamped on it when it was
relaxed. He sometimes quietly told that he had done
more with the planters in a few words over a game of
chess, or a hand at picquet, than he could effect by his
best sermons. He sat now keeping Langley company
with an excellent Havannah.

The turn of conversation is often singular. A moment
before they were discussing the flavour of cigars; now
they spoke of the consequences of sin. The captain was
curious to know if, with a new course of life, all past
crimes and errors were truly forgiven. Mary listened with
more anxiety than marked the tone in which the question
was put; for the past had so little the captain liked to
look back on, that he contrived to banish it from his
remembrance altogether. The minister replied, undoubtedly, that to the repentant, sin was forgiven; but he
remarked that, in some way or other, a punishment was
attached to the original crime, from which it could not
escape. " Sin is pardoned, without doubt," he said ; " but
believe this, that not one guilty action can be committed
which will not meet with a strict reckoning, and for which
a full and severe penalty will not be exacted in this world
or the next; sometimes by mental, sometimes by bodily
agony. To no man is it permitted to greatly offend with
impunity."

The captain thought this doctrine carried a great deal
too far. He was for a scheme of general amnesty, such
as is granted by tottering states, which confound weakness
with mercy, giving out that it fails to punish, not from
impotence, but from an excess of charity and good-nature.

The scene and the conversation had hitherto been

commonplace enough, though the changes which passed
over Mary's face, as she listened to the argument, threw
in that touch of poetic feeling which is often found in the
most ordinary occurrences.   She knew herself deeply
interested in the topic; for there were passages in her
father's life, darkly hinted at sometimes by him, which
chilled her blood when she thought of them.

The captain grew warm, and applied the argument, as
heated persons will do, to himself.   "Look here, now,"
said he; "suppose that I, when I wasn't so wise as I
am at present, had a cargo of slaves on board? Well,
we'll say the ship leaked, that she wanted lightening, that,
no matter how, it was necessary to turn them out; do you
mean to say now, that I should be punished for that when
I took up with better notions?"

"I should say," replied the minister, regarding the
case quite hypothetically, "that in this world or the next
would a fearful punishment be awarded you."

The captain grew a little paler.   As for Mary, she
gave a faint scream; it was not without great difficulty
that she could further suppress her feelings.

"Tush, man!" said Langley, roughly, "I have done
such things in my time, yet what am I the worse for
it now; where's my accuser?"

A voice that filled the room with terror, said, distinctly, "Here!"

All eyes were instantly turned to the spot whence that
voice issued.

The Nubian stood in the door-way, his figure dilated
beyond the grand proportions of nature.   For the second
time the glance of these two men met, and the captain,
though his accuser was unarmed, felt that he was a lost
man.

His courage did not desert him, though horror almost fioze his blood, and deprived him of sense. He rose to meet the Nubian's gaze. "With what," he said, "do you charge me?"

The black said, simply, "With murder!"

Langley advanced to grapple with his accuser; but Mary, quick as light, threw herself on the Nubian, beseeching him to withdraw at once, telling him that he had accused her father—that he was in error—that he knew not what he was about.

Never had the Nubian seemed more calm, as he said —"Almost I would to God I did not. Gentle girl, you speak to me in vain, I am but the agent of Heaven. The cry of the blood that wretched man has wantonly spilt has risen to the Almighty throne. The hour of retribution has come!"

Four men entered the room at these words. The Nubian said to them, "Behold your prisoner!"

His terrible calmness carried conviction to Mary's heart. She tried to struggle with her dread—to address the Nubian. In vain; her faculties were paralyzed; she sank senseless at his feet.

He raised her with the mingled reverence and love due to a divine being; with such tender care and holy awe must the Christians of old have touched the body of a martyred saint. He threw back the bright masses of hair from her pallid face, and touched her temples with some water at hand.

Langley fiercely grappled with the men who held him. "Villains!" he shouted, "let me go; that fiend would kill father and daughter at one blow!"

The Nubian had laid the fainting form on a couch, and knelt beside it. He raised his eyes, and said, in

U

tones of deep pathos, "Thou hearest—gracious God—thou
hearest! still am I doomed to suffer!"

"Detested monster!" exclaimed Langley, "why didst
thou come here to destroy our peace?"

The Nubian answered him not. He saw in the
brightening colour of Mary's lips signs of returning life.
"Guard well your prisoner," he said to the men. Then
grasping the hand of the minister, who, during the few
minutes of this dreadful scene, had been motionless with
astonishment, he bade him watch over her. "I will not
shock her by my presence. It may be, I shall never see
her more." He bent down to imprint one kiss on her yet
cold hand, and left the room, answering not one word to
the fierce reproaches of his enemy.

The Nubian had recognised the captain of the slaver
the instant Langley set his foot upon the shore. His
mind was torn by the storm of contending passions. The
horrors of that night of massacre, setting the seal of blood
to the long career of desperate cruelty and wickedness he
had witnessed, was never absent from his mind. He made
no vow of vengeance, but he prayed Heaven to make him
the human instrument of its justice. For this end he
conceived that in his labour he was gifted with supernatural strength. Accident, or, as it seemed to him, Providence, had thrown in his way two of the seamen of the
slave-ship. These men, as less guilty than their principal,
he had constantly kept in the island, in the full belief that
at no distant time would the captain be delivered into his
hands, that their testimony might be joined to his own
against him. If he came not to that island within five
years, the Nubian resolved to wander over the earth in
search of him. That time was within three days of its
accomplishment when he saw Langley land.

The struggle of his soul ended in the conquest of the sterner passion. A voice within him cried out for ever—"Justice—justice!" With all haste he departed for Kingston. For the event that had arrived he had long been prepared. His own testimony, express and clear, was supported by that, equally decided, of his witnesses. When the depositions were taken, he felt secure that no mortal power could deprive justice of its victim. "This day," he exclaimed, as he left the court, "have I built up the scaffold on which that man shall die!"

As the intelligence of Langley's crime became known, it excited the greatest horror and detestation. He was examined and committed for murder. By the advice of his counsel he reserved his defence; his advisers frankly told him they saw no chance of his escape, if the Nubian pressed the prosecution against him with the same vigilance, and the witnesses all appeared on the trial. Mary had never left her father since his capture. Those words filled her with hope. She believed she had the power to save him, and that belief filled her with courage.

Christian now resided in the capital. He still persevered in his business with all his former regularity, though he felt the time was at hand when he should no longer continue it. Mary proceeded to his dwelling, and was directed to his private room. She entered it unannounced. He was standing at a desk, apparently wrapped in profound thought, with his face shaded by his hand. Before him was a small miniature, which Mary instantly recognised as one of herself, that, at the earnest request of the minister, she had sent Christian in return for his continued course of kindness and benevolence during her absence. From beneath his hand large scalding tears fell on the glass of the miniature. He presented no other trace of emotion. His large form was as rigid as if it had been carved of stone.

Mary seized the moment as most favourable to her wishes. The life of her father was at stake; with that thought what had she to do with scruples? She laid her hand softly on the Nubian's shoulder. He started back for an instant, then gazed upon her with a look of indescribable love, admiration, and reverence. Mary, who knew the usual reserve of his manner, and had prepared herself for opening the interview, was surprised and affected when he threw himself at her feet, and raised his hands to her in an attitude of supplication.

"Pure and beautiful being!" he said, in tones of the deepest feeling, "how can I ever hope for thy forgiveness? yet how can I live, how can I die, without it?"

Mary felt that the barrier of reserve she dreaded to encounter was broken down by the Nubian's action in an instant. She addressed him with the simplicity of times past.

"My forgiveness, Christian! Oh, you may obtain more than that! Save my father, as you yet may easily, and you shall have my regard and gratitude for ever."

Anguish was written in every line of his face, as he replied—"This is not my act, but God's. I am but the instrument he wields in his hand."

"Christian! Christian! beware how you mistake the impulse of revenge for the dictate of Heaven! Vengeance is not yours! Come, you have been deceived by bad spirits! Hear what it is I ask of you—only this, that you take no part against my father. Fly! leave this island at once. I—I, who saved your life,—Christian, I speak not this boastingly, but as a claim to your gratitude, —I beseech, I implore this of you, as the greatest boon that one creature can ask of another."

He groaned as if his spirit were racked by mortal agony. "This is torture!" he said; "but it cannot conquer me. Lady, if you had seen what I have seen, the long train of fainting captives, the horrors of that hold, dark, suffocating, filthy, in which fever raged, and the dead and living lay together, the massacre of that night, which even now turns my brain as I speak of it, you could no longer doubt that the justice of Heaven cries aloud for atonement." He sprang to his feet, having his mind filled only at that instant with all the crimes he had witnessed, and the sense that he was the chosen agent to avenge them. "He must die!" he said, firmly—"die, that the awful warning may be carried through all lands —die, that human justice may be vindicated—die, that the cry of innocent blood may be silenced—die, that the oppressor over all the earth may know God reigneth in heaven!"

The hope of Mary fainted in her breast as those awful words, delivered with the vehemence and fire of inspiration, fell upon her ear. Yet she made one effort more to turn the Nubian from his purpose. She raised her eyes to his, and waited till she saw them melting with tenderness and affection.

"Christian," she said, "though I have never breathed my thought into mortal ear, nor hardly looked on it myself, yet I know well with what feeling you have regarded me. I have your love, such love as men feel for a chosen bride." She saw him start, and fix on her a gaze of passionate love. "My hand, my faith pledged on the altar, shall be yours, if you consent that we fly together. Think! will not a life of wedded love, my father's years of penitence, be more dear to you than a moment of vengeance?"

The Nubian turned from her for the space of an instant. When he looked on her again, his face was more
tranquil. "Angelic creature!" he exclaimed, "worthy,
not of love, but of worship, thou art more beautiful than
my dreams ever painted thee. Never did I adore thee as
in this hour. No mortal heart can ever conceive the
temptation thou hast offered to my soul. To save thee
from an uneasy thought, I would have died—I would
have deemed all the torture to which man could put me
repaid by one kind word from thy lips. Yet we part now,
and for ever. Wretched that I am, I dare not ask thy
pardon."

He led her out unresistingly, but his keen sense saw
that she shrank from the pressure of his hand. This
alone was wanting to complete his agony. As she passed
from his dwelling, his strong frame fell heavily to the
ground.

*   *   *   *   *

A gibbet stood long on a promontory of the Jamaica
coast. The chains clanked dismally as the sea-breeze
caught them. In that case of iron swung the bones of
the murderer Langley.

*   *   *   *   *

The Nubian, true to his purpose, stayed to see his victim die. He had previously settled his affairs as one who
was about to quit the world, giving his last instructions to
a trusty agent. A ship waited for him till the execution
was over. His parting words were only that his mission
on earth was accomplished. No one knew whither he
went.

The pure and gentle Mary parted from her father only
at the foot of the scaffold, when his spirit seemed wholly
Heaven's. With the good minister she quitted that

island, which now presented to her only images of terror. Her heart was too confiding to live long without an object. When time had softened her grief, a lieutenant, poor, but high-minded, gained her affections. He had previously been unfortunate, but now all things prospered with him. He rose rapidly in rank; his promotion was secured by purchase; he could never learn whose was the wealth that advanced him, that cleared off his incumbrances, and that made him a happy and a prosperous man. His sweet wife, though ignorant of the agent, suspected the source; but the thought was too full of painful recollections to be willingly indulged in.

A few years since, there came reports of a deadly conflict between a party of Africans in a province of Nubia and a band of savage slave-dealers. The Nubians were victorious, but their leader received his death-wound in the struggle. One of those who survived him, and who, it seems, had his confidence, took from his breast a miniature, and transmitted it by a safe hand to England. It reached Mary, then a fond wife and mother, with a few words from the seaman to whose care it was consigned, telling how he who wore it fell. It was the miniature she had given to the unfortunate Nubian, and was now stained with his heart's blood.

If in spirit he ever hovered over earth, he must have rejoiced as he saw that that picture, so dearly prized in life, was sometimes dimmed by Mary's tears.

FIFTH EVENING.

On the morning of the day which ushered in the Fifth
Evening of our revels, there had arrived at the Hall an
accomplished literary friend of the host, who had been
long absent in the East, travelling over every step of
those lands which sacred and classical lore, combined with
the beauties of Nature and the wealth of Art, have rendered the richest in the world, both in moral and intellectual associations, and who had since given to the world one
of the best books ever called forth by that most fertile of
all travelling themes.   The Lady Eva had lately been
reading these charming records of "the Crescent and the
Cross" with delight and enthusiasm, and the moment
their accomplished writer entered the library, she entreated him to aid her Tale-telling project by something
about "the land of the sun." He sought at first to excuse himself from the task, by alleging that what he had
told of the beautiful lands he had lately visited was the
simple, unembellished truth; that he had seen, and then
described what he had seen, for the use and convenience
of those who might follow him; whereas what the Lady
Eva required of him was a fiction, an effort of the fancy or
the imagination; and even if he had succeeded in the
former case, it was, so far, an evidence that he might fail
in the latter.   But the Lady Eva would hear of no excuse.

" Surely," said she, " you must have seen, in those far-off lands and strange conditions of society, enough of that kind of truth, which for us, here at home, will have all the air of fiction."

On this hint, the gentleman she addressed, with graceful courtesy, proceeded to relate

ZOË:

AN EPISODE OF THE GREEK WAR.

I.—GREECE AND HER LEADERS.

" No gospel announces the glad tidings of resurrection to a fallen Nation—once down, and down for ever."—W. S. LANDOR.

So spoke a true Poet — yet, for once, not truly : Time is the iconoclast of aphorisms, and every day demolishes some such unstable " eternal truth."

Hellas, in her shroud of slavery, heard the Isrāfil voice of Freedom, and awoke ;—her spirit burst its bonds, and

" Greece was living Greece once more ! "

When the Revolution first broke out, the glow of war was not yet chilled in Europe : youth was still emulous, and age still proud, of glory won under the Lion and the Eagle standards. Many a young student, to whom Thermopylæ and Salamis were more familiar names than those of Torres Vedras and Trafalgar,—when he heard that armies were marshalling in Greece and Thessaly, believed that the heroic age was to return : and many a veteran, in whom the force of imagination had long yielded to that of memory—the memory of privations and hard knocks —

listened, nevertheless, eagerly to the first note of war, and found the trumpet had lost nothing of its spell.

No sooner had fame transmuted the Greek "Insurrection" into the "WAR OF INDEPENDENCE," than volunteers of all nations, ranks, and professions, hastened to the standard of Ypsilanti. Some of these modern paladins were sincere enthusiasts, and had abandoned a life of luxury and ease for this romantic cause; but by far the greater number consisted of needy and profligate adventurers: both classes—the seekers of glory or of gold— were equally disappointed in the capabilities of the Grecian camp; the latter were forced to share the life and hardships of the Klepht and Palicar; the former either obtained at once a leading rank, or retired from the service in disgust. All these adventurers were ultimately formed into a regiment called the "Philhellenic Band," which early distinguished itself in the field.

Early in the year 1822, the young Senate of Greece was assembled at Epidaurus. The members sat, like the Areopagites of old, in the open air; or lay couched on the fresh grass, in the shelter of some olive-tree. Their appearance was as various as their attitude; some wore the venerable beard, the flowing robes, and even the turban of their Eastern oppressors; some were clad in the graceful national costume, adopted from Albania; with crimson cap and broidered vest, and sash well filled with pistol and yataghan. Their appearance was imposing and strangely picturesque, as they sat or stood—grey-beard and warrior grouped together—on the slope of a gentle hill that commanded a wide-spread view of the country in whose cause they were assembled. It is true that the classic Land beyond that glorious Gulf lay still in slavery; but those who gazed upon its beauty there had pledged their lives for its redemption; and when was such a pledge kept truly, and in vain?

In all Greece, a more fitting place for such assembly could scarcely have been found: beneath them lay the Saronic gulf, winding round Salamis and old Ægina:— beyond—though purple shadows wrapped Piræus and the plains,—the Acropolis of Athens stood out against the evening sky, with its marble temples gleaming in the setting sun's last smile. That sunset streaked with gold the violet shadows of the mountains over Marathon, while far to the eastward it glistened on the sea; and even in the darkling west one magic ray had lighted up the citadel of Corinth, through the very shadows of Parnassus.

Even this Assembly, usually so turbulent and discordant, seemed influenced by the quiet of that evening hour. No voice was heard but that of the orator, through whose melodious, but warlike words, there stole at intervals the happy song of the wild bird, or the murmur of the waves. Occasionally, perhaps, when a friend was accused, or a native city threatened—some armed senator would start to his feet; and, with flashing eyes and fierce eloquence denouncing the accuser, fling back the charge: but tranquillity was soon restored.

A short distance from the assembly, a guard of the Philhellenic Band lay scattered among some orange-trees that shaded the ruins of the temple; all were asleep, except the sentries, and their young officer, who was leaning on his sword, and engaged in conversation with a stranger of very different appearance. The latter wore a sort of undress uniform like that of a Russian officer of rank, but this might have been assumed from its convenience and simplicity; there was no disguise, however, in the military carriage and dignified bearing of the wearer.

His cap was drawn down over his keen, but thoughtful eyes ; and heavy moustaches performed their part in concealing the expression of the mouth, and giving a character of stern repose to the whole countenance: his dress was handsome, but uncared for; his sword and spurs alone were bright. His young companion, the Philhellene, presented a striking contrast to the stranger in every respect: the graceful and noble costume of Greece was carefully arranged about his light, athletic figure, and his richly-mounted arms were brightly polished. Though war and weather had scarred his cheek and bronzed his brow, his eyes still shone with enthusiasm; his whole bearing was calm and proud, but there was that in his look which told of unbroken energy and resolution.

"Shall I, then, announce you to the Senate ?" inquired the young officer.

"By what name ?" asked the stranger, with a smile.

"I know not, though this is our second meeting. But I feel that I am in the presence of one who alone seems superior to the unhappy circumstances of the time; and who will assuredly, soon or late, control the destinies of our country."

"Of *our* country ?" repeated the stranger, in the English language, but slightly tinctured with a foreign accent.

"Yes," replied the Philhellene, "it is my country by adoption, as I believe it to be yours. I have already told you how I relinquished high prospects in England, to become a nameless adventurer in a cause which I still hold sacred—how suddenly my first illusions vanished when I found myself in the camp at Yassey. You also know how my comrades perished at Dragastan,—that I, as one of the few survivors, obtained command in the Philhellenic Band

—and this, with the exception of our naval expeditions, forms my whole history. My zeal in the cause I serve, if less enthusiastic, is more firm than ever :—my fate is now identified with that of Greece : avarice and cruelty, treachery and selfishness, may sully her fair fame; but when I think on all that she has already done,—on all that she may yet perform,—I can still afford to *hope* as well as to *remember.*"

The stranger appeared to listen with interest to this confession; and, after a pause, rejoined, " It is of such men as you that our country stands in need. I love your nation, but abhor your government. Had England but conceded the right of nationality to Greece, it would have been worth more to our cause than a hundred victories. But of this we will speak no more — It is well that we retain some of our illusions ; they may be converted into truths, and are necessary to veil our corruption : as your comrade, Chaussevigne, once observed to me, ' Greece is like the dome of the Invalides, at Paris—all glittering with gilding, but we know what there is below.'* But, see ! here comes one in whom all the characteristic vices and virtues of this people are combined."

As he spoke, a Greek officer, showily dressed and accoutred, was challenged by the sentries, and then, dismounting, made his way to the assembly. " That is Theodore Colocotronis," resumed the stranger ; " brave, avaricious, sanguinary, and coxcombical. I thank the Turks that they have left our old men the dignified appearance of nonchalance with which they receive him : he comes from Nauplia, with tidings of defeat. But here comes a man of another stamp — Suli's heroic chieftain,

---

* Michaud.

Marco Botzaris. See how proudly he wears that stained capote over his simple vest; no herald's escutcheon in your kingly courts ever bore a nobler blazonment than the soils upon that shaggy skin. By heaven! they rise to meet the rugged mountaineer—there is virtue still in Greece! Their courtesy is well rewarded; he brings tidings of the surrender of Corinth by the Turks. With what classic brevity, but force, he tells his tale. Look well upon him; for such men live short lives in times like these."

"And by what means, may I ask, have you become acquainted with events that these hurried men have only just had time to tell?" inquired the Philhellene, whose interest and curiosity were strongly excited by his strange companion.

"Some day or other you shall know," said the latter, "but not now. Here comes a friend of yours, the bravest, yet most diffident man that sails the seas. Farewell, for the present; tell Ypsilanti, when the assembly rises, that he who gave you this ring awaits him at Piadi; then keep the trinket — it may serve you yet." So saying, the stranger left him; and almost at the same instant Canári grasped his hand hurriedly but affectionately, as he passed to deliver his report to the assembly. The slight and delicate appearance of this naval hero gave little token of the hardships he had braved; and when he timidly related to the assembly how he had steered his fireship into the midst of the Turkish fleet, and exploded her under their very guns—his faltering voice and downcast eyes appeared to belie his daring deed. His story was soon told; he exchanged a few words with the President, and in a few moments more had flung himself down by the side of the Philhellene — his timidity had passed away, and he was once more the frank, bold-hearted seaman.

"Norman! my friend, my brother!" he exclaimed,
"I have glorious news for you to-night. We sail at midnight for Myconé, the isle of love, and wine, and beauty ;
there, even your stately step shall flourish in the Romaika,
and your cold Northern blood shall glow with night's dark
wine.* Then, on for Scio! to avenge our slaughtered
friends :—the butchering Turk holds his feast of lanterns
on Friday night, and by all the gods of your mythology
and my mother-land, he shall have a light he expects not."
As he spoke thus, his eyes flashed fire, and his voice was
in tune with the trumpet's blast. "But more than all
this," continued the volatile Greek, changing once more to
a joyous mood—"more than the wine which cheers the
body, or even than the vengeance that refreshes the soul,—
I have found for you a heroine at last;—not one of those
exemplary old women who is ready to set fire to a powder
magazine, though herself and her children be a-top of it†
—but a real, romantic heroine—brave, beautiful, eloquent,
and even rich. What! nothing but your old incredulous
smile? I tell you, had you heard and seen her, as I have
done, you would abandon those dreams and reveries of
yours for a bright reality that transcends them all, and
forget that the world contained aught else but her. It
was she who roused the Eastern Islands to resistance, and
inspired them with resolution to be free."

The Philhellene listened with interest to a rhapsody
well suited to those stirring times, and inquired how long
his friend had known the subject of his glowing eulogy.

* The " Vino di Notte" is made in the Cyclades, of a grape so delicate,
that, if gathered by daylight, it ferments, and becomes worthless.
† This was a circumstance of frequent occurrence in the Greek war—
when the men were slain, and nothing remained for their wives and children but the brutality of the Turkish soldiery.

"I'll tell you, my boy, how it happened. You know how reluctant Tenos and Myconé have shown themselves to join our cause, or even to afford supplies. Last week, though I left my mark upon the Turkish fleet off Scio, my own ships did not come out of action exactly as they went into it; and I was obliged to seek Myconé, to refit. I found the little harbour almost deserted, and there was scarcely a soul to speak to. One surly old fellow remained, however; and he told me that the whole village was gone to the orange grove, where the ruined temple stands. And there I found them—men, women, and children—crowding round Módena Mavroyéni.* Now, I'm not fond, myself, of hearing a woman talking to more than one person at a time, but—before I had looked and listened while my pulse beat five, to that inspired girl— I only wished that all Greece could have heard her, too.

"She stood upon the ruined temple's marble steps, surrounded by the Primates of the island, who looked like priests of old, attendant on their deity; and never yet did priest or Pagan picture a divinity of more glorious form or inspiring voice. She spoke of Greece, and the cause became divine; of slavery—and I felt its chain upon my neck; she spoke of our ancient valour—I thought I had been a coward until then, and was invincible thenceforth. She spoke of freedom, and her voice sounded like a Marathonian trumpet. She told of our slaughtered brethren, and her own slain sire, and the people wept; and then she spoke of vengeance!—vengeance—fierce, terrible, and swift! Vengeance—that would sweep the Ottoman from the face of the earth, and carry Freedom on its wings!

---

* Her story, as well as those of all the persons in this tale, is historical.

" She ceased—for a moment there was silence, as the ear strove to catch some echo of that thrilling voice : but then burst forth from every pent-up bosom one glorious shout—high, vehement, prolonged—that reached the Turks in their distant citadel, and told them their accursed rule had ceased for ever !"

The Philhellene caught instantly the enthusiasm of the sailor, and grasped his hand—"There spoke the spirit of old Greece !" he exclaimed. "This is what I have longed to hear and know. I sail with you to-nignt, and if my faith in the regeneration of Greece has ever languished, I will kindle it anew on the altar of Módena Mavroyéni !"

" Not by that name, however," rejoined his mercurial friend; who now, half ashamed of his own enthusiasm, sought to amuse himself with that which it had awakened. " My heroine disclaims the half Italian title she received from her Fanariote father, and now styles herself, simply, ' Zoë,'—a name by which her mother used to call her."

The assembly soon broke up, and the friends separated —to meet at midnight on board the galley of Canári.

II.—LOVE AND WAR.

" And yet in times so stormy, in a land
Where Virtue's self held forth a bloody hand,
To greet armed Power—in such times as these,
Still Woman's Love could find a way to please."
Philip Van Artevelde.

MERRILY the light mystico* of Canári bounded over the starlit sea—winged by her snowy sails spread widely

* The mystico is a light, long boat, peculiar to the Archipelago ; it is adapted both for sail and oars, and has extraordinary speed.

x

to the breeze.   Strenuously, too, her stalwart seamen bent
to their oars—changing at every sweep the purple water
to phosphoric foam.   Will was in their work; for, whatever the vices of the Greek, his country's name was then
on every lip—her cause in every heart.   Swiftly they sped,
for the mission of Canári was an urgent one, though now
that Delhi of the seas lay wrapt in such deep luxury of
repose as none but men of eager action know.

The Philhellene kept watch for his wearied friend;
and found his own imagination strangely haunted by that
Island Girl; whose image would still present itself to his
excited fancy, and block up, as it were, every avenue to
other thought.   Hitherto, everything Greek, except Greece
herself, had disappointed him; although during his brief
but stirring career he had left no opportunity of adventure
unessayed—

> " Woman, the field, the ocean—all that gave
> Promise of pleasure, peril of a grave—
> In turn he tried."

Little more than twelve months had elapsed since Norman first joined the gallant but ill-fated Ypsilanti, in
Moldavia; but, in trial, disenchantment, and experience,
those months had done the work of years.   He believed
that his worldly education was now complete—that he at
length saw life in all its clear and cold reality.   Vain
thought! such knowledge is denied to man.   Every one
has his own "reality," which to his neighbour seems the
veriest illusion;—and who is to decide?

However war, wealth, ambition, and woman's self, may
be argued down to an illusion, and lose their charm when
applied to the cold touchstone of experience—Nature's
glory will never lose its power over a heart in which

enthusiasm has once existed. This even our adventurer could feel, as the Day-god—born anew at Delos—rose gloriously from his native isle, and shot his golden arrows over earth and sea : lightly they glance from the Ægean's silvery shield, but pierce and scatter the pale mists on Sunium's Promontory, and the proud Athenian hills.

As their first warm shower fell upon Canári's cheek, he sprang to his feet. For a few minutes, he gazed proudly and fondly on the view before him, then knelt devoutly, and prayed to a little image of the Virgin.

" Well ! my volunteer !" he exclaimed, as he rose from his devotions; "the galley makes good way, and we shall make Myconé by nightfall. Now, tell me what you think of our expedition ; and, first—of Zoë ?"

" First inform me who it was you found me with, last night, at Epidaurus—the stranger whom you saluted so respectfully ? "

" That's exactly what I cannot tell you," said the sailor, looking serious ; " he knows more of our affairs than any man in Greece, yet he never drew a sword in our cause. He is one day at St. Petersburg ; another, at Stamboul ; a third, in the heart of the Morea ; dictating, not only wisely, but bravely, to our vacillating president."

" He seemed unwilling to be seen last night," observed the Philhellene, " and Ypsilanti would scarcely wait to hear and grant my application to join your expedition, after he had heard his message."

" And yet they say the prince hates the very ground this stranger shadows," replied Canári : " he feels his superiority, and fears his superseding him as president. I have heard it whispered, that this man is Capo d'Istria ; and that—cold, cautious, and subtle—he only waits until the more forward men of Greece have rendered her cause

illustrious, to put himself at the head of her affairs. Now
let us change the subject; and thank the gods that we
have only Turks and war to deal with, instead of place-
hunters and politics."

" Agreed — in good time, too; for yon blue speck on
the horizon is the island of your lady-love."

" Nay, she's no love of mine," rejoined the sailor.
" Think you I should babble about her I loved, even to
your cold ear ?   Moreover, Norman, she's as proud as
Lucifer, though lovely as his own bright star.   And yet,"
he added, musingly, " I am the only man on whom she
was ever seen to smile : but then it was in pity."

" What ! *you*, Canári — the flattered favourite ashore,
the fearless and the feared afloat — *you*, scorned by a village girl ?"

" Nay — not scorned; neither is she is a village girl.
Her father was one of the first families of the Fanal,* and
came to Myconé only to avoid the persecution consequent
on the war.   Even here, however, it pursued him; and
he was put to death by Hassan Pasha when the Turkish
fleet arrived.   From that hour his daughter became
changed; — no longer the timid girl, who seemed to shrink
if the rude breeze disturbed her veil; she went from house
to house — rousing the spirit of the people to revolt by
her own sad story and her wondrous eloquence.   At
length, hearing that the dastardly Council of the island
was about to send submission to the Porte, she appeared
among them; followed, as I told you, by all the inhabitants of the village.   The beauty, zeal, and unexpected
appearance of the heroic girl, gave to her mission almost
a supernatural character.   The senate heard her, as it

---

* Constantinopolitan Greeks, called " Fanariotes,"from the " Fanal,"
the name of the district they inhabit.

were, reverentially; and, as her glowing words fell burning
on their age-chilled hearts, they warmed to nobler views :
each senator forgot his corporation craft, and felt—thought
—voted—as an individual MAN. Myconé was free, and
Zoë was the angel of its freedom!

"And now, to come to *my* part of the story:—The
island was to furnish its share of ships and seamen to the
fleet, and Zoë was the first to contribute the two best
galleys in the harbour. My name was somehow whispered round; and, turning to me, she poured on me alone
those words and looks that had overpowered the whole
assembly. *What* she said, I know not; but *how* she said
it, I shall remember in my dying hour. When she ceased
to speak, the people turned to me, expecting a reply. You
know my failing—my utter inability to speak before a
crowd. My heart felt bursting with a thousand thoughts,
but *I*—stood trembling like a beaten slave. That importunate assembly seemed now all eyes—and now all ears—
and now seemed all gasping for my words as if for breath;
still, I was silent as the dead. Then it was she smiled.
No smile of scorn, Norman; but one of gentlest, kindliest
encouragement, as she exclaimed, 'Our Canári prefers to
speak by actions, rather than by words; his silence accepts
the command that shall speak in thunder to our tyrants!'

"With these words she ceased—the enthusiasm that
had hitherto sustained her, seemed to fail; she drew her
veil timidly, but gracefully, about her, and retired. Then
my words came fast and free enough; for I felt, when *she*
was gone, as if there was no one left. I swore that those
very galleys should fire the ship of Hassan Pasha, and the
false Turk shall confess to-morrow that Canári keeps his
word!"

Merrily still flew the light mystico over the sunny sea,

as the island she was bound for seemed to rise from the
waves to meet her. Gradually its bold and beautiful outline became more clear; then its bosomy hills and shadowy
glens became developed; the myrtle and olive groves came
into view; and, finally, the temple, the snow-white cottages,
and the people on the shore.

The mystico shot swiftly into the harbour; but before
the friends had landed, they could discover, from the
excited crowds ashore, that something unusual had happened. Groups of long-robed elders or white-kilted youths
were scattered round, each listening to some speaker who
was declaiming violently. Women sat upon the rocks, with
hair dishevelled and faces hidden in their hands; while
little children pressed unnoticed to their sides. Bustle
and confusion prevailed along the quays; and high above
the town the blood-red banner waved upon the Turkish
citadel, whence salvos of artillery proclaimed some victory.

The moment his flag was recognised, loud welcoming
cries of " Canári ! Canári !" resounded from the populace.
Crowds pressed eagerly about his galley as she took the
ground; and before he had landed, he learned from a
thousand voices that Scio was laid waste, and all its inhabitants were massacred by the Turks.*

Canári was well used to hear of death and horror.
From his youth up, he had been accustomed to wrestle
with the storm, and grapple with destruction in its most
ruthless form : but this murder—so terrible, so universal
—for the moment seemed quite to overwhelm him. He
thought of the kind, the beautiful, the loved, who had so
often welcomed him to their delicious island, now cold in

---

* Ninety thousand Greeks were slain on this occasion, out of a
population of 110,000; and the loveliest island in Greece blighted into a
wilderness.

a bloody death; polluting with their unburied corpses the
scenes that they once blessed! He sank upon his knees;
and, clasping his trembling hands upon his burning brow,
remained for some time in a silence that none dared to
interrupt. Then, starting to his feet, his form dilated,
his eyes flashed lightning fire, and his pale lips quivered
in a vain attempt to give utterance to the storm of passion
that raged within him. No words would come, though
he laboured fearfully to speak; but at last he raised his
bugle to his lips, and blew his well-known battle-note—
so wild, and long, and fierce, that his very comrades shrank
before him, and the Turks were startled in their lofty
citadel.

Not all the tongues of ancient Greece could have
spoken more eloquently, or made a more powerful appeal,
than that one trumpet-blast. All the heroic feelings that
had slumbered for a thousand years in Hellenic blood
were roused to action by its spell. The whole people
crowded once more round Canári—boys, and warriors,
and grey-haired men—and demanded vengeance, as if it
was only his to give. "And vengeance ye shall have!"
exclaimed the sailor. "To-morrow's dawn will bring us
arms from the Morea—to-morrow night, we sail for
Scio!" Then, knowing how necessary it was that this
excitement should be sustained, he continued—"To-night
for the banquet—the funeral feast to our lost friends; to-
night we will keep festival like our ancestors; and like
them keep the morrow for revenge!"*

Welcome was that word. The Myconians were of old
renowned for hospitality, and the elders now hastened to
occupy their fevered minds with a new excitement: the

---

* " Let us dine merrily, for we sup with Pluto."—*Leonidas.*

young men hastened to the ships, and employed themselves
under Canári's orders, in preparing them for sea.   Meanwhile the Philhellene wandered alone among scenes that
seemed everywhere to speak of Zoë ; and pondered whether
even her spirit could save Myconé from the fearful doom
of her sister island.

And now evening was come : not, as in our northern
climates, with damp, cold shadows falling upon cloaked
people, hurrying to the shelter of their houses; but " softly,
beautifully bright ;" genial as the noontide, refreshing as
the dawn — thoughtful, tender, and inviting.   The sea-
breeze wafted fragrance from the orange-blossoms, as it
made music with their boughs ; and fluttered through the
long, dark tresses of many a Grecian maid.

Where a soft green hill sloped gently to the shore,
Canári and his comrades held their festival in the open
air.   No one could have judged, from their gay, joyous
bearing and frequent laughter, that such was merely the
light foam upon the torrent of one deep, dark passion, that
rolled beneath.   Unlearned as were most of the island
Greeks of that time, there was a classic instinct amongst
them that seemed to induce imitation of the customs, and
even of the garb of ancient times.   The white wide tunic,
with its close vest, whose embroidery was an armour in
itself — the long hair that floated round the shoulders,
the brazen helmet, the greaves, and even the trumpet that
characterized the naval Greeks, might have been worn at
the siege of Troy.   Like their ancestors, too, they made
this funeral feast ; like them, they quaffed the rich red
wine of Scio, and poured libations to the manes of the
dead.   But when they came to drink Canári's health,
their toast was peculiar to their own time and people.

" Sudden and glorious death !"* was drunk to their leader with as much enthusiasm as if it involved length of days and peaceful happiness.

And so the festival went on. The people of the island had decreed a crown of honour to Canári, for his last successful expedition against the Turks, and now he was to receive it.

As is usual all over the East, whether Christian, Moslem, or mere Pagan, the men banqueted alone. But now the sounds of a distant serenade were heard from beyond the grove, through whose vistas a procession of Greek maidens was seen advancing to its music. Ordinarily, the melody of these festive Islanders was of the soft and gentle character that seemed suited to their clime ; but now it had caught the warlike tone of the roused people's mind, and the clang of the Moorish cymbal, with the loud roll of the throbbing drum, gave strength to the soft breathings of Æolian flutes. This contrast (and yet union) of the martial with the festive spirit of the hour was everywhere apparent. In the harbour, the fire-ships lay dancing on the playful waves, bedecked with flags and streamers, fluttering thoughtlessly over the volcanoes that slept below. The revellers along the shore were equipped for war ; helmets wore the Bacchic wreath ; and many an arm that raised the sparkling glass was stained with soils of the armourer's forge. At intervals, the watch-cry of the sentries broke upon the ear, through the merry chattering of children ; and the peaceful olive-groves below reposed in the shadow of battlemented cliffs above, surmounted by the Turkish citadel and its crimson flag.

But every eye was now fixed on the graceful procession

---

* I know not how I can better translate the Greek toast of " καλη μ>λυβl," — a good (or handsome) bullet.

emerging slowly through the old temple's columned porch,
that spanned their pathway. As they advanced, the men
rose from their grassy seat, and gathered round Canári,
who stood with folded arms, in embarrassed suspense. To
him, that bright array of graceful women was more unwelcome than the fierce columns of the Turkish host; and
she who led them more formidable than all else. Her
companions wore the rich and varied attire of their
country; their leader alone was arrayed in simple white,
airily enfolding her stately form. All the others wore
chaplets of bright flowers, but she was crowned with a
simple myrtle wreath. On she came — with a calm though
timid air: high-souled maidenly virtue shone in her eyes,
and endowed her glorious shape with majesty. The revellers paused in their wild glee, and bacchanals grew reverent
before her; for she looked like an angel descended from a
higher sphere on some gracious mission to fallen man.
And such, indeed, she was — from the lofty sphere of
thought in which her spirit dwelt, she had brought freedom's aspirations, and conferred them on her tyrant-
trodden countrymen.

A hundred voices whispered " Zoe !" as she came,
slowly, and more slowly, until she paused before Canári:
then, as he knelt with folded arms, she placed a chaplet of
oak-leaves on his helmet, and said, in a voice that, gentle
as it was, reached every ear; " Myconé, grateful to her
hero, sends you this." The acclamations that burst from
the excited crowd were hushed instantly, when her lips
were seen to move again, as she raised the white-cross
banner.—" For what you have already done, Canári, our
people offer you this crown; for what you are about to do,
they entrust you with this sacred symbol, the standard of
regenerate Greece. Confident that, in your keeping, its

glory is secure, we add only the injunction of the Spartan
—'H τᾶν, ἢ ἐπι τᾶν'."* Air loves sweet sounds, and
wafts them carefully along. The Grecian echoes caught
those classic words, so breathed by classic lips, and poured
them into every listening ear of that widely-circling crowd.
Once more a shout of acclamation rent the sky, and once
more was hushed, as Canári, losing his timidity in enthusiasm, rose suddenly, and gave the flag to Norman.

"By him," he cried—"by him that banner shall be
carried more nobly, though not more proudly, than by me.
Grecian-born as I am, my country claims my life and
service as a right; but here is one who has dared as much,
and done far more than I—who has shed his blood for us
on the hills of Epirus, and the Ægean seas; who for us
has abandoned his own prosperous England—*his* home,
and that of Freedom!" Once more the acclamations rang
in generous echo to that generous speech, and the Philhellene was startled to find that every eye was bent on him.
His proud self-possession soon returned; and as there is
nothing more imposing to an excited audience than perfect calmness in the person who addresses them, his words,
sincere though few; his manner, modest though manly;
instantly riveted attention. But he soon found himself
speaking for one alone—that beautiful being who stood
before him, with her large, soft, inquiring eyes fixed
radiantly on his; her exquisitely chiselled lips seeming
to quiver with the echo of each word he spoke; and the
rich, warm blood betraying every emotion of her heart in
her changing cheek.

Why should we pause on such a scene?—It is over;

---

* "With it or upon it." The words and allusion of Germanos,
Archbishop of Patras.

and the people are dispersed along the shore; each group
sustaining its excitement in a different mode: here a circle
of young islanders whirl rapidly in the Romaika dance, to
which the surrounding crowd keep time with clapping
hands and martial song;—there a party of revellers,
crowned with ivy, sustain the island's Bacchic character,
as they drink deeply to the health of Zoë and the gallant
stranger.   Gathered round the old elm-tree, the elders
are assembled in debate on the equipment of the morrow's
expedition; and many a doomed sailor is strolling along
the shore, with his arm encircling some slender waist that
shall never feel that pressure more.

It is the invariable result of times of common and
intense peril, that the usual conventionalities of life are
dispensed with, and the fetters of formality relaxed.   The
Greek islanders were never remarkable for demureness;
and now, by universal consent, every disguise abandoned,
life wore, openly and honestly, its best and truest feelings
—as it might be, in its last hour.   Old feuds were forgotten, decaying friendships were restored, and lovers no
longer shrank from free confession, or feared observant
eyes.

Softly and gloriously the summer moon shone over
that fair island and its joy-tranced people—joy all the
deeper and more intense from its uncertainty: but a
brighter light was shining, and a deeper joy was basking
in its ray, where Zoë wandered with the stranger by her
side.   Norman was deeply versed in all the graceful
learning of that lady's land: a scholar's fame had long
been his, and his aspiring mind had grasped at all that
ever came within its reach.   And yet how much had he to
learn from this simple island girl!   What was the value
of all the light that ever beamed from philosophic page,

compared with that now shining from *her* eyes? How
.dark and objectless seemed life till then—how eagerly and
devotedly he gave himself up to a first, deep, reckless love!
And Zoë—how changed was *she* within that hour! Till
then, her every thought was engrossed by her orphan
sorrow or by patriot pride: the first passion to which her
young heart awakened was thirst for vengeance on her
father's murderers; this became sublimed into zeal for her
country's cause; and feeding thereupon, her soul grew
strong. Then, finally, came Love—the master passion
that absorbed all others—shining out suddenly, like sunrise in those Eastern skies: no struggling dawn—no long
protracted contest between light and shade—but flashing
forth upon her soul like lightning, and filling at once its
whole horizon.

Man seeks, however vainly it may be betimes, to preserve the "Divide et impera" system in his passions;
and in *his* heart, ambition, pride, and glory may share
their rule with Love. With woman—Heaven bless her!
—the master passion is a despot, and one that "brooks
no brother near the throne:" whatever it may be—love,
pride, anger, or revenge—it rules alone.

And thus it was with Zoë—Nature's own wayward
child: but a few hours ago, her every thought was occupied with glorious abstractions, that seemed to leave no
room for another emotion in her mind: unconscious of her
rare endowments, to her it seemed as natural to speak
eloquently as to feel deeply. She had never known what
it was laboriously to strive for, and lingeringly to acquire,
influence: she appeared, and her power was felt—she
spoke, and it was omnipotent. To her ardent but modest
mind, this influence seemed simply owing to her mission
as Priestess of the glorious creed she preached.

And then came Norman, clothed with all the attributes most attractive to her imagination; with a spirit so calm and self-possessed—yet enthusiastic as her own; with all the prestige of the most daring deeds, yet the gentleness and reverence towards woman that combines with bravery so well. His eloquence, earnest and commanding, made the exclamatory harangues of her own people appear to be mere angry prattlings: and then his devotion to her—so sudden, trusting, and entire: the critical and exciting times in which she lived—all these things "rent moments into immortalities," and made the passion of the hour appear mature.

Night went, and morning came full swiftly to that island people; but most of all, to the palace were Zoë entertained her guests. Apart from the gay and thoughtless crowds, she sat beneath a lofty alcove, looking out upon the sea. Eastern luxury was there, blended with the refinements of civilised Europe. Italian art had decorated with frescoes the light, graceful architecture of the Saracens; silken cushions were piled upon the porcelain floor; silver lamps shed soft light upon a sparkling fountain; and around it vases of flowers, exotic even there, breathed perfume.

And Zoë gazed upon the paling stars, and the brightening hills, and the shadowy form of the Turkish mosque, that showed where the beleaguered Moslems still kept their ground. The eyes of the Greek maiden wandered over the sea, and rested long and earnestly on the galley that bore the banner of the Cross. In a few short hours it was to bear the stranger, now her lover, to danger and perhaps to death: but *he* was by her side; and he also gazed thoughtfully upon that tranquil view, and proudly on that fateful banner.

"To-morrow night," he whispered, "that flag that floats serenely now, shall ascend to the skies on the explosion that destroys the Pasha's ship. But not more high or suddenly will it soar, than the hope that now breathes softly in your ear, to claim reward when we return."

"When *we* return!" she repeated. "Alas! the charmed life Canári bears may be proof even to this desperate chance—*he* may return; but he may come alone!"

Just then the bugle of Canári blew; and thenceforth prompt, energetic action, took the place of thought and reverie. Eager and armed crowds now hastened to the shore, and Norman's step was not the last that trod Canári's deck. Still the little fleet waited for the morning's breeze; and at the earliest dawn the Patriarch of the island came, with his priesthood in all their sacred pomp, to bless the expedition. The

"Full of hope, misnamed forlorn,"

confessed themselves devoutly; and bent humbly beneath the absolving hands, before they mustered at their respective posts. In each of the fire-ships an altar was raised, and garlands of flowers adorned the rigging. Who could imagine, as he looked upon those ministers of peace —surrounded by every sacerdotal sign, and voice of hymns, and festive wreaths—that destruction's fiercest devil crouched below? Every cavity in these ships was charged with explosive matter; hand-grenades lay in piles along the decks, and a battery lurked among the grappling irons, the first strain of which was to explode it: the subtle Greek-fire—penetrating and quenchless—was laid in tubes from stem to stern; and a curtain of bullet-proof, to defend the firemen, lay ready for tricing up the shrouds when the ships were about to act.

The breeze blows merrily, the harbour is deserted, the open sea is gained, and galley and fireship strain eagerly for the scene of action. Day fades, and evening comes. Scio looms before the invaders through the evening's gloom, and soon they open on the bay where the Turkish fleet lies crowded in fancied security. The Grecian galleys come to an anchor along the unprotected southern shore; but the fire-ships that are to begin the action sail on to the north, in order to command a leading wind.

Meanwhile, the triumphant Moslems held their festival in the desolated homes of the slaughtered islanders. A thousand bonfires along the shore gave light to groups, rejoicing tranquilly according to their fashion. Every Turkish ship was clearly visible by the light of innumerable lamps hung amongst the rigging: and conspicuous above all was the admiral's flag-ship; on which three bright-green lanterns showed that Hassan Pasha held his orgies.

By the last light of evening, two little brigantines, bearing the Crescent banner, were seen slowly entering the bay. On they came, tranquilly and unnoticed, till, instead of bending their course toward the merchantmen, they were observed to steer straight for the centre of the Turkish fleet. That fleet had already experienced the fearful havoc of the Greek fire-ship, and at once a cry burst from every watchman —" The Greek! The Greek!" Instantly the Moslem joy was hushed; hurried and confused commands were issued aboard of every ship; cables were cut, and sails were instantly let fall.

Just then, one of the two dark little craft that had caused such panic in that stately fleet, was seen to haul her wind; for a moment she remained motionless, while the crew of her doomed consort got on board, and left

Canári and his friend alone to work her. A small caïque —*their* only hope of safety—towed astern; and on went the little brigantine gallantly through the heart of the Ottoman fleet. Cannon opened upon her from every quarter; and a thousand bullets whistled round the white-cross banner that now proudly streamed from her mast-head, as she swept calmly, but swiftly on. Canári holds the helm, and Norman leans against the foremast with folded hands, in one of which is visible one burning spark. The brig passes on silently through the confused and drifting fleet, and winds her way steadily towards the towering ship of the admiral. Now she is under her very counter—and now her gunwale grates against the sides; the grappling-irons fasten in the main-chains—the little spark has been planted and makes quick harvest; a hundred dusky hands strive to shake off the irons; but the grenades explode, annihilating everything but the grim hooks that they protect, and the stanchions to which they cling.—"Now, Norman, our task is done!—Away for life and Zoë!" shouted Canári, cheerily, as he leapt, followed by his friend, into the caïque, that soon shot clear of the fire-ship and her gigantic victim. The latter had cut her cables, and now drifted to and fro, as if struggling to get free from her destroyer;—vainly as the tall giraffe attempts to fly from the tiger that bestrides him while it tears his sides! The caïque paused upon her oars, and watched for the explosion. It came full quickly;—for a moment the brig recoiled,—then seemed, transformed into fire—to plunge into the Moslem ship: instantly was the fiery invasion met, echoed, and repelled, by another explosion, louder and more terrible by far; the huge three-decker and her destroyer disappeared from the ocean and mingled their blazing fragments in the clouds.

By that sudden flash were seen a thousand turbans

Y

floating about on the dark water : one — only one — small
boat was seen escaping, and Canári's eagle eye caught the
Pasha's standard at its stern. A gesture was enough : the
caïque shot along through the sparkling shower that hissed
around it, towards that boat. It struck the barge ; the very
shock gave impetus to the force with which the assailants
sprang on board, and their swords descended as they came.

A moment is gone by ; that boat contains no living soul.
The caïque skims again lightly towards the open sea ; and
the insignia of the ruthless Pasha are amongst her trophies.

That night and its morrow are passed by. Evening
comes again, with all the soft beauty that it wore when the
lovers looked out upon Myconé's bay. Softly and gloriously once more the moon shone over that calm scene,
and thoughtfully did Zoë once more gaze upon its beauty.
Long had she striven to sustain her spirit with heroic
thought and Tyrtæan song ; but suspense had tranced
her into silence, only broken by the beating of her passionate heart. The lute lay neglected by her side, flowers
were torn and scattered round her ; the very horizon she
had watched so long seemed like some iron circle pressing
on her brow, and she buried her face in her clasped hands.
A ripple is heard — a caïque shoots along the waves, and
lightly touches on the marble stairs — a firm but slow step
is heard — and Canári comes — but comes alone !

III.—PEACE.

" But song of bard, or sage's lore,
   That land ennoble now no more ;
   It is not Greece—it must not be ;
   And yet look up—the land is free ! "
                          AUBREY DE VERE.

LONG years of sanguinary struggle and fearful vicissi-
tude had passed by ; Greece was left desolate of her beauty.

her wealth, and her bravest children—but she was left
FREE. Her patriot people either slept in honourable
death, or lived in liberty.

In the early spring of 1833, the beautiful harbour of
Nauplia was crowded with ships of war; the conquering
flags of Navarino—English, French, and Russian—floated
from their spars; and salvoes of artillery welcomed to her
shore the monarch of regenerate Greece!

And such was the result of what cold-hearted, calculating Europe denounced twelve years before as a hopeless
struggle; as if any noble cause were *ever* hopeless! Twelve
years before, and Ypsilanti might have said—

> " Lo! with the chivalry of Christendom,
>   I wage my war—no nation for my friend;
>   Yet in each nation having hosts of friends!" *

And now the most powerful nations in the world were
emulous of doing honour to the cause they had so long
denounced.

Almost all the Greeks of the Morea, whom the war had
spared, and many of those from Livadia and the islands,
were assembled on the shore to greet their king. Infinitely various was their appearance and array; as Primate,
Klepht, and Palicar, in coloured robes, or snow-white
tunics, and scarfs, and arms, and armour of antique
fashions, crowded round the path their sovereign was to
take. Some clambered about the broken bastions, or over
fallen columns, to command a better view. Greek matrons,
in their festival attire, thronged each safer spot of ground;
holding their unconscious infants up, as if they could see
also through their eyes. The pathway to the citadel was
kept clear, not by soldiers, but by Greek maidens, upon

* Henry Taylor's admirable drama, " Philip Van Artevelde."

whom none of those wild warriors of the hills would dare
to press; and little children sang hymns of joy and welcome as they strewed the ground with flowers.

Facing the place of disembarkation, the ground was
broken by military operations, or their result; the road
to the citadel wound among huge rocky fragments, whose
mossy eminences afforded resting-places to gay groups.
Beyond this space rose the Acropolis, backed by the wide
sweep of the hills of Argos and the mountains of Arcadia.

Another loud salvo of artillery shook the sky, and
announced that Otho had landed in his new kingdom,
whilst a universal shout of enthusiasm from his new subjects welcomed him to Greece. The graceful and classic
costume of his adopted country became his light and
youthful figure well; and he trod the sacred soil with a
firm and noble step. His eyes glanced eagerly around;
but, alas! there was no generous fire, no proud inspiration
there! His salute was courtly, but cold; and while Grecian warriors pressed to catch his notice, he chattered
lightly to his Bavarian friends.

He was, however, the gift of the Great Powers to
Greece, and it behoved her to be grateful. And so her
enthusiastic people felt for a little while. No foreboding
of worse than Turkish tyranny, renewed under a Christian
form, then shadowed their glad hearts; mirth and revelry
resounded everywhere, and the first festival of freedom
was well kept.

That evening—when the sun had set, the breeze blew
off the land, and the fever of rejoicing was at its height—
a lonely galley held her way from the festive shore, on,—
over the darkening sea. She steered the same course
that the galley of Canári held long years before, and
reached the same haven in the harbour of Myconé. The

islanders were celebrating their king's arrival with their usual zeal in the cause of pleasure; but the pilot of the galley made no pause among the revellers. He soon found himself alone among the orange groves; and near the ruined temple found the object of his search — a grave.

A tomb of Parian marble bore a simple symbol; but while an inhabitant remained, there was no epitaph needed to tell the stranger that beneath its shelter reposed the chivalrous valour of the Norman, by the side of the passionate but pure beauty of the classic East.

Canári, too, has long since found a sailor's sepulture among the islands that he died to save. There he lies in honour — shrouded only by the dark Ægean that he loved so well.

* * * * * *

At the conclusion of the Eastern traveller's narrative, with which all the company professed themselves much gratified, the Lady Eva turned appealingly to a young lady who sat near her, and intimated that the more her own sex would assist in this novel celebration of her birthday revels, the more she should, in after-life, recur with pride and pleasure to the recollection of this happy year. "And I know you *can* tell stirring stories," she added, archly and beseechingly; "for SAINT ETIENNE revealed this fact to me one long winter night of last year."

The appeal was successful; a drawing was quickly chosen, and presented by the Lady Eva, and the result was

THE TERRACE GARDEN.

IN the southern provinces of France, the climate is almost Italian. There, along the range of the maritime Alps, the vegetation is luxuriant as that of Italy; the air-tints of that sunny region possess all the magic glow of the sweet south, and the short twilight following the summer day is as soothing to the soul and sense as that which heralds the night upon the shores of Naples. It was an evening in the month of August, 1790; the sun was slowly sinking towards the blue waves of the Mediterranean, along whose sleepy and slowly heaving swell his last rays fell in a broad tract of light. Large volumes of copper-coloured vapours rested on the western horizon; a few white, feathery clouds flecked the deepening azure of the high vault of heaven, and already the young moon glimmered above the crests of the distant mountains. A bold promontory stretched far into the glassy waters of the gulf of Lyons. A thick wood of aged oaks, with a few tall pines rising proudly above their broad masses of foliage, clothed the promontory from its summit to the verge of the steep rocks skirting its base. Midway up the ascent stood the château de Montauban; it was a stately pile of Gothic architecture, with the dark ivy, the growth of three centuries, clinging to its grey stone, mantling the highest turrets, and almost hiding the sculptured shields of noble blazonry surmounting each deep-arched gate and window. The château was surrounded by terraced gardens, with their groves of orange-trees, their thickets of roses, their stone vases filled with exotic shrubs, and their fountains sparkling in the evening light. Long flights of stone stairs led from the upper to the lower terraces, until they

descended to the lowest, which was scarcely raised above the shore of a small cove, where the rippling waves, dancing in between the cliffs, washed murmuring over the pavement of the terrace.

Two persons stood hand in hand upon the lowest terrace, and looked silently over the scene we have essayed to picture. One was a young man, who might perhaps have already attained his twentieth year. His figure was tall and graceful, but cast in that athletic mould which showed that he had already acquired the full strength of manhood. His head was set on with the proud grace often seen in the works of the antique sculptors; his features were aquiline, and strongly marked, possessing the haughty and somewhat stern beauty of the Roman statue. His eyes were dark and fiery as those of the mountain stag; and his hair, which curled closely round his forehead, was black as the raven's wing. His dress was the plainest garb of the Alpine hunter; but the easy dignity of his whole air and mien proclaimed his right to rank with the highest nobles of France. He was certainly a handsome man, but his almost faultless beauty repelled rather than attracted interest. His countenance too truly mirrored his spirit, and betrayed the feeling of disgust and lassitude which follows the excitement of premature passions. The freshness and the illusions of life were lost, he had lived too quickly, and the clear, keen observation of men and their motives,—the cold, selfish spirit of worldly calculation, had succeeded to the expansive generosity and warm-hearted confidence of youth. His wealth had enabled him to purchase the bitter knowledge of the worthlessness of the world, and to buy pleasure which had destroyed happiness.

His companion was a girl, apparently about one year

younger. Her fairy form, beautifully rounded, but almost
infantine in its fragile lightness, her long auburn hair,
falling in waves over her shoulders, her soft and dark-grey
eyes, shadowed by their black lashes, and the rosy and
transparent bloom on her fair cheek, gave to her beauty a
witchery which had won for her the name of the Fée
de Montauban. She leaned upon her companion's arm,
and looked fondly into his eyes, which were fixed upon
her with a gaze of equal fondness.

"To-morrow!" she said, with a sigh: "so soon—so
very soon!"

"To-morrow!" he replied, with a look of fierce impatience; "it is even now too late."

"Adhemar, why will you leave us? There is no hope
of glory now—nothing but danger."

"And duty, Madeleine," he added. "Would you, the
last scion of our race, would you wish your brother to dishonour our name, and to stain that noble shield, which
has been borne untarnished since our ancestor won his
spurs on the fields of Palestine, and received them from
the hand of Philip Augustus?"

"But the court can claim no duty at your hands," said
Madeleine; "you never sought power or rank from the
favour of the king. Not one of our ancestors ever received
any honour from the court."

"True, Madeleine. The name of a Montauban was
never heard in the ante-chamber of some lowborn minister,
whose arrogance marked the depth from which he had
crept, as well as the height to which he had climbed. No
Montauban was ever seen in the degraded levée at the
ruelles of the fair favourites, the only mediators whose
intercessions with our kings could obtain the royal favour
for the nobles of France. Never were our names heard

there; but when did a Montauban desert his sovereign in the hour of danger?"

"But the danger now lies in the hatred of men so far beneath you, that it is a degradation to contend with them," said Madeleine.

"A pack of wolves may be as destructive as a lion; shall we spare them in contempt?" replied Adhemar de Montauban. "Enough, Madeleine, I must go. I must take my place by the side of the king. I will not lurk here, as if I feared to avow my principles. I will not emigrate; for emigration is only a cowardly desertion of our duty, our country, and our king. I am an aristocrat; I have a name to uphold, and a property to defend, and the *canaille* shall know that I may die, but never shrink from the struggle."

"Yet the poor peasants have been very miserable," said Madeleine; "perhaps they only seek for justice. Dear Adhemar, do not call them *canaille*."

"My sweet Madeleine, you argue like a woman. A moment since you spoke as if the blood of the rabble would stain my sword, and now you speak of them as very moderate, estimable people. You do not know what you want to say."

"I know that I want to keep you here with me, and safe," said Madeleine. "For the rest, I do not understand anything about politics; your vassals are happy, for you are very kind to them; but on other properties near my convent I saw the peasants very wretched; they were starving, and yet they were obliged to work for their lords without payment for their labour."

"Tush, Madeleine, you must not deduce principles from solitary facts. There are a few tyrants among our noblesse, perhaps, but most of them are kind to their vassals, and considerate of their welfare; their kindness gives as favours all that the laws could grant as rights to the peasants."

" Yet, Adhemar, it is hard to think that one must ask as a favour what ought to be a right; it is dreadful that the lives of thousands, or at least their welfare, should depend on the caprice of one,—yes, Adhemar, even of you."

" Do you accuse me of oppressive conduct?" said Adhemar.

" Oh no, you are too noble, too kind, to be severe to your dependants," said the young girl, with a look of ardent love and pride; then, seeing that Adhemar looked annoyed by her words, she changed the conversation, and added, " Will you not consult our grandfather, Adhemar ? "

" He is in his dotage," said the Marquis de Montauban; " I have consulted a better counsellor, Edouard de Lorency. He advises me to go,—he accompanies me."

Madeleine trembled; a deep blush passed over her cheek, and then it ebbed away and left her very pale. Her brother observed not her agitation, and he went on speaking with bitter energy.

" We go, and though it may cost us our lives, yet we will prove that we are aristocrats and patriots also. Patriotism and self-interest are one in our feelings. What is the welfare of a country to a man who has nothing to lose by its ruin ? What is dishonour to a man who has no name ? "

At this moment a servant informed Adhemar that his lawyer was awaiting his pleasure in the library.

" He comes to take my instructions before I leave the country, perhaps for ever," said the Marquis; " I would De Lorency were here."

Madeleine remained alone. She leaned on the pedestal of a sculptured vase, which was filled with some rare Indian plants. Their drooping branches bent over her head, and their bright and perfumed flowers rested on her hair and on her brow. Her eyes were fixed on the setting sun, but her thoughts were abstracted from all around her. A light footstep reached ner ear — she started; a smile played on her lip, and a rosy flush rose even to her temples, but she did not turn her head towards the terrace stairs. Monsieur de Lorency was at that moment descending those stairs. He was about thirty-five years of age, but he looked much older. A wound received in America had caused his dark brown hair to assume a touch of grey. His figure was very fine, but his commanding presence was somewhat injured by the slight stoop which always bent his head. A deep furrow was traced upon his broad and thoughtful brow, and a shade of melancholy gravity rested on his clear grey eyes. He was not happy. The last representative of a noble but fallen house, he had experienced the neglect and the coldness of the world, and in return, he looked upon that vain world with haughty scorn; and shrank from the pleasures of that society, in which he felt that he was received without a welcome. When chance threw him among those who were only his equals in birth, although more richly favoured by fortune, he met them with a reserve which would have repulsed any advance towards intimacy. Though generally silent, he possessed great conversational powers, but he spoke with a cynical bitterness which sprung from wounded pride and the galling feelings of high-born poverty, and which effectually repelled the interest which his high character as a soldier, and his powerful talents as a political writer, would naturally have excited.

"Mademoiselle de Montauban," he said, "I come to take leave of you."

The tone of deep sorrow in which he spoke contrasted strangely with the cold formality of his words. After a pause, he added, in the same low, broken voice, "Your brother has told you that we must leave you to-morrow."

"Why do you persuade him to leave me?" said Madeleine.

They were silent once more. She still looked along the darkening sea, while his eyes were fixed on her with a look of painful thought; but though her face was half averted from his gaze, she felt that it was fastened upon her, and she dared not turn towards him.

"Your brother asked my advice; he placed his honour in my hands. Could I deceive him? If my advice has caused you grief, I implore you to pardon me. And oh! Mademoiselle de Montauban, do not hate me."

"When may you return?" said Madeleine.

"I know not," he answered. "Adhemar has hope; he thinks the cause of royalty may yet triumph. I have no hope; the cause is lost. Our king has no energy; our nobles have deserted the country; our priests are infidels; the popular party wish for revenge for past injustice, as well as for the obtaining of the recognition of their own rights; the royalists wish to uphold every oppressive abuse of law, to which they give the name of justice. How can peace ever arise from these discordant elements?"

"No, no," said Madeleine, "there can be no peace. I shall never see Adhemar again."

She burst into tears, and hastily extending her hand to De Lorency, she murmured a few words of parting regret. Lorency took her hand, touched it with his lips, lightly, courteously, and timidly, and allowed her to leave him without one word which could betray the truth which he but too deeply felt, that thus to part with her was worse than death. Slowly she ascended the terrace stairs; when the last flutter of her white robe was lost beneath the gate of the castle, Lorency caught the branch of the ipomea which had touched her hair—he plucked it from the plant—he pressed it madly to his lips, and hiding it in his bosom, he hurried to the château, in search of Adhemar. He found him in the library with the lawyer.

"I sent for you, Edouard, to consult you about the settlement of my property. My father's will fixed my majority on my twentieth birthday, so I have been of age for some months."

"I know you have had that misfortune," said Lorency, trying to force his attention to the business to be laid before him.

"I wish to secure all that I can dispose of to Madeleine, in the event of my dying, or, to speak more correctly, in the event of my being killed in the civil war which I foresee. She requires a guardian; now my mother's father is almost the only relation we have living of her family. My father's family have quarrelled with me, because I announced my intention of settling everything on my sister. I will not name any of them her guardians. Our grandfather is already in his dotage, so that he cannot discharge that duty. Will you accept it? It is a strange request, but you are my only friend."

"I cannot, Adhemar—I will not!" replied Lorency.

"You will not!" said Adhemar, impatiently; then seeing that De Lorency was pale as death, and fearfully agitated, he took his arm, led him out on the terrace, and said, "Tell me, De Lorency what has agitated you thus?"

"Your own words, Adhemar. You ask me to be a father to your sister, to watch over her, to see her every day, and to sign the contract which will make her the wife of some man whom she may love, but who never could love ner as I have loved her from the moment I first saw her."

"She has rejected you?" said Adhemar, inquiringly.

"No; she dreams not that I have dared to love her. I will not pain her by confessing the misery she has inflicted. I am too proud to acknowledge a hopeless love, even to Madeleine."

"Hopeless! I do not think it hopeless," said Adhemar; "a woman might love you, if you loved her, but I never could have suspected you of so much condescension. Your pride——"

"What has pride to do with love?" said Lorency. "My pride is the consciousness that I love her more than life; more than all, except my honour. She is young; I am old. You have shown me how old I am, by asking me to be her guardian; her father, as it were. I am poor; she is rich. I will not tell her what anguish she has caused me."

Adhemar made no answer. He left the Baron de Lorency upon the terrace, and sought Madeleine in her dressing-room, where he heard she was sitting. Her head was bent upon the cushions of the sofa, over which her hair hung in disordered tresses. At the sound of Adhemar's voice she looked up, but large tears stood gathered on her eyelids. Adhemar drew her to his breast. "Madeleine," he said, fondly, "Edouard de Lorency loves you; but he fears that you would banish him from your presence, if he dared to confess it. Will you forgive his presumption for my sake, and allow him to plead his own cause?"

"I knew that he loved me," said Madeleine, hiding her face upon her brother's shoulder, "and yet he was so cold and so distant, that he made me very unhappy. I could not speak to him when he treated me so coldly, and then I saw that he was hurt and miserable; and yet it was not my fault."

Adhemar kissed his sister once more, and returned to De Lorency, who was pacing the terrace in extreme agitation.

"I have seen Madeleine," said Adhemar; "she has long known that you loved her."

"And therefore she treated me with cold disdain," said Edouard; "I knew that my love was madness."

"Must I offer her hand to you?" said Adhemar. "Go to her, plead your cause, and come back to me when she has given you your sentence."

Half in desperation, half in hope, De Lorency sought Madeleine. The conscious blush and the unconscious smile which greeted him when he spoke to her, answered all his doubts. He threw himself on his knees at her feet, and poured forth his love, his hopes, his fears, and his joy. Before Adhemar interrupted him, he had told her the story of his life. She was his first and his only love; and she had promised to repay the years of suffering he had endured, by a whole life of happiness. Adhemar was delighted. Edouard was his only friend, and he was now the guardian of Madeleine, so that he was freed from a great responsibility, and Madeleine was secure in a husband's protection.

The will of the late Marquis de Montauban had fixed the twentieth birthday of Adhemar as that on which he should come of age; it had also given to Madeleine a noble fortune, coupled with a condition that she should

not marry until she, too, had attained her twentieth year
Adhemar and De Lorency, therefore, left the château immediately after the fiançailles of the Baron with Madeleine.
She remained alone with her mother's father, who had
long lived with his grandchildren. Months passed on
slowly, sadly, over the lonely château. The smile faded
from Madeleine's lip, and the bloom withered from her
soft cheek; her step lost its elasticity, and her low voice
took a sadder tone. Her grandfather had sunk into the
utter imbecility of extreme old age. She watched over
him with patient tenderness, soothing the fretfulness of
his feeble mind with gentle fondness. She busied herself
much amongst the peasantry of her brother's estates; her
charity relieved their wants, and her assistance was ever
ready to second the efforts of their industry. Their gratitude rewarded her kindness, and while political miseries
destroyed the peace of all around, there was prosperity and
quiet on the territories of Adhemar de Montauban. These
occupations filled her days, but still she was unhappy.
Her brother and her betrothed lover were far from her,
exposed to every danger, and resolved to share to the last
the perils of their fallen sovereigns. Day by day Madeleine watched and waited for the hour which brought her
letters with a sinking heart and a dread which was almost
despair, for each day might bring the announcement of
the arrest or death of those she loved. And when their
gloomy and hopeless letters came, they gave no happiness,
for they could only tell of escape from the dangers of one
day, and promised no safety for the morrow.

At length, the flight, capture, and imprisonment of the
royal family, left Adhemar and Lorency at liberty to return to the château De Montauban. Madeleine was happy
once more. Neither Adhemar nor Edouard had been

denounced by the republicans; they lived quite alone, received no visits, and busied themselves in the construction
of a small harbour at a point where Adhemar's land joined
those which still remained in the possession of De Lorency.
This harbour was of the utmost advantage to the fishermen
of the coast, and they were grateful to the Marquis, who
had undertaken the work at his sole expense. Adhemar's
tenantry loved him; De Lorency's were equally attached
to him, although his poverty had hitherto restricted the
exercise of his charity among them. The curés of both
parishes had taken the constitutional oaths; the municipal
officers of the commune were Adhemar's dependants; so
that everything seemed to promise them safety during th
troubled times which were fast approaching.

The Reign of Terror desolated France, but as yet the
family of Montauban had escaped. Madeleine's twentieth
birthday was at hand, and she had promised Edouard to
give him her hand upon that day. At length the day
came, and Madeleine was conducted to the municipality by
her brother. De Lorency awaited them there. The legal
ceremony was performed, and De Lorency returned with
his bride to the château, where the curé was to perform
the religious ceremony at the altar of the old chapel.

Greatly were they astonished when they learned that
the priest had not arrived. He had not sent a letter, nor
even a message, of explanation. De Lorency ordered a
horse to be saddled, and instantly mounting, rode to the
house of the curé. He was not there; he had left home
early, saying that he would visit some sick persons, and
then proceed to the château. De Lorency returned to the
château. A vague feeling of alarm spread from one to the
other; even the aged servants of the house shared in the
undefined apprehension. The evening came at length.

z

Adhemar, according to his custom, was playing draughts
with his grandfather, which was the only amusement 'n
which the poor old man still found pleasure. De Lorency
and his bride walked out upon the terrace. The night was
beautiful, a moonlit summer night, and Edouard led her
down to the shore. The bright waves curled playfully
over the base of the low terrace; the perfumes of the
garden flowers filled the air, and the nightingales answered
each other from the trees. A deep-hushed quiet reigned
over all around; and as Edouard's arm encircled the form
of his bride, as his low voice whispered vows of passionate
love, Madeleine forgot the vague apprehensions which had
haunted her during the day, and surrendered her soul to
hope and happiness.

"Tell me that you love me, Madeleine!—oh, tell me
once more that you love me! I can scarcely believe in my
happiness."

"You know that I must love you now, Edouard; it is
my duty," said Madeleine, playfully, while unconsciously
and fondly she clasped her hand in his.

"Coquette! is it thus you play with my love?" said
Edouard, in the same joyous tone of perfect happiness.
"Nay, dearest Madeleine—" He paused, and instinctively
he clasped her more closely to his breast; for at that moment a dark speck appeared amid the moonlight on the
water. It came quickly on; it was a boat. It was pulled
by one man, but aided by the wind it darted quickly over
the waves, and in a few minutes its keel grated on the
sand beneath the terrace. The boatman sprung upon the
terrace, and De Lorency recognised the good-natured,
honest Pierre Huguenin, the Mayor of the commune, and
one of the most attached of Adhemar's tenants.

"Monsieur de Lorency, I come to warn you. A party

of gens-d'armes from Marseilles have arrived at my house ; they have seized the poor curé, and have orders to arrest you and the Marquis. Fly while you have some hope of escape ; cross the frontier into Italy."

Madeleine sank almost fainting on the steps of the terrace. The hardy peasant looked upon her with sorrowful compassion. He had that morning united her to him who now knelt beside her in mute despair. The orange wreath was yet unfaded on her brow, and yet, ere morning dawned, they should part, perhaps for ever! De Lorency felt that the bitterness of death was crushed into that one thought.

"Monsieur, call the Marquis; I dare not venture into the château ; all your servants may not be true to you."

Casting one look of agony upon his bride, Edouard ascended the terrace stairs; in a moment he returned with Adhemar.

"You have been denounced, Monsieur le Marquis, and accused of maintaining a correspondence with the émigrés. The gens-d'armes arrived at my house about two hours since; they brought in the priest, whom they arrested upon the road from Marseilles. While they went to search his house, I got away, and came across the bay to warn you of your danger. Do you suspect any of your dependants of thus betraying you ?"

"I have never confided a single secret to any of my people," said the Marquis, "therefore none of them could betray me. This is a groundless charge, and I know the inventor of it. Boileau, my attorney, is the traitor. I detected some unfair charges in his last account, and therefore, about a week since, I dismissed him from my employment."

"He has been in close conference with the officer of the party at my house," said the Mayor Huguenin

" Now, farewell; saddle your fleetest horses and fly to
the frontier. I will conceal Mademoiselle Madeleine in
my house; she will be safe as if she were in a chapel."

" No, she shall share our fate," said De Lorency; " it
would be cruelty to leave her alone, even in safety; fear
for us would kill her. Leave us, Huguenin; you may be
compromised; for our safety you have risked your own."

" No danger for me," said the Mayor; " they know the
attachment of your tenantry, and, to avoid all danger of a
rescue, they will not visit the château till midnight. Their
intention of arresting you is kept a secret. I was not
informed of it by any of them, but I overheard the conversation of the officer with Boileau. And now, farewell!"
he said, as the Marquis gratefully wrung his hand.

At that moment the tramp of horses was heard rapidly
approaching. Huguenin hastily pushed off his skiff, and
pulled her round into the shadow of the rocks.

" Fly, Madeleine; Huguenin will protect you," said
Adhemar, thinking only of her safety.

" Never!" replied Madeleine; " I will share your fate,
your prison, or your grave. What have I on earth but
you?" And as she spoke, she took her brother's hand, and
the hand of her husband, and clasped them to her breast.

" Madeleine, my own in life and death!" exclaimed
De Lorency.

Slowly, and yet firmly they returned to the château.
It was already in the possession of the police. They had
assembled the domestics in the saloon, where the old Marquis de Laferté was seated beside the deep chimney, where,
as was his pleasure, a fire was burning, although it was
summer. He looked from one to the other of the strange
faces round him with a childish terror, and seemed to feel
the presence of dangers which his feeble mind could not

understand. Madeleine placed herself by his side; and there they sat, helpless age and defenceless innocence, alike unrespected by the tyrants of the hour. De Lorency was calm, though his eyes were fixed on his bride with a look which spoke all the anguish of his disappointed hopes of happiness. Adhemar de Montauban stood proudly amidst his enemies, and his haughty and searching glance turned from one to the other, until it rested on the traitor Boileau with an expression of bitter scorn. The traitor did not quail; he was triumphant, and he felt no regrets. The officer commanding the detachment seemed somewhat embarrassed; he saluted Adhemar with courtesy, and with evident reluctance informed him that he was his prisoner.

He was a young man, and he shrank from witnessing the misery which he had unwillingly inflicted. Adhemar almost pitied him.

" My sister will accompany us, Monsieur ?" he said.

" I have received no orders respecting Mademoiselle," replied the officer. " You and M. de Lorency alone are named in my orders."

" To what prison are we to be conveyed ?"

" To Lyons," said the officer. That word contained the sentence of death.

Adhemar turned suddenly to Boileau, and said, bitterly, " Traitor ! why are you here ?"

A few words from the officer of the gens-d'armes explained all. Boileau had received from the Comité de la Sûreté publique a commission resembling that of Canier and Lebon. He was thus arbiter of the destiny of his former master. Adhemar had doubted his probity; he had dismissed him with contempt from his employment, and he was now at his mercy.

De Lorency stood in silent despair near Madeleine, who had sunk back fainting upon her chair.

" Monsieur," said Adhemar, " will you permit my sister to share our prison ?"

The young officer hesitated, spoke to Boileau in a low voice, and said, " I dare not exceed my instructions. I will retire for a few minutes, as you may wish to take leave of your family."

He left the room, followed by his men ; the terror-stricken servants also retired to the outer hall, but Boileau remained, as if he would enjoy the misery of his victims. He seated himself coolly, and fixed his eyes inquiringly on Madeleine. De Lorency saw not, heard not, knew not aught that passed around him. His soul, his senses, every faculty of his mind, every feeling, was absorbed in his love and his despair. He drew Madeleine to his breast, and covered her pale brow with kisses, while he strove to recall her to consciousness by the fondest vows of impassioned love. Adhemar pointed to Boileau, and said with an expression of contemptuous disgust, " De Lorency, take Madeleine from this chamber, which is now unworthy of her presence."

" Stay, Citoyen Lorency," said Boileau ; " La fille Montauban must hear what I have to say to her. The destiny of all present will depend on her reply."

" Hence, Madeleine, this is no place for you," said De Lorency, as he felt that she attempted to extricate herself from his arms.

" Your fate depends on my answer," said Madeleine ; and suddenly recovering her clear reason, with the noble energy of woman's self-devoted love, she placed herself before Boileau, and said, " Speak ! I am ready to hear you."

" Your brother disgraced me ; he deprived me of the employment by which I lived ; I have obtained my revenge. He never trusted me, but I suspected his correspondence with the émigrés. I tracked his messengers ;

I know all; I have a copy of his last letter to Coblentz; but though his life is in my hands, you can save him if you will. Consent to be my wife, and I will destroy the proofs against your brother, and even facilitate his escape. His estates must be forfeited, but his life will be safe."

Madeleine could not speak. Boileau continued, calmly and unpityingly, " I know you love that man; he, too, shall be saved. Now I leave you; in half an hour I return to you, then I must receive your answer."

" Hear it now—I am the wife of Monsieur de Lorency!"

" A ceremony can be set aside," said Boileau. " Consult together, and decide."

He left the room. Adhemar laughed bitterly. " Consult, and decide," he said. " An honourable consultation, truly! He proposes to dishonour my sister, to rob me of my lands, to brand me as a coward; for none but a coward would accept life purchased at such a price."

De Lorency silently took from his pocket-book the certificate of his legal marriage with Madeleine; with a quivering lip he read it over, and then let it fall into the fire. Adhemar sprang forward to snatch it from the flame, but it was too late.

" Madeleine," said De Lorency, " you are free; save your brother, if you can; sacrifice yourself—think not of me. I have death in my power; I need but say before my judges, ' Vive le Roi,' and I shall escape from my tortures."

" Madeleine," said Adhemar; " Madeleine, hear me. I am not happy; I loved, and was betrayed. She whom I loved with the whole burning passion of a virgin heart, deserted me. She married another, more powerful, more wealthy; I need not name them; she became a duchess. I met her again; love, hatred, revenge were busy in my bosom; my life was a hell upon earth. The syren spread her snares for me; I sacrificed my conscience, my honour, all for her. I deceived her husband, and he was my friend; I outraged heaven, I braved hell, for that woman; I thought her very treachery to the man whose name she bore was truth to me. Fool! dupe that I was! She gratified her vanity by my public subjection to her caprices, and then she discarded me. Since then, as you know, I have led a life of expiation for my career of guilt. I have only sought to fulfil my duties,—I love not life; let me die!"

Boileau entered the room : he approached Madeleine, and asked her to inform him of her decision.

"Take our estates—take all—but spare their lives; I cannot marry you!"

" Without your hand I should have no title to the estates; and more than this, where were my revenge? Your brother disgraced me; the disgrace must recoil on himself through you. Once more, girl, choose; will you save them ?"

" I am Edouard's wife; I cannot save them!" said Madeleine, in agony. She sank upon the floor; De Lorency raised her in his arms and carried her into another room.

" Madeleine! my own Madeleine! it were worse than death to resign you to another. In a few days I shall be murdered by those demons at Lyons. Swear to me never to wed another; let me carry your love to the grave."

"I swear it!" said Madeleine; "but can you doubt it? Could I give to another the faith I have pledged to you? But we shall not be parted for ever; I cannot outlive you, my love is a part of my life."

"De Lorency, they call us," said Adhemar. He

clasped his sister to his breast, and rushed out of the room. The agony of that moment was unfelt by Madeleine; she had fainted. Edouard's hot tears fell upon her death-like cheek, as he pressed his lips to hers in one last kiss. He laid her on the sofa; he cut off one long curl of her hair, and thrust it into his bosom; then cutting off a lock of his own hair, he laid it beside her; and not daring to linger, lest she should return to the consciousness of her misery, he hurried from the castle.

Days, weeks passed on, and brought no ray of hope to Madeleine. Her heart was broken; her youth was blighted; her beauty withered; but her mind was calm, and her courage had risen to the energy of desperation. She seemed to live apart from the things of the world; the only tie that still bound her to life was the care of her helpless grandfather. The estates of the Marquis were confiscated, and Madeleine and the old man were driven out into the world, without a home, without support save from the charity of the former vassals of their house. Huguenin received them; he served them like a menial, and was almost grieved when Madeleine thanked him for his kindess.

The old Marquis had not known the danger which surrounded his family for many months. Even the arrest of the friends had made no impression on his feeble mind; they were absent, but he heeded it not, as their visits to Paris had accustomed him to their absence. His removal from the château had at once aroused him from his unconsciousness; he felt that danger and sorrow were around him, and he trembled like a timid child awaking alone in the darkness of the night. He clung to Madeleine with touching dependence. He was wretched if she left him for a moment. He would often say to her, " Where is Adhemar? where is Edouard? Write to them, Madeleine;

tell them to come home to-morrow. Why have they left me alone?"

And Madeleine would seek to soothe his fretful impatience, and then retire to hide the bitter tears that answered his vain appeal.

At length the old man's life seemed to decay. Gradually he sunk towards the grave. Before he had been one month in Huguenin's house, he died. Madeleine watched by his side. He died without pain. No priest could attend the bed of death, but Madeleine prayed for the parting soul.

Madeleine saw him laid in the grave, among the mouldering crosses in the village churchyard. The turf was laid on again, and the peasants stood round in silence. Madeleine looked on them with a sad smile of resignation.

"My friends," she said, "you have been very kind. I cannot thank you. May Heaven reward you here and hereafter!" The tears burst from her eyes, and she sunk on her knees upon the new-made grave. The paroxysm did not last long. She dried her tears, and rose from the sod. "I am free now—farewell!—I go to Lyons."

Huguenin tried to dissuade her from this resolution. She was firm, and he was obliged to yield. He could only place her under the care of the post-office courier, conveying letters to Lyons. That night she left Montauban.

Lyons—La ville affranchie—Lyons, whose very name had been blotted from the map of France, was then suffering all the horrors that the diabolical cruelty of republican vengeance could inflict. Day after day, wholesale executions decimated the population. The Place de Terreaux rivalled the Place de Grève in its horrible celebrity; but there was this difference: the people of Lyons looked on in terror, because they dared not shun the spectacle; the mob of Paris went to see executions performed, and looked on the Grève as the Spaniards do on the bull-ring, or as the Romans did on the arena. At Lyons, the executions were not so well performed, as some of the Parisian amateurs said. The victims were shot at the side of their common grave. Sometimes the firing party missed their mark, and, instead of mortal wounds, some were only slightly hurt. They were despatched with the bayonet. Then all were thrown into the grave, and the earth cast back on the yet warm bodies of the victims.

Madeleine was placed by the courier in the house of Huguenin's sister, the wife of an officer in the garrison; Madeleine was therefore safe in her protection. Day by day she visited the Court of the revolutionary tribunal; she wandered round the prisons, to which she had tried in vain to obtain admittance. She followed the condemned, as they went out to death, but she saw not those she sought. Were they already dead? It was a fearful doubt. If she could but see them once more, even on the verge of the grave!

One day, as she returned from the place of death, a man called her by name; she stopped—and Boileau was at her side.

"To-morrow you will see them. I have purchased Montauban. I shall be rid of my rival to-morrow, and I will forgive your refusal, and take you home, if you consent."

Madeleine laughed a wild maniac laugh, and turned from him without speaking. She was almost maddened at that moment.

"She is mad!" he muttered, as he pursued his way; "and yet, how beautiful she is, after all!"

Madeleine did not return to her friends that night.

"To-morrow"—it was her only thought! the Place de Terreaux, her only world! She sat on a stone—the hours passed on unheeded; the silence, the cold night air, calmed her fever; her mind became clear; her thoughts were solemn, but not despairing.

Day dawned slowly over the devoted city. Madeleine knelt and prayed. How long she remained on her knees in prayer, she knew not. The measured tread of the soldiers and the roll of the cart-wheels called back her thoughts to earth. The grave was already dug—the soldiers took their ground—the condemned were placed on the verge of the grave, about to receive them. Adhemar and De Lorency were there, calm, proud, unmoved, as if they were upon an ordinary parade; with their hands clasped in the last pressure of brotherly love, they waited for death. Madeleine sprang forward, burst through the ranks of the soldiers guarding the prisoners, and sank at the feet of her husband and her brother.

"I am come, I am come," she murmured; "Heaven has heard my prayers. We shall die together."

"Heaven is merciful," said De Lorency. He raised her to his breast, and then looked up to Heaven with unspeakable thankfulness. Still clasped in De Lorency's embrace, Madeleine placed her arm round Adhemar's neck, and drew him towards her. No one thought of separating them. One victim more was nothing They repeated together one short prayer, and then calmly awaited death. Not a hand quivered—not an eye quailed. The word was given; "Vive le Roi!" cried the victims. The report of the muskets drowned their voices. All was over!

THE next picture which the Lady Eva had chosen for the close of the Fifth Evening's séance, was one which had, more than any other, puzzled her own fancy as to a fitting theme for its illustration ; and she had, in her pretty perplexity, handed it to an admired and popular writer, whose pen had equally distinguished itself in prose and verse—whose active fancy and powerful imagination had shown themselves capable of evoking " sermons from stones, and good from everything."

But the request was fruitless; his prose muse was "not i' the vein," and his poetical one had already promised an illustration of a drawing reserved for the concluding evening's sitting.

In this dilemma the Lady Eva turned to the lady whose imagination had already illustrated two designs, chosen during a previous evening ;* and an appeal, from which there was *no* appeal, presently produced the tale entitled

CONSCIENCE.

THE Château of Riechoffen is situated on a steep eminence, six leagues from Strasburgh. Its park and gardens are the admiration of the neighbourhood ; and few travellers are allowed to pass through the village of Riechoffen without being asked to visit the superb château. To the lover of the picturesque, the surrounding park, or rather, the two parks, which form part of this rich domain, offer much to excite admiration ; while to the amateur and connoisseur, the valuable paintings, the splendid carvings, and the countless objects of *virtù*, which enrich the

* " The Fortunes of the Glengary," page 90.

interior of the château, render an admission within its
walls a matter of great interest. Two days in the week
are set apart for the reception of strangers; but the
urbanity of its present venerable owner, the good and pious
Count Riechoffen, renders admittance easy to all travellers
who, pressed for time, cannot wait for the appointed public
days.

The Count and his beloved partner were for many years
regarded as friends by all their vassals; and when the
death of the Countess cut short the domestic happiness of
their lord, not an eye in the village but wept for the loss
of one so endeared to them; not a family for leagues
round that did not sympathize in a grief, which they felt,
from the Count's age and character, must be irreparable.

The only child of their marriage—the Count Wilhelm
—was absent at the time of his mother's death ; and though
he hastened home on the sad news reaching him, he did not
long remain with his widowed father; and as his absences
from Riechoffen were supposed to be errands of pleasure,
people marvelled that he did not, after this mournful event,
remain to share his father's solitude.

Whatever might be that father's feelings on his son's
departure, he never betrayed either surprise or anger in
speaking of it. Indeed, few were admitted to his presence
during the first year of his widowhood; the chaplain, who
lived in the château, was his only companion; the closet
adjoining the chapel, where reposed the remains of his lost
wife, his habitual dwelling-place. During this period of
mourning, the gates of the domain were closed to all
visitors; but after the year had passed, the Count received
a few friends, and strangers were again permitted, on two
appointed days in each week, to view the château—all but
the closet and chapel, to the former of which the Count

always repaired during the hours in which company were admitted to the other parts of this superb edifice.

During Count Wilhelm's second visit to his home, which took place three years after the death of his mother, he mentioned his wish to marry, and confided to his father that the object of his attachment, an Italian lady, though rich in youth and loveliness, was without fortune. The Count Riechoffen received this intelligence with unfeigned pleasure; and the lady's want of fortune was agreeable to him; for, aware of the sordid avarice which disfigured his son's character, and rendered him unlike either of his noble parents, such a proof of disinterested attachment delighted him, and putting his arm affectionately round his son's neck, he said—

"A bride of your choice, my dear Wilhelm, wants no adventitious aid of fortune to ensure her the welcome of a daughter in my heart. Pure and good, I feel she must be; or my son would never have chosen her to succeed his mother, as mistress here."

"But she will not live here," replied Wilhelm. "The thought of this cold clime frightens her; our rude sports would terrify her. Born and educated in her own sunny land, she would be lost in this cheerless abode, where neither the charm of music nor the sound of revelry are heard."

The Count Riechoffen's tall form seemed to dilate, his usually pale cheek became suffused with the crimson flush of anger, his voice was less firm than usual, as he replied—

"My son, have you forgot the sad loss which hushed the glad and happy sounds that for many years were wont to resound within these walls? Could revelry have intruded into the house of mourning? Since your angel mother's spirit ceased to bless this abode, what has it been

to me and to yourself but a place of solitude and desolation? Wilhelm, the object of your love is an orphan;
what ties can she have to keep her from her husband's
paternal home? Your mother, my peerless Thérèse, left
parents and other kindred to share the home which, by
her love and the bright excellence of her character, she
rendered for nearly thirty years a blessed and a happy one.
My son, I would not be harsh, but I must not conceal
my opinion from you, that the woman who regards and
esteems a man sufficiently to entrust her happiness to his
care, should have no minor reserves of climate and of
dwelling. Where her husband's duties call him, there
should be her sunshine; and, methinks," added the Count,
looking round the rich apartment in which this conversation took place, and extending his glance over the broad
domain seen from the open window, " it were no difficult
task for the most fastidious and refined in taste to reconcile themselves to this spot."

Wilhelm perceived that this was no moment to pursue
the point; and though firmly resolved never to relinquish
the charms and pleasures of an Italian residence, he saw
the necessity of concealing this determination for the present, and therefore replied—

" It must be my task, as it will be my interest, to
erase from Giuditta's mind all the gloomy impressions it
has conceived of our German austerities, both of climate
and manners."

" Bring her here at once," interrupted his father, "and
she shall not have to complain of a German welcome.
These halls shall once more echo with mirth and song!
It is *her* son's bridal I would keep," he added, in a tone
as if intended for his own ear alone, " and her pure spirit
will hover round us!"

Nothing could exceed the liberality with which the

noble Count Riechoffen provided for his son's establishment on his marriage. Besides the income he settled on him, which was an independence, he caused a suite of rooms in the château to be newly decorated and set apart for his and his bride's use, and the lonely widower was seen again to smile as he talked of the approaching arrival of his children. But this was an event long protracted, and for many months excuse followed upon excuse.

On one of the public days, the Count Riechoffen, who had retired, as was his wont, to the closet adjoining the chapel, was surprised, on passing from it into his library, to find seated on the carpet, and playing with some flowers, of which she was making a garland, a little girl, apparently about three years old. As the Count approached, the child looked up. Her dark hazel eyes filled with tears, her cheeks assumed a deeper hue, but as if trying to persuade herself not to be frightened, she said, " Mamma, come back !"

The Count stooped down and endeavoured to take her hand, but she withdrew it ; and, no longer able to control her emotion at the presence of a stranger, burst into tears. For a long time she sobbed as if her little heart would break, occasionally screaming, "Mamma, mamma, come and take Rèse away !" The Count Riechoffen, distressed at the child's agitation, knew not what to devise to calm her. He did not summon aid, for fear of still further alarming her by the entrance of another stranger. At length he asked, would she go with him and look for mamma ? The child nodded assent, but still cried bitterly; and thus they proceeded into the garden, but no mother was to be found. The child kept running wildly from side to side, till, quite exhausted, she sank on the grass, and nothing but her hushed sobs were to be heard. Day

A A

was closing; the Count watched over her till she fell
asleep, and then, lifting her in his arms, he bore her
gently to the house, summoned his late wife's maid, and
gave orders that the child should be taken care of, and put
to bed.

The strange truth had flashed across Count Riechoffen's mind — some cruel mother must have left that sweet
child, never meaning to return.   At first, his heart was
full of indignation and bitterness against the parent;
but some good angel whispered him that perhaps some
wretched mother, heart-broken and forsaken, had committed her only treasure to his protection, and might even
then be dying — her last earthly thought, a hope that he
would befriend her innocent babe.   " Poor, wretched
mother!" he exclaimed; " what must have been the suffering and the grief which could have induced thee to part
with such a child!"   And from that hour Count Riechoffen felt an affection for the hapless creature he supposed
to have been cast by Providence on his care.   So true it is
that, in a noble breast, pity is ever allied to love.

For some days the little girl continued to weep at
intervals, and to run from room to room searching for her
mother; but as time wore on, her childish grief gradually
subsided, and she no longer looked on Count Riechoffen
with terror, but received with pleasure his warm caress.
The name by which she called herself completed her conquest of the Count's affection.   Thérèse, the name of his
lost — his idolized wife, could not be heard or uttered by
him with indifference.

Week after week and month after month passed, and
yet Wilhelm and his bride arrived not.   This delay had
at first grieved the Count, but the current of his thoughts
had been changed; his warm and affectionate heart had

found another interest, and he had become so attached to the little Thérèse that she was seldom allowed to leave his side. On the evening that he had discovered the poor little girl in the library, he had summoned to his presence the old housekeeper, whose office it was to do the honours of the château, and recount all its wonders and all its riches to visitors. But she had retired early to rest, in consequence of some slight indisposition. He was, therefore, forced to content himself with a message from her, to the effect that she had not noticed the entrance of any child among the crowd of strangers who had that day visited the château.

A governess had been engaged for the little Thérèse before Wilhelm and his bride arrived; and as the Count Riechoffen did not care to expose his little favourite to the haughty indifference of his daughter-in-law, she never appeared in the reception-rooms during their residence, which did not exceed six months.

Much as Count Riechoffen had desired to love his son's wife, and anxious as he had felt to propitiate her regard, not a symptom of affection, not a trait of attachment, rewarded his constant solicitude for her comfort. The Countess Wilhelm was not even respectful or courteous to her husband's father. She was a spoiled and capricious beauty, without one redeeming quality of heart or mind. Her lapdog was her idol; her Italian waiting-woman her companion and intimate. The respect entertained by a populous neighbourhood for this noble family, and the veneration in which the late Countess's memory was held, induced every one to proffer civility and attention to her son's wife; but Giuditta's manner was either so imperious and reserved, or so supercilious and impertinent, that she

became detested and shunned by all the ladies in the
neighbourhood.

Her husband, over whom she tyrannized with all the
little cunning of an ignorant and uneducated woman,
seemed completely weary of her, and would make long and
distant excursions from home, under the pretext of wild-
boar hunting, but, in reality, as was evident to his father,
to escape from Giuditta's silly persecution, and Count
Ricchoffen saw them depart on their return to Italy, from
the home which he had fitted up for their permanent
abode, without one feeling of regret; and when he again
saw his lovely adopted child, his innocent and pure-
minded Thérèse, enjoying herself and running, with childish glee, through the suite of rooms she had been for-
bidden to approach during their stay, he felt that on the
child of a stranger,—the child, perhaps, of shame—the
forsaken one of its mother—on that child did the aged
Count feel that his happiness depended, far more than on
his own and only son.

We will pass over the years of Thérèse's childhood and
her early girlhood, during which time no inquiry had
been made for her, and no clue presented itself to discover
who she might be. With her growth the beauty of Thérèse increased, and at sixteen she was one of the most
lovely beings ever beheld. Rather above the middle
stature, she was slight, but gracefully proportioned. Her
fairy hands and rounded arm, her swan-like throat and
beauteous shoulders, might have inspired the poet, and
offered a study to the sculptor. Her small and finely-
shaped head lent another charm; and the expression of
her dark and melting eyes betrayed the meekness and
mild benignity of her disposition. The affection, the ten-

der and watchfu assiduity, which marked the conduct of Thérèse to her benefactor, was beautiful to contemplate. The joyous innocence of her heart imparted freshness to his feelings, and her young and ardent nature seemed half reflected on his care-worn and dispirited countenance. They were all in all to each other. Thérèse remembered no other affection, and Count Riechoffen had found all that remained to him on earth weak when compared to his fondness for this sweet and loving child.

About this period the monotony of their lives was broken by letters from Italy, stating the dangerous and hopeless illness of the Countess Wilhelm, who had imprudently swallowed a large draught of some iced beverage immediately after dancing. The next post told of her death, and announced Wilhelm's intention of bringing her remains for interment in the family vault beneath the chapel.

Count Riechoffen had never mentioned Thérèse in his letters to his son, and therefore, when the mournful procession arrived, he judged it best that she should not appear till the solemn rites had been concluded, and he had acquainted his son with her residence at the château.

There was such a change in Wilhelm's appearance, that his father became alarmed on seeing him, and again his former tenderness for the child of his departed wife was resuming its sway; but the unbecoming manner in which he received his father's confidence respecting Thérèse, the coarse and unfeeling remarks he uttered, sent back the warm stream of returning love to the old man's heart, and he turned to the gentle Thérèse with yet fonder affection, as he exclaimed, " How different would have been my sainted wife's conduct! Alas! how unworthy is Wilhelm to have been *her* son!"

Count Wilhelm's residence at the château was of short duration; but he proposed to return in the winter, and asked permission to bring with him a young man whose father had, some years before, on his death-bed, confided him to his care, leaving Wilhelm sole executor and trustee to the very large fortune he would inherit on attaining his majority. A little less than a year was still wanting ere this event would take place, and his guardian expressed a wish that it should be passed under his guidance.

Count Ricchoffen acquiesced in this proposal; but how little did he foresee the results to which it would lead!

Ere the winter had set in, Count Wilhelm and his ward arrived. With the appearance of the latter the Count Ricchoffen was extremely pleased; there was a manliness and frankness in his manner, which found a ready sympathy in the mind of his aged host. Had not his youth forbad the idea, he might have been supposed the Count's own son, from the assiduity with which he sought to enter into his tastes, and render himself agreeable to him.

Wilhelm was frequently absent for weeks together. At first he had invited Adolphe di Sanvitalli to join these hunting excursions; but finding that they were either entered upon with distaste, or declined entirely, he ceased to disturb Adolphe in what he termed his frivolous occupations. But did Count Wilhelm really know the nature of that occupation which bound the young and ardent Sanvitalli's heart and soul to the château of Ricchoffen? Did he pause to consider the natural consequence of his constant association with a young and lovely woman, who, for the first time, was made sensible of her power to please?

Constantly thrown together, their lives passed in the

exercise of those kind and pious feelings which arise in the hearts of all who devote themselves to soothe and divert the aged, how could it be otherwise than that Adolphe and Thérèse should become attached, and firmly and irrevocably so, before either of them was aware of the existence of such a sentiment? A proposal of marriage was made for the latter by a gentleman of fortune residing in Strasburgh; and this proposal being communicated by Count Riechoffen to his son, led to a discussion so loud and angry, on the part of Wilhelm, that Adolphe, who was in an adjoining room, with the door open, could not avoid hearing it. The first sentence which fell from the Count's lips seemed to unlock the secret of his own heart. "He is not worthy of her," said the old nobleman, "or I could better make this sacrifice; but to resign Thérèse, to part with that beloved child to one who cannot know her worth, is impossible. And yet," added he, "my death would leave her unprotected, though not unportioned."

"No, of that I make no doubt!" exclaimed Wilhelm, sneeringly; "she has not stolen into your affections without taking care to get provided for; the itching for money is inherent in these low-born brats, and I dare say your paragon has been, from time to time, well tutored. However, my advice is to close at once with this offer; nothing so respectable may again occur."

"Are you mad, Wilhelm?" inquired his father; "or of whom are you speaking? Of Thérèse's birth nothing is known; but her virtues and her Christian graces may stand in lieu of the proudest blazon that displays itself on a royal escutcheon. She has been to my failing years their prop and support; she has entwined herself around my heart; and had I a grandson who would make her happy, on him would I bestow her, as the best and choicest blessing I had to give."

While the Count had been speaking, Adolphe di San-vitalli had entered unperceived. Springing forward, he caught the Count's hand, and, falling at his feet, exclaimed, "Would that I were that grandson, to be considered worthy of such a blessing! but even as I am I would fain entreat it at your hands. Oh! I beseech—I implore you, let my love, my admiration, for your Thérèse, be considered my guerdon for endeavouring to become worthy of it."

"Hold, sir!" interrupted Count Wilhelm; "do you forget that I am your guardian, and that it is my consent alone which can avail? Hear me, Adolphe; sooner than consent to your thus disgracing the noble name you bear, I would——"

At that moment the object of this discussion appeared. It was the hour for prayer, and she came, as was her daily wont, to attend her benefactor to the chapel. The sight of her seemed to paralyze Wilhelm's tongue. Was it shame at beholding the orphan girl, against whom his unmanly speech was directed? or did her appearance recall some recollection, which sent the blood from his cheeks, and rendered him mute and confused?

Count Ricchoffen arose, and passing his arm through Thérèse's, said, "Come, my children, let us go to the house of prayer; and may we, in the exercise of our devotions, recover our serenity." They passed to the closet, and perceived that the servants were assembled in the chapel, where the chaplain was already in his desk, waiting their entrance to commence his exordium. Thérèse took her seat, as usual, on a low chair by the Count. Court Wilhelm sat opposite to them, looking gloomy and

disturbed, and occasionally stealing a furtive glance at Thérèse; while Adolphe remained standing behind her chair, his eyes alternately wandering from her beauteous head to his guardian's agitated countenance. The Count Riechoffen appeared absorbed in thought, his arms folded, and resting on his crutch-handled cane.

The service was scarcely concluded, when a message was brought to Count Wilhelm, desiring his immediate presence in the apartment of the aged housekeeper, whose office it had been for more than forty years to conduct strangers over the château, and whose health had been for some months fast declining. On entering the apartment, he found the old lady propped up in bed with pillows; her eyes were sunk, her face livid, and her whole aspect bespoke the near approach of death. She motioned to him to approach, and desired every one else to withdraw.

" Count Wilhelm," said she, " know you the name of Müller ?" He started, and turned pale. " Know you," she continued, " the fate of poor Constance Germain, on whom you bestowed, by marriage rite, the name of Müller?"

" Oh, tell me of her !" cried Wilhelm, thrown off his guard by the abruptness of the question.

" It is thirteen years since she breathed her last, praying for her destroyer, and blessing those who had fostered his child."

" What mean you, Agatha ?—His child? my child? Gracious Heaven ! why was all this kept from me ?"

" Why ?" returned Agatha—" do you ask me why? As the supposed Wilhelm Müller, Constance had loved and worshipped him she thought her husband; but from Wilhelm Riechoffen, who she discovered to be her betrayer, she scorned to seek relief, and so she sank heart-broken to the grave."

"But her child, Agatha—her child! Oh, tell me—
that did not surely perish too?"

The feeble spark of life seemed fast fading in Agatha's
bosom. Large drops of perspiration stood on her forehead. The exertion had been too much, and the unhappy
man who stood by her bed, in all the agony of shame and
remorse, feared that her spirit would depart without resolving his torturing doubt respecting his child. Some moments elapsed before Agatha could again articulate. At
length she said, almost in a whisper, "Thérèse is that
child," and then she sank back in a swoon, from which
she never recovered, and in a few minutes life had fled.

On leaving this scene of death, Count Wilhelm retired
to his own apartment, where he remained inaccessible to
every one for that day. When he joined the family next
morning, an extraordinary change was visible in his appearance; the usual sternness of his countenance was gone; a
look of melancholy reigned in its stead, and his impetuosity
seemed wholly subdued.

*   *   *   *   *   *

It may be supposed that Adolphe di Sanvitalli did not
neglect the opportunity afforded him by his guardian's
seclusion, of urging his suit with the gentle Thérèse;
and, having won from her frank and ingenuous heart an
acknowledgment of regard, he had no difficulty in obtaining the Count Riechoffen's sanction to their engagement,
though its fulfilment could not take place till he attained
his majority, which event would render his guardian's
opposition vain. But it soon became apparent that all
objection on Count Wilhelm's part was at an end. To his
father and to Adolphe he made full confession of his early
sin, but Thérèse knew not that he was her father, till
some months after she had become a wife.

SIXTH EVENING.

WHEN the company entered the library on the sixth evening, those who had hitherto noted with interest the varied and expressive countenance of the youthful Queen of the Revels, could not fail to observe that, on *this* evening, her features were less radiant with the sunshine of hope, less alive with the eloquence of expectation, than they had been during any previous evening of the week — a week in which the Lady Eva might be said to have lived the life of many years; since, during the course of it, she had for the first time experienced that truest sense of existence which springs from a consciousness that others live, as it were, for the time being, in and through us.

Heretofore, she had enjoyed that vague and visionary species of happiness which, however blessed it may be as the appointed lot of childhood, leaves no more trace behind it than does the passage of a beautiful vessel through a sunny sea. But during this eventful week, the Lady Eva had, for the first time, become one of a company of noble and cultivated men and women. Many of them she knew to be distinguished among their fellows for gifts and acquirements, before which the nobility of birth and station bows down in willing homage. She had seen such a

company for several successive evenings, devoting their
thoughts and intellectual energies to themes of which she
felt that *she* was in some degree the originator; and the
thought seemed to have communicated to her a species of
intellectual life and consciousness that she had never felt
before.

But now that the eventful week was verging towards
its close, a reaction to the previous excitement had cast a
cloud upon her fair brow, which the entrance of the guests
did not at first dispel.   On each of the preceding evenings
she had manifested an anxiety amounting almost to impatience for the commencement of the Revels, but now, as if
desirous of delaying it, she did not for some minutes even
approach the table around which they had been wont to
congregate; and when at length she did open the gorgeous portfolio which contained the few drawings yet
to be illustrated, it was with a sigh that she commenced
the task—for on this occasion she evidently felt it
one—of indicating the course of this *last evening's*
entertainments.

She took up a design depicting the descent of a mountain cataract into the rugged vale below, and handing it
to the accomplished writer, who had promised, on the
previous evening, to illustrate it by a poem, she besought him, with almost a starting tear—more difficult
to be resisted than the sunniest smile—not to disappoir
her.

The result of this petition was,—

THE ASSAULT OF THE DEVIL'S BRIDGE.

[IN 1799, the French army under Moreau, making their retreat, on the advance of the Russian troops under Suwarrow, from the valley of Schollenen, broke down the bridge over the River Reuss. The attack was one of the most memorable of the Mountain War. The French fought gallantly, but were overwhelmed, and the pass was won at the point of the bayonet.—September 24.]

I WOUND my way down Schollenen;
In purple lay the solemn glen.
Night hastened; yet the western blaze
Oft turned my step, oft fixed my gaze;
A shaft of flame, each pinnacle
Shot upward from the forest dell;
Along the hill the heather dun
Lay crimsoned in the full-orbed sun;
And every rill that down it rolled,
Threaded the crimson web with gold.

All loveliness, and calm around;
No cloud in heaven, on earth no sound,
Save tinklings of the Alpine fold,
Save where some distant convent tolled,
Or when some mountain falcon's cry
Touched on the sense, and then swept by;
All dewy freshness, earth and air;
(The hour, by Nature made for prayer!)
All pure, as if those scenes sublime
Had never echoed woe or crime!
But glance upon the rocky ridge,·
Where spans the chasm that slender bridge,
So light, so lofty, and so lone,
As if by spells across it thrown—
Where, seen between us and the sky,
Stands the chamois with fearless eye;
Where, by his fawn, the fallow deer,
Scarce to the breezes bends his ear;
And the rock-eagle feeds his brood,
King of the mountain solitude!

Yet, once beneath this golden sun,
The sternest work of war was done.

'Twas autumn-eve, and all was still—
A trumpet sounded from the hill !
'Twas answered from the covert green,
That darkens down yon rich ravine—
'Twas answered from yon oak-crowned dell—
'Twas answered from yon marble cell,
Where by old Time, or tempest reft,
Bursts the bright river from its cleft,
'Twas answered from the mountain snow—
War was around, above, below !

Anon was filled the valley wide,
Anon was filled the mountain's side ;
With tossing flag and trumpet clang
From slope to slope the squadrons sprang,
And still, to shout and war-horn wild,
Battalion on battalion filed—
Still bayonet-point and sabre-blade
Swelled upwards from the valley's shade.
There, as they rose, the eye might trace
The deathless marks of tribe and race :
Harnessed with sabre, mace, and bow,
The Bashkir, son of storm and snow ;
Fierce as the wolf upon the track,
Winding his steed, the brown Cossack ;
There, silver-sheathed, from neck to knee,
The Georgian's knightly panoply ;
There, rider of the Desert sand,
With turbaned brow, and lance in hand,
The fiery warriors of the Khan,
Who steeped in blood thy shores, Japan—
Who stormed thy giant wall, Cathay—
Then, wild as panthers in their play,
Rushed where the towery Kremlin flings
Its shadow on the tombs of kings—
Then, homeward swept, an ebbing flood,
Leaving behind but wrecks and blood,
Waiting till some new Tamerlane
Shall loose the living tide again.

But, charge for charge, and blow for blow,
Was thy bold tactic, brave Moreau!
Along the river's rocky edge,
Along the Grimsel's lofty ledge,
Beneath the forest's twilight shade,
Ploughing the host, his cannon played.
And still the Russian answered well.
Thick poured his storm of shot and shell ;
Yet vain his toil to storm the ridge —
Crushed in the torrent, lay the bridge.
Across that chasm, alone might spring
The mountain goat, or eagle's wing —
Still flowed the gore, and pealed the gun,
Nor yet the mortal Pass was won.

Night fell. Beneath the cloud of night
Still thundered, raved, and bled, the fight.
But hark ! — a warning horn is blown,
And see ! — a rocket upward thrown !
Bagrathion, bravest of the brave,
Has climbed the rock and stemmed the wave,
Where, bounding from its snowy tract,
Plunged in the vale the Cataract.
Torn by his fire from flank to flank,
The Frenchmen fell in rank on rank —
On Russia's banner rose the sun,
Fixed on the ridge — the Pass was won !

At the close of this poem, there was a flutter in a part
of the room where a young gentleman, recently from
college, was deprecating, with the most candid air in the
world, the solicitations of a group of ladies who had clustered about him. It appeared that he had betrayed to one
of them, quite unintentionally, during the animated recita-
tion just concluded, the interesting fact, that this poem on
Moreau had called to his recollection a statelier piece of
versification which he had himself composed on a famous
hero, equally brave and energetic.

Such a discovery, at such a moment, was not to be suffered to escape. It was rapidly whispered from one to another, and so reached Lady Eva at last, who, with that sunny and most arbitrary wilfulness which was not to be denied, resolved upon putting the gallantry of the detected poet to the test of her persuasive appeal—as yet, invariably successful.

And that young poet came of a race distinguished alike by gallantry and genius, and had given abundant promise that, at no remote day, he would vindicate its fair reputation proudly in his own person; for he had already won high collegiate honours, and obtained applause for fugitive productions displaying a lively imagination and cultivated taste. But these effusions were only the graceful fruits of leisure moments, snatched from the severer studies to which the loftier ambition of his intellect was steadily directed. It was not possible that the Lady Eva could fail in urging her request in this quarter, and after some playful hesitation, the Collegian commenced his heroic lay.

CHARLES THE TWELFTH.

Ask ye what meet reward remains to grace
The hero-monarch's last sad resting-place ?
What lingering trophy of his proud career,
When Death's stern arm breaks down the strong man's spear,
Is left, his memory from reproach to save,
And wipe the stain of carnage from his grave ?
'Tis the bright hope of glory, that afar
Shines through the mists of time, his leading star,
And still delusive lights o'er field and flood
His onward course to untried scenes of blood.
When on some hard-fought field the victor's eye
Views one vast scene of hopeless misery —
When from their wasted homes, in suppliant prayer.
A nation's voice sounds mournful on his ear,

And Conscience speaks within his breast once more —
" Behold thy works, and tremble, Conqueror !"
'Tis then that Glory tempts his wavering mind ;
" One aim be thine !" she cries — " to rule mankind ;
Let not a few weak tears thy course delay,
Once shed, then past, mere evils of a day,
While in all future time thy brow shall be
Wreathed with the crown of Immortality,
Thy name in pæans chanted, and enroll'd
With storied chiefs and demigods of old."
False Syren ! in an angel's radiant guise
Thy form first charm'd young Charles of Sweden's eyes
When from beleaguer'd town and tented field,
East, West, and South, the hostile trumpet peal'd,
Robed as his country's genius didst thou stand,
The sword of Vasa gleaming in thy hand.
Shall then the Dane resume his hated sway,
The scourge of Sweden in her evil day ?
Shall the rude Russ and wolfish Polack hold
Proud Mora's stones, where kings were crown'd of old,
And heroes worshipp'd, and pollute the home
That rear'd the conquerors of imperial Rome ?
" Sleeps Balder's spirit ? from its mystic fire
Starts not the buried sword of Angantyr ?
Wake, Thor and Odin, fathers of the strong !
Sound from your clouds Valhalla's battle-song,
Inspiring, like the loud Orthian strain,
That fired embattled hosts on Ilion's plain,
The scorn of coward ease and fleeting breath,
The joy of battle, and the thirst of death."
They heed not, — by deep fiord and pine-clad steep
The fabled gods of Runic legend sleep ;
Nor needs the call ; in living strength and wrath,
Heirs to the glory of the unconquer'd Goth,
Their home the camp, their breath the battle-cry,
Forth pours the might of Swedish chivalry.
Train'd from their hardy youth in fight to dare
The ravening wolf or grisly mountain-bear,
To brave the Northern Ocean's wildest wrath,
Or scale, mid storms, the dizzy glacier's path,
They burn with Lützen's fame their name to twine,
And cleanse in blood the wrongs of Vasa's line.

Exult, young monarch ; but ere shadowy night
Shuts out the beauteous vision from thy sight,
Let one last glance of fond remembrance fall
On the rich beauties of thy capital.
The setting sun hath thrown its latest ray
On each fair isle and undulating bay,
Yet casts one golden beam of lingering light
Where thy proud palace rears its massive height.
Far to the right, in all a monarch's pride,
The mighty Baltic rolls its gladsome tide ;
There, in calm beauty, Mälais waters lie,
The cradled mirror of the northern sky,
Reflecting rock and wood, and castled steep,
And park and pleasance in its bosom deep.
Ere darkness o'er the lovely landscape roll,
Gaze, till that scene be graven on thy soul,
And let each treasured memory of the past
Be centred in that look — for 'tis thy last ! —
Last to the martial thousands muster'd there,
Who, as the deep drum beats for vesper prayer,
Raised loud the hymn that roll'd o'er Lützen's field
" God is our fortress !   God our sword and shield :
— Weep for thy humbled crown, thy purple torn,
For thy proud boastings, Denmark, only mourn ;
In the first chafings of his mighty wrath
The Swede hath swept thee headlong from his path.
Bow down thy vanquish'd head, and, stooping low,
Proud Frederic, crave existence of thy foe ;
Nor bootless plead ; o'er realms unwasted reign,
And live, despised and spared, to plot again.
On to fresh victory with lightning speed !
East calls to West, in her extremest need :
Mark, where their wary chief arrays for fight,
In strong-fenced camp, the hardy Muscovite,
And strives by skill and vantage-ground to meet
The fiery onset that knows no retreat—
Such onset as of yore, on land and wave,
Sires of the Swede, the bold Berserkir gave.
Headlong they close ; in vain, with murderous aim,
The battery opes its countless mouths of flame :
First in the breach, as foremost in the field,
Advancing still where valour's self might yield,

The warrior monarch cheers his vanguard on
'Gainst tenfold odds, and Narva's field is won.
Speed on thy course, brave King; what need to tell
The tale of daring deeds recorded well,
That swell'd the spring-tide of thy young renown,
And hurl'd in turn each leagued aggressor down?
Yet, nobler, worthier of immortal lays,
The kingly virtues of thy better days;
To give to Poland's best and bravest son
Her sceptre, from an alien despot won;
To hear the peasant's prayer; with liberal hand
To heal war's waste amid a conquer'd land;
Release the captive soldier, free to roam
Back to his native fields and scatheless home,
And bid the voice of veteran thousands yield
To God the glory of each stricken field—
These are the deeds which die not: Time may raze
To dust old thrones and kingdoms; but such praise
Outlives e'en Time, and radiant mounts on high,
A living wreath to meet Eternity!
Hadst thou then known, that He, whose mighty word
Can raise the weak, and break the conqueror's sword;
Whose will the instinctive universe obeys,
Had mark'd the narrow circle of thy days;
Hadst thou then paused on that prophetic thought,
Then had the sword (thy country's battles fought)
Been sheathed in honour; and thy name alone
Had proved the bulwark of thy realm and throne.
Yet ere the tide of ruin o'er thee roll,
Tear the dread lust of conquest from thy soul:
It may not be! Hard were the miser's part
To ope the dried-up fountains of his heart;
Hard for the desperate gamester's gloating eye
To shun the hazard of the fatal die;
But harder yet, when Victory has shed
Her lustre on some youthful monarch's head,
For his proud heart to bow its cherish'd will,
And spurn her fading chaplet, and be still.
    Alas! how changed from all the knightly ruth,
And free, bold courtesy of earlier youth!
Caress'd and fear'd by Europe's mightiest powers,
On Lützen's plain his conquering banner towers;

But vain 'he boast, to match *his* purer name,
Whose glorious death gave you rude stone its fame.
Pride prompts to wreak on Dresden's vanquish'd lord,
Insults more bitter than the headsman's sword :
Pride, rising in his guardian-spirit's room,
With hand yet red from Patkul's felon doom,
Waves high the torch of war, and calls — " Arise !
On, great of soul ! fulfil thy destinies.
On ; crown again thy Stanislaus' brow ;
Kings be thy liegemen, and their monarch thou.
Let Russia's humbled eagle northward fly
To her rude eyrie in the Polar sky,
And Fame inscribe thee on her shield of gold,
' Stay of the weak, and tamer of the bold.'
Away ! though howling deserts round thee rave,
Though to thine eye one vast unbounded grave
Is spread, though hostile elements arise
To stay thy course, and bar thee from thy prize.
Away ! thine ancient foe at length must feel
The full outpourings of thy wrath ; thy heel
Shall crush his suppliant neck ; thy word must give
' The last poor boon that bids the vanquish'd live.' "
How fond the boast ! the cherish'd hope how vain !
The stern Czar waits him on Pultowa's plain,
With strength matured, and purpose firm and cool,
And learning conquest in reverse's school.
No backward look, no quailing heart, was there ;
All skill could prompt, or reckless valour dare,
That day did Sweden's king, with soul that rose,
In combat or retreat, o'er Nature's throes.
But who the God of battles may withstand ?
Fall'n is thy star ; a feeble, faithful band
Alone of all thy veteran host is left,
To guard thee still, of all but hope bereft ;
Aping the empty mockery of state,
A suppliant at the generous Moslem's gate.
Again he comes ; let wondering Europe tell,
How desperate grew the strife ere Stralsund fell !
Still burning for some deed of high emprise,
He calls to arms ; at once new legions rise :
His home unvisited, he parts again,
To strike to earth once more the traitor Dane

In his own den to tame him, as of yore,
Return with honour, or return no more.
Why sudden pause upon the rampart's height,
Yon thunders, volleying through the dead of night?
And hark, what stifled murmur fills the air?
No sound of onset or retreat is there;
No, 'tis the muffled drum, whose requiem-tone
Proclaims a mighty spirit quench'd and gone.
Peace to thy shade! in such majestic mould,
Heaven forms the master-souls who win and hold
Man's free unbought allegiance: those who guide,
For weal or woe, Time's ever-moving tide.
Shall the strong heart's indomitable fire;
The Spartan mastery of each gross desire;
The friendship firm and true; the courage high
In life and death; the unshaken constancy;
The mind that left its impress on an age;
Serve but as themes to Mockery's pedant page,
Marr'd though they were, and warp'd to purpose vain,
By the mad pride that work'd the angels' bane?
No! turn we to that Isle of knightly name,
Sacred to Valour, Loyalty, and Fame,
Where mingling with the dust of chivalry,
By great Gustavus' side his ashes lie.
The sword his cold hand grasp'd in death's embrace,
Finds on his tomb its well-won resting-place;
High o'er his head, a martial nation rears
The banner'd trophies of a thousand years:
Around, each warrior-knight, each patriot king,
The heroes of the North, are slumbering.
And may not Fancy deem, nor deem in vain,
That still their spirits haunt yon sacred fane?
And, as we view each chief's time-hallowed bier,
Should some far trumpet steal upon the ear,
Or the faint breeze, or hour of even-song,
Rustle one banner's drooping folds among;
Let fond Imagination catch the sound,
And paint each warrior-spirit hovering round;
While the rapt pilgrim owns with pleasing dread,
The viewless presence of the mighty dead.

AFTER the foregoing poem, there remained of the
twenty-four beautiful drawings but three unillustrated;
these three the Lady Eva took up, examined, and admired
separately. " There is a person present," said she, " to
whom I would wish to confide the illustration of these
three designs. They are each beautiful in their conception, finished in their execution, and, in the hands I
desire to place them, cannot fail to elicit a spirited and
dramatic tale."

The eyes of the company involuntarily followed the
direction in which the Lady Eva's were turned. Not an
instant's doubt prevailed as to the accomplished author to
whom she intended to appeal. Could her choice have
'allen more happily than on a refined Critic, able Historian, and admired Dramatist? Every one present thought
of his " History of Russia," his " Lives of the Poets,"
except those who more immediately recollected "Marriage"
and " Mothers and Daughters." A murmur of applause
ran through the assembled group, as the Lady Eva approached, and gracefully proffered the three drawings.
" But," remarked the gentleman thus silently invoked—
" but, Lady Eva, this is to be your last tale, and surely
——" " True," she interposed, with a heavy sigh, " it
is to be my last tale, and therefore do I beseech you to
make it, what indeed you can scarcely fail to do, one which
shall render my Birthday Revels long remembered by all
our Friends."

While the Lady Eva was speaking, the gentleman she
addressed had taken the drawings from her hand, and,
after a careful examination of each, and a few minutes'
reflection, related the following tale, which he entitled—

LOVE TO THE RESCUE.

Prelude.—1656.

A RICH autumnal sun was setting over the scanty waters of the Vesle. The broad plain through which they rippled, monotonous and dreary enough in ordinary circumstances, acquired a sort of tender beauty under the influence of the mellow light, which invested the whole scene with a touching and melancholy interest. The sombre colouring of the season and the hour heightened the peculiarly mournful character of that dismal stretch of country, in the midst of which stands the ancient city of Rheims, whose tall spires, and low, fantastic roofs, could be discerned by the rays which sparkled on their points and angles, long after the faint twilight had deepened into dusk on the surrounding level.

Upon the highroad which crosses this plain, leading in a direct line to one of the principal gates of the city, a solitary traveller was laboriously pressing onwards towards his destination.

His costume was not that of France. The broad-leafed, conical hat, the short cloak, slashed doublet, and falling band, indicated not only the country whence he came, but the party to which he belonged. English royalists, however, were at that time so well known on the continent, through exile and misfortune, that their dress provoked little curiosity. The traveller bore evident marks of suffering and fatigue; and, although the urgency of his journey was apparent, in the impatient anxiety with which he every now and then quickened his pace, he frequently paused for momentary rest;—perhaps, also, to indulge

in the contemplations suggested by a locality where the
chivalry of England had formerly won many a brilliant
triumph.

He was scarcely more than twenty-five years of age;
but mental affliction, while it could not wholly disguise
his youth, had stamped a painful gravity on it, which
made him appear much older. A hardy frame, capable
of bearing up manfully against toil and privation, was well
associated with the earnest spirit which imparted so serious
an interest to his face; certainly not the interest of a fine
outline, or handsome features, for he possessed neither—
but that sort of interest which grows upon the visible
signs of a strong and faithful nature battling against
adversity.

The traveller had now reached the ruins of a Roman
amphitheatre, at a short distance outside the walls of the
town. Utter darkness had supervened upon the last gleam
of sunset, which palpitated for a moment on the edge of
the horizon, and vanished; and the mass of houses, ramparts, and spires before him, would have been undistin-
guishable in the common gloom, which obscured all objects
alike, but for the reflexion of the city lights dimly suffused
on the sky. Guided by this beacon, he hurried forward,
and at last gained the triple archway of the Porte de
Mars.

It happened to be high holy-day at Rheims—the day
of the patron, St. Remi. Hundreds of people, in their
gayest attire, were crowded into the streets, especially
round the old, unsightly church, which has nothing to
commend it to the admiration of the inhabitants, but the
tradition of a fabulous antiquity, and a pious catalogue
of miracles. Sedan-chairs, heralded by flambeaux, were
in movement in all directions, conveying beaux and old

ladies to supper-parties or vespers ; and the more commodious avenues of the town were thrown into an absolute
uproar of delight by itinerant mummers, dancers, show-
men, and ballad-singers. A huge model of the tomb of
the Consul Jovinus (for Rheims boasts of having given a
consul to Rome in the fourth century) occupied a conspicuous position in the Place Royale, illuminated inside
with candles, and containing some wonderful reliques,
which the populace were invited to inspect, on payment of
a trifling douceur. Bands of music struggled hard to be
heard above the miscellaneous din, and everybody seemed
to be fiercely intent upon extracting the utmost possible
hilarity from the saintly festival.

The stranger hustled his way as well as he could
through the tumult; nor did he altogether escape some
broad witticisms upon the dinginess of his garments, and
the shape of his hat. The people seemed to think that
one who made so grotesque a contrast to their merriment
had no business amongst them ; a fact which was still
more poignantly impressed upon him by his own bitter
thoughts.

It was by no slight exertion that he succeeded at
length in effecting his escape into a quiet alley under the
ramparts, disturbed only occasionally by stragglers from
the main streets, or idlers hastening to join the revel.
Pursuing this narrow track to the end, he emerged into
a small open space, dotted with a few skeleton poplars.
Here he paused for an instant to make sure of his route.
The monastic repose of the spot assured him that he was
in the ecclesiastical quarter of the town. In the opposite
angle a massive building stood out darkly against the sky,
and the stone cross which surmounted an antique fountain
in the centre of the place, satisfied him that he had

fortunately hit upon the right point, without exposing himself to the delay of an inquiry.

Rapidly crossing over, he struck into a paved passage under the shadow of the houses, and stood before a low door deeply sunk in the building. The echoes of the carnival he had just left behind floated down into the stillness, and were little calculated to strengthen his resolution, now faltering on the threshold of the very place he had sought so eagerly—the object of his long and weary travail. His hand trembled as he touched the handle of the bell, and the agitation which he in vain endeavoured to subdue, was not likely to ensure the most favourable reception from the sacristan, who opened the door.

" The archbishop ?" inquired the stranger; " I would see the archbishop."

" An unseasonable request," returned the sacristan.

" But my business is urgent—I have come a long distance to see him—travelled night and day—I am exhausted by fatigue and indifferent entertainment by the way—but that's nothing, nothing ! The reverend father will not be offended when he knows my business."

" Your name ?" demanded the sacristan.

" It would be of no avail. A stranger craves audience —'tis business of life and death—I entreat you—my need presses."

" To-morrow—to-morrow," replied the other; " his grace is at prayers."

" The better for my hopes," responded the stranger, " for mine is an affair that pleads to Heaven for help. Oh, God ! what may not happen before to-morrow !"

The intense anguish with which these words were uttered, softened the habitual indifference of the sacristan. " Well," he replied, scrutinizing the stranger, at the same time, from head to foot, "come in, at all events. His reverence will scarcely see you to-night—but as you say your business is so urgent, I must see what can be done. Come in—come in."

The stranger grasped his hand with a look of fervent gratitude, and followed him into the house, or, as it was then called, the Archiepiscopal Palace.

The venerable archbishop, a descendant of the famous Sir Peter de Craon, was not so difficult of access as the sacristan would have had the stranger believe. The audience was granted at once; and the stranger was received with an encouraging condescension, which greatly puzzled the more ceremonious notions of the sacristan.

" From England, my son ?" inquired the prelate, whose benignant manner at once gave assurance to the visitor.

" Yes, reverend father ; nor have I pressed couch since I left Southampton."

" To what end, my son, have you undertaken so toilful a journey ? Speak freely. You will find friends here, and countrymen."

" Thank God for that," replied the stranger ; " for I left none but wolves and oppressors behind. Pardon me, your grace, for begging audience at this late lour ; but my heart is racked with fears for one who is — perhaps *was* ——." His voice sunk as he approached the inquiry upon which all his anxieties were concentrated.

" The Prince Charles ?" demanded the archbishop.

" No, reverend father ; he is safe in Paris. But one who perilled and lost all in his righteous cause. I believe there are English monks under this sacred roof ?"

" Several."

" And amongst them—Father Jacques ? Does he still live ?" And his eyes had already gleaned the answer

before the archbishop had time to shape it into utterance.
" Blessed be the Lord, for all his mercies ! "

" He still lives, my son."

" But broken in health—feeble—worn out with sorrow ?   I have heard as much, and my only hope was to be
with him in his last hours.   I am in time for that ? "

" He is ill, indeed—very ill," resumed the prelate.
" If you bring good tidings——"

" I bring none—none.   In England, we have abandoned all hope.   The adherents of the royal party are
scattered and disheartened.   No man dare avow his faith
there.   Nothing remains to us but prayer and death.   Our
kingdom in this world is gone for ever."

" Such despondency at your age, my son," replied the
archbishop, " is an offence against the justice of Heaven.
The time will come when the rights of the throne and the
church shall be vindicated in full ; but England must look
for restitution to its young blood, animated by the memory
of hoarded wrongs, and years of tyranny.   And when that
time comes——"

" I will do my duty," returned the cavalier, " should I
survive to witness the glorious issue of our sufferings.   But
your grace will forgive my present impatience.   I have
endured much in the hope I had scarcely ventured to
indulge, of seeing Father Jacques——"

" Not to-night.   You need repose and refreshment ;
nor would it be wise to risk an interview without some
preparation.   We must postpone the meeting till morning ;
and in the meanwhile confide fully in me.   I must not
conceal from you, that, in his precarious state of health,
any sudden communication might be attended with the
worst results."

The stranger was too much impressed with the necessity of acting upon this prudent advice, not to obey the archbishop's injunctions implicitly. The sacristan, who still felt some uneasy doubts about a visitor whose business was so importunate and mysterious, could scarcely contain his astonishment when he found that supper was ordered in the closet for his grace and the cavalier; but all his speculations, fertile and ingenious as they were, suffered total shipwreck upon afterwards discovering that his lordship and the stranger had remained in close council until a late hour of the night. The worthy sacristan could not for the life of him comprehend it; nor was he much enlightened the next morning when he was required by his grace to conduct the stranger, by a private passage under the cloisters, into the choir of the cathedral.

The cathedral of Rheims is one of the oldest and most magnificent in Europe. Its clustering columns, rich arches, statues, and monuments, scarcely require that additional appeal to the imagination which it derives from its remote historical associations; and it is impossible to tread its stately nave and noble transepts, to gaze upon its ponderous towers flanking the entrance, or to listen to the chimes of its mighty bells, smiting the roof and walls like peals of thunder, without being filled with awe. The solemn emotions which the majesty of the scene stirred in the mind of the stranger, lifted him for a brief interval out of the thoughts which had hitherto absorbed all his faculties. He stood close to the font where Clovis is said to have been baptized — upon the spot where a long succession of kings had received their crowns, under the sacred responsibility of a religious trust; he was surrounded by costly tombs and sculptured effigies, wonders of art and mementos of eternity, peculiarly impressive in the hush of the sombre light that fell upon them from the painted

windows; and as the swelling notes of the distant organ
soared through the lofty pile, he was profoundly moved,
and, sinking upon his knees, surrendered up his spirit to
silent prayer.

He was not alone in the cathedral. A few solitary
communicants might be seen in some of the side chapels,
where the service of the mass was performing; and upon
the steps leading to the choir, at the back of which the
stranger had taken up his station, an aged monk was engaged in offices of devotion. Through illness and infirmity
his limbs were incapable of long sustaining the painful
attitude of supplication in which he first addressed the
throne of grace, and he sat down exhausted upon the steps.
But his mind was still abstracted in pious meditations, and
absorbed by the outspread volume of divine truth over
which he reverently bent his head.

The action was carefully noted by two of the brotherhood, who loitered in the transept, apparently for the purpose of observing the motions of the monk. When he had
concluded his orison, they drew near. The stranger had by
this time become a dumb spectator of the scene, the issue
of which he watched with intense interest.

A brief salutation, in the customary form of a blessing,
apprised the monk that he was addressed by the affectionate
greeting of his spiritual superior.

"Thanks for your holy care," he replied; "I need it
all. I feel more and more every day how swiftly the vain
shows of this world are gliding from my eyes. The shadows of the grave are thickly gathering round me."

"Not so, Father Jacques," mildly responded the archbishop; "we must be hopeful in our reliance on the divine
mercy."

"I trust I am so," answered the monk; "and if a con-

trite spirit, chastised by much suffering, and bowed to the dust by bereavements, may hope to be acceptable, I have hope, reverend father, of rest and comfort—hereafter!"

"And why not of a tranquil passage to a future life? There are manifold blessings in store for us all—human sympathies, which it is our duty to nourish."

Father Jacques raised his eyes, and looked inqr'ringly at the archbishop. He felt that there was a meaning in the words beyond the mere expression of general consolation they seemed to convey.

"It is not well, father," continued the archbishop, "to abandon wholly our interest in worldly ties. We forsake the world's pleasures, its pomps and its vices; but our hearts are human, and must yearn with human love to the last."

"You speak strangely," returned the monk.

"Yet not without reason," resumed the prelate. "The world you have renounced must contain some objects of interest for you."

The monk grasped the speaker's arm convulsively. "To the purpose, I entreat your grace," he exclaimed. "You never spoke thus before. Pardon this weakness—but I am very feeble."

"Well—well—be composed," said his grace; "I have received some intelligence, which, under Divine Providence, will bring comfort and happiness to you. But you must be calm, and shew me that you can bear joy as patiently as you have borne affliction."

"Calm—calm—calm!" And he added, with a wandering look, as if the communication had bewildered his senses—"Joy for me?—for me—a shattered creature!"

"Let us retire from the nave," said the archbishop, "and you shall hear the good news."

Conducting the old man between them, the venerable prelate and his coadjutor led him to a stone bench close to the choir, within hearing of the stranger, who still remained concealed behind a pillar.

"I received some information from England last night," observed the archbishop.

"Ah! the regicide is dead?" inquired the monk.

"No — Cromwell still lives, more confirmed in his power than ever."

"That is ill news, my lord," responded the monk, drawing a deep and heavy sigh.

"Yes—ill news for England. But you have relinquished all interest in such concerns. It was not of that I desired to speak," he continued, cautiously.

"You put me on the rack. What is the news that touches me? I am as one dead to the world, and nothing in the world can affect me."

"You have kindred, Father Jacques?"

A shudder ran through the frame of the old monk, but with a violent effort he commanded his emotions. "Kindred? Not one—not one! Distant relatives, perhaps— strangers to my heart. But kindred is something more than blood. No, no; I have no kindred!"

"My information, Father Jacques," observed the archbishop, "says otherwise; and I am disposed to credit it on many accounts."

"Unless the grave can give back its tenants, reverend father, your information must be wrong."

"We shall presently see," returned the other, at the same time motioning the stranger to draw near. "There came to me here last night," he continued, "a young man from England; one who has still, even to his very habit, maintained his allegiance to the sacred cause of the Stuarts.

Your family was known to him; their history through the war, their sacrifices in defence of the king. He knows all that has happened, to the very hour when he left the shore. And he tells me——"

"God of mercy, have pity upon me!" ejaculated the monk, clasping his hands, and gazing into the archbishop's eyes, as if he would read the sequel in their depths.

"He tells me that one still lives whom you have believed to be dead—one close to your affections."

"Where is he?" demanded the monk. "Let me question him."

"He is here," returned the archbishop, as the stranger, with hesitating step, approached and stood before Father Jacques.

The old man rose from his seat, and peered into the face of the stranger, but could recognise nothing there to assist his conjectures. "Speak!" he cried.

"Your blessing, father!" exclaimed the stranger, in a broken voice, as he flung himself on his knees before the monk.

A bubbling cry escaped the monk, as he raised the supplicant totteringly from the ground, and looking again intently into his features, went on, in a low and almost inarticulate tone: "You are a stranger to me; you bring back old times and old faces. Your garb is like that of my youth. It gladdens me to look upon it! And you have suffered, too? You look so harassed! And tears—tears for me! 'Tis a blessed sign in one so young! And you bring tidings to me? No, no! But you come from England; that is something. To breathe the air with you is like home again. I am foolish to talk so. Your name—your mission? Will you not speak to me?"

c c

The stranger was too much overcome by the piteous aspect of the monk to trust himself with words, and, turning away his head, tried to conceal his agitation. The monk reiterated his question.

"No matter, for the present," said the stranger; "we shall have time to talk by-and-by. I bring you joyful news, which I shall relate in full—news that I can vouch for. You are no longer friendless—your name is not extinct. There lives one who may yet revive it with honour in the old place."

This intimation, although it might be dark to others, seemed to be perfectly intelligible to the monk. But it produced a fearful effect upon him. The expression of wonder and incredulity which spread over his features as the stranger uttered the last words, was rapidly succeeded by a sudden pallor. He was stricken with paralysis, and must have fallen to the earth, had not the stranger clasped him strenuously in his arms.

He was conveyed to his chamber in a state of insensibility. For three days the stranger, refusing all rest, watched by his bedside. And during that agonising interval, the monk gathered strength enough to listen to the voice of him who watched, and to reward his care with blessings.

At the end of three days, the stranger, wan and haggard, and with the wretched aspect of one upon whom a brief period of concentrated grief had done the work of years of common misery, was led out of that chamber of mourning.

The monk was dead.

I.—A HAWKING PARTY. 1661.

Two milk-white palfreys and three horses, all richly caparisoned, stood in front of the entrance to Lynton Hall. It was precisely the sort of morning that old Latham would have chosen to try a flight of falcons. The sky was slightly overcast by a light fleece of snowy clouds, which prevented the eyes of birds or sportsmen from being perplexed by the sun, and there was just wind enough abroad to give freshness to the atmosphere without presenting much resistance to the plumage of hawk or heron.

The falconer had gone forward in advance with his stage of hawks, making an accompaniment to the music of their bells, by trolling the words of a ditty, which was at that time in the zenith of its popularity :—

> " The soaring hawk from fist that flies,
>   Her falconer doth constrain
>   Sometimes to range the ground unknown,
>   To find her out again ;
>   And if by sight, or sound of bell,
>   His falcon he may see,
>   ' Wo ho !' he cries, with cheerful voice—
>   The gladdest man is he !"

The falconer knew as well as the writer of the ballad how to prize his falcons, and he broke in, every now and then, upon the ditty, to cry, " Wo ho !" to his birds, and in especial to stroke with a feather the dark plumage of a stately peregrine, upon whose execution in the approaching sport he evidently laid great stress.

The track lay through one of the wildest and most romantic valleys of Devonshire ; and when the falconer had gained a particular spot, where the rendezvous was appointed, he scaled a rock to ascertain whether the party were in motion. A flutter of bright colours through the trees announced their rapid approach. Presently a noble greyhound, swifter than the fleetest steed, swept past, and in a few moments more, the whole valley was animated by the presence of the equestrians, who, unable to restrain the high spirits of their horses in the clear morning air, came scampering and bounding over the sward.

The ladies of the party were Lucy Montagu, the heiress of Lynton Hall, and her light-hearted cousin, the Lady Catherine Gower, a maid of honour, who had ventured upon an exile of a few weeks from Whitehall, in the hope of retrieving her complexion in the breezes of Devonshire. They were attended by the young Lord Nevyl, whose estates lay close by, and two gentlemen who were then visiting at Lynton. From the skill with which Lucy Montagu and Lord Nevyl applied themselves to the exciting preparations for the sport, it was manifest that they were thoroughly familiar with its mysteries; which was more than could be said for the rest of the party, who merely looked on, with a vague and indulgent curiosity, while the merry falconer began to unloose his birds.

"The peregrine first, Hugh Clark," exclaimed Lucy Montagu, as she touched the falcon with her glove; "and see that her jesses are safe."

The falconer was hardly pleased to risk his favourite's reputation on the first flight, and would fain have substituted a fussy little hobby, which, with the impetuosity characteristic of its species, was impatient to be on the wing. But the lady was anxious to show the best of the sport first, before the attention of her guests was exhausted.

The whole party had now dismounted; and Lord Nevyl was busy helping with the birds.

"Shall I take the peregrine, Miss Montagu?" he inquired.

"If you please, my lord," returned the lady; "and I will second you with my own ger-falcon. Give her to my hand, Hugh. There—gently. Wo ho, pretty bird!" And stretching our her closed hand, carefully protected by a richly-embroidered glove, the well-accustomed hawk stept upon it with an air of gentle dignity, that excited the admiration even of Lady Catherine.

"It is wondrously beautiful," she exclaimed, "and seems quite familiar with you."

"So she should be, Catherine; for I may almost say I trained her with my own hand. Is it not so, Hugh?"

"Ha," replied Hugh, "your ladyship will train a hawk with any falconer in England. Your ladyship took this bird in hand from an eyas. I remember the first time your ladyship hooded the beauty. There is such an art in that!"

"But can the creature see?" inquired Lady Catherine.

"Of course not, Catherine," returned Lucy; "we should have no control over them if we did not keep them blinded till we start the prey. Don't you admire my rufter, and its handsome crest of pheasant feathers? You shall learn presently how to fly a falcon from the hood;—only keep silence, and watch!"

Lord Nevyl, who was prepared with the peregrine on his fist, with the leather end of the jesses wound tightly round his hand—for it was a bird of enormous height and power—listened with evident delight to the pleasant lore of Lucy Montagu. Even the two gentlemen, Piers Everington and his brother Charles, both members of the new parliament, seemed to grow interested in these preliminary details.

The whole party now moved noiselessly towards the river which brawled through the rugged bed of the valley, expanding at this place into a sort of basin, with a broad strand at the opposite side. A few straggling tall trees on the margin indicated the heronry, to which all eyes were now anxiously turned.

"Which way is the wind, Hugh?" inquired Lord Nevyl.

"Down the river, my lord," returned Hugh; and silently motioning to leeward of the heronry, he led them down through the bushes for a considerable distance. Piers Everington was grievously perplexed by this trouble-some manœuvre, and inquired the reason of it.

"Why, simply," said Lucy, to whom all these devices were mere matters of course, "because the heron on its return must fly against the wind, which gives an obvious advantage to the falcon."

"Very curious, indeed!" returned Piers Everington, not a whit enlightened by the explanation.

"You see how accomplished Miss Montagu is in this royal pastime," said Lord Nevyl. " She might boast, with Spencer's Sir Tristram,—

> ' Ne is there hawk which mantleth on her perch,
> Whether high towering or accoasting low,
> But I the measure of her flighte doe search,
> And all her prey and all their habits know.'"

"Hush!" interrupted Lucy, "there is a heron on the wing."

Hugh Clark shaded his eyes with his hand, to note the action of the distant bird, and, after a moment's observation, confirmed the announcement. " Down, down in the bushes!" whispered Hugh; and the whole party

to the great reluctance of some of them, crept under the shadows of the brushwood as well as they could.

Lord Nevyl, having measured his distance with a practised eye, let fly the peregrine, who, the moment she was released, discovered her prey, and, fluttering her head, ascended in a series of spiral gyrations into the air. The instinct of the heron was no less rapid. She saw her danger, and strained her whole muscular power to ascend higher and higher, disgorging her food at the same instant to lighten her weight. She was considerably above the peregrine, whose circular flight, however, gradually lessened the distance; but the heron still soared, and kept the ascendancy. Now was the time for the ger-falcon to come into play. With a single touch of surpassing dexterity, Lucy slipped the jesses, and snatched off the hood, and the stately bird shot into the air, taking still wider circles, the peculiar action of which had the effect, to the unskilful spectators, of making it appear that the pursuers and the pursued all took different directions. But presently, as the hawks gained upon their prey, the artifice by which they thus diminished the atmospheric resistance, became perfectly intelligible, and it was soon evident that their apparently divergent flight was directed steadily to one point.

The peregrine is now close upon the heron; another grand sweep in the air, and she is above her. The spectators become as agitated for the issue as the plumed combatants themselves. The peregrine mounts higher and nigher, to secure a more effectual stoop; the heron, with unerring instinct, feels that life or death depends on the next half second of time, and, lowering her wing, watches with fearful interest the motions of her enemy. The stoop is taken; as swift as light the peregrine makes her blow,

but the heron has evaded it by shifting her station: and
the hawk has no sooner shot past her than she takes to
her wing again, and soars upwards with increasing energy,
but it is only to encounter the ger-falcon, who has all this
time been ascending upon her track. The powerful wing
of the ger-falcon leaves her no chance of escape. Higher
and higher they mount, until at last they fade into specks
hardly distinguishable from each other ; but the falcon is
still to be detected by her gyrations, and the superior
speed of her flight. The interest of the struggle deepens
in intensity as the falcon ascends far above the heron, who
now, fierce in her agony, and seeing all hope of escape in
that direction at an end, comes precipitately down, prepared to transfix the pursuer upon her up-turned beak.
But luckily the peregrine diverts her from her purpose by
a sudden lurch, and the ger-falcon drops upon her prey,
which she seizes with fatal velocity, the peregrine binding
to its fellow at the same time. The three birds, now
twined and convulsed in a fearful contest, descend together
rapidly to the earth.

"To horse !" cries Hugh Clark, dashing into the river,
towards the place where the birds were likely to drop.
Lucy and Lord Nevyl were already in their saddles, and
across the river before the astonished lookers-on had recovered their surprise at the suddenness of the challenge.
Of course Lady Catherine, and the two members of parliament, were left far behind, while the sport carried their
friends into a remote part of the valley.

Hugh Clark had secured the heron just as Lucy and
Lord Nevyl came up; and as they were now approaching
a closer part of the valley where pheasants were to be
found, they determined upon trying a kestrel, or wind-
hover, which was then much used for pheasant hawking.

Dismounting again, Lord Nevyl and Lucy walked forward, while Hugh Clark selected a favourable spot for the flight. It was a gorge in the steep rocks, out of which issued a waterfall, the river tumbling and foaming through the dark ravine below. The pheasants, who kept the open country, were often to be found here on the summits, and sometimes lower down, tempted into occasional excursions by the stillness and solitude of the place.

The young lord was not sorry to be left alone with the beautiful heiress of Lynton Hall, and her beauty never appeared so resplendent in his eyes as amidst such scenes as these; her singularly picturesque dress setting off to the greatest advantage that pure colour and charming frankness of expression, which had never yet been deteriorated by the fashionable excesses of a town life. The proximity of his residence had gradually rendered him an intimate at Lynton Hall, and the refinement of his tastes enabled him to discover intellectual merits in Lucy Montagu, which he esteemed even beyond her beauty. It was not surprising that Lord Nevyl should be in love with Lucy Montagu; but it was very surprising that he did not know it. There is a curious sophistry in certain minds, by which they contrive to mystify themselves into prolonged delight through this season of ambiguous passion, still loitering dreamily on the confines of self-confession, which they continue to evade as long as they can, by one deception or another, as if they were afraid it would all of a sudden put an end to their delicious doubts. But confessions must come at last; and they often come at very unexpected moments. Sophists of this class are generally surprised, when they least expect it, into the full sense of their own happiness.

"How charming is the solitude of this place!" exclaimed Lord Nevyl. "Your fair cousin scarcely appreciates our wild scenery."

"How can she?" replied Lucy; "she has lived in London all her life; yet she is not spoilt by it. She has such delightful spirits, and is so natural, in spite of her courtly tastes."

"I can understand her character; but she would never be happy out of the sphere in which she moves."

"You are greatly mistaken. Lady Catherine is the most unselfish of all persons. She delights in conferring happiness on others. But how can you know anything about it? We are all enigmas, and must be found out, like other puzzles."

"Not all, Miss Montagu," said Lord Nevyl, with a tone of earnestness, which appeared rather unusual to Lucy Montagu. "At least," he continued, "one fancies once in one's life that one has found——"

"Oh! one fancies a thousand things," interrupted Lucy; "but character is not to be solved by fancy."

"Then what is the key to this exquisite mystery?"

"Why, I suppose," rejoined Lucy, laughing at the odd conceit, "keys to mysteries are something like keys to locks, and every mystery must be opened by its own key."

"But there is a master-key, to which they all yield alike."

"You absolutely make me curious, Lord Nevyl; pray what may that be?"

"Sympathy, Miss Montagu; before which hearts are laid open, as it were, by a touch of enchantment." He ought to have said "love," for undeniably that was what he meant; but Lord Nevyl did not yet exactly know what he meant.

" Oh, people may have sympathy in common pursuits,
and yet make great mistakes in extending their inferences,"
returned Lucy; "but the argument is a little too subtle
for me.   And see, Hugh is starting a pheasant."

Lord Nevyl was grievously vexed at the interruption.
He secretly wished all the pheasants in England safe under
cover.   But there was no time for refining upon lost
opportunities.   Lucy was already at the entrance of the
gorge, with a kestrel clambering on her hand, while Hugh
was directing her attention to a distant spot, to which he
thought he had traced the flight of the pheasant.

" It will presently rise," said Hugh; " be wary."

The bird rose almost at the moment, and it was not
until Lucy had released the kestrel, which mounted with
that singularly graceful flight, for which this tiny species
is so remarkable, that they discovered the prey to be a
heron, and not a pheasant.   The disadvantage was great
between the pursuer and the pursued; and it was curious
to observe how swiftly and courageously the kestrel ascended, and distanced its prey, which, hoping to elude the
pursuit, kept beating about in the brown shadow of the
rocks.   The hurried cry in the air of *pli, pli, pli,* evinced
the eagerness of the hawk, until it attained its greatest
altitude at a vast height above the affrighted heron, when
the sound ceased.   Lord Nevyl, apprehensive of losing the
bird, notwithstanding that he still heard the tingle of its
bells, hurried upon a rock in the middle of the stream to
lure it back, while Lucy prepared a second kestrel to be in
readiness in case of need.   But these precautions were
unnecessary.   The kestrel was suspended apparently motionless in the air, although a steady observer, accustomed
to this peculiarity, might detect a slight, tremulous quivering of the wings, by which it sustained itself.   They held

their breath to watch the issue. Like a flash from the
sun, the kestrel darted down, and struck its prey. The
execution of this movement was perfect. Both the birds
were now struggling in the water, from whence they were
quickly rescued by Hugh Clark, who, to do him justice,
understood his part of the science quite as well as the
kestrel herself.

"We have lost our friends," said Lucy, who, very pro-
vokingly, seemed to become aware of the fact now for the
first time. Lord Nevyl wished all the friends, as a moment
before he had wished all the pheasants, safely under cover
—anywhere but in his way. "We had better rejoin
them," she added, making a signal for the horses, which
were in charge of a servitor at a little distance.

A spectator seeing these two young people riding hastily
back to come up with their party, might have supposed
that they were very anxious to escape from each other's
company. A part of the way there was not a word spoken,
and when they did risk a little conversation it was reserved
and constrained. There might be no great difficulty in
guessing at the thoughts that were passing through Lord
Nevyl's mind, taking sundry contradictory shapes, unconsciously moulded by his wayward and poetical temperament. But it was not quite so easy to speculate on Miss
Montagu's thoughts. There was nothing to be gathered
from her manner, which was most tantalizingly *insouciant.*
The enigma to which she compared her sex was never more
vexatiously represented than it was by Miss Montagu herself during that short ride; at least Lord Nevyl was of that
opinion.

They found their friends higher up the valley, trying
some hopeless experiments with two or three hawks which
had been left with them by the falconer. Mr. Piers

Everington had been cruelly lacerated by a little merlin, which he had incautiously unhooded, out of sheer curiosity, without liberating its jesses; and Mr. Charles Everington was in no little consternation at having lost a hobby, which he had suffered to go in quest of game on its own account, and which had disappeared amongst the trees. Whether Hugh Clark ever recovered the hobby we know not, but it is certain that he muttered an infinite variety of hard words as he went, swinging his lure, in search of the fugitive.

These little *contretemps* brought the hawking to a stand-still; and as there was no concealing the *ennui* of the visitors from London, it was agreed on all hands to suspend the sport for that day, and return to the Hall. The gallop home was cheering enough. Lady Catherine was in florid spirits, and threw everybody, except Lord Nevyl, into ecstasies with her brilliant wit and sinister repartees. Even his lordship felt grateful to her for sparing him the necessity of talking.

It was twelve o'clock—a clear hour before dinner—when they arrived at Lynton Hall. Little time enough for maids of honour and courtiers to make their toilets. But Lord Nevyl required less preparation; nor was he in a mood to fret himself over details of that kind. He dressed quickly, with an uneasy nervousness, and descended to the drawing-room. To his utter astonishment, Lucy Montagu was there before him.

She was as calm as ever—as frank, as lively, and even more lovely than usual. The enigma became mcre and more perplexing to Lord Nevyl, who was never so embarrassed before in the whole course of his life. The inexplicable self-possession of women!

Lucy bantered him upon the celerity of his toilet.

She was unconscious of the greater despatch with which she had dismissed her own. But he was too abstracted to perceive the advantage which this slight oversight threw open to him.

"I am afraid I have interrupted you, Miss Montagu," ne managed to say, at last, as awkwardly as he could say it. Lucy had been reading a large folio, bound in vellum, with ponderous clasps. "What have you been reading?"

"Drayton," she replied—"my favourite Drayton. They say he is only a bad geographer, with just enough of imagination to lead him astray; but I love his fantastic style, and the sweet glimpses he gives us of pastoral romance."

"Your unerring taste is sure to detect the beautiful and the true, even in the tangled wilderness of the Polyolbion. Drayton has always been one of my household divinities, but I shall prize him for the future more highly than ever."

"I suppose I ought to be obliged by so delicate a compliment," replied Lucy, with a very sunny smile; "but it is quite useless to attempt to flatter me into the notion that my taste is a criterion in such matters. I dare say Drayton is an indifferent poet enough."

"But it is possible, Miss Montagu," said Lord Nevyl, who was now beginning to recover his composure—"it is possible, even if your taste were in error, which it cannot be, that still I might like Drayton the more, because——" There was a tremulous pause on the word.

"Because?—well?" And in a mischievous spirit of badinage she was half inclined to laugh.

"I mean," he resumed, "that one cannot help loving everything that interests those who ——" Miss Montagu hastily turned over half-a-dozen leaves all at once.

"I don't like his Barons' Wars," she interposed, "nor

his ——" She tried to flutter over a few more leaves, when Lord Nevyl gently arrested her hand. It trembled for an instant in his.

" You will banish me, perhaps, from your presence for ever, Miss Montagu, for my presumption; but—" he released her hand—" I cannot, I dare not any longer dissemble my feelings."

"My Lord Nevyl!" she exclaimed, slightly averting her head, "I beg——"

"It is in vain!" cried Lord Nevyl, passionately—"in vain! My long pent-up secret has found utterance at last. Pardon me that I have dared to love you. It was not your beauty, spiritual and radiant as it is, for which alone I loved you; but that which is more beautiful than beauty — that intellectual grace which raised you nearer to the divine nature."

" I cannot hear this," replied Lucy; "it is so strange — so unexpected——"

" Yet to me so long familiar! And I fancied, too, that you must have seen it—that love could speak tongue-tied. How often in the summer nights, when you used to sing some of those broken lyrics of the old troubadours, I fancied, in the tones of your voice, a sweet spirit responding to my silent heart. How I have dreamed of the future—the felicity of realising the mission of the affections. This thought has consumed me day and night. Pardon—forgive the passionate devotion you have inspired. One word—one little word of hope!" And flinging himself on his knees, he clasped the powerless hand of Lucy Montagu.

In that brief moment she has passed into a new state of existence. Her imperial will, her happy caprices, the bright heedlessness of youth—what have become of them?

Absorbed in the one new image of life—new, startling,
confounding.   It is the first time the thought has taken
an actual form in her imagination.   Her sense of things
becomes dazzled and bewildered.   She will neither desire
him to hope nor despair.   She needs help and direction
more herself.   She cannot answer; she will think—think
of what?   Everything is changed.   She is no longer the
being of fugitive trifles—on a sudden the half-formed
fantasies of all her timid wishes assume vital shapes, to
which she must give grave audience; her fairy Ideal has
become disenchanted into the Real.   What is to come of
this?   Does she love any one else?   No!   Does she love
at all?   It is the crisis of her life—this perilous second
of time!

Fortunately for the trembler, a step, light, quick, and
buoyant, echoes on the staircase.

"My cousin!" exclaims Lucy, trying to disengage her
hand, but not until Lord Nevyl has impressed it with a
fervent kiss.

The door is flung open, and Lady Catherine bounds
into the room.

II.—ARRIVALS AND AUGURIES.

LYNTON HALL was a sumptuous pile, which might be
traced back from small beginnings to the age of Elizabeth.
Enlarged and embellished from time to time by different
hands, it presented a singular and fantastic specimen of
that wilful confusion of styles which prevailed in England
down to a much later day.   Moorish arches and Gothic
windows, richly crusted with ornaments, were picturesquely
heaped upon the flat surfaces and quaint zig-zags of the

old Saxon architecture; while Italian terraces, stepped
parterres, embroidered with flowers, and transpicuous alleys,
through which the sun played at gambols with the dancing
shadows, completed the heterogeneous but costly ensemble.
During the Interregnum, Lynton Hall, in common
with all other country mansions, yielded to the dreary
influence of the time. It was kept in solid repair, but
that was all. The fine arts had nothing to do but stand
still; there were no accessions to the picture gallery; no
new statues, fountains, or garden luxuries; no improvements, interior or exterior. All was cold and lifeless.
The same policy that abolished fans, feathers, and girdle-
glasses, and shut up the play-houses, had also spell-bound
the residences of the gentry in a long and dismal lethargy.

The Restoration acted like enchantment upon the
sleepers. It was the signal of a universal release from the
hypocritical dulness, which sat like a nightmare upon the
spirits of the young and hopeful. The whole population
started up to enjoy the national holiday, like children suddenly released from the stupefaction of the conventicle.
Lynton Hall participated in the general rejoicing.

Sir Edmund Montagu was a puritan—firm, inflexible,
and sincere. The nobler and the graver elements of the
character belonged to him. Lady Montagu, inheriting
royalist principles from her family, had sufficient good
sense to suppress their manifestation under the Protec-
torate; but the death of Cromwell dissolved all obligations
of that kind, and rendered the resumption of the splendour
and the gaieties proper to her station a matter of policy,
as much as it was, on her part, a matter of choice and
feeling.

The chambers of the Hall rang with the clamour of

D D

changes befitting the altered spirit of the period. Artists
from London, anticipating the advent of the meretricious
Verrio, had already, with exuberant fancy, poured out a
whole mythology of gods and goddesses upon the ceilings
and walls of the principal rooms, galleries, and staircases ;
and the poetry of invention was tortured into endless
deformities to find out new devices for emblems and portraits cut in pyramidal yews and bosky shrubs. The long
walks were buttoned up with rows of pots of la Reine
Marguerite, every verdant niche had its stone nymph or
dryad assigned to it, and every vista was closed with a
sparkling fountain or a classical group. Day after day
heaps of new things arrived from London, and the ladies'
apartments were literally strewn over with flirting hats,
martial gloves, Colambor fans, angel-water, May-dew,
and French petticoats. Sir Edmund did not consent to
this revolution ; he submitted to it, or, rather, he tried to
endure it. Guests were come, and more were coming, and
it was in vain to resist the overwhelming tide of change.
Christmas, too, was coming—the traditional season of
English hospitality and merry-making. The tranquillity
he loved was shaken to its centre. There was no repose
for him in the remotest corners of the house. The echoes
of the turmoil followed him everywhere.

On the morning succeeding the incident just related,
he penetrated through a levée of foreign artists to the
chamber of Lady Montagu, and found her busily occupied
inspecting a fresh consignment of perfumes, salves, and
washes.

"A rare tumult this morning, madam," he exclaimed ;
" when may I look for peace ?"

" Well, well," replied Lady Montagu, " it is nearly

over; but positively we did require a little improvement, it is so long since the place was touched. Besides," she added, trying the effect of a good-natured appeal to his pride, " you would not have us give a mean reception to my niece, Lady Catherine, and Sir Dudley Perrot, and the other court people who are to spend the Christmas with us ?"

" And so," retorted Sir Edmund— " and so, because your niece, a maid of honour — save the mark ! — and some jackdaw courtiers are about to make profligate revel in our house in the solemn Christmas time, I must be scared in my retirement by a hurricane of feet and tongues, as if Tartarus had disgorged its demons at my gate !"

" Nay," exclaimed her ladyship, " you must be just. I never murmured at the painful suppression of my own feelings, through the long and bitter years during which the friends of my youth were banished from their homes, confiscated, and hunted like dogs. Nor do I triumph now in the deliverance that has come to pass ; I only ask that we may be allowed to resume our natural position. And not even this for my own sake, but for the sake of others."

" Others ? " said Sir Edmund.

" We have a daughter," returned Lady Montagu ; " you would not sacrifice her ?"

" I would have her in all things worthy of my name."

" And of our rank and wealth," added Lady Montagu.

" Rank and wealth !" he reiterated ; " by what signs do you judge of our rank and wealth ?"

" By the ample dowry I brought you," she replied, in a tone of surprise, " and these broad lands."

The gloom darkened on his features, while he demanded, " To what does this lead ?"

"Have you not observed of late," she answered, hesi-
tatingly, "the frequent visits of Lord Nevyl?"

"Lord Nevyl!" cried Sir Edmund, in a tone of crush-
ing contempt.

"It is scarcely just," returned the fair advocate, "to
quarrel with his title. You received honours yourself from
the hand of the Protector. But, in truth, it is only my
own suspicion, — although I confess I think such an
alliance——"

"Because he is a lord!"

"No, not that; but because he is every way worthy of
Lucy, and because his estates lie close to our own."

"And you would prudently consolidate them. Keep
within your own province, good housewife. It is a wise
and needful caution. I would have my blood spread —
healthily drawn out in distant air, not bound up in close
deeds and tenures. Has Lucy spoken to you of this?"
he inquired, with a searching look.

"Never!" replied Lady Montagu.

"Nor you to her?" he demanded.

"Never!"

"Then keep your counsel locked up in your own
breast. We must have speech again upon this clever suspicion of yours. Hearken to the din of footsteps — more
visitors — more lords and peacocks!"

It was as he anticipated. More visitors were arriving,
and their approach was announced by a bevy of bedizened
lacqueys, whose clamorous entry made a greater uproar
than that of their masters. Lady Catherine, through
whose introduction or invitation most of the court people
were attracted to the tranquil shades of Lynton, entered
the room to communicate the intelligence, just as Sir
Edmund had uttered his imprecation against the peacocks.

She saw he was angry, but her brilliant spirits and high breeding were not to be put out by other people's ill temper.

"They are coming, dear Lady Montagu!" she exclaimed, running over, caressingly, to her aunt.

"Who?" inquired Sir Edmund, in a freezing tone of discouragement; but his sour reproof was thrown away upon the lively maid of honour.

"Who? Some of the choicest beaux and gallants, of course; gentlemen of the privy chamber——"

"And ladies of the privy chamber?" interrupted the questioner.

"No—no ladies."

"Well, there's some grace in that," resumed Sir Edmund; "but if I must receive these people, pray, Lady Catherine, enlighten me upon their names and qualities."

"Well, there is Mr. Giles Moreton, a poet, who has written verses on his majesty's restoration, a great favourite with the king; and Mr. Plympton, remarkable for nothing but his chocolate coat, lined with rose-coloured silk, and his lisp; Pettingal, a beau of the first water, who is said to consume more carnation wash and Spanish paper than the whole four women actors, boarded by Davenant, in Lincoln's Inn; and—and—Sir Dudley Perrot."

"A goodly company!" exclaimed Sir Edmund, with a groan. "And who may this Dudley Perrot be?"

"Sir Dudley! My court fool. You shall be my confessor," she added, with a *malice prepense*, eliciting a still deeper groan from Sir Edmund, at the ghostly office she assigned him. "Sir Dudley is a lover of mine, poor motley! He is a sort of country squire—as ignorant of town life as one of his own great Flemish horses, yet aping it at all points, like a monkey. His father, who was in some

kind of trade, expended a fortune in the service of the
king—and so, by way of a set-off, his majesty knighted
the fool."

"A royal way of paying his majesty's debts!" ejaculated Sir Edmund.

"But you must not suppose," continued Lady Catherine, "that I invited Sir Dudley. The truth is, he followed me. He follows me everywhere, like my shadow.
One wants a motley, you know, to play off one's humours
—so we must be civil to the poor, harmless popinjay.
But, dear Lady Montagu, you and Sir Edmund must
hasten to receive them;" and she ran on, with a vivacity
that fairly overthrew the gravity of Sir Edmund, until she
hurried them both out of the room, to meet the approaching guests at the door.

The three first-mentioned gentlemen made their appearance in succession, and were received with a ceremonious
formality, in which the true courtesy of the host was no
less apparent than his puritan coldness. Sir Dudley
remained behind. He hung back in the avenue to adjust
his sword and ruffles, and to put on an elaborate periwig,
which his valet carried in a bandbox.* Having satisfied
himself, by a careful review of his person in a pocket-glass,
that his costume was perfect, he advanced to the house
with an awkward sidling air which produced infinite merriment amongst the people assembled within. Even Sir
Edmund could hardly suppress a smile at the first glimpse
of the attitudes into which he managed to distort his
grotesque figure.

---

* In the county of Berks there is an approach to one of the old
mansions which is still called Wig Avenue, from the circumstance of being
the spot where the gallants used to put on their flowing wigs, before they
presented themselves at the house.

The guests had already gone forward, and Sir Edmund and Lady Montagu still lingered at the entrance, when their attention was attracted by the person of an aged man who stood at the extremity of the terrace, apparently soliciting their notice by strenuous gesticulations. Hugh Clark, who happened at the moment to be bestowing a philosophical lesson on one of his hounds, ordered the ill-clad supplicant to be gone about his business; when Sir Edmund, rebuking the falconer's harshness, advanced, with Lady Montagu on his arm, to inquire into the old man's necessities. There was, at least, that one vital virtue in his republican creed, that it recognised the claims of manhood in the poor, as well as in the rich.

The man was an ancient pensioner who had long subsisted on the bounty of the family, and who enjoyed a sort of reputation amongst the common people for his skill in casting nativities and telling fortunes—practices which were at that time in high estimation even amongst the educated classes.

"One word in your ears," hoarsely whispered the mendicant.

"As many as you will," cried Sir Edmund, who, without being what is called superstitious, desired rather to conciliate than to provoke people of his stamp—"what fortune is in the wind to-day, good Master Sachell?"

"Ill fortune. I came to warn you. Beware—beware!"

"Tut—tut. You must not alarm Lady Montagu."

"I tell you to beware, Edmund Montagu. Danger, and evil, and woe hover over your house."

"What means this?" demanded Lady Montagu, flushed, and not a little terrified at the strange intelligence.

"Mere fantasy," replied Sir Edmund, hastily, scowling at the same time upon the prophet.

"No—a living truth," uttered the mendicant, in a still deeper voice. "You will heed my words hereafter. Beware who comes into your house, and who goes out. Beware, Edmund Montagu!"

"No more of this," cried Sir Edmund.

"As I have eyes to see, and ears to hear," persisted the mendicant, "I saw and heard—not in a vision—but the living——"

"The beggar's brain is crazed," exclaimed Sir Edmund, fiercely, drawing Lady Montagu at the same moment towards the house. "Begone, knave! and practise your sorceries elsewhere."

The mendicant turned and moved slowly away. Lady Montague was fascinated to the spot, and continued to gaze after him, while at every step he looked back with haggard emotion to reiterate the terrible warning. His receding figure, tall and macilent, and clad in ominous black, presented to her affrighted imagination the aspect of a messenger of fate; and as she passed the threshold of the door, the one appalling word, "Beware!" struck like a knell upon her heart.

III.—A DRAWING-ROOM AFTER THE RESTORATION.

THERE is a great movement in Lynton Hall: a gathering of company, a dazzling concourse of guests. Pages in rich liveries fill the vestibule; and a cavalcade of coaches, most of them drawn by six barbs, make a brave stir in the old avenue. There is a grand reception at Lynton Hall to-night, including, in addition to the visitors from court, the principal gentry of the surrounding country.

The drawing-room, voluptuously decorated, and hung at either extremity with purple serge, bound with gilt leather, is like a scene of enchantment. A flood of light streams down on all sides from innumerable painted lamps, multiplied every instant into ten thousand flashing rays, scintillating from the jewelled costumes of the crowd.

The vast extent of the apartment affords ample space for the various amusement of all. Groups of dancers occupy one end, and small parties are scattered over the other, engrossed in a variety of pastimes. In one place there is a constellation of bright faces gathered round a table, enjoying, to their hearts' content, the merry fright of a little linnet, Ringing Whittington (as it was called)— the poor bird being imprisoned for the purpose in a cage, on the top of which were arranged a number of bells, which rang Whittington as he sprang about trying to escape from the tingling music produced by his own motions. In other places, gentlemen are engaged in lansquenet and ombre; some are employed in the fashionable relaxation of building houses with cards; and sundry little circles are deep in lively games of forfeits, so much in vogue at court, especially that ingenious perplexity, " I love my love with an A," which yields so many excuses for the wit and gallantry of the beaux; and that artful romp, called "Hunt the Slipper."

The Lady Catherine and her fair cousin have drawn round them a crowd of gallants. Lucy Montagu is dressed simply, but richly, in white satin, looped up with pearls, her bright brown ringlets, without any ornaments, flowing in profusion over her shoulders. The maid of honour is somewhat more elaborately attired in a peach-coloured bodice, lavishly brocaded, fitted tightly to the shape, open down the front, and fastened with brilliants, a delicate lace tucker peeping over its snowy round above. She seems perfectly conscious of the costliness of that sweep of lustrous silk, short, full, and lavishly plaited, and those puffed sleeves, gathered high up in front with clusters of diamonds, showing, under a fall of the finest cambric, trimmed with lace, one of the daintiest arms in the world. Her dark hair floats in long tresses over her bosom, and is further enhanced by a garniture of diamonds, and a dazzling flutter of " heart-breakers," disposed with consummate art.

Mr. Giles Moreton was paying a thousand unmeaning compliments to Lady Catherine. He said that Crashaw must have seen her in a vision, when he spoke of—

> " Tresses that wear
> Jewels but to declare
> How much themselves more precious are !"

" Nonsense !" exclaimed Lady Catherine; " never quote poets to me. There is not a lurking flattery in one stanza that I will not match with a piece of downright insolence in another. Suckling settles the question at once with a most honourable candour—

> ' There's no such thing as that we beauty call,
> It is mere cozenage all.'

What think you of that, Pettingal ?" she added, as the fop advanced with a mincing air. Beau Pettingal was one of the most distinguished butterflies of his day, and came out on this occasion with surpassing absurdity, in a slashed suit of amber-coloured velvet, and gigantic silver buttons, an enormous peruke, an immense laced steinkerk, a huge sword-knot, and a profusion of ribands of various colours, streaming from all available points on his breast, knees, and shoulders.

"Odds life!" quoth he, aping the favourite exclamation of his Majesty—"your ladyship is right. There is no
faith to be placed in poets; the only true exponents of
beauty are the painters."

"The alternative is questionable, Mr. Pettingal," cried
Lucy, "for the painter too frequently runs into the
extremes of grossness or affectation. He rarely ventures
on the ideal, without exposing his want of true taste by
some ludicrous exaggeration."

A simper ran through the group. Lely and Kneller
were the most popular of all the court flatterers—the
former from the luscious redundancies of his pencil, and
the latter from the refinement of his wit, which added a
personal interest to his reputation as an artist. The
courtiers evidently thought this judgment of Miss Montagu's somewhat dangerous, but Lord Nevyl, who was
close at her side, came gallantly to the rescue.

"Miss Montagu's criticism is unanswerable," he observed; "take Lely for example—he is not merely wanton
but fantastical. He has a marvellous hand for draperies,
but then he seldom knows what to do with them; and his
most charming nymphs are to be found reposing in brocade
on green hillocks, or trailing their embroidery through
swamps or sheep-walks." The justice of the remark was
irresistible, and elicited an universal titter.

While desultory conversations of this kind were going
forward in different parts of the room, servants were
moving about amongst the guests with trays of agreeable
beverages; and even the most delicate of the ruffled gallants paused in their badinage to sip rosa solis, usquebaugh,
or flip, or to linger gracefully over a tart and whipt sylla-
bub. The progress of these delectable luxuries broke up,
for an interval, all the little knots of talkers, and gave a

temporary diversion to the gentlemen, who speedily became scattered over the room.

The group round Lucy and Lady Catherine was gradually dispersed, even Lord Nevyl being carried away by the general movement. While the cousins, thus left together, were freely discussing between themselves the topics suggested by the scene, they were surprised by the appearance of a person whom they had not noticed before, passing slowly through the crowd, apparently towards the place where they were seated. His deportment was stern and severe, whilst his dark and faded attire contrasted strangely with the gay colours and sumptuous apparel of the rest of the guests. The cousins observed his motions with curiosity.

"Do you know him?" inquired Lady Catherine.

"No," answered Lucy; "he is certainly unbidden, whoever he may be, or he would never make his appearance in such a costume."

"Yet he has the air of a gentleman," cried Lady Catherine; "a likely fellow, well-formed, almost handsome; somewhat soiled, to be sure—a little the worse for the wear, and, perhaps, for want of a change—but still a gentleman."

"He comes towards us," said Lucy; "he is absolutely going to speak to us."

The strange visitor approached, and making an obeisance to Lady Catherine, addressed her in a tone of perfect good breeding. "A gallant scene, fair mistress."

"For gallants, truly," replied the Lady Catherine, with a slightly haughty curl of her pretty lip.

"I scarcely expected to see so rich a company in Lynton," observed the stranger, after a pause, taking no notice of the gentle repulse.

"You did not? And why not, may I ask?"

"Why? Because," said the stranger, with a faint effort at vivacity, " I thought you were all puritans here."

" He evidently thinks he is addressing you," whispered Lady Catherine to her cousin; "leave him to me." And she raised her voice, and continued: "Puritans? You are mistaken. I am a stanch royalist."

"You are? Amazement!"

" I see nothing very amazing in it," she replied; " you are a royalist, too, I presume?"

" Yes, an unfortunate one. I have lost my estate, or, at least, been kept out of it by my loyalty, while you——"

" While I have been preserved by my loyalty in mine," she interrupted; adding, in her own thoughts, that if it would help her to a holier estate she should be still more obliged to it.

The visitor gazed earnestly upon the beautiful form before him. Lady Catherine was not easily subdued by earnest looks, but she felt that she had never before encountered an expression so thrilling as that which filled his eyes while he gazed upon her. The silence that succeeded perplexed her excessively, but she was opportunely relieved by her court fool, Sir Dudley Perrot, who came up with a jaunty leer on his face, just in time to enable her to recover her composure. Sir Dudley's figure was a caricature in itself; his glittering buckles, and pink stockings, his flirting glass, and his forest of curls, and the excess of tawdry jewellery and rich tissues which he had contrived to collect about his person, betrayed the vulgarity of his low ambition, which took delight in transcending the worst taste of the tavern braggart and box-lobby fop. To drown the stench of the tobacco, in which he indulged to the height of the fashionable vice, he was drenched in perfumes, and scented the room like a civet cat.

Interposing between the unknown visitor and Lady Catherine, he stooped down to speak to her, with a familiarity which was instantly punished by the uplifted fan, with which she sheltered herself from his rudeness. The stranger measured him from head to foot with a glance of ineffable scorn, without altering his position, until Sir Dudley, dismayed by so unexpected a reception, slunk back into the crowd.

At this instant Sir Edmund Montagu approached. He had not observed his new visitor before, and the sudden apparition of a stranger so unceremoniously garbed, excited his astonishment. Lady Catherine, with instinctive tact, softened the reception which she anticipated Sir Edmund would have given a decayed royalist under such unpropitious circumstances, by volunteering to introduce him.

"A stranger, Sir Edmund—Sir Edmund Montagu."

The visitor turned full upon the host. His face had undergone a sensible change. The colour forsook his cheeks, and then returned, and fled again. His eyes dilated, and his lips trembled.

"I bid you welcome, sir," said Sir Edmund.

"Welcome to Lynton! Thank you—thank you!" replied the visitor, in a low, agitated voice.

"Your name, sir?" inquired Sir Edmund. "I believe I have not the honour——"

"You forget me?"

"Forget you!" echoed Sir Edmund.

"I am not surprised at that," continued the stranger: "stranger things have happened, and stranger still may happen yet"

"Do you know this gentleman?" said Sir Edmund, turning to his niece.

" I do not remember," she replied, " having seen him before."

The stranger moved a few paces away, out of hearing of the ladies.　Sir Edmund followed him, like one under the influence of a spell.

" Sir Edmund Montagu," said he, " this is not a place for explanations.　Give me a private audience, where we shall be free from interruption.　Alone—we must be alone."

The warning which had been so mysteriously conveyed to him by the old mendicant, now, for the first time, flashed across Sir Edmund's memory.　Could this intruder be concerned in it ?

"What is your business with me, that I should grant this meeting ?" he inquired, scanning the person of the stranger ; " I know you not."

" I am unarmed," replied the other, calmly, " you perceive—a civilian, and by no means in condition to do you personal mischief," he added, while a cold smile rippled over his features.

" Do you threaten me, sir, in my own house ?" demanded Sir Edmund, betraying the apprehensions he was so anxious to conceal.

" Threaten you in your own house !" repeated the other ; " surrounded by your well-furnished guests and retainers—a single man, without arms !　You mock me, Sir Edmund Montagu.　Do you refuse this interview ?"

" Suppose I do ?"

" Then you must abide the consequences.　I demand a private meeting for *your* sake, not for my own.　For *your* sake, Sir Edmund," he repeated, laying increased emphasis on the expression.

" For my sake ! The proceeding is strange—inexplicable. I will trust you, sir, but—" and he still hesitated —" you must clear up this mystery. Follow me !" and Sir Edmund went towards the door.

The stranger turned to the cousins, who were considerably interested in the dumb show of the abrupt dialogue, and making a graceful bow, followed Sir Edmund out of the room.

Lady Catherine's wonder at this sudden retreat was heightened, rather than abated, by Lucy's declaration that she never saw her father look so agitated before. Her ladyship's curiosity was tantalized to the utmost stretch of endurance, and she resolved to sift the mystery as soon as the stranger returned.

The gorgeous revel did not break up until long past midnight. Lady Catherine looked in vain through the assembly for Sir Edmund or the stranger; neither of them re-appeared for the remainder of the night.

IV.—THE UNBIDDEN GUEST.

"You forget me ?" said the stranger, as he strode into the old library after Sir Edmund, who, carefully closing the door, motioned him to a seat.

Sir Edmund pushed aside a cresset lamp which burned on the table between them, and gazed earnestly into his face. " As I look at you, dim remembrances come back upon me," he observed. " Be brief. We are out of the reach of interruption here—your name?—your business ?"

"They are one," returned the other. "My name is Walter Stanley."

"Walter Stanley!" ejaculated Sir Edmund, with a wild and incredulous glare.

"You have not seen me since I was a boy, and I have passed through a life of hardship since. It is not very astonishing, after all, that you should forget me."

"I recognise some resemblance in your lineaments," said Sir Edmund, "but it is such as might be common to many men. I will treat you with no discourtesy. Your name may be Walter Stanley—there are, doubtless, a hundred Walter Stanleys; but the boy of whom you speak is dead."

"Yet was he identified only a few days past by one of your own pensioners."

"Sachell!" exclaimed Sir Edward; "he identified you? A conspiracy—a base imposition. Have a care, sir, how you proceed any farther in this business!"

"It was not my desire," said Stanley, "to be recognised by any person in this neighbourhood until I had first communicated with you; but some men have quicker wits than others. The mendicant knew me at a glance."

"And upon this evidence ——"

"No, I stand here upon legal proof. Listen to me calmly. You have flung a vile imputation upon me. No more of that, for my blood, long fevered by wrongs, is hot, and may master my discretion. Command your passion, and hear me."

"You sue for hearing fairly," said Sir Edmund; "but still be cautious in your utterance."

"For upwards of a century, Sir Edmund Montagu, Lynton Hall was the seat of the Stanleys. The armorial eagle still looks down from its mural escutcheon. It is

E E

now twelve years since they were expelled from their
home, from their country, and reduced to beggary."

"The hand of Heaven," interposed Sir Edmund,
"smote them down for their sacrilegious defence of an
impious tyranny."

"And the hand of Heaven," said Stanley, "has raised
them up again to re-assert their rights. Be patient, and
listen. My father, devoted to that cause which you
denounce, raised three regiments for the king; his house,
this house, was thrown open to the cavaliers during the
horrors of the civil war; he would have poured out his
heart's blood as freely as he expended his treasure in that
sacred service. But it was not to be. When regicide
crowned the last demoniac triumph of a godless rebellion,
my father's name was proclaimed, and his estates were
confiscated. He shared that destiny with others, and he
bore it with what resignation he might. The prolonged
misery of siege, and battle, and privation, had already
destroyed my mother; there was nothing left to him
in this world but his only son, Walter Stanley, who
now ——" Overcome by strong emotion, the speaker
covered his face with his hands. Sir Edmund awaited
the sequel in profound silence.

He continued: "My father left England. He was
compelled; his friends were numerous, but as powerless
and helpless as himself. It was his earnest desire that
I should receive an English education, and he left me
behind, under the guardianship of one who was bound
to him by many ties of gratitude; and while you, Sir
Edmund Montagu, were in the enjoyment of my rightful
inheritance, conferred upon you by the Usurper, I, the
heir of Lynton, was doomed to the penury of a humble
roof, gathering such niggard knowledge as my scanty

opportunities afforded, and eking out the crust of bitter poverty under a false name, as if I were the son of a criminal. That was the justice — that was the mercy, of Cromwell."

"It was the public necessity," exclaimed Sir Edmund, "which demanded such sacrifices. You blame Cromwell for cruelties which were forced upon him by the universal cry of the people. Blame, rather, the tyranny of which Cromwell was but the retributive avenger."

"We shall apply the argument presently," returned Stanley; "for so surely as Cromwell avenged what you call the tyranny of Charles, so surely will the second Charles avenge the iniquities of Cromwell. But to return to my story. My guardian was poor, timid, oppressed — a man of peaceful life, and unfit for the difficulties of the trust which was reposed in him. Three months had scarcely elapsed after the usurpation, when my guardian, scared by frightful rumours on all sides, spread a report of my death. He hoped to secure my safety by this cunning stratagem, little calculating on the consequences it was destined to produce. The report reached my father before it was possible to communicate the explanation. The blow nearly killed him. The last link of his affections was snapped, and he retired from the world to bury his miseries under the ascetic offices of the priesthood. Years passed away: he had not seen me since my childhood. All inquiries after his retreat were fruitless, for he had resolved, upon entering the church, to close up every avenue by which he could be traced to his seclusion. At last the secret was discovered through the agency of a monk, who had undertaken, on behalf of the royalists, to collect the names of English exiles who had taken refuge in the religious establishments of France. He was living,

but on the threshold of the grave. I lost not an hour on
that melancholy journey. The shock was too much for
his enfeebled spirit; and he died in my arms at Rheims,
but not," he concluded, " till he had placed in my hands
the evidences of my birth, and documentary proofs of my
inheritance."

This communication, to which, circumstantial as it was,
Sir Edmund had listened with painful interest, was followed by a long pause. Sir Edmund rose from his chair
and paced the room in silence. At last, Stanley broke in
upon his gloomy reverie:

" This was my business, Sir Edmund. Shall it be
quietly, and if you will permit me to say so, amicably
adjusted, or must I seek other means of restitution? I
come here to claim my right — to enforce it, if need be."

" Mr. Stanley," replied Sir Edmund, " it was by no
intrigue — by no subterfuge or treachery, I came into possession of Lynton. I served the Protector — he rewarded
my services by a grant — an honourable, open grant. I
am not prepared to admit that such a grant would be
reversed by the sovereign under any circumstances; but
I wave that — I bow to the decrees of a higher tribunal,
who, in its inscrutable wisdom, seems to have brought us
thus face to face together under this roof. Satisfy me
that your claim is just. I am ready to take that course
which my obligations as a Christian gentleman point out;
without exposing you to the waste or the delays of law."

" Nobly spoken," responded Stanley, deeply affected
by a display of magnanimity which his habitual sense of
oppression hardly led him to anticipate.

" You see me moved," observed Sir Edmund, " but
do not mistake me. To myself such a sacrifice, so unexpectedly demanded, so wholly unlooked for, would

signify little. My own desires are few and simple, and enough remains behind to satisfy even larger wants than mine. But this touches me deeply on account of others rather than myself."

" Your daughter ?" said Stanley.

" My daughter !" repeated Sir Edmund, in a voice choked by emotion. " Who shall break this news to her ? It will crush her for ever; reared in the lap of ease, and so unfit to struggle against reverses !"

Walter Stanley's features relapsed into a suddenly grave expression while Sir Edmund spoke. It had never occurred to him that the recognition of his established right would doom the daughter of Sir Edmund perhaps to penury.

" My position is hard," he said; " I never contemplated the issue you place before me; nor would I willingly be the cause of inflicting sorrow upon that bright and joyous spirit. Is there no middle course—no compromise ?"

"Compromise !" rejoined Sir Edmund, proudly; "none. Justice is whole and entire, and must not be paltered with."

" Pardon me," said Stanley, " if the strange events of this night, so fraught with import to my future life, should make me bold. I have seen your daughter. Her frankness, her kindness to me, have inspired me with an interest which I dare not disregard."

" The feeling is creditable, Mr. Stanley; but you must see how impossible it is to consider such feelings. I can accept no boon on her account."

" Nor would I have you. I offer none. I would rather ask a boon at your hands and at hers."

Sir Edmund smiled at the youthful generosity of the speaker

"Forgive the earnestness with which I urge my plea," continued Stanley. "Your daughter has always considered Lynton as her inheritance; let her still do so."

Sir Edmund was so utterly amazed at this proposition, that he almost doubted whether he had heard it correctly. Stanley continued:

"I have seen her gracing with her beauty her place of pride and power. I came with dark thoughts and heavy misgivings into the bright assembly, of which she was the brightest star. While fops and fribbles looked contemptuously upon my worn doublet, she—she alone spoke freely and encouragingly. Her words fell upon me like sweet music. Can I, dare I, for my own advantage, even for my own right, fill the heart of that gracious being with sorrow?"

"Yet, Mr. Stanley," said Sir Edmund, "to that issue it must come at last."

"No, no," cried Stanley, with increasing animation; "I know not how to shape my thought into language. But it is possible we might reconcile the difficulty with honour on both sides. I offer Lynton to your daughter, but," hesitating for a moment, "not unencumbered."

"Do I understand you rightly?" demanded Sir Edmund.

"If Miss Montagu be free in heart, as—till this night—I have been, allow me only the opportunity, grant me the happiness above price, of laying my inheritance at her feet. How could it be else so worthily disposed?— and God speed the wooing! If it be otherwise—Lynton, so newly won, after years of suffering, will have few charms for Walter Stanley!"

It was impossible to doubt the depth and purity of the feeling which suggested this proposal; and Sir

Edmund, alarmed in his pride at so unexpected a suit from one whom he now saw, for the first time, under the most unfavourable influences, could not but secretly respect the disinterestedness of his conduct. The plan certainly offered an available escape from a very serious calamity, and there·was little in Stanley's personal bearing, and still less in his character, so far as this interview had searched and developed it, to which, under such circumstances, he could fairly take exception.

" You consent ? " demanded Stanley, who saw that Sir Edmund was revolving all these considerations in his mind.

" I make no promise for my daughter," replied the other — " I can make none. But you must feel that a declaration of this nature demands some pause. If my daughter — but I can depend nothing on such a contingency. Give me a little time for reflection, and be assured, Mr. Stanley, that whatever may be the result, I am not insensible to the generosity and candour with which you have acted. I am harassed and exhausted. No more — but good night ! "

" When may I trespass on you again, Sir Edmund ? " inquired Stanley.

" To-morrow," said Sir Edmund.

Stanley retired; and when he closed the door, Sir Edmund flung himself into a chair, and gave way to the distracting conflict of feelings which, up to that moment, he had successfully struggled to suppress.

V.—A GLIMPSE OF ORANGE FLOWERS.

THE next morning Lucy Montagu received a summons to attend her father in the library. He looked wan and dishevelled. The mental agony of the night had wrought a visible change. But his manner was more collected, and even kinder than usual. She saw that something extraordinary had happened, little suspecting to what purpose it tended.

Sir Edmund opened the communication cautiously, preparing her slowly for the final announcement that Lynton —the scene of her happiest years—was about to pass into the hands of another. She received this intelligence with a degree of fortitude that extorted his admiration. Women are the best philosophers on such occasions. They submit to reverses with less resistance than men; perhaps from the passive resignation of their nature, perhaps from that happy unconsciousness of the greater evils of life to which the larger ambition of the other sex is so sensitive. Instead of murmuring at the impending misfortune, Lucy Montagu had the wisdom and the tender courage to point out many sources of consolation in the coming time.

The conversation naturally reverted from Lynton to its new possessor.

"A man of honourable mind and generous impulses," observed Sir Edmund.

"I rejoice to hear," said Lucy, "that he is so worthy of his inheritance."

"And this youth," resumed Sir Edmund, "trained up in adversity, with a noble heart and enlightened tastes, enters upon his possessions almost as sorrowfully as we shall relinquish them. His joy is turned to bitterness, from the painful reflection that in claiming his own rights he inflicts unhappiness upon us—upon *you*."

"Upon *me!*" repeated Lucy.

"I am not surprised at the interest he takes in *you*," he continued; "and that, for your sake, he even hesitates in the fulfilment of the duty he owes to himself."

"Dear father," exclaimed Lucy, "you speak in riddles!"

"He saw you last night—you received him with kindness. The sudden contrast between your position and his, and the thought that he had come like evil destiny upon you to destroy that happiness which you wore so graciously, have touched him deeply."

"Did he say this to you, father?" she inquired.

"Oh, yes!" he returned, "and a great deal more, not so readily syllabled by the sullen lips of an old man like me. Lucy," he added, taking her hand, and gravely watching the growing flush on her cheeks, "there is a way by which you can secure Lynton. This young enthusiast, Walter Stanley, has spoken frankly on the subject."

"You lay a fearful responsibility upon me, father," she answered.

"I cannot recall," said Sir Edmund, "a single instance in which you have forgotten your duty to me. You will not forget it now. Walter Stanley would make you mistress of Lynton."

Poor Lucy was stunned by this terrible news, and the tone in which it was delivered clearly implied that her father expected her full acquiescence in the proposal. If she ever had any intelligible doubts as to the state of her feelings towards Lord Nevyl, they were now dispelled on the instant. She tried to speak, but the attempt only rendered her confusion the more apparent.

"I know what you would say," interrupted Sir Edmund; "the proposal is sudden, and Mr. Stanley is a stranger. I know the plea you would make—your tender age; and, perhaps, some pent-up feeling hitherto concealed in the modest secrecy of youth. I feel all that—understand it : but time will soften all, and reconcile you to my wishes."

"Oh, father!" exclaimed Lucy, "what can time do but prolong the misery of such a union?"

"It is at least unjust to assume so much before you have given Mr. Stanley an opportunity of making himself known to you. How if you misjudge him?—if hereafter you should discover that you had formed a false estimate of one who at least deserves a more grateful reception at your hands? You must consider these things. I will not take your answer now. See Mr. Stanley; know him —then let me have your resolve."

"It cannot be!" uttered Lucy, in a voice of involuntary agony.

"It must be!" rejoined her father, sternly. "You fancy I cannot detect the mystery that lies coiled under all this reluctance. Shall I refer the question to Lord Nevyl?"

The abruptness of this appeal to a feeling which Lucy innocently believed the whole world to be ignorant of— that delusion, so natural, so precious to the young—overwhelmed her. Tears started into her eyes, and she made some foolish excuse about her dress to conceal the tremor of her hands. Her secret was betrayed as plainly as if she had confessed it in so many words.

"We will talk no more of this at present," said Sir Edmund. "We shall have ample time for reflection on all sides. But take with you my parting words—that if this be a sacrifice, it is made for those who are best entitled to your self-devotion; for those who have nursed and tended your childhood, who love you, Lucy—God alone knows how fondly! Bless my child! No tears, no tears; but prayer—prayer for strength to do our duty!" And, kissing her forehead, he led her to the door.

Poor Lucy fled to her chamber, with a heart almost

broken by her first, strange grief; and when she had wept until her eyes ached again with their unaccustomed anguish, she ran to seek her cousin. It was a difficult confidence, too ; for it involved the necessity of a confession which she could hardly prevail upon herself to make, even to that faithful friend.

The Lady Catherine was shocked at the discovery — especially shocked, at finding that the visitor of the night before, about whose business she felt so much womanly curiosity, should have turned out such an exorbitant monopolist of the chattels of Lynton ; not content with the estate, but demanding in addition the living spirit of the place. She tried to banter Lucy about Lord Nevyl, and about Walter Stanley, and invented a little romance about the gallant rivalry for her hand, between Lynton Hall and Nevylswood. But her sunny mirth was at fault for once. It was the saddest mirth she had ever volunteered ; and she felt how idly her gaiety played round the drooping head that rested on her bosom. Yet, in the midst of all, she persisted in asserting that, come what might, Sir Edmund Montagu should not coerce her sweet cousin's affections. She was ready to answer for the firmness of Lord Nevyl, at all events.

Walter Stanley was punctual to his appointment. Sir Edmund received him in the library, having previously requested the presence of the ladies in the drawing-room. The meeting was constrained on both sides ; but it was clear that Sir Edmund had kept his pledge, so far as it rested with himself. It was no less clear to Walter Stanley that Miss Montagu had given an unfavourable reception to his suit. He had anticipated this. How could she otherwise treat the presumption of a stranger ?

Still he cherished the forlorn hope that time might subdue all objections.

Sir Edmund was perfectly candid upon all these points. He told him that he had communicated with his daughter, but that, in the surprise of so startling a proposal, it was not to be expected she should be prepared with an answer. His suit was at least unprejudiced; beyond that, he could say nothing for the present.

The presentation in the drawing-room of this stranger, who had come to dispossess the whole family of the Montagues, was embarrassing enough. Stanley, whose part on the occasion was, perhaps, the most difficult of all, went through the trial with excellent self-possession; and he certainly looked to considerable advantage in a more cavalierly costume than that which he had displayed on the preceding evening. His fine person and manly bearing disarmed much of the hostility which must have been involuntarily betrayed towards one of a less imposing presence.

He was first presented to Lady Montagu, then to Miss Montagu, then to Lady Catherine. At the last introduction, he changed colour, and could hardly control the dismay produced upon him by the announcement of her name. He had committed an irretrievable error—he had mistaken Lady Catherine Gower for her cousin. The mistake was so obvious in the altered expression of his looks, and in the hesitating words which faltered on his lips, that Lady Catherine, with her quick instinct, saw in a glance what was passing through his mind; and, overruling all frigid forms of etiquette on the sudden impulse of more generous thoughts, sprang forward, and, placing her hand upon his arm, exclaimed, "Mr. Stanley, you mistook me for my cousin! It is so! You mistook me for Miss Montagu?"

Stanley could hardly answer that it was so, with a thousand flurried apologies, fluttering from his heart into sundry broken phrases, when Lady Catherine threw herself into the arms of her cousin, hiding the tears that gushed for joy from her bright eyes.

It was so—and the trouble passed from the heart of Lucy. But it was only a transfer of the new embarrassment, for Walter Stanley did not love that gracious being less because she happened to be only the cousin of Lucy Montagu. Nor did Lady Catherine's interest in the stranger cease because he had shown so noble a spirit in the first hour of his regenerated fortune. And time did in this case, what time usually does when young hearts are left free to the discovery of mutual feelings—love grew upon love, and was crowned in the end with its pure and enduring reward.

And how ran the course of wooing with Lord Nevyl and the fair Lucy? To say the truth, Lord Nevyl had very romantic inspirations on the subject, and—if that were possible—became more devoted than ever to the disinherited heiress of Lynton. There is some perplexity in this wilfulness of the universal passion, which the world may never be able to unravel; but it is not less certain, on that account, that there are some natures which prefer love for its own sake above all human blessings, and which take delight in manifesting the singleness of their devotion. Lord Nevyl's heart was moulded in this graceful shape, and he dowered his happy bride with all the more lavish tenderness, that she might never feel the loss of that fortune which he neither needed nor desired.

And Lynton Hall and Nevylswood were once more restored to prosperous friendship and close neighbourhood of the affections, revived in younger spirits and sustained with cheerier usages. Sir Edmund and Lady Montagu retired upon an estate they possessed in Wales—enough for their ambition, which now reposed, not in their own future, but in that of their child. Welcome visitors were they in the joyous Christmas time to their old haunts in Devonshire!

For the rest of the personages who have flitted through this narrative, nothing need be said, for nobody can care to trace their useless destinies. But we must add, that old Sachell, the mendicant seer, was handsomely pensioned by Lady Catherine Stanley, for his delightfully dismal warning; that Sir Dudley Perrot fell in a duel, which he sought for the sole purpose of helping up his reputation at court; and that Pettingal, the beau, expired of a carouse with Buckhurst and Sedley, at the Rose Tavern, in Drury-lane.

The voice of the narrator ceased, and as he turned to make obeisance to the Lady Eva, he found that she had crept close to his side, where, on a low ottoman, she had silently taken up a position of fixed attention. A few bright tears trembled in her long lashes. She seemed hardly conscious that the story was done—the last story! The whole group had insensibly drawn round her. Their interest was divided between the incidents of the tale and the fluctuating emotions so eloquently expressed in that sweet face.

It was the last story! The portfolio was exhausted, and there was no further excuse for drawing on the imagination of the assembly. Even the elastic spirits of youth, — so prompt with ready resources, so unconscious of difficulties, — failed at this trying moment. There was a slight movement on the ottoman; Lady Eva had slowly unclasped her hands, and thrown back the rich curls which fell in graceful negligence over her fair shoulders. She looked as if she were about to speak; her lips stirred, but she was still silent. Everybody understood her thoughts; — the Birthday Revels were over!

The happy circle that had been so long spell-bound under the enchantment of these pleasant legends, now gradually broke up the silence, and gathering about the fair girl, overwhelmed her with thanks and congratulations. It had been a week of pure enjoyment, to be set apart amongst their most delightful memories; and they assured her, that when they should have separated, as they were too soon about to do. upon their several engagements of duty or amusement, tne recollection of the intellectual pleasures of which she had been the creative spirit would linger with them gratefully through many a future year.

This was some consolation to the Lady Eva, at the close of her Birthday Festival; but she was for exacting a sort of promise, that, when the time came round to celebrate the same event again, they would re-assemble to enact a similar round of votive gaieties. She would have had it a life-long holiday, if she could have had her own way, little dreaming of the changes that might happen in the interval to others and to herself; the new ties that might be formed, the new interests that might grow up, the blanks that might fall in, the sympathies that might be weaned from fiction to reality, from the regions of poetry and romance to that world of living struggle, whose stern experiences too often extinguish both heart and fancy!

Still she was not to be denied ; and so they promised ner, with such conditions as might be reasonably allowed on all hands, that they would cheerfully attend her next summons, and dedicate their best efforts to renew the charms which had shed such a refined fascination over these six happy EVENINGS AT HADDON HALL.

THE END.